A native New Yorker, William Hjortsberg has lived in the mountains of Montana for the past twenty-five years. He is the author of seven works of fiction and has several screen credits, including *Legend* (directed by Ridley Scott) and *Angel Heart*, based on his novel *Falling Angel*. He is currently at work on a biography of Richard Brautigan.

Nevermore

WILLIAM HJORTSBERG

PHŒNIX

A PHOENIX PAPERBACK

First published in Great Britain by Orion in 1995
This paperback edition published in 1996 by Phoenix,
a division of Orion Books Ltd,
Orion House, 5 Upper St Martin's Lane, London WC2H 9EA

A CIP catalogue record for this book is available
from the British Library.

ISBN: 1 85799 445 0

Printed and bound in Great Britain by
The Guernsey Press Co Ltd, Guernsey, C.I.

FOR MAX AND MITCH

Author's Note

Nevermore is a work of fiction. Although several of the characters are indeed historical personages, they too are intended as fictional creations. At times, I have included as dialogue actual written or spoken opinions regarding spiritualism. In each case, the appropriate speaker is acknowledged and his words enclosed in quotation marks.

The action of the novel is set over a period of several months in 1923; however, I have taken certain liberties with actual chronology and for narrative purposes have borrowed events from both previous and later years. For example, the famous séance in Atlantic City took place in 1922, during Conan Doyle's earlier lecture tour of America. Houdini's underwater endurance test actually occurred in 1926 in the Shelton Hotel swimming pool. The business of the folding rule found in the medium's cabinet involved a Boston woman named Mina Crandon in 1924.

For information on the lives and times of my characters, I am indebted to the following works:

Botkin, B. A., *New York City Folklore,* New York, 1956.

Carr, John Dickinson, *The Life of Sir Arthur Conan Doyle*, New York, 1949.

Christopher, Milbourne, *Houdini: The Untold Story,* New York, 1969.

Conan Doyle, Sir Arthur, *The Edge of the Unknown,* New York, 1930.

Ernst, Bernard M. L., and Hereward Carrington, *Houdini and Conan Doyle,* New York, 1932.

Gresham, William Lindsay, *Houdini,* New York, 1959.

Higham, Charles, *The Adventures of Conan Doyle,* New York, 1976.

Hoyt, Edwin P., *A Gentleman of Broadway,* Boston, 1964.

Silver, Nathan, *Lost New York,* New York, 1967.

Silverman, Kenneth, *Edgar A. Poe,* New York, 1991.

White, Norval, and Elliot Willensky, editors, *AIA Guide to New York City,* New York, 1967.

Wilson, Edmund, *The Twenties,* New York, 1975.

In addition, I would like to acknowledge several friends for supplying me with books, information, encouragement, and editorial advice. My thanks to Hannelore Carter, Richard Cosgriffe, Bob Dattila, Marsha Landreth, Charles Levendosky, Christene Meyers, Bruce Nims, Lyndon Pomeroy, Paul Sandberg, and John Tauranac.

WILLIAM HJORTSBERG

And rays of truth you cannot see
Are flashing through Eternity—

a Bostonian
1827

NEVERMORE

1

HOCUS POCUS

The magician stood alone in the shadows backstage. Short, stocky, and middle-aged, he parted his dark shock of wiry gray-flecked hair straight down the middle. A surprising number of men still sported this Gay Nineties barbershop quartet look at the start of the Jazz Age, the brave new tommy gun decade when flappers and bathtub gin became as American as apple pie and the G.A.R.

Despite impeccable tailoring, the magician's evening clothes looked perpetually rumpled. He had never been known as a fashion plate. When just a teenager first starting out, he wore suits several sizes too large, like a kid in hand-me-downs. Perhaps this was deliberate, a misdirection worthy of a master in the arts of deception. Watching him, one never suspected the starched dickey and wrinkled soup and fish concealed an athlete's body honed by years of diligent exercise.

It was not his nature ever to be idle. Waiting in the wings before his turn, listening to the house orchestra play an Irving Berlin medley, he kept his hands busy with a pair of lucky silver half-dollars. He rolled them from knuckle to knuckle across the backs of his hands, a flourish as difficult as any known in magic. The coins moved with delusive ease, round and round, propelled by an imperceptible flexing of his tendons. His eyes slid shut. His head slumped forward. He looked like a man in a trance, the rotating coins part of the deepest meditation.

The magician was the headliner, the most famous name on the big-time vaudeville circuit, topping the bill at the Palace, one thousand, eight-hundred simoleons a week for two shows a day. He listened to the applause surging and crashing beyond the footlights like storm-driven surf. The orchestra's string section trembled on the last notes of "A Pretty Girl Is Like a Melody" as if overwhelmed by the frenzied clapping. "Conrad and Speers," the ballroom dancing team, were getting an enthusiastic hand. The magician had never seen their act, but the reaction to their finish gave him great pleasure. A warmed-up audience meant his own reception would be enormous.

"Dapper Dave" Conrad and Violette Speers traipsed off hand in hand, pausing behind the stage right tormentor. Draped in shadows, the magician watched them exchange hissed insults, their faces sudden savage masks of hate. In a moment, it was time to waltz back on for a final bow, and the frozen smiles snapped into place like instant makeup.

Conrad and Speers were an act in one. They performed on the apron between the footlights and a painted drop, making entrances and exits without a curtain, timing their calls precisely. Smiling, ever-smiling, they swirled into the wings in each other's arms as the applause died and the majestic house curtain descended.

A stagehand hauling the show drop aloft whispered: "You two were a panic. Knocked 'em dead." Conrad and Speers stalked past him without a word, heading for their dressing room dour as prisoners walking the last mile. The magician watched, not comprehending how they endured such hell on earth. The years he and his wife had worked as a double were the happiest in his long career. A momentary smile eased his stern expression.

The interlude, a lively jazz tune, segued into the familiar strains of his act intro, jogging the magician out of his dime-museum memories. He made one last check backstage, his fierce, slate-blue eyes taking it all in. His equipment stood in place between a sequence of drop curtains. Everything had functioned smoothly when he and his assistants tested the props earlier that day. He saw Collins and Vickery in position and the rest of the team waiting on their marks. Ever the perfectionist, the magician scanned the stage; his hawk's gaze detected that the new girl had forgotten her plumed turban. Mary, her name was. Mary something. No time to mention it now. He made a mental note to dock a five-spot from her pay.

The act drop rose and the lights came up. Iris, the showgirl longest in his troop, stood center stage, waiting for the applause to die down. The magician slipped a silk packet smaller than half a stick of gum into his mouth, concealing it between his cheek and lower jaw. Years ago, he made these himself, staying up late into the night, winding silk in the flickering gaslight of a hundred nameless cheap hotels.

They were manufactured for him now in lots of a dozen by Martinka and Co. As a boy, he'd often wandered into the famous magical supply house, unable to afford even the cheapest five-cent trick; now he owned the entire business lock, stock, and barrel. The tiny custom-made packet nesting inside his mouth seemed a talisman, his entire career wound within its minute coils.

When the applause crested, Iris began her lilting spiel: "Ladies and gentlemen, direct from a triumphant tour of the British Isles and star of the recent smash hit motion picture *The Man from Beyond,* the Palace Theater proudly presents the world famous escapologist, that magnificent master of mystery . . . the Great Houdini!"

A fresh tumult of applause greeted the magician. He strode onto the stage, framed by a bright pair of follow spots, his slightly bowlegged walk in no way detracting from his inherent dignity. His grave demeanor suggested ancient ritual: a priest at the altar; yet his words had the easy confidence of a man utterly at home in the limelight.

"Thank you, ladies and gentlemen . . . " A brief nodding bow acknowledged the ovation even as his hands went up to silence it. "A great pleasure to be back in my hometown, entertaining the finest and most discerning audience on the face of the earth." The faint hint of a smile and a lifted hand stifled ripplings of renewed applause. "I got my start more than a quarter of a century ago, playing engagements on the Bowery at Coney Island and in Tony Pastor's great theater, which some of you must remember, down on Fourteenth Street in the old Tammany Building . . . "

As he spoke, a lithe showgirl named Wilma wheeled forward a cloth-draped table with a round glass fishbowl as a centerpiece. He asked a member of the audience to loan him a handkerchief and a dozen eager hands fluttered with silk and cotton in abject surrender. He was charming them now, a sudden smile erasing the years, the handsome face a boy's mug once again. "And just to show I have nothing up my sleeves . . . " With a quick tug, his celluloid cuffs pulled away, along with the sleeves of his tux, both fastened with snaps above the elbow.

The first trick was all deft patter and mechanicals. He showed them the clear glass fishbowl, rapping and tapping to prove its solidity. Wilma pulled the paisley drape aside, displaying the table's bare legs. Houdini placed the borrowed handkerchief in the bowl. It vanished in a flash of igniting magnesium paper, deftly palmed from Iris when she'd handed him the hankie.

Rewarded with renewed applause, Houdini's dazzling smile grew several degrees brighter and he milked the hand, pulling yard after endless yard of rainbow-hued silks from out of a seemingly empty bowl. Wilma gathered up the excess, winding it around her slender waist with a ballerina's twirl. The impossible multicolored flow continued uninterrupted, accompanied by a crescendo of clapping, until at last the borrowed handkerchief appeared, knotted in the middle of this silken harlequinade, and it brought down the house.

Houdini had the audience in his hip pocket. There was nothing to the trick. They loved it because they watched a legend, a wizard who walked through brick walls and leaped manacled into icy rivers. Prisons on three continents had failed to contain him. In 1906, with much ballyhoo, stripped naked and searched by the authorities, he had escaped from the condemned cell that had held Charles Guiteau, assassin of President Garfield.

Over the years, he had accepted every challenge. Padlocked into water-filled milk cans, nailed in crates and piano packing cases, sealed inside giant paper envelopes and iron boilers welded shut on stage, he escaped from them all. He was once chained within the carcass of a huge squid found on a Cape Cod beach. It stank with formaldehyde and he nearly suffocated, but in five minutes he was free.

For more than a quarter century, each escape had appeared more impossible than the last. A thousand times he'd stepped sweating and disheveled into the spotlight, a testament to unimagined heroic exertions. More baffling still, when the volunteer committee removed the cloth screen, the confining challenge would be standing intact on stage, ropes and chains in place, padlocks still fastened.

His mystery and daring captured the imagination of an entire generation. At almost fifty, the magician retained energy equal to that of a man half his age. The week before, to publicize his Palace opening, he'd eagerly hung upside down, trussed by his heels, five stories above a vast crowd on Times Square, wriggling out of a strait jacket in under three minutes.

"Five years ago, ladies and gentlemen, I made an elephant disappear several blocks from here on the stage of the Hippodrome, the world's largest theater." Houdini said this without the shadow of a smile, invoking a cathedral hush within the gilded auditorium. "Tonight, I'm going to perform the world's smallest wonder . . ." Scattered applause indicated old-time fans recognizing the introduction to "The Needles," a trick Houdini had performed with success since before the turn of the century.

A request was made for a volunteer from the audience and Iris ushered a portly gentleman with a golden Shriner's crescent dangling from his watch chain onto the stage. Houdini bantered with the man, breaking the ice by asking his name and where he lived, making him feel at ease. He showed Mr. Elmer Conklin, of 809 Lexington Avenue, a paper of sewing needles and a small spool of thread. "Are these anything other than common everyday items which might readily be purchased at the five-and-dime?"

"They are not, sir." Mr. Conklin nervously handed them back, hooking his thumbs into the pockets of his blue serge vest.

"Observe carefully. Houdini swallows them."

Mr. Conklin watched, amazement overcoming his stage fright, as the magician mouthed the needles and thread. Back in the summer of '95, when Houdini and his wife had toured with the Welsh Brothers Circus, an old Japanese acrobat had taught him to regurgitate at will. So blasé he often fell asleep while performing as the bottom man of a balance-pole act, Sam Kitchi was a swallower, ingesting ivory balls, coins, watches, and once, to the amazement of the young magician, a live mouse. Houdini practiced for weeks with a peeled potato tied to a string, strengthening his throat muscles, perfecting the art of retroperistalsis.

The magician focused his raptor's stare on a bewildered Elmer Conklin, swallowing in quick succession the needles and thread, followed by the packet from Martinka's. Gripping them halfway down his esophagus, Houdini invited the volunteer to examine his mouth with a flashlight provided by Iris.

"Glad I'm not a dentist," the stout man stammered, unwittingly getting a good laugh as he peered at the magician's molars. "Folks, there's not a thing in there I can see. . . . Talking about under his tongue and everything. I'm satisfied his mouth is empty."

Iris took back the flashlight. Wilma handed Houdini a brimming glass of water. "Hot work always makes me thirsty," the magician quipped, drinking down the liquid without apparent difficulty. "Now, ladies and gentlemen, you and Mr. Conklin have just seen me swallow a needle-book and a spool of thread. I return them to you . . . thusly . . . "

Houdini regurgitated the gag from Martinka's. The needles and thread remained clenched in his throat. He plucked at the end of his tongue, pulling a single thread from his mouth. Threaded needles dangled every inch or so, a lethal silver fringe glittering in the spotlight. Houdini's arm extended full length, prompting wild applause from the astonished audience.

Iris took hold of the thread and backed away from the magician, suspended needles unspooling continuously from his mouth as she gracefully crossed the stage. Houdini basked in the ovation. The cheers surged through him, more powerful than the transports of love. Iris held her slender arm high in the air, pinching the end of a fifty-foot parabola curving back to the magician's open mouth. All along its length, hundreds and hundreds of needles winked and gleamed, flashing reflected light like fangs in the savage, ghostly smile of an invisible monster.

2

MONKEY BUSINESS

A quiet night at the Twenty-ninth Precinct, unusually quiet for a Friday, although business most often picked up after the theaters let out. Manning the desk, Sergeant Heegan remembered the grand old days before Prohibition when the Tenderloin was the beat of a rookie's dreams. Not that the payoff from the speaks wasn't every bit as choice as back when torpedoes like Gyp the Blood and Monk Eastman brawled, bribed, and bought the house a round. Just a bit too genteel and refined nowadays to suit Heegan's tastes. He preferred his sin out in the open.

Graft, on the other hand, needed to stay under the table, and when roly-poly Leon Fishkin waddled in off the street, bold as brass in his ritzy cashmere topcoat, offering up a thick envelope adorned with the embossed logo of the Zebra Club, the desk sergeant tossed it back in his bloated face, telling him to stick it where the sun don't shine. Much offended, the portly bootlegger stormed out of the station house, sputtering like an overheated Tin Lizzy.

"The nerve of that fat louse, waltzin' in here and wavin' his dough around like a come-on man at the two-dollar window, when any dumb jerk knows how the pickup is made." Sergeant Heegan addressed his remarks to a lone cop typewriting in the bull pen behind the booking desk. Busy hunt-and-pecking his way through a robbery report, with his tie and collar removed, the sandy-haired detective didn't glance away from the noisy Remington Standard No. 10 or offer as much as a grunt in reply.

Never satisfied with an inattentive audience, the desk sergeant shrugged and turned back to the *New York American*, folding the newspaper to the sports section, his lips silently forming Damon Runyon's account of a sparring match between former heavyweight champion Jack Johnson and Luis Angel Firpo, the Argentine contender. Heegan whistled between his teeth in grudging admiration. Seemed the old dinge completely bamboozled the "Wild Bull of the Pampas."

It was only an exhibition workout but, round after round, not a glove landed on the Negro. Johnson was forty-four, two years younger than Heegan. The middle-aged Irish cop considered himself one tough customer in spite of the silver frosting his thin red hair, yet deep in his heart he knew for damn sure no money on earth could induce him to step into any prize ring with some dago bone-crusher like Firpo.

The telephone rang, shrill as his old lady on a nagging fit. "Damnation!" Heegan set the paper aside and reached for the candlestick instrument. "Twenty-ninth Precinct," he barked into the mouthpiece, "Heegan speaking." The operator connected him with a near-hysterical woman. Her frantic voice echoed like the insistent buzzing of a hornet trapped in a bottle. The desk sergeant held the black, bell-shaped receiver several inches from his ear. Although often accused of being a touch deaf, Heegan had no trouble making out every word.

"I saw it with my own two eyes," the woman screeched. "My apartment faces the street on Thirty-eighth. It came right along as big as you please and turned the corner onto Ninth Avenue."

"A gorilla, you say," Heegan inquired with more than a trace of a smile.

"A great big hairy ape!" The woman's descriptive powers were doubtless enhanced by all the hoopla for last year's Eugene O'Neill hit on Broadway.

"You sure it's not just some drugstore cowboy in a raccoon coat?"

"Officer! Will you please listen to what I'm telling you? This was a kind of monkey. It had a young woman in its arms."

"Carrying a woman . . . ?"

"I saw her long blond hair trailing down over the shaggy black arm. Horrible . . ."

"Madam, sounds to me like you've observed a frolicsome couple on their way to a costume party."

"This is not Halloween!"

"A simple masquerade, ma'am. Don't go troubling yourself with thoughts of any gorillas."

"Shouldn't you alert the Zoological Society and all menageries and circuses?"

"I'll be doing just that, ma'am. Have a pleasant evening." Sergeant Heegan hung the receiver on the hook and laughed out loud. "Get a load of this," he hooted, spinning around in his oak swivel chair. "Some dumb Dora thinks she's seen a gorilla on Ninth Avenue . . ."

The bull pen was empty. Rows of deserted desks and shrouded typewriters stood mute as mausoleums. Heegan was alone. He spun back to his sports section, untroubled by solitude. After a year spent perched like a lighthouse keeper atop the ornate traffic tower at Fifth Avenue and Forty-second Street, he never again felt lonely. The tower went up in 1920, the first of several similar structures bedecked with spread-winged bronze eagles and cornucopia-framed clock faces, standing in the middle of the avenue at intersections ten blocks apart. These were the earliest electric traffic lights in the city.

The sergeant leaned back in his chair, drifting away into memory. Switching the red, yellow, and green beacons had always made him feel important. High above the passing swarm, snug from bad weather, he pitied those poor bastards standing all over town directing traffic with white-gloved hand signals, their apple cheeks puffing, a cacophony of whistles steaming in the chill air.

On most days, the exhaust haze had hung so thick Heegan could barely see the towers nearest him, north and south along the avenue. When he had started on the force, automobiles were an exotic rarity and high winds often whirled tons of dried horse manure, powdered by passing carriage and wagon wheels, into poisonous shit storms so dense you couldn't see your hand in front of your face, let alone take a decent breath. Some things about the old days were not quite as grand as the desk sergeant might have wished.

"Goddamn that dumb kike!" Heegan bellowed, his face redder than his hair.

"Not so dumb as to be without friends in City Hall." Captain Boyle looked more like a bishop than a policeman, his immaculate hair white as an altar cloth; the lean greyhound face shrewd and intelligent. He spoke in a whisky-mellowed whisper. "How many of your friends are pals with the mayor?"

Subdued by the quiet, patient voice, Sergeant Heegan adopted a more conciliatory posture, like a choirboy caught throwing spitballs. "I know I was way out of line, Captain, but the sight of him there, waving that money around like he was rubbing our noses in it, well, it just got my blood up . . ."

"You've too much heart, Jimmy, that's your trouble." The captain remained genuinely fond of Heegan, was in fact godfather to his oldest son. Both men knew he would never rank higher than sergeant and, although neither ever mentioned it, the bright gold badge gleaming on Francis Xavier Boyle's breast provided a constant rebuke. "Heart's a grand thing, but when you're dealing with the public you've got to use a little more of what's up here." The captain tapped a manicured forefinger against his temple, chuckling inwardly at the image of the sergeant's head thumping hollow as a melon at the same touch. "You know I'll have to take you off the desk . . . ?"

"That sheeny bastard!"

"Relax. He was after your stripes." The captain handed Heegan an envelope. "Report down to homicide at headquarters."

"Headquarters? What the hell'm I gonna do down there?"

"I'm sure you'll find some way to make yourself useful."

* * *

Sergeant Heegan heard the captain's words echoing in his mind all through the afternoon. Every time he refilled the detectives' coffee mugs from the big graniteware pot kept percolating on a hot plate in the squad room lavatory, he thought about making himself useful. No one at homicide knew what to do with him. Several other uniforms served as drivers and in menial backup capacities. None ranked above corporal. So, Heegan brewed the coffee and hung around trading lies with the plainclothes dicks when they weren't out on call or busy interrogating suspects and typing endless reports. He had no complaints. In another year, he'd have his pension.

Just after dark, a call came in ordering every available man over to an address in Hell's Kitchen, cutting short Heegan's rambling blarney once again. On his way out the door, a detective caught the sergeant's doleful glance. "You waiting for some engraved invitation?" he asked. Heegan made a pistol of his index finger and aimed it at his heart: Who, me?

"No law says you have to sit on your ass all day long."

Sergeant Heegan followed the detectives down the long, narrow stairs. There was nothing for him to do, but it had to be an improvement on watching the coffee boil. He rode up front beside a uniformed driver in an open five-passenger 1918 Ford with a canvas top. They set out in a black caravan of four automobiles.

Just for the hell of it, Heegan cranked the siren and they wove through traffic with a great wail, other vehicles pulling out of the way. An unnecessary noise, in the absence of any emergency: the dead meat didn't care if the cops arrived on time. Technically, it was against regulations, but nobody told Heegan to knock it off. The siren's scream made the jaded detectives feel important.

When they pulled up at an address on Thirty-ninth Street, just east of Tenth Avenue, a small crowd had gathered on the sidewalk. Three patrolmen stood by the entrance. The detectives sauntered inside, leaving Heegan in charge of the uniforms, who now, with the addition of the drivers, numbered seven. The sergeant paced off a thirty-foot perimeter in front of the tenement, telling his men, "Don't take no naps and keep the rubberneckers back of this here line." Task accomplished, he made straight for the action, bustling through the building with a hefty swagger.

The body sprawled in the courtyard out back, a dirt lot adrift in trash and almost as crowded as the street, with detectives milling everywhere. A camera on a tripod tilted down into the roped-off trapezoid enclosing the corpse. In the bright magnesium flare of flash powder, Heegan saw a gray-haired woman, shirtwaist stiff with dried blood, her splayed limbs contorted like those of a broken doll flung from some great height.

Heegan made himself inconspicuous on the fringes of the activity, picking up what he could from overheard conversation. Two elderly tenants talked with detectives about the victim. Her name was Mrs. Esp. She was a widow; spoke with some kind of accent. Lived with her daughter on the fourth floor. Other than that, the two wheezing geezers, a man and his wife from the look of it, didn't know beans. Widow Esp was something of a recluse. They never saw that much of her. The daughter, on the other hand, came and went every day. Had a secretarial job downtown. Lovely young thing, with long golden hair. Not bobbed the way some of them are wearing it.

Heegan edged away from their babble, wanting a closer look at the corpse. The photographer had done with the late Mrs. Esp: having shot her from a dozen different angles, he folded his equipment into a black suitcase. Another man coiled the barrier rope. Several bored detectives leaned over the body, gazing down at her with no seeming interest.

She was a mess. Thick clumps of hair had been yanked free by the handful, laying bare a raw, abraded scalp. Her blotched and bruised face twisted disagreeably, the backwards stare making her look all the more like a twisted doll. Heegan marveled at how deeply her throat had been slashed. The cut ran from ear to ear.

Alone among all the others, a slim, dapper man in a battered

"Open-Road" Stetson and double-breasted topcoat stared, not at the body, but straight up at a shattered fourth-floor window. "Long drop, Mr. Runyon," quipped a detective at his side.

Heegan took a good look at him. So, this was William Randolph Hearst's blue-ribbon sportswriter. He knew the word along Broadway was Damon Runyon liked to hang out with shady characters. Gamblers. Torpedoes. Small-time grifters. Cops. For all of that, the sergeant had never laid eyes on him before.

"It's the sudden stop that kills you, Charlie," Damon Runyon said. He was a small man, with a thin, unsmiling shark-slit mouth. His round glasses gave him an owlish look, the glint of the lenses masking the ironic twinkle in his eyes. The detective chortled appreciatively.

"Turn her over." Lieutenant Bremmer gave the orders. "Let's see the rest of the damage." Heegan glimpsed him earlier in the day, rushing in and out of his office. The lieutenant was built like an energetic fire-plug, one of those small men who made up in authority what he lacked in stature. Two detectives immediately took hold of the body and everybody watched as they gently lifted it.

Mrs. Esp's battered head tore loose from her shoulders, falling with a soft thud into the shadows. Even the most hardened cop gasped in horror. "Eight to five she was already dead when she hit the ground," smirked Damon Runyon.

About this time, the wagon arrived from the morgue. Bremmer had the team bundle the stiff on a stretcher but told them not to load her until he and the boys had a look upstairs. Heegan went along with the pack, trooping up four flights. They found the door to the Esp apartment locked tight. "Give us a hand here, Sergeant," barked "Bulldog" Bremmer. Grateful for something to do at last, Heegan reared back his beefy leg and splintered the door open with a single kick.

The front room was a kitchen. An oak icebox dripped in one corner. A coal scuttle stood between the blackened range and a bathtub covered by a worktable. This was an Old Law tenement with a single toilet in the hall serving all four apartments on the floor. The men pushed inside, finding the place a shambles, broken furniture strewn like pieces of kindling. An overturned flour bin powdered most of the floor but the detectives failed to find a single white footprint.

The back room was in even greater disorder. Twenty-dollar gold pieces lay scattered about, along with a bundle of silver spoons tied with silk ribbon and several broken bits of costume jewelry. A cotton mattress torn from the bed was bunched against the wall. Mother-of-pearl grips smeared with gore, a gleaming straight razor lay on the only unbroken chair, pointing to the blood splattering the cheap patterned wallpaper. The shattered window frame gaped with night. A gusting breeze sent several torn clumps of gray hair drifting across the bare floorboards like tiny spectral creatures.

Lieutenant Bremmer turned the central gas jet higher. At first glance the room looked unoccupied, a fireplace on the side wall seemingly unused, as no ash collected on the grate. Oddly enough, considerable quantities of soot had fallen onto the hearth. Bremmer bent over for a look. A long strand of blond hair hung out of the flue.

"Christ almighty," he muttered, reaching up to tug a slender arm down from the chimney. The head and shoulders of a young woman followed, badly scratched and mauled. Discolored bruises banded her pale throat. Hanging upside down, her staring blue eyes and wide-open mouth spoke of a final uncomprehending horror.

Damon Runyon leaned forward among the detectives. "I'll be damned," he said with a lopsided grin. "Rue Morgue . . ."

"What's that?" asked Heegan, standing at his elbow. He thought he'd heard him say "rumor."

"Just like the Poe story."

Sergeant Heegan didn't know what the newspaperman was talking about. He had never heard of Edgar Allan Poe.

3

A VARRAY PARFIT GENTIL KNYGHT

The knight and his lady stood arm in arm at the stern rail of the *Mauretania,* watching the long white line of wake describe their course across a blank and nearly motionless sea. It was very cold. Bundled in heavy overcoats, she with her ermine stole wrapped tightly around her neck, they remained the only couple on deck under a moonless, cloud-free sky. The clarity of the air magnified the myriad stars and rendered the horizon sharp and straight as a razor's edge, the obsidian sea abruptly divided from the silver diadem of sky.

He drew her close and whispered into the fur-muffled ear. "It was on just such a night as this that the *Titanic* went down. And not so very far from here, I should reckon." His voice rumbled gently with a laconic Scots burr.

"Is it only a decade ago?" she said. "It seems absolute centuries."

His heart surged with emotion, not because of what she implied: a whole world swept away; each of them losing a beloved brother to that devastating war; his son, Kingsley, gone as well. They had been through so much together, yet he felt neither sadness nor loss. He no longer believed in the finality of death. If there was such a thing as eternity, he knew in some mysterious way it was connected to the profound love he shared with this fair, stalwart woman who had remained by his side through it all.

He was sixty-three years old, his wife fourteen years younger, although she looked to be still in her late thirties. Theirs had been a love at first sight during the Queen's Diamond Jubilee more than a quarter century before, and the fire of it burned more fiercely now than on that first damp spring morning so long ago.

She interrupted his musing: "Will there be any danger of ice?"

"I should think not." The knight wrapped a bearlike arm around his fair lady. "They steer a somewhat more southerly course these days. Still, it's all fate, isn't it, really?"

"At least we should be together." She nestled tenderly against him and he knew she was thinking of Mrs. Isidor Strauss, who had refused to enter a lifeboat, saying she had spent forty years with her husband and would not part from him.

"I wonder how poor old Stead spent his last moments . . . ?" He referred to W. T. Stead, once editor of the "Review of Reviews," his Boer-sympathizing adversary back in the days of the South African War, later a friend and companion on the spiritual path, lost along with more than fifteen hundred other souls in the *Titanic* disaster. "Perhaps at tonight's meeting we might make contact."

She smiled up at him. "I know if we don't, it shan't be from want of trying."

Never noticing their burnished reflections in the gleaming cherry-wood paneling, so intensely did they stare into each other's eyes, the dignified couple made their way along the first-class passageway. Steam heat transformed the interior of the great ship into a balmy summer evening, and they removed their topcoats, he gallantly carrying both over his arm.

The knight was a tall man, well over six feet, with the burly build of a heavyweight boxer. In spite of his years, he moved with an athlete's innate grace. Carefully trimmed now, his thick, white walrus mustache had swept to dark, dashing cavalier points when first they met. She thought him then the most handsome man she had ever laid eyes upon and nothing in all the years spent together had ever altered her original opinion.

Their stateroom was on the port side of A Deck. It was spacious, yet dainty in its "posh" appointments. Although not bound for the Indian Ocean, they had shared a quiet laugh about "port out, starboard home" upon embarking. He hung up their coats. She sat at the vanity, brushing and rearranging her dark gold hair. She caught his reflection over her shoulder and smiled.

Her husband was one of the most famous men on the planet, his beloved books translated into dozens of languages; his plays, the toast of the West End. He received his knighthood not for these literary accomplishments but for service to Crown and country during the Boer War, something altogether more noble. Far from being a bookish chap, he was an avid sportsman, an expert amateur boxer, and a champion cricketer. She admired him enormously.

The smiling knight rested his powerful hand on his lady's pale shoulder. She pressed her cheek against it, kissing his fingers. Neither her pride in the man nor her admiration for his varied abilities compared to the enormity of her love. When they met she was a girl of twenty-four with a passion for singing and fast horses. She still craved a spirited mount and galloped fearlessly through the woods surrounding their Sussex estate. And her fine mezzo-soprano voice, trained at Dresden and Florence, continued to give her husband great pleasure.

She sang for him on that first rainy afternoon so long ago and she remembered the joy in his bright blue eyes. He was in his prime then, a jovial bull of a man, bursting with energy and ideas. Already celebrated, he wore his fame lightly, taking more joy in bowling a century on the cricket field than in all the kudos of the literary establishment. He was also married, "Touie," his wife, an invalid. She loved him anyway: utterly, completely.

If he had been a different sort of man, one to whom honor mattered little, he might have divorced his ailing wife, or baser still, taken his new love for his mistress, and she surely would have followed his lead. But, he did neither, compelled by a code he'd honored all his life. He would not abandon his wife; neither did he deny his love. Although wiser heads counseled her never to see him again, no romantic heart ever argued with her choice. For the next decade, their relationship remained platonic. They saw each other often, chastely, and with discretion. And whenever he stormed at the unfairness of it all, she smiled and said she didn't mind as long as they were together.

Nine years went by with dignity and decorum, and when Touie succumbed peacefully to the tuberculosis that doomed her long before, he mourned for another twelve months. He was now a knight of the realm. This meant little to him. The happiest day of his life was when at last his lady became his bride. And although the "Flaming Youth" of a more cynical postwar generation might smirk at the thought, she took pride after such a long and secret courtship in being still a virgin when she stood beside him at the altar.

A passenger liner at sea provided a succinct microcosm of the society left behind on land. Down in the depths of the stokehole the black gang toiled in sweat and misery, shoveling coal round the clock into furnaces under the great boilers that drove the ship. Over them, the steerage passengers dwelt in dormitories little better than prisons. The spare, efficient quarters on the next level housed the crew. No frills or fancy ornament here. Servants were not expected to aspire beyond their station.

High above the throbbing engines and catacombed human hive, the stately corridors of wealth and privilege surpassed a humble immigrant's most extravagant dreams. The steamship companies provided fantasies as grand as any concocted in the motion picture studios of Hollywood. Shielded by riveted iron plates, surrounded by teakwood decks, magnificently arrayed beneath the four looming red stacks, the *Mauretania*'s handsome public rooms included cafes modeled on the Orangery at Hampton Court, tiled Turkish baths with marble columns, a gentlemen's smoking chamber in the manner of Renaissance Italy, grand ballrooms and dining rooms spanning every French style from François I to Louis XVI.

Launched five years before the *Titanic,* sister ship to the *Lusitania,* the *Mauretania* first won the Blue Riband for speed in 1907. The prized ensign remained affixed to her foremast fifteen years later. Still the swiftest craft afloat, she was a stately survivor from a grander and less gaudy age. The same might well be said of the knight and his lady ascending the main staircase, so completely did they embody the virtues of a lost time. The year before, he had been made an Earl and Knight of the Garter. They were known, at least by sight, by all the passengers. Everyone on the stairs nodded an amicable greeting.

In the Louis Seize library, where the bookcases were so like those in the Trianon, they paused to chat briefly with the Duchess of Marlborough, whom they'd met at a séance in Kent. Knowing that her friends, the Burlieghs, were among their guests, they invited her to join their party, and she accompanied them into the adjoining writing room.

The rest of the group had already assembled. "Here's Sir Arthur and Lady Conan Doyle just now," barked bluff Brig. Gen. Sir Nevil Soames. After genial greetings, the knight introduced the duchess to those she didn't know: a couple from the United States, Mr. and Mrs. Frederick Randell; and the spirit medium, V. T. Podmord, a noted clairvoyant. The steward brought drinks and refilled coffee cups. Lady Jean chatted with the duchess and the Randells, who owned a chain of "drug stores" in some improbable place called the Midwest.

Sir Arthur joined General Soames, Lord and Lady Burliegh, and the ethereal Mr. Podmord, a thin young man so pallid as to be nearly translucent. "Dreaming true is the only psychic power I possess, outside of healing," Sir Arthur said, replying to a question from Lady Burliegh. "Thank God for that."

"What? No desire to have ectoplasm oozing from every pore?" The brigadier fixed young Podmord with a dubious eye. "Tell him what he's missing, tell him of the rapture and the joy."

The clairvoyant's cheeks flushed. "Perhaps Sir Arthur possesses powers of which he is unaware . . ." His reedy voice piped in suppressed indignation. "Or wishes to deny."

"Of whatever small talents I lay claim to, Mr. Podmord, I can certainly assure you that there are none which escape my attention." Sir Arthur's cerulean eyes danced, lively with imagination. "It's the responsibility I couldn't bear. To be so close to the spirit realm, to hear all those pleading voices, greet so many distant shades. . . . It would quite consume my life, I'm afraid."

"It already has," Soames remarked. "Lecture tours in Australia. America, again. And book after book on spiritualism. Give us more of *The White Company* and *Micah Clarke*."

Sir Arthur felt secretly pleased. The brigadier had praised the historical fictions, his own two favorites among his work. Unlike most enthusiasts, Soames did not urge him to produce more bombast about the odious Sherlock Holmes.

"Might not one be insensitive to his psychic gifts and, at the same time, unconsciously make use of them?" Lord Burliegh wondered.

"Rubbish!" snorted General Soames.

"I shouldn't be so quick to condemn." Sir Arthur smoothed his mustache. "First, hear the evidence. In a long life touching every side of humanity, far and away the most intriguing character I have ever encountered is Houdini."

"The music hall magician?" chirped Lady Burliegh, anxious to demonstrate her familiarity with popular culture, although unsure of the reference.

"The same. I have never met his equal in courage. All the world knows of his daring. Why, he has performed feats the average man trembles to contemplate. Moreover, it is impossible to think of his many miraculous escapes without imagining some form of dematerialization has taken place."

"Is not this same trickster leading a campaign against spiritualism?" pouted V. T. Podmord. "Is he not the greatest medium-baiter of the age?"

"He has lately embarked on a very public vendetta, attacking every medium, whether false or true, with equal fervor." Sir Arthur sighed. "I believe this serves Houdini a two-fold purpose. First, he has never been adverse to publicity, however lurid. But, more importantly, there is no better smoke screen than just such an antispiritualist posture, not if you are trying to conceal being the greatest physical medium of all time."

Brigadier General Soames swirled his brandy and shook his head. "Why should an entertainer wish to conceal his greatest selling point? Especially one who so courts the press?"

"Houdini is a great student of the history and literature of magic. He, more than anyone, is aware of the fate suffered by those conjurors whose tricks were found to be accomplished through supernatural means. The stake awaits the warlock."

After the steward cleared the table, they all gathered around. "I've had sittings with Hartlepool, the trumpet medium," Sir Arthur said to Lord Burliegh as the ladies took their seats and the steward closed the drapes. "And with Gladys Piper, the flower medium, not to mention the Bangs Sisters of Chicago. All with remarkable results."

"We've used the Bangs," Mrs. Randell commented. "Very inspirational . . ."

The steward retired, shouldering a tray piled with cups and glasses. He turned off the lights and closed the double doors on his way out. It was pitch dark. Shadows masked the gray sycamore paneling and gilded furniture. Sir Arthur had arranged for the disbeliever, Brigadier General Soames, to be seated as far from the medium as possible. It was essential at these times to give the sensitive psychic support and he made sure Lady Jean was placed on Podmord's right. His wife had the gift of "inspired writing." Her faith was a beacon.

Following a short prayer, Sir Arthur spoke of the *Titanic,* mentioning they presently passed through water where more than a thousand bodies had drifted for days, if not weeks. He quoted Thomas Hardy's poem on the calamity, telling them that his friend, the journalist W. T. Stead, who perished in the accident, had also known the poet. "If his spirit is at large, perhaps he will reveal himself to us here tonight."

Although Stead had not been personally acquainted with anyone else present, both General Soames and the Burlieghs had friends among the passengers lost on the *Titanic*. V. T. Podmord expressed his opinion that this would "most exquisitely facilitate contact." All the psychic signs were auspicious and they sat together holding hands in the dark as the great ship steamed on its course through the icy sea. Other than occasional small talk, nothing of interest occurred.

4

ISIS IN SEARCH

Her hair gleamed midnight black. When she was a farm girl in New Hampshire, it had hung past her waist, but now, fashionably bobbed, it curved like a raven's wing along the ivory line of her jaw. Blessed with striking features (high sculpted cheekbones, large wide-spaced wave-green eyes, a prominent nose with nostrils delicate as seashells, lips full and red, parted by a slight overbite, giving her smile a perpetually mocking air), she ignored her detractors, who joked about a predatory look, calling her "fox-faced" behind her back. Most people, men especially, found Opal Crosby Fletcher impossibly beautiful.

Born in the final year of the old century, she seemed to belong more to that vanished time. Her rural upbringing kept her distant from the stunning changes bedazzling a new era. Like many imaginative youngsters, Opal had played with an imaginary friend, sharing secret confidences with him. Other children played with invisible fairies and nonexistent talking rabbits. She insisted her phantom playmate was the spirit of a priest of Ra from Old Kingdom Heliopolis, that the secrets he whispered inside her mind were prophetic.

At first, Opal's casual remarks regarding next week's weather or the sex of unborn calves seemed nothing more than playtime babble, but the accuracy of her predictions soon made it impossible to deny her gift. Word of her prescience spread. Neighbors dropped by the Crosby farm in North Conway daily, seeking advice from the little girl. Stories appeared in the state's newspapers and strangers by the drove crowded onto the white frame farmhouse's elm-shaded front porch.

Inevitably, this led to offers from a legion of one-ring circuses and fly-by-night carnivals. The elder Crosbys were seriously tempted. Their dairy business remained marginal at best, and any extra income seemed a blessing. Young Opal rejected all such commercial considerations, believing divine gifts were not to be sold for profit. A wealthy investor arrived from Boston, waving a big check in exchange for advice on future stock market developments. Opal refused to help. Her inner voice remained obstinately mute.

The onset of puberty brought about changes beyond the merely biological. At fifteen, Opal announced she was the reincarnation of Isis, ancient Egyptian fertility goddess, and conducted her first séance in the town meeting hall. Looking more innocent schoolgirl than pagan goddess, her dark beribboned braids tumbling across a home-sewn gingham dress, Opal was bound and chained within a sealed wooden cabinet.

After volunteers extinguished the kerosene lamps, manifestations began almost immediately. Bells rang, trumpets blared, tambourines and chairs levitated. Many present in the old colonial building claimed they saw luminous spirits hovering among the hand-hewn rafters. The story ran in the *Manchester Union* and was picked up by several big-city newspapers. The myth of "Isis reborn" began to spread.

This time, more substantial offers arrived. Telegrams from Edward F. Albee, head of the Keith Circuit, and Martin Beck of the Orpheum Circuit proposed national vaudeville tours. Broadway beckoned when both Flo Ziegfeld and Charles Dillingham sent personal representatives to New Hampshire, contracts in hand. To poor farmers like the Crosbys, the suggested salaries seemed astronomical. Opal would earn more in a month than the dairy farm took in during an entire year.

It didn't turn out that way. Lacking their daughter's clairvoyance, the Crosbys imagined a glorious future in the "Follies" or the Hippodrome's "Big Show." Isis made other plans. Barely sixteen, the fertility goddess eloped with a sixty-three-year-old textile tycoon.

Walter Clarke Fletcher descended from an old New England family, a long line of merchants and ministers; doctors, lawyers; Yale men, Episcopalians; one a colonel in the Continental Army. His grandfather had built a small woolen mill on the Housatonic. At the start of the Civil War, his father owned three more and finagled a government contract for military blankets. By the time the ink dried at Appomattox, Gordon Prouty Fletcher was a millionaire many times over. Educated abroad, young Walter broke the family's Old Blue tradition. On the continent, he developed a taste for vintage wine, baccarat, and women who were decidedly not Episcopalian.

On his return to the United States in 1894, Walter left the Fletcher estate in Hartford and commissioned architect Richard Morris Hunt to design an imposing chateau for him in New York, on the corner of Fifth Avenue and Eighty-fifth Street. To this home overlooking Central Park he brought a succession of wives, who raised half a dozen children, none of whom interested him any more than did the textile business. They all survived his indifference and, by some miracle, so did his ever-expanding woolen mill empire. Not even persistent bad luck at the gaming tables made any appreciable dent in his enormous fortune.

The children were all grown by the time Walter Fletcher carried his new teenage bride over the threshold into the vast, echoing marble pile on Millionaire's Row. As his life was already something of a scandal, none of his blue-blooded neighbors did more than cluck and gossip at this latest development. Other than the usual polite society page squib, scant mention was made of the event in the city's newspapers. The *Daily News*, first of the sensationalist tabloids, remained three years in the future and, although no less cynical and hard-boiled, journalists in those days exercised a certain sense of decorum.

Whatever the prurient might have imagined regarding an aging roue ravishing an innocent farm girl, the truth evaded their wildest dreams. Opal was no timid victim. On their wedding night, she stalked Walter Fletcher across his opulent bedchamber like a tigress. Her kisses tore at his lips. Her knowing touch and erotic crooning murmurs suggested much experience, and he thought himself in the arms of a prostitute until he found he had forced a virgin and came away matted with her blood.

From the very first night, Walter remained Opal's love slave. In his private moments, he reflected on his long libertine life, thinking it a bit of a chuckle to be so thoroughly besotted with his wife. He followed her around like an adoring lapdog, marveling at how prim and decorous she seemed in public. Her newly sophisticated wardrobe erased any vestige of the rural milkmaid and yet, even in sleek Chanel dresses and gauzy Schiaparelli gowns, Opal always appeared chaste and demure.

Another story blossomed in the privacy of their boudoir. The wonder of those silken nights thrilled him to the core: the electric touch of her firm, youthful breasts, nipples gone hard from the warmth of his breath hovering before a kiss; the delicious sweetness of her pouting mouth, her wet, flowing orgasms; the languid magic of pliant limbs enfolding him in an embrace more mysterious than anything he'd ever known, for all his profligate ways. She held him under a spell with the faraway look in her emerald eyes. Ageless, inviolate, she stared into his soul as if across an immutable chasm of lost time.

She definitely improved his standing in society. Although their invitations were accepted at first out of curiosity, everyone coming to meet the new Mrs. Fletcher went away charmed by her quiet, unassuming manner. And what began as mere polite inquiry regarding tales of divination in New Hampshire evolved into weekly séances in the Queen Anne library on the second floor of the big house on Eighty-fifth Street. It became quite the thing to do. In no time at all, young, dark-haired Opal assumed the mantle of psychic consultant to the Four Hundred.

For the best part of five years, life for Mrs. Fletcher remained a constant round of luncheons, concerts, tea dances, nights at the opera, theater openings, and charity balls. Although raised on Elbert Hubbard and the folksy poems of Edgar Guest, Opal now quoted Freud and Amy Lowell. She was a quick study. Whatever lingered of the naive country bumpkin added an appealing edge of self-mockery to her air of fashionable world-weariness.

Mr. Fletcher sported a smug smile his friends found most irritating.

Proud of his new, unearned respectability, he delighted whenever he detected glowering envy in the eyes of fellow members at the Century Club. Opal was a strange girl, quiet and introspective. She required a daily quota of solitude. No complaints from Walter, as she never nagged about his club life or the times he came in late. He didn't stay out all that often, intoxicated more by sleeping with his wife. She twined her downy, slender arms around him, resting her cameo head upon his chest, and dreams more magical than any from childhood transported him through the night.

His luck at cards remained unchanged. He was in the habit of losing frequently at Canfield's Gambling House, an establishment operating outside the law since before the turn of the century. "You know what they say . . . ?" His eyes always twinkled when he pushed his last stack of blue chips across the felt-covered table. "Lucky at love . . ." One day, moments after the words left his mouth, he keeled over backwards in his chair. As he lay sprawled on the Persian carpet, his final thought concerned the arched and deeply coffered ceiling. It looked to him like a muffin tin. Everyone said Walter Clarke Fletcher died a very happy man.

The family did not contest the will. The cotton and woolen mill empire went to his children. Opal was left the house on Fifth Avenue, a rustic camp in the Adirondacks (where they'd often made love on a bearskin in front of a roaring fire), and a trust worth five million. She looked very becoming in black, more mysterious when seen through a veil. Two years after the funeral, she still wore no other color.

On frequent trips to Paris, accompanied only by a personal maid, Opal remained unstained by any hint of scandal in spite of her secret private love life. The weekly séances in the library continued whenever she was in town, her guest list more exclusive than the social register. The city's most prominent citizens believed this slender girl from the country to be a reincarnated goddess.

On New Year's Day, a thirty-three-year-old revivalist named Aimee Semple McPherson dedicated the Angelus Temple in Los Angeles, a structure crowned with an electrically illuminated rotating cross visible for fifty miles. Three months later, she filled all five thousand seats weekly and Sister Aimee's Foursquare Gospel began broadcasting over the radio. Opal Crosby Fletcher didn't listen to radio. She read H. L. Mencken in the *Smart Set*. His mocking report of the "supernatural whoopee" the "booboisie" reveled in out in sunny Southern California made her sit up and take notice.

Not long afterward, Opal announced her plan to build a temple to Isis. It was to be a sanctuary of spiritual harmony, a garden with trees and sparkling fountains, surmounted by a five-story glass pyramid. Under the apex, surrounded by flower beds, reflecting pools, and ancient Egyptian sculpture, the plans called for a windowless onyx chamber: the shrine of Isis in Search.

At first, she informed only a select inner circle and received immediate offers to bankroll the entire venture. These she politely declined. Her spirit-voice told her the cost should be shared among many. To that end, she proposed renting an auditorium and conducting a public séance, admission free, donations welcome. If this proved successful, Opal was not opposed to a return engagement.

Erte designed the posters. They featured a stylized Isis in a striking black-and-silver geometric-patterned robe. Two out of an edition of five hundred were displayed outside Liederkranz Hall, leased by Opal Crosby Fletcher for the final Friday in April. Four hundred and fifty were mailed out with the invitations. The remainder she gave to her office staff, servants, and a group of schoolchildren on their way to a field trip in the park.

Attracted by considerable press coverage, a mob showed up outside of the theater on East Fifty-ninth Street on the night of the séance. Free tickets waited at the box office, first come, first served, for the key social event of the season. Every seat was taken, standing room filled to capacity.

On the bare stage, a single spotlight focused on a stark wooden crate draped in black. For better than half an hour the audience rustled and coughed until, at last, the spotlight dimmed and Isis swept out from the wings, her fashionable outfit covered by the flowing robe pictured by Erté, a multibranched silver candelabrum in each hand.

No applause greeted her. A distant cello played Bach offstage. After setting the candelabra on either side of the proscenium, Opal stood at the center of the apron, wrapped in her metallic robe. She opened her arms in a regal welcome. "All peace be with you, friends . . ." Her clear, musical voice filled the hall. "Half of you are here by invitation, another five hundred tickets were given away at the door. Isis, who speaks through me, has commanded a temple be built to celebrate her search for the dismembered Osiris. I come to you for help. If you would like to make a donation, all necessary information may be found in your programs.

"I've never invoked the spirits before so many. Eight years ago, I conducted a séance in the town meeting hall of North Conway, New Hampshire. The cabinet my father built for that event is here tonight. I will be restrained within it. And with my deep appreciation, I would now like to greet the distinguished committee verifying my confinement."

A gilt-edged group filed onstage to a patter of polite clapping: two Whitneys, the wife of a Whitney and the cousin of William K. Vanderbilt, along with Reverend and Mrs. Nathaniel Porteous, he the rector of the Cathedral of Saint John the Divine. The men moved the wooden crate downstage as the lights came up.

It was built along the lines of a steam cabinet, with folding doors on the slanted front and a single aperture on top to permit the medium's head to emerge. An ordinary wooden chair sat inside. Leather straps dangled from the arms and legs. "These were made from horse hobbles on my parents' farm," Opal said, as two committeemen fastened the buckles, securing her. The others thoroughly searched the cabinet. They announced it to be empty, closing and padlocking the doors.

The committee placed a battery-powered bell box, a tambourine, and a trumpet on the stage and retired to their seats. The house went dark. Candlelight revealed the cabinet's shadowy bulk and Opal's head showing above it, her eyes closed.

A restless hush gripped the auditorium. The cello fell silent. The candle flame wavered in the sepulchral silence, as if disturbed by wind or the unseen passage of invisible visitors. One by one, the candles mysteriously went out. Blackness enclosed the hall like a coffin lid.

Brrring! The bell box rang.

A woman in the balcony screamed.

The bell box rang a second time and a stern voice cried out: "Fraud!"

This caused a general stirring as the shadow of a man was seen to rise from the darker mass surrounding him. "This is fraud!" he declaimed, pushing his way toward the side aisle. "Turn on the lights!" He hurried toward the stage. "I demand the lights be turned on immediately!"

The authority of the voice and the implicit danger of the situation compelled the light man to bring the dimmers up, showcasing the energetic man bounding onto the stage. "It's Houdini," someone whispered. A general commotion ensued, though a far cry from his usual reception. This was not his audience. Most of this crowd never attended vaudeville. They considered it something vulgar to amuse the servants.

"I am Houdini." The magician faced the audience with fire in his eyes. "What you have just seen was accomplished by trickery. Would the committee please come back on stage."

Opal said nothing as her high-society committee filed up the side stairs. From the moment the first disturbance snapped her out of her trance, she stared directly at Houdini, eyes burning into him.

The padlocks were unfastened. "Examine every inch of the cabinet," Houdini exhorted the committee members unfolding the doors. Opal remained strapped to her chair. While the buckles at her wrists and ankles were unfastened, she at last made eye contact with the magician. He felt her intensity glowing with electric energy, like Tesla's arcing artificial lightning. In the end, it was Houdini who looked away first.

Opal stepped from the cabinet. Committee members examined the interior walls and corners. "Nothing has been altered," announced one of the Whitneys.

"Call that a search . . . ?" Houdini stepped forward and removed the chair, which had sat upon a colorful square of Moroccan carpet.

Picking it up, he pointed to a folded carpenter's rule on the cabinet floor. "Here is your fraud!"

The immediate outcry swept the hall like a tropical storm. "An eight-foot rule," Houdini called out, gaining some measure of quiet. "Unfolded, and gripped in the teeth, it easily reaches the bell box from the cabinet."

Several in the audience hissed and booed. Opal stepped forward to silence this disturbance. "Dear friends," she said, "I deeply regret what has happened here tonight and the debate I know will follow. I am confident of the gift I was born with and trust you will give me another opportunity to share it with you. For the moment, I beg you to understand the impossibility of any contact in an atmosphere so charged with hostility."

A wan smile softened her features. For a moment that touched their hearts she was a little girl again, standing before them in all innocence and simplicity. Then, with a graceful swirl, she was gone, gliding into the wings.

The audience made no general rush for the exit; most people stayed put, engaging in vigorous conversation. In any event, they all ignored Houdini. He hurried off the stage and up the aisle, leaving William K. Vanderbilt's cousin puzzling over the folding rule. Bunch of stuffed shirts and swells. He'd performed for heads of state, for Teddy Roosevelt himself. Real royalty, not this pack of parvenus and robber barons.

In the lobby, departing members of the press surrounded Houdini standing in line at the coat check counter. More his kind of crowd. He liked newspapermen and they liked him, knowing he was always good for some copy.

"What made you spot her as a phony?" asked a reporter sporting a pearl gray derby.

"Boys, take it from me, there's not one of 'em that's on the level." Houdini tugged on his topcoat. "I used to do a spook show myself back in the old days, so I know all the angles. Over the years, I never saw a medium I thought was on the up and up."

Outside, a light rain glazed the pavement. Waiting under the marquee, besieged by autograph-seekers, the magician missed the first few taxis. These folks had earlier picked up free tickets at the box office. After satisfying a dozen fans, Houdini waved his arm at an approaching Yellow cab. Just as the magician opened the door, a jasmine-scented figure swathed in black Alaskan seal swept past and stepped inside. It was Opal Crosby Fletcher. Her eyes bored into his. "Get in," she said. "I'll give you a lift."

He wondered afterward what made him hesitate. "Come on," she said. "I won't hurt you."

Houdini climbed in beside her. He smelled the rain glistening on the rich ebony fur. "Are you headed uptown?" he asked stiffly.

"I want to talk with you." Opal pulled her coat closed around her. "Let's go someplace quiet and have a drink."

"I don't drink," he said, regretting the unintended hint of sanctimony.

"Coffee, then. We'll have a bite to eat. Driver! Fifth Avenue and Forty-fourth Street."

Like many of its new neighbors—the speakeasies and blind pigs operating out of brownstones and basement apartments since the passage of the Eighteenth Amendment—no name or electric sign identified the establishment occupying the distinguished turn-of-the-century building on the northeast corner of Fifth and Forty-fourth. After one hundred years of doing business at nine different locations in Manhattan, none was needed. This was Delmonico's.

A row of bronze lamps budded from the narrow stone balcony surrounding the tobacco-yellow building. The cabby signaled for a turn well ahead of the brightly lit corner. He pulled to a stop on Forty-fourth in front of the ornate wrought-iron entrance. A doorman rushed out with an umbrella. The lady paid.

Houdini never felt comfortable in places like this. The headwaiter deferred to Mrs. Fletcher as to visiting royalty as he led them into her favorite dining room. Although fame ensured him first-class treatment everywhere, the magician knew a Jew was not truly welcome in this bastion of wealth and privilege. Once, back in '04, he had brought Bess and his mother here to celebrate the conclusion of their first successful European tour. The chill formality and polite disdain left a bad taste in his mouth in spite of the exquisite food. Fortunately, Mama didn't speak English and had a wonderful time, always enjoying any display of her son's phenomenal success.

"My late husband and I ate here at least once each week," Opal said, setting aside her bill of fare. "Either here, or at Sherry's . . ." She glanced about her. "Such a wonderful place. A pity it's also going out of business."

Houdini followed her gaze around the elegant room. More than half the tables stood empty. It didn't take a mind reader to figure out that Prohibition meant the end for most of the plush old establishments like Sherry's and Delmonico's. "It belongs in another time," he said.

"Yes," she said. "And, so do you. And so do I."

She stared at him again with her burning intensity. He thought of all the cheap sideshow hypnotists, crystal readers, carny mitt-camp operators, and gypsy fortune-tellers he'd encountered in the course of a long career. He and Bess had even had an early success working a mentalist turn, wowing the rubes with their "telepathic" powers. What had once aided them did the same trick for Opal. She looked so fresh and guileless, the dew not yet dry on her petals.

At the same time, Houdini felt something unsettling about her. She possessed a certain power. He thought of Mesmer, then reminded himself she was half his age and might easily have been the daughter he never had.

"I was raised on a farm, Mr. Houdini," she said, a disclosure utterly at odds with her beaded black Patou evening dress. "My folks didn't talk much, but when they did, they got straight to the point." She fitted a black cigarette into a long, gold-tipped ivory holder. "You put that ruler-thing in my cabinet."

She waited, leaning slightly forward, her carved ivory holder extended, ignoring the long silence, until at last a waiter stepped up and lighted her cigarette. Suddenly realizing his bad manners, Houdini made a hapless gesture of patting his pockets and stammered, "I . . . er, don't smoke . . ."

This produced a sly smile from Isis as she exhaled. The smoke smelled of cloves and spices. Definitely not tobacco.

"I know you did this, not because I am psychic," she continued. "I know it because I know nothing else. If I am innocent, then you must be guilty." She paused to inhale. "You . . . or someone else wishing to discredit me."

"Those who prey on the tender emotions of the bereaved deserve no less." He saw no hypocrisy in this statement, nor any humor in his lofty, second-bill comic father tone of moral indignation.

"You condemn me without a trial." Her eyes, shining with unwavering truth, never left his.

"All right. I admit I made the plant. It was a cheap trick." The magician cringed inwardly at this confession. Any violation of his strict Boy Scout sense of fair play brought on tidal waves of guilt, but he quickly took refuge in the iron-clad sanctuary of a puritan morality. "I know you use a gag. They all do. The Davenports did. The Fox Sisters. . . . All of them."

"I invite you to a private séance at my home. You may set whatever controls you wish, provided you forsake any further . . ." She smiled at him through a drifting garland of smoke. "Sleight-of-hand."

"Agreed!" Houdini slapped the tabletop for emphasis, causing polite heads to turn a few tables away. He pretended not to notice, but lowered his voice all the same. "Here is my card."

She set it beside her bread plate, tracing her fingertips over the embossed lettering. "I'll have my secretary make the necessary arrangements."

He found himself lost in her eyes again and attempted awkward small talk, groping for a way out. "Isis in Search. . . . Catchy name for a church." Was there no escape from those eyes? "What're you searching for?"

"You . . . ," she said.

5

MEOW!

Show people were a clannish lot. The vagabond nature of their profession, together with a caste system based on talent and luck, set them apart from the daily grind. Most were further isolated by lifelong poverty and, in spite of a faddish era's unending appetite for "stars," by the general disapproval of polite society, who still smugly remembered a not-so-distant time when actors were expected to use the trade entrance.

Entertainers remained a separate class, speaking a backstage lingo as obscure with slang as the argot of the underworld. Like criminals, they lived life on the lam, holing up in show business ghettos such as flourished in a number of rooming houses and cheap hotels along the side streets intersecting Times Square.

For every headliner lodging at the Astor, there were a hundred second bananas, chorus-line hoofers, and small-time ventriloquists crammed into drab run-down rabbit warrens like the Hotel Stanley, at 124 West Forty-seventh Street, just off Sixth Avenue. Rooms here could be rented daily, but most tenants paid by the month. Cheaper that way, and if an act got lucky and went on the jump for ten weeks in the sticks, the management could always be counted on to credit them with time already paid.

Located one crosstown block from the "Great White Way," the Stanley was a short walk to the shoebox offices of third-rate booking agents and song publishers. Local coffee shops and cafeterias catered to show people, especially during the off-hours when the legitimate world toiled. In fair weather, old-timers living in the neighborhood gathered along "Panic Beach," a strip of sidewalk fronting the Palace Theater, trading jokes and gossip, reminiscing about back when they "wowed 'em in Trenton" or "brought down the house in Philly."

Maude and Chester Marchington had lived off and on at the Stanley since before the war. Their two-room suite wasn't much improvement over the room they'd had on Thirty-second Street more than twenty years ago when they were newlyweds. In 1900, Herald Square was the heart of the theater district and Maude worked as a showgirl in the Floradora Company, dancing alongside fifteen-year-old Evelyn Nesbit, who later gained notoricty as "the girl in the red velvet swing."

That's what the press called Evelyn at the trial of her millionaire husband, Harry K. Thaw. He murdered Stanford White, her former lover, in the rooftop garden restaurant at Madison Square Garden. The famous architect died on top of his favorite design. Back then, Chester sported handlebar mustaches. A job as a singing waiter at Rector's was as close to show business as he would ever get on his own. Maude always said she was happy not to have married a jealous, sadistic millionaire, to have found instead a loving man with "a set of million-dollar pipes," who didn't go around bumping off everybody who'd ever gotten fresh with her.

Her appraisal of Chester's talents proved somewhat inflated. The two-act they put together during the summer of the Thaw trial, the "Merry Musical Marchingtons," never rated higher than fifth billing on the three-a-day. Now they took whatever bookings they could get, performing at weddings and bar mitzvahs; working summers in Coney Island and the occasional split week at small-time Loew Circuit theaters in the Bronx and Brooklyn. For the most part, they hung out on the pavement outside the Palace or lingered over coffee at the Somerset with friends from the old days, out-of-work jugglers and comedians.

"With those earphones stuck on his head, he don't care what kind of howling goes on next door." Maude addressed her remarks to the hotel's daytime manager, a ginger-haired young man named Bloom, decked out in so many freckles he looked camouflaged. "It's bad enough I got to listen to the El roaring by outside, all day long and half the night . . ."

Her angry stare focused not on Bloom, but Chester, slumped in his ratty armchair, fiddling with the dial of a little single-tube reflex circuit Crosley 50. Ever since he first bought an experimental crystal set five years ago, he'd been addicted to radio. Maude thought it just another fad. She still called it the "wireless," wisecracking that it had less future than their act.

"I don't hear anything," Bloom said.

"Just wait." Maude pointed at the wall. "It's like someone is getting skinned alive in there."

They waited. An uptown train rattled by on Sixth Avenue just as the howling started. Bloom couldn't be sure. There was too much racket.

"Shhh!" Maude put her finger to her lips like a schoolteacher.

Bloom remained quiet. He kept glancing at the door, thinking this a waste of time. Suddenly, the most unearthly shriek came through the wall, a wail of torment echoing all the way from the depths of Perdition. Bloom jumped, giving a mouselike squeak of terror. "What'd I tell ya?" Maude's knowing smirk once carried to the back row of Keith's Union Square.

"My goodness! Whatever could that possibly be?" Bloom did not look like a happy man.

"Ain't it your job to find out?"

"Six-D is Mrs. Speers's room. I believe she's out on tour."

"So, you gonna wait till she gets back? Me and Marconi here gotta put up with that caterwauling in the meantime?"

The tortured howl made Bloom's flesh crawl. "I'll get to the bottom of this," he said.

Maude Marchington followed Mr. Bloom out into the hall and watched as he rapped his knuckles on the door to 6-D. No answer.

He shrugged his shoulders and knocked again with somewhat less enthusiasm.

"Either you do something about it, or I'm calling the cops," Maude said.

"The passkey's in my office."

Maude waited by the elevator until Bloom returned. Less than five minutes had elapsed. "It's just as I thought," he said, the scissor gate rattling shut behind him. "Mrs. Speers informed the front desk she was leaving Tuesday, to go out West for twenty-eight weeks on the Orpheum Circuit."

Bloom was a catty sort and knew this last information would hit a nerve. He got to observe tenants twice in their careers: first on the way up, and later, on the way down. Mrs. Speers had played the Palace at the beginning of the month and was clearly ascending. The same could not be said for Mrs. Marchington.

His remark had its desired effect. Maude remained silent, following him down the dusty hall to 6-D. Bloom imperiously inserted the passkey. When the door swung open, the morbid wailing diminished. They both stood apprehensively on the sill, peering into an empty room.

Not precisely empty. Aside from the usual run-down furniture and threadbare carpet, an H & M wardrobe trunk and several suitcases stood in line along the wall by the door, waiting for the express men to come and collect them. Maude stepped inside first. An unfamiliar sweetish smell hung in the air. Bloom sniffed, wrinkling his nose, trying to place it.

"So, she went on tour and din't take no luggage," Maude sneered.

"Perhaps she changed her plans." Something definitely wrong here, aside from the unearthly noises. Bloom struggled to put his finger on just what it might be.

Maude glanced around, a disgusted expression souring her features. "Nice to see the management doing all this redecorating," she said. "They wouldn't tumble for as much as a can of paint when we asked for something to be done about our dump."

That was it. Fresh wallpaper. Bloom ran his fingers along a moist seam. He smelled the drying paste. Someone had recently papered the room. Bloom couldn't imagine Mrs. Speers doing such a thing. She was never coming back to this fleabag.

A low moan filled the room, like a child weeping. Bloom and Mrs. Marchington stood stock-still, transfixed by the desolate wail. Gradually, the sound amplified, building into a demonic shriek more terrifying than anything either of them had ever heard before.

It came from within the wall. Bloom pressed his ear against the spot. There was an empty resonance when he drummed his fist on the new wallpaper. The wall was hollow. Bloom stepped back in disbelief. "A closet," he said, thumping along the outline of an invisible doorway. "There should be a closet . . ."

"What . . . ?" Maude had never been a quick study.

"Wait here!" The day manager bounded out of the room.

She shrugged. "Who's going anywhere?" But, she didn't like being left alone with that awful sound and stepped half out into the hallway, watching Bloom run to a fire safety station down by the elevator. A red-painted axe hung above a red sand bucket and the accordioned pleating of a folded canvas hose. Bloom seized the axe and rushed back to 6-D. He pushed past Maude, his eyes wild and white.

Maude watched from the doorway. Bloom paused, breathing in short gasps like a cornered animal. He surveyed the wall, taking some mental measurement, and with a wild cry, swung the axe over the top of his head. The excess force proved a miscalculation on Bloom's part. The opening to the former closet had been sealed with nothing more substantial than sheets of cardboard, plastered and papered over, and the axe ripped through it as if it were stage scenery.

Flung off balance, Bloom dropped to one knee. The axe hung from a long, ragged tear in the wall, its weight slowly pulling the upper portion of damp plaster and cardboard away from the opening, peeling it back like the lid on a tin of deviled ham. And, sure enough, packed inside was the dead meat.

Held upright by coathooks in the closet wall behind her, Violette

Speers's corpse stood at stiff attention, the top of her head split apart deep into her brow. A clotted mingling of brains and blood caked her hair, forming a stiff crimson wig. Her left eye hung completely out of the socket, dangling down her cheek like a stranded tadpole. Maude Marchington screamed.

Her scream echoed within the closet. Perched on the dead woman's shoulder, a scrawny, one-eyed black cat squinted out into the unaccustomed light. The hideous creature opened its red maw and howled.

6

THE WRITING ON THE WALL

Sir Arthur Conan Doyle stooped to lift a volume of Heroditus from a footlocker piled with books. He slipped it into the careful line already arranged along the back of a rather too-small desk in his corner suite at the Plaza Hotel. He always traveled with a reference library, endeavoring to maintain a regular writing schedule even when engaged on a speaking tour. Nowhere near enough room on the desktop for everything he brought. If he spoke to the management they would make every effort to accommodate him, but he decided against any fuss. It didn't matter where he wrote; railway carriages and waiting rooms had always served as well as his study. He piled the extra books against the wall, thinking of all the great literature composed on lap desks over the centuries.

The little writing table stood in the semicircular corner alcove and warm morning sunshine angled in on the eastern side. Sir Arthur glanced out a north-facing window at the new spring green showing in the trees of Central Park. Aside from the hotel's fine service, he most enjoyed the Plaza's splendid location. Such spots were at a premium in New York, a thoroughly inhospitable city, in Sir Arthur's opinion.

Never comfortable in any town, Conan Doyle preferred the capitals of Europe, where the inconveniences were offset by rich historic tradition. Compared to the amenities of London (charming irregular streets, unexpected squares and parks by the dozen, and the decidedly human scale of its white-and-black Edwardian buildings), the rigid grid of Manhattan closed in like an urban purgatory. Looming skyscrapers crowded out the sun, and thoroughfares snarled with motor traffic and a never-ending pedestrian manswarm.

Grand Army Plaza remained a pleasant exception. Here, the constricted canyon of Fifth Avenue opened onto a three-sided square in a splendid preamble to the liberating expansiveness of the park itself. Sir Arthur turned to the east-facing windows and took it all in. He always made a point of learning the local geography, seeking to inform his fiction with an exact sense of place. Last year, on a previous trip to America, Scully, the doorman, had pointed out the surrounding landmarks.

The circular fountain, surmounted by a graceful bronze statue of "Abundance," delighted him. Pulitzer, the newspaper chap, paid for the whole thing, a gift to the city. Sir Arthur preferred it to the "Eros" fountain, stranded like a damsel in distress amid the congestion of Piccadilly Circus.

The crown jewel of the square was the extravagant building to the south. Cornelius Vanderbilt's turreted mansion rivaled the royal palaces of Europe. A spiked, ornamented iron fence surrounded the carriage entrance facing onto the plaza. It took thirty servants to run the place, Scully told him, with a certain note of vicarious pride.

Sir Arthur marveled at the vulgar ostentation of America's merchant princes. All along Fifth Avenue, facing the park north of the plaza, a mile-long row of chateaux and palazzi, each deserving a country estate, crowded together cheek by jowl like an overdressed chorus line rudely competing for the limelight. How ironic that a nation priding itself on creating a classless society tolerated this obscene nouveau-riche overindulgence.

A brisk knock interrupted his musing. Sir Arthur consulted his pocket watch. Right on time. He opened the door to admit a waiter wheeling a serving table with a proper hot English breakfast housed under covered platters. He praised the young man for the hotel's excellent service and ushered him out with a tip. Breakfast in bed was a luxury he and his wife enjoyed when traveling. At home, such utterly sybaritic behavior remained a rare holiday treat, but in foreign hotels it seemed just the ticket.

Sir Arthur rearranged the crystal bud vase, fanning fringed ferns around a single red rose. Satisfied with the arrangement, he pushed the breakfast table into the darkened bedroom.

The knight pulled back the heavy drapes, flooding the pale yellow room with sunlight. Smiling, he bent to awaken his lady with a kiss. She roused, her smile drowsy, her heavy golden hair unpinned and tumbling across her breasts. "Lovely morning," he said. "No less lovely than you."

Jean drew him down beside her on the bed. "You're lovely," she purred, her voice thick with sleep.

"Am I, indeed?" He kissed her slender neck and the strap of her nightgown slipped from her shoulder. A soft, chaste kiss, yet her flesh blushed pink at his touch.

"Indeed, indeed, indeed . . ." Her nimble fingers unfastened the buttons on his waistcoat.

"I say," he protested, "there's breakfast waiting."

"You're all the breakfast I need."

Her probing kiss silenced any further discourse. By the time they got around to the porridge, coddled eggs, broiled tomatoes, kippered herring, bacon, and buttered toast, everything was soggy and cold.

The knightly couple had separate schedules that day. Sir Arthur arrived back from interminable meetings in a thoroughly disagreeable mood. He had barely enough time to bathe, shave, and dress before their dinner engagement. Winding uptown through Central Park in a cab restored his robust good humor. The invitation to the home of Mr. and Mrs. Harry Houdini had been a long-anticipated pleasure.

Before the start of Houdini's much-publicized war on psychics, the two men corresponded frequently on the subject of spiritualism, and when the magician toured England in 1920, Sir Arthur provided introductions to a number of well-known mediums. Thanks to these letters,

Houdini obtained over a hundred psychic sittings in Britain, insisting he was an impartial observer. Midway through his tour, when the April daffodils bloomed in saffron profusion about the countryside, the great Self-Liberator journeyed down to Windlesham, the Conan Doyles' home in Crowborough, for a well-remembered luncheon.

They had hoped to get together again last year when Sir Arthur first lectured in America, but Houdini's busy vaudeville schedule made this impossible until the very last moment. Two nights before sailing back to England, the Conan Doyles were guests of the magician at the Earl Carroll Theater for a performance of Raymond Hitchcock's "Pinwheel Revue." The occasion was a celebration of Mr. and Mrs. Houdini's twenty-eighth wedding anniversary.

Sir Arthur remembered a splendid evening. "Hitchy," the irrepressible master of ceremonies, introduced him to the audience and urged Houdini onto the stage where, after an uncharacteristic display of modesty, the magician agreed to perform his famous "Needle Mystery." Houdini stopped the show. Sir Arthur never forgot the startling appearance of all those glittering threaded needles. There had been no time to prepare any sort of trick. Clearly, he had witnessed a supreme psychic manifestation.

The cab pulled to a stop in front of a four-story brownstone house at 278 West 113th Street. Every window glowed with electric light. In contrast with its more somber neighbors, the building declared itself boldly on the dark street, a bit of the Great White Way transplanted uptown. "Quite festive," observed Lady Jean.

Houdini himself opened the door mere seconds after Sir Arthur pressed the buzzer. His welcome warm and effusive, the magician ushered them into a wood-paneled foyer where a slender Oriental servant took their coats. A tiny, dark-haired woman with bright intelligent eyes and a broad, full-lipped smile stood shyly to one side. Two small energetic dogs scampered about her feet.

"Mrs. Houdini," Conan Doyle called in his bluff, hearty manner. "Delightful to see you once again. You're looking quite splendid." Stooping, he tousled a furry canine neck.

"Welcome, welcome," Bess said, taking Jean by the hand.

"And this is the brother of the great Houdini," the magician trumpeted like a carnival barker, pointing to a square-jawed man in the doorway behind his wife. Not a hint of irony in his voice. Houdini gestured expansively at his newly arrived guests. "Dash. I want you to meet the man who gave the world Sherlock Holmes: Sir Arthur and Lady Conan Doyle."

The knight caught his lady's eye as the "great" man's brother stepped up to shake hands. He detected a definite twinkle, but she kept her face blank as a card player holding trumps.

"Theo Weiss," the brother said, by way of introduction. "My friends call me Dash."

"Dash it is then, what?"

Houdini suggested his wife and brother might want to get Lady Conan Doyle some refreshment and keep her company until the other guests arrived. His gracious manner belied his impatience. "I know Sir Arthur is anxious to have a look at the library."

In fact, the magician was the one who was anxious. His extensive collection of books and memorabilia dealing with magic, witchcraft, conjuring, spiritualism, and the theater was his pride and joy. He believed it to be the finest library of its kind on earth and was always eager to show it off to an appreciative audience.

"If it's no trouble," said Sir Arthur, "I should be pleased to do some browsing."

Houdini bowed the knight toward a set of double doors, his "Alphonse and Gaston" manner unintentionally comic. The library occupied a huge room on the ground floor. Shelves of books rising to the ceiling lined all four walls. They surrounded hundreds of other stacked volumes. The two men wove between a waist-high colonnade as if negotiating a maze. Houdini showed Sir Arthur his proudest treasures: David Garrick's diary, a Bible autographed by Martin Luther, Edgar A. Poe's portable writing desk.

This simple wooden box held Conan Doyle's imagination. The writer placed his fingertips on the weathered mahogany surface. As a doctor, he had often felt for a patient's pulse with just such a gesture. What lingering trace of genius might still be detected by those with a gift for divination? Although he believed passionately in a spiritual afterlife, he sadly lacked the sensitive's nature and could not make contact unaided.

Conan Doyle showed great interest in the number of books dealing with spiritism, but expressed disappointment on discovering that by and large they were written by antagonistic critics. "You certainly have all the nay-sayers," he chided with a gentle smile. "Have you no room for statements of belief?"

Houdini frowned, unwilling to acknowledge any deficiency in his library. "Not everything has been properly cataloged. There are many crates of books still stored in the basement. Upstairs, in my study, I keep a collection of holograph letters. Perhaps you'll find them more intriguing. I've many by Lincoln; also, Edmund Kean, Jenny Lind, Disraeli . . . many others."

"Anything by spiritualists?"

"Of course . . . Ira Davenport. D. D. Home."

"Home, you say. By Jove, I'd be keen to have a look at those."

"Your wish is my command, Sir Arthur. Please follow me." Houdini led the way out of the library, grinning like a schoolboy.

On the second-floor landing, a peculiar piece of furniture caught Sir Arthur's eye. A sturdy oaken chair, extremely worn, with sweat-stained leather straps hanging from the arms, legs, and back. He had seen a similar contrivance once before, nearly ten years ago, on the eve of the war, when he made a tour of Sing Sing Prison as the guest of Warden Clancy.

"Ah-hah!" Houdini cried, noting the author's curiosity. "Worthy of Madame Tussaud's Chamber of Horrors. The very first electric chair ever used at Auburn Prison. I saw it originally as a youngster at a dime museum where I was showing. When it came up at auction a few years back, I couldn't resist the temptation."

Sir Arthur visibly recoiled from the grotesque device, as if facing some malignant creature crouching to attack. "Odd to have such a thing

in one's home," was his only comment. Conan Doyle remembered sitting
cheerfully in the chair in the death house at Ossining back in 1914, smoking a
pipe and fitting his head into the small steel cap. One thing to enjoy a bit of
gallows humor; quite another to display such a hideous instrument as
household decor.

The magician remained oblivious to any implied criticism. "At
first, I thought to use it in my act. You know, with a time deadline like
when some of your naval petty officers challenged me to escape tied to
the muzzle of a cannon with a twenty-minute fuse. Twelve years ago in
Chatham. A good many paid to see me blown to kingdom come. Made
sense to figure I'd draw a big crowd to watch me burn."

"A bit macabre for family entertainment, don't you think?"

"Exactly. That's why I dropped the idea. Used a hot seat escape as
one of the cliff-hangers in 'The Master Mystery,' but it was just a prop."
Houdini continued on up the stairs, leading the way to the third floor.
"Over seventy men died in that contraption," he said.

The magician's study was at the end of the hall. Sir Arthur paused
along the way. Something odd about the bedroom on his right. Great
gathered drapery folds suggested the Orient, as did hanging silks, carved
furnishings, tasseled lamps. A candle flickered on a small shelf, illumi-
nating the glass-framed Kodak portrait of a kindly gray-coifed matron.
The same pleasant face stared out of a larger photograph resting against
the cushions on the brocade-covered bed. No one lived in this room. He
was gazing into a shrine.

"My beloved mother's room." Houdini stepped past him toward the
bed. "Sometimes I come in here and lay my head down on the counter-
pane, just as I used to lay against her breast and listen to the beating of
her heart."

The appalling frankness of this confession was offset by the magician's passionate sincerity and Conan Doyle, who knew himself to be
also a bit of a mama's boy, felt touched by it. "Contact is possible, you
know," he said. "Such I sincerely believe."

"I cannot imagine a greater happiness. If willpower alone could
bring her back, she would be with us now."

"There are guides."

"In a lifetime of searching, I never found one who wasn't a phony." Houdini's manner abruptly changed. "It's all hokum." The mournful attitude dropped away and he marched out of the room grim with determination.

Sir Arthur followed amiably. "You must keep an open heart," he said. "I have spoken with the Ma'am, my own cherished mother, on several occasions since she passed over."

Houdini's study resembled the lair of a mad alchemist. Bizarre magic show memorabilia in bright carnival colors stood among wooden filing cabinets stacked like gargantuan children's blocks. Crates, trunks; folios crammed with posters; bound programs shelved along the walls. The chaos had an apparent order; the magician produced the Davenport and Home correspondence with a minimum of searching.

Sir Arthur examined the thick folders. Far too many letters to read in one sitting. He asked if he might come back at a more convenient time and peruse them.

"My collection is at your disposal." Obviously pleased, Houdini made no effort to conceal a smug smile. "I also have hundreds of letters from Harry Kellar, who was with the Davenports on their first tour."

"Thank you, but no. Kellar was a stage magician. I mean no offense when I say I am interested only in the genuine article, not a trickster merely duplicating the effects of a séance."

"Why, Sir Arthur, I am nothing but a trickster, yet I have always been keenly aware of your interest in me."

The briefest moment of recognition ignited when their eyes met and they looked beyond the common ground of achievement and genius into the comic heart of human folly. Both men laughed, sharing the unspoken joke. They didn't know one another well enough to be comfortable with such informality and the mirth soon subsided into more familiar postures.

"Depend upon it, my dear Houdini, my admiration for you goes far beyond an appreciation of your conjuring abilities." Sir Arthur stood, legs spread, arms behind his back, like an officer at parade rest; like a rugby coach embarking on a pep talk. "I am convinced, above all your protests, that you possess supernormal powers. I have the testimony of

Mr. Hewat Mackenzie, one of the most experienced psychical researchers in the world, that when he stood near to you on stage, during an escape from a padlocked iron milk can filled with water, he clearly felt a great loss of physical energy of the sort experienced by sitters in materializing séances. I accept this as evidence of your ability to dematerialize."

Houdini was at a loss for words. How could this great man of letters believe such bunk? Further proof that the better a man's education and the more impressive his brain, the easier it became to mystify him. The milk-can escape was a gag. Dash still featured it in his act. It pained him to think anyone he so respected could be such a sucker. "I give you my word of honor. The escape you mention was a trick."

"Then what about the time you escaped from regulation handcuffs at Scotland Yard? That was no stage presentation."

"All right. I'll tell you about it. I've published most of my handcuff secrets." Houdini lifted a heavy crate off a steamer trunk. He made it look easy. "It was my first trip to London. Spring of 1900. I was trying to get a booking at the Alhambra. Dundas Slater, the theater manager, liked my audition, but as it was a challenge act . . ." Houdini opened the trunk lid. Hundreds of jumbled manacles and handcuffs glittered inside like a pirate's treasure chest. "He suggested in an offhand manner that Scotland Yard might be the most infallible test of my skill."

"And you accepted immediately!" Sir Arthur beamed with boyish playing-field enthusiasm.

"I came prepared to demand that exact challenge."

"Because you knew you possessed the power to dematerialize."

"Because I knew a little secret about the darbies used by Scotland Yard." The magician showed a sturdy pair of handcuffs to Sir Arthur. "Jersey Giants. See the broad arrow and crown. That marks 'em all. They have a simple spring lock. My study of the mechanism revealed a strategic flaw." Taking the knight's hand, Houdini quickly snapped the cuff shut on his wrist.

"I say . . . ," protested Sir Arthur.

"I discovered if Jersey Giants were tapped sharply at a certain point . . ." Houdini locked Conan Doyle's other wrist. ". . . against a hard surface, they would simply snap open. The morning of the Alhambra audition, before putting on my trousers, I strapped a sheet of lead to my thigh. It proved an unnecessary precaution at the Yard, as Superintendent Melville shackled my hands behind my back around a stone pillar. He said: 'This is the way we handle Yankees who come over here and get into trouble.' He then suggested to Slater that they return in an hour and release me.

"I said, 'I'll come with you.' One good knock and I was free. Slater signed me on the spot."

Sir Arthur stared uncertainly at his manacled wrists. "I hope you have the key."

"No need." Houdini showed him the critical point on the mechanism. "Go ahead. Rap 'em hard against the edge of the desk."

"Like this . . . ?" Sir Arthur brought his wrists down smartly against the desktop. The handcuffs popped open as if by magic.

"Simple, when you know the trick." The magician flourished his fingers and plucked a silver half-dollar out of midair.

"Skillful conjuring is an excellent distraction." The knight dropped the Scotland Yard darbies back into the trunk. "Focuses attention away from your true psychic powers."

Houdini shrugged. "Nothing I can say will set you straight. I have prepared a mysterious entertainment for later this evening. The supernatural is not involved. Everything I do is the result of preparation, practice, knowledge, study, more practice, and physical abilities of an extreme sort. Maybe a little curtain-raiser might convince you."

Houdini sat in his desk chair, hooking his arms over the back. "Let's assume my hands are tied behind me. In my line of work, you gotta be able to use more than hands."

Astonished, Sir Arthur watched Houdini slip out of one shoe and sock, deftly untying the other shoelace with his toes. Second shoe off, the nimble toes of both feet went to work retying the shoelace in a neat bow.

"Absolutely amazing!"

"No, Sir Arthur, this is amazing." The magician lifted his right leg into the air, bending it toward him, contorting like a yogi adept. When it seemed impossible a human limb could twist any farther, the foot arched down and slipped into his outside jacket pocket. It reemerged in a graceful uncoiling, a needle-book and spool of thread gripped between his toes.

Must never go anywhere without those props, Sir Arthur thought. Always prepared to perform on popular demand.

Houdini dropped the needles and thread on the floor between his feet. Sir Arthur watched in wonder, scarcely able to believe his own eyes as the magician removed a needle from the folded paper and carefully threaded it with his toes.

"Capital!" cried the excited knight.

"Purely physical." Houdini bounded to his feet like a prizefighter coming out of his corner. "My body is a trained instrument. Given time to prepare, I can withstand any blow." The magician braced his legs, thrusting out his chest. "Go on. Hit me. I'm ready. Hit me as hard as you can."

"You can't be serious?"

"Go on. . . . Give it your best shot."

Sir Arthur placed his hands behind his back. "I used to be quite keen about boxing. Grand sport. Wouldn't want to sully it with this sort of foolishness."

"Okay . . ." Houdini relaxed his stance. "It was just meant as a demonstration. Wanted to show you what the physical body was capable of. Watch this. Learned it as a kid in the carny."

Arching backwards, limber as a dancer, Houdini bent all the way to the floor and picked the threaded needle off the carpet with his teeth. Snake-supple, he returned upright. "Worked as an acrobat, tumbler, contortionist. . . . Watched an Indian fakir do this." The magician thrust the needle through his cheek.

"Dear fellow . . ." Nonplussed by this extraordinary behavior, Sir Arthur sputtered in Colonel Blimpish protest, even as his keen medical eye observed the needle's passage to be completely bloodless. "No more, I beg you."

"Harry, dear . . ." Beatrice Houdini stood in the doorway of her husband's office. "We don't want our dinner to get cold."

"Coming, Mrs. Houdini." The magician picked up his shoes. "Just showing Sir Arthur some of the tricks of the trade."

The other dinner guests were the magician's attorney, Bernard Ernst, and his brooding, overweight wife. They engaged in immediate shoptalk. Conan Doyle deduced very quickly that Theo "Dash" Weiss also performed as a magician, using the stage name "Hardeen." He toured on the rival Pantages Circuit with an act so similar it incorporated Houdini's famous milk-can escape, which his brother no longer performed. The Weiss boys joked about cornering the market in the escape business. Hardeen's success discouraged any serious rivals. Strictly a family enterprise.

"When we bought this house twenty years ago, there were almost no Negroes living in Harlem," Bess Houdini told Lady Jean. "This was a nice German neighborhood back then. Still is, really. The colored live mainly above 125th Street. Of course, there's an Irish section up here, too. And Italians on the East Side."

"The bottom dropped out of the upper Harlem real estate market in 'ought-five," Houdini interjected. "Speculators built too many new apartments, especially around 135th Street. Wanted to recoup their losses, natch. Fill up those vacancies. So, they started renting to Negroes. Cheap crooks're getting one twenty-five a month for places that used to go for forty bucks."

"It wasn't something you really noticed until after the war," sighed Bessie. "That was when you really started to see the change. Used to be such a quiet residential place."

The conversation turned to the subject of the movies, something they all had in common. A film version of Sir Arthur's novel *The Lost World* had recently been produced in Chicago with spectacular special effects footage depicting ancient dinosaurs. Houdini, veteran of a serial made in Yonkers and two Hollywood films, had started his own motion picture company in New York a couple years before. Another family enterprise. Dash took time out from his career and pitched in. Houdini was president as well as writer, producer, director, and star. Two new films were released. Both did poorly at the box office.

"I quite enjoyed *The Man from Beyond*," commented Sir Arthur. "The escape from the brink of Niagara Falls was spot on."

"Maybe so," Dash fixed his brother with a cocky smile, "but *Haldane* was strictly from hunger."

Houdini ignored any implied challenge. "I shoulda done the Egyptian picture instead . . . *Mistero di Osiris*—" Suddenly brought up short, the magician cocked his head as if hearing a faraway sound, drifting away into thought. Everyone waited for him to finish speaking and the conversation dwindled, inhibited by his distraction.

Conan Doyle cast about for a way out of the embarrassing silence. A framed photograph of an early flying machine hung on the opposite wall. The box-kite tail was emblazoned with the name HOUDINI in bold capitals. "Using aircraft for advertising." Sir Arthur indicated the picture with a nod of his head. "Pure twentieth-century thought. I, for one, applaud it."

"That was my own machine," Houdini said. "A Voison. Santos Dumont design. Had a British E.N.V. 60.80 horsepower petrol engine."

"By Jove, I didn't know you were an aeronaut to boot." Sir Arthur's enthusiasm infected his grin.

"I was the first man to make a successful airplane flight on the Australian continent. March 16, 1910."

Sir Arthur kept his grin in place. How absurd to speak in headlines like some demented town crier. Wouldn't the celebrated Dr. Freud have a field day analyzing this man's ego?

Houdini pointed to a bronze plaque on the opposite wall next to the photograph: a winged globe in relief. "The Aerial League of Australia awarded me that trophy. I was touring down under. Next to shut. "

"Beg your pardon. . . . Next to what?"

" 'Next to shut' is the featured turn on a vaudeville bill," Dash interjected. "Shut is closing."

The magician firmed his jaw, still posing in the cockpit. "Shipped the Voison from Germany with all my gear. Put a mechanic on the payroll, too."

"Do you still fly?" inquired Lady Jean.

"Took a spin in a Stinson four years ago. Out west making *The Grim Game.*"

"Amazing aerial photography in that." Sir Arthur positively beamed. "Your leap between two aeroplanes while handcuffed is the most reckless feat of daring I have ever witnessed."

"The midair collision was unplanned. Turned out to be a lucky accident. Willat kept the camera running in the third plane and we worked the footage into the story."

Sir Arthur, entranced with the memory of viewing this daring moment at the cinema, stared up past the ceiling. "The way they spiraled down through the sky, locked together, like giant insects spent at the climax of their nuptial flight." Everyone around the table smiled at the daring sexual allusion so discreetly phrased. "You were fortunate no one was injured."

Houdini nodded agreement. "The planes separated mere moments before crash-landing." The magician made no mention of the piano wire safety harness, or of the double who made the jump that day. Houdini had watched on the ground, his arm in a sling, having fractured his left wrist in a three-foot fall during a jailbreak sequence filmed the day before. This was a closely guarded secret. Always best never to let the truth get in the way of legend.

Bernard Ernst patted the leather cigar case jutting from his breast pocket with affectionate anticipation. "Houdini was quick to gauge the import of moving pictures," he said. "Why, if he was to have done that plane jump stunt before an audience, the most he could hope to draw is ten, maybe twenty thousand. On film, millions get to see him."

"So, where were the millions for *Haldane of the Secret Service?*" Houdini made a face of mock nausea. "I'm all through with pictures. Maybe they are the future. I know all the vaude houses are showing two-reelers as part of the bill these days."

"Vaudeville is dying," Mrs. Ernst said. "That's the pity of it."

"What can you do about it?" The magician shrugged. "Mourning the past is a waste of time. Far better to prepare for the future. When my touring contract is over next year, I plan on putting together a full evening show and playing nothing but legitimate theaters. Thurston's been working that side of the street pretty successfully for fifteen years now."

"Perhaps this is an impossible question to answer . . ." Lady Jean's melodious voice captivated everyone at the table. "But . . . I'd be interested to know what you consider your most difficult escape."

Houdini's expression suggested pensive cogitation. How the man thrives on attention, thought Conan Doyle, shifting his gaze to his wife's lovely smile.

The magician ignored the servants clearing the table. "I will merely repeat what an old friend once said to me. For two and one-half years, starting when I was fourteen, I worked as an assistant necktie cutter for H. Richter's Sons. Five-oh-two Broadway. Twelve hours a day. I cut linings only. Assistants were not permitted to handle the better goods. It was then I first practiced card sleights and other tricks.

"Years later, after making a name for myself as a magician, I returned to Richter's cutting floor on a sentimental visit. My old partner came up to me and said: 'You know the greatest escape you ever made? It was escaping from this necktie factory.' "

Everyone laughed, including the Ernsts, who presumably had heard the story often before. Bernard Ernst laughed loudest of all. Conan Doyle watched Houdini's broad smile, pleased to note this pompous, heroic man also had a sense of humor.

Coffee and dessert were served in the drawing room. The gentlemen had permission to smoke. Sir Arthur stuffed his pipe as Ernst warmed a cigar over a candle flame. Houdini posed by the fireplace. "I have prepared a test for Sir Arthur," he said, picking a schoolboy's slate off the mantel. "Please examine this." He handed the slate to the knight.

Conan Doyle drew on his pipe, turning the slate over and over. "Appears to be exactly what it is."

"You'll notice two holes bored in the corners of the wooden frame." The magician produced twin lengths of brass wire with S-hooks wound onto either end. Hooking one into each hole, he handed the wires to Sir Arthur. "Hang these anywhere you see fit, so that the slate dangles freely in space."

Conan Doyle rose and hooked one wire over the top of a picture frame. The other, he attached to the spine of a large book on a shelf standing opposite. The slate swung in the middle of the room.

Houdini used his coffee spoon to stir the contents of a small bowl. "White ink," he said. "You may taste it if you wish."

"I'll accept your word as a gentleman."

The magician took four small cork balls from his pocket and placed them in a line in front of the bowl. "Pick one at random and cut it in half."

Conan Doyle selected the left-hand ball. It was about three-quarters of an inch in diameter. He sliced it in half with his penknife. Pure cork throughout.

Houdini dropped the other three in the bowl of ink, stirring them with the spoon until all were evenly coated. "We'll let these soak for a while. Sir Arthur . . . ? Have you a bit of paper and a pencil about your person?"

Conan Doyle pulled his notebook from an inside jacket pocket. "Always carry the tools of the trade." He slapped the small leather-bound volume against the palm of his hand.

"I would like you to leave this house. Walk as far as you wish in any direction. Once you are satisfied you are alone and unobserved, write some phrase or quote on a piece of paper. Then, fold it, put it back into your pocket, and return here. We promise not to drink all the coffee."

Sir Arthur felt exhilarated as he walked east on 113th Street. He loved games of every sort. Delighted in mystery. His pipe glowed red as a demon's eye with each excited puff. He turned uptown on Seventh Avenue and paused beside the B. S. Moss Regent Theater on the corner of 116th. Tearing a leaf free from his notebook, he wrote down words from the Old Testament that popped randomly into his head: "Mene, mene, tekel, upharsin . . ."

The knight was back in the Houdini parlor before ten minutes had elapsed. Everyone stared at him. He felt in their curiosity his own isolation; guardian of the secret message.

"You have done as I have instructed?" asked the magician.

"Yes."

"Good. I have devised this test, Sir Arthur, to teach you what can be done in the realm of the miraculous by means of pure trickery. The illusion you're about to see is one to which I've dedicated a great deal of thought, working on it, off and on, all winter. I assure you, it's accomplished entirely through natural means. I want you to remember this demonstration and be careful in the future when endorsing phenomena as bona fide supernatural just because you are unable to explain them.

"Your wife and the others will swear nothing has been touched in here." The magician handed the knight a spoon. "Please, choose one of the three remaining balls."

Sir Arthur scooped the middle ball out of the bowl, cupping his free hand beneath the dripping white ink.

Houdini stepped aside and pointed at the hanging slate. "Carry it over and hold the spoon against the left-hand side."

Sir Arthur did as he was told. He lifted the spoon to the black stone surface and the wet, white cork ball stuck to it by some inexplicable power. Houdini held himself erect, fierce as a falcon. Like a trained snail, the ball commenced to roll across the vertical face of the slate, leaving a cursive white trail behind.

Sir Arthur held his breath. The gravity-defying ball appeared to spell out words as it rolled. The knight pulled on his spectacles, just to be sure. The stark white letters blazed across the slate as the ball dropped free to the carpet:

MENE, MENE, TEKEL, UPHARSIN . . .

7

HEEGAN OF HOMICIDE

Sergeant James Patrick Heegan knew he had no cause for complaint. Ever since transferring downtown to headquarters he didn't have to do a blessed thing all day long. A precinct desk assignment had been soft duty, but at least the department expected him to keep his ass in the chair. Not to mention occasional paperwork. In exile downtown, he felt completely useless.

The second or third day, Lieutenant Bremmer motioned him aside in the hall. "Listen, Sarge," he said. "I don't really care why you're here. I know it's politics. Some other bullshit. I don't want it to be my problem. Far as I'm concerned, you don't exist. You hear me?"

"Every word."

"I'm cutting you a lot of slack, Heegan. Just don't rub my nose in it."

The sergeant punched in and pulled his shift, stayed reasonably sober, and kept his uniform buttoned; aside from that, no one gave a damn what he did. As the weeks drifted by, he got better at brewing coffee. The younger detectives treated him like some kind of comic strip flatfoot. He didn't mind, accepting their teasing as a form of shorthand affection. Occasionally, he'd go out on call with them to break the monotony, but for the most part he just sat around and read the papers.

Heegan hunched inconspicuously over a late edition folded flat before him at an empty desk in the squad room, looking for all the world like a man engrossed in an official homicide report. The publication schedules of the morning and afternoon newspapers conveniently divided his day. He logged quite a few hours in local luncheonettes and coffee shops, but as the lieutenant requested, didn't rub the department's nose in it.

Sergeant Heegan discovered a way out of his malaise one morning while reading the *New York American*. As always, he started with the sports section. Beneath the comic strip "Bringing Up Father" he read a humorous Damon Runyon poem about spring training. Heegan had smiled at Jiggs and Maggie but the poem made him laugh out loud. Runyon's byline dominated the page. Along with "Runyon's Rhymes" and his daily column, "Says Damon Runyon . . . ," there was also an article on the state boxing commission.

Heegan read every word. An interview with Giants manager John J. McGraw occupied most of Runyon's column. The bottom paragraphs carried a bold head:

MURDER BY THE BOOK . . . ?

Next to a championship fight or the World Series, there's no sporting event boils the blood of your correspondent any hotter than a complicated murder mystery. Lots of recent ink slung concerning the demise of Broadway Butterfly Dot King last March 15, but hardly anybody has much to say about the more recent axe-slaying of 26-year-old hoofer Violette Speers.

Of course, the late Mrs. Speers is no former Ziegfeld girl and didn't have $30,000 in jewels to steal. Just a second-stringer found walled-up in a cheap room at the Hotel Stanley. Entombed with a howling cat, says the back pages. Sound familiar? Only if you're wise to the Tales of E. A. Poe.

Being a Poe fan, the death of Mrs. Speers brings to mind a double homicide I am privileged to observe

from baseline seats about a month ago. The losing side
is Mrs. Esp and her blond daughter. Widow Esp with
her throat cut. The daughter is stuffed up the chimney.
Exactly like "The Murders in the Rue Morgue."

Have asked Nick the Greek, known to make a little
book from time to time, what odds he offers on the Poe
Connection.

"Long shot," he says to yours truly. "But if someone
spots an orangutan hanging around Broadway, all bets
are off."

Heegan read these paragraphs over and over. He knew an orangutan was some kind of big monkey. He also knew he was on to something. The sergeant tucked the paper under his arm and told the duty
officer he was going out for a couple hours. No problem. Take a long
lunch. Didn't even look up from his paperwork. A stray dog would
attract more attention.

Heegan headed straight for the nearest branch of the public library.
He spent the afternoon with a one-volume edition of Edgar Allan Poe's
stories. The newspaper writers the sergeant liked, guys like Ring
Lardner and Runyon and Arthur "Bugs" Baer, never made him feel stupid
for not knowing something, whereas Poe's snooty ornate prose deliberately mocked his ignorance. He plodded on, page after page, slowly
reading "The Murders in the Rue Morgue," "The Black Cat," and "The
Mystery of Marie Roget."

Around three o'clock, the sergeant brought the book to the front
desk. The librarian showed him last week's newspapers and he quickly
found the story of the Violette Speers murder in a copy of the evening
World. What he remembered the squad room boys telling him was all
there along with a whole lot more. When Heegan got to the part about
the one-eyed cat, he felt his sphincter tighten with excitement. He
wasted no time finding a public phone and placed a call to the editorial
offices of the *New York American*.

Sergeant Heegan showed up at Lindy's on Broadway and Fiftieth

Street promptly at five. The place was bright and brassy, bentwood chairs and white-tiled floors, an all-night delicatessen alive with the clatter of blue plate specials. Even in the slow of the afternoon, most tables were occupied with swells in snappy pinstriped suits and broad-brimmed fedoras. Heegan noted their sudden interest in studying the menu when a uniformed cop sauntered past.

The sergeant found Runyon in a back booth with a lean, stoop-shouldered, dark-haired man he spotted for a lunger first thing. They both drank coffee. The newspaperman didn't recognize Heegan from the night of the Esp murders. No reason why he should. "If you're Damon Runyon, you probably ain't used to being in here this early." The policeman enjoyed feeling one up on him as they shook hands.

"Sergeant Heegan, allow me to introduce my illustrious colleague, Mr. Thomas Aloysius Dorgan, known to his intimates and the world at large as 'Tad.' "

The bright-eyed consumptive made no effort to rise. "Mr. Runyon and I are embarking upon an evening of pugilistic appreciation. The dark and dangerous Mr. Harry Wills is topping the card at the Garden."

"I know you," Heegan said as he sat down. "Tad . . . the cartoonist. 'Indoor Sports.' 'Silk-Hat Harry.' 'Judge Rummy.' "

"Tad is much more than a mere cartoonist." Damon Runyon pointed a manicured finger. "This man is a great sportswriter and philosopher. He has given our language that immortal phrase: 'Yes, we have no bananas.' "

"Yeah . . . ? Well, he shoulda done the lingo a favor and kept his mouth shut."

"Hear that, Tad? The sergeant is a harsh critic."

Dorgan slumped in his chair. "Gotta roll with the punches . . ."

"Mr. Runyon, the reason I called you was on account of what you wrote in your column today." Heegan took a couple sugar cubes out of the bowl and popped them in his mouth.

"You got something on the Esp murders?"

"The night before the two stiffs was discovered . . ." Heegan crunched his sugar. "I was on the desk at the Twenty-ninth and a call come in from some woman claims she sees a gorilla carrying a blond down Ninth Avenue."

Runyon caught Dorgan's eye. "By gorilla, I take it you're not referring to the mugs who patronize this fair establishment."

"She was positive it was some kind of ape."

"What was the woman's name?" Damon Runyon took a slim lizard-skin notebook from the inside breast pocket of his natty suit.

Sergeant Heegan cleared his throat. "I . . . er, can't recollect. I was transferred down to headquarters shortly after that."

"You made a record of the call?"

"Why, certainly. . . . Everything according to regulations, that's always been my creed." Heegan tried to look sincere. "Go by the book and you'll never have no regrets."

"No problem, then . . ." Runyon jotted a couple numbers down and tore the page free from his notebook. "That's where you can reach me. Top one's my home number." He handed the slip of paper to Heegan. "Call anytime, night or day, soon as you get that woman's name and address."

"You think it's something big then?"

"Brother, if this dame is on the up and up, it'll be the biggest thing since Lefty Louie and Gyp the Blood iced Herman Rosenthal out front of the Metropole."

"That was before your time, wasn't it, Al?" cracked lanky Thomas Aloysius Dorgan.

"Nope. It was 1912. I got here from Denver two years earlier." Damon Runyon fixed Sergeant Heegan with his mirthless grin. "The cops made a bad job of the Rosenthal rubout."

Heegan didn't really want to hear about it, but he nodded in agreement. "Yeah. . . . Lieutenant Becker."

"Charlie Becker went to the chair. That was some story."

"I'll get you the name of the monkey woman." Heegan pushed out of the booth.

"Headlines, sergeant." The sportswriter made a tent of his thin fingers. "Big fat headlines."

"Extra! Extra!" giggled Tad.

Heegan had his work cut out for him. He paced the cracked bluestone sidewalk on Thirty-eighth Street between Eighth and Ninth. Identical six-story tenements stretched before him on either side, every building fronted by iron fire escapes. For the life of him, he couldn't remember whether the woman said she lived on Thirty-eighth or Thirty-ninth. Maybe he'd get lucky.

When you lack manpower better use brainpower, Heegan thought, trying to save on footwork by estimating the buildings too far back for a tenant to see the corner of Ninth without sticking her head out the window. That calculation cut the block in half. For the next hour, the sergeant rang the superintendents' doorbells. Lucky thing it was dinnertime.

All the supers gave him the same thing: a list of single women living in apartments facing the street. Heegan figured a married woman would have got the hubby to call the cops. And if the breadwinner wasn't at home, a frightened housewife would surely have made mention of it. It had to be some nosy old biddy with nothing better to do than stare out the window at the world passing her by.

For the next three hours, Sergeant Heegan interviewed spinsters, widows, showgirls, and prostitutes. The hookers got defensive right away when they saw the badge, but he asked everyone the same questions and the part about the gorilla made them all smile. Each denied calling the police on the night of April second.

Only four names remained on his list. Heegan had resigned himself to covering Thirty-seventh Street when he came to Millicent Cooper's apartment. He knocked with a lack of subtlety learned from twenty-plus years on the force. The sound of his pounding fist boomed inside.

"I'm coming! I'm coming!" The shrill voice had a nagging familiarity. "You don't have to break it down." The pint-sized woman who opened the door was wrapped in an embroidered Chinese gown, her long white hair pinned above her wrinkled pug-dog face with a tortoise-shell comb. "The neighbors are going to think it's an alky raid and you're coming in with a sledgehammer."

"Excuse me, ma'am." The sergeant tipped his cap. "Are you Mrs. Cooper?"

"Every inch of me." Millicent Cooper smiled, a rictus caricaturing joy painted on her sad sagging face. "I'd invite you in, officer, but I'm having some friends over for a game of Mah-Jongg." An arching Siamese cat pushed between her legs and stared cross-eyed up at Heegan.

"No need, Mrs. Cooper. Just procedure. Did you by chance tele-phone the police on the night of April second?"

She nodded, pulling the braided sash tighter. "When I saw the gorilla carry that woman. Are you the officer I spoke with?"

"No, ma'am. I'm just following up."

"Who is it, Milly?" a female voice yelled from another room. A sec-ond Siamese appeared next to the first, rubbing against Millicent Cooper's legs. "Pung!" shouted another voice with mock-Oriental enthusiasm.

"A policeman," she hollered back. "About that gorilla!"

Heegan wrote on a scrap of paper with a pencil stub. "The woman was blond?" he asked.

"That's right. Long blond hair. Hanging down unpinned. Like she was unconscious. What was that all about, anyway?"

"We're still looking into it, Mrs. Cooper." Heegan licked the tip of his pencil. "Would you kindly tell me your telephone number?"

"Hudson six four three four." For a moment, youth gleamed again in Millicent Cooper's eyes. "I'm pleased to help in any way I can."

"That's much appreciated." Sergeant Heegan touched the visor of his cap. "Thank you, Mrs. Cooper. I expect you'll be hearing from others in the department as the investigation continues."

"What investigation . . . ?"

Heegan started down the stairs, not wanting to tell her much more. A third voice screeched from inside the apartment: "Millicent! Your play!"

Mrs. Cooper looked confused. "Excuse me." She glanced over her shoulder. Two more cats joined the milling pack around her feet.

"Evening, ma'am." Heegan bounded off down the stairs, his heart light as a bird taking wing into the cool night sky.

Over at the Twenty-ninth, Eddie Hallenbeck had the desk. Heegan waited until things were quiet, grabbing a bite at Jack's across the street from the Hipp before heading for the precinct house. It was quiet all right. Made the morgue feel like a six-day bike race. Hallenbeck seemed glad for some conversation and Heegan happily obliged, embroidering fanciful tales of headquarters high jinks.

It looked like they might jaw all night and Heegan almost offered Hallenbeck a sawbuck to take a powder for an hour. Instead, good old Eddie asked the Sarge to do him a big favor and keep an eye on the desk awhile. He'd be right back. Heegan told him to take his time.

The sergeant settled into the familiar swivel chair and waited ten minutes or so after Hallenbeck's departure before getting out the April blotter. Turning to April 2, he saw his usual double and sometimes triple spacing between the entries.

Heegan dipped a pen in the ink well. In the appropriate spot he wrote: "9:25 P.M. "Call from Mrs. Millicent Cooper. 355 West 38th St. Hudson 6434. Saw a gorila (?) carrying a woman down the street. No manpower available." His precise unornamented script matched all the other surrounding entries. Heegan placed the big ledger back in the desk drawer. It had been a long, long time since he felt this good.

The sergeant didn't go straight home when Eddie Hallenbeck got back from sneaking around. Heegan went downtown to headquarters. The squad room stood empty, but a number of half-empty coffee cups indicated the crew had recently gone out on a call. He pulled the cover off a typewriter and settled down to puzzle things out.

Twenty minutes of laborious one-finger probing yielded a memorandum for Lieutenant Bremmer:

> THIS ITEM FROM RUNYON'S COLLUM. ON THE NIGHT OF THE ESP MURDERS I WAS ON THE DESK AT THE 29TH. I LOGGED A CALL FROM A WOMAN WHO CLAIMED TO SEE A GORILA CARRY A BLOND DOWN 9TH AVE. HAVE READ THE ED POE STORY. IT IS THE SAME IN EVERY WAY AS THE ESP CASE.
>
> SGT. J. P. HEEGAN

Heegan unscrolled the page from the typewriter carriage and attached the bottom half of Damon Runyon's column with a paper clip. He carried it into Bremmer's office and set it square in the middle of the green blotter on the lieutenant's desk.

Back in the squad room, the sergeant picked up a phone and gave central the newspaperman's home number. Heegan remembered that Runyon was going to the fights, but, in his exhilaration, didn't realize it was so close to midnight.

A woman answered. "Mrs. Runyon . . . ?" he asked.

"Speaking."

"Is Mr. Runyon at home?

"Mr. Runyon is never at home."

"Do I take you to mean that he's not available for messages?"

"You can take it any way you like. If I see him, I'll say you called." Her voice sounded slurred. "Just who in hell exactly should I say is calling?"

"Heegan of homicide."

The sergeant hung up grinning. He snapped a match alight on his thumbnail and set fire to the cigar he filched off Bulldog Bremmer's desk.

8

--·--·--·--·--·--·--·--·--·--·--

THE GAME IS AFOOT

Sir Arthur sat at the foot of his bed shortly after dawn. A faint line of light described the edges of the heavy drapes drawn across the windows. Jean remained asleep, warm and safe beside him. He thought of Houdini, the white cork ball in the pocket of his dressing gown gone gray from constant fingering. Conan Doyle had cut the other two in half and found nothing. He knew bisecting the final ball would yield the same result. Had a magnet been involved, Houdini certainly would have switched the spurious original through sleight-of-hand.

It wasn't how the magician made the balls behave that troubled him. Nor the slate. He'd examined the slate and by all outward appearances it was utterly ordinary. This, of course, did not rule out possible trickery. Things are often not what they seem at first glance. Conan Doyle took pride in his keen powers of observation. To his practiced, diagnostic eye all the equipment Houdini used in his "demonstration" looked to be normal everyday household items. Even so, he knew a magician's art depended upon the assumptions of the gullible.

The impossibility of what he'd witnessed was not what puzzled Sir Arthur. How did Houdini know the secret words he had written? The knight wrestled long and hard with the mystery, finding no solution other than the one suggested by common sense and logic: the magician was a true medium, possessing unimagined powers.

He'd talked it over with Jean and she agreed with him, convinced of Houdini's supernatural abilities. What a pity so formidable a warrior could not be enlisted in the cause of spiritism. He squeezed the white cork ball in his fist as if to wring the magic from it by sheer strength.

Not wanting to wake his wife, Sir Arthur eased up from bed and padded barefoot out of the room. Always an early riser, finding the quiet morning hours ideal for work, he followed an unvaried routine. First, the bathroom. While urinating, Conan Doyle made a mental list of the many matters requiring his attention that day. Sadly, the schedule had no room for an afternoon ride with his wife. Friends recommended a stable nearby and he and Jean had twice gone for an invigorating gallop along the bridle path twisting through Central Park.

Little likelihood of repeating such happiness in the days ahead. The coming fortnight promised a nightmare of appointments and timetables. Starting tonight, he had lectures scheduled for Carnegie Hall, Columbia University, Cooper Union, and the Brooklyn Academy as well as travel to New Haven, Boston, and Providence. These engagements established the pattern of his life for the immediate future: numberless strange hotel rooms, interminable luncheons, and the constant presence of the press. Sir Arthur banished such whining from his thoughts. With six months of the tour still to go, keeping up morale remained a high priority. His mission deserved no less of him.

He looked forward with great pleasure to a spell by the sea in two weeks' time. Especially so because the children would be joining them in Atlantic City. Much as he adored having Jean all to himself for a bit of a "honeymoon," he was happiest when surrounded by his family. The thought of future horseplay had him grinning.

Sir Arthur stepped from the bathroom in a very jolly mood. A pot of fresh-brewed tea waited just outside the door to the suite. Fetching the tray provided a pleasant start to his days at the Plaza. He picked the tea service off the hallway carpet, smelling the oven aroma of new-baked rolls nested beneath crisp white linen, and when he turned, closing the door behind him, he saw the figure of a man, seemingly without substance, seated in a chair by the writing table in the rotund alcove.

Sir Arthur took a step toward the luminous figure, a creature of mist encased in a corona of moonlight. Gray dawn shadows blunted the corners of the room. Sir Arthur blinked, fearing a hallucination. The figure remained in the corner. He was dressed in the manner of a dandy from the first years of Victoria's reign. His tousled hair and hastily knotted cravat suggested weary dissolution.

Sir Arthur returned the specter's stare. He knew those doleful mourner's eyes, the ironic brow and clipped mustache. It was a face steeped in melancholy. It was Poe.

"I say . . ." The shock of recognition staggered Sir Arthur. Could the emanation have resulted from touching the portable writing desk in Houdini's library the other evening? Was there some magic involved? He set the tray down on a coffee table by the couch. When he looked back up, the apparition had vanished.

Even before seven o'clock in the evening, numbers of taxicabs and private automobiles stopped to discharge passengers on Fifty-seventh Street in front of Carnegie Hall. The first of Sir Arthur Conan Doyle's scheduled lectures in New York City had completely sold out and the spiritualist audience, unlike the usual procession of concert-goers, made a point of arriving early. Those bringing topcoats out of habit carried them folded over their arms, for the eastern seaboard sweltered in the grip of a heat wave in early May and the evening felt exceptionally humid, much more like summer than springtime.

Mr. and Mrs. Harry Houdini alighted from a Checker cab and mounted the steps to the lobby at a few minutes before eight. Long years in show business had ingrained a habit of never arriving at any performance until just before the curtain. They had spent too many idle hours backstage to ever be comfortable killing time in an audience.

Houdini collected their complimentary tickets at the box office and headed with Bess for the auditorium. A brusque diminutive man intercepted them. His bald pate gleamed as if buffed with furniture wax.

"Harry! Harry!" he called in a clipped British accent, rushing forward out of the last-minute crowd. "A word with you please." Seeing Bess, he bowed in a grandiloquent manner. "Mrs. Houdini, I presume."

The magician bristled, adopting an icy, imperious air. "Mrs. Houdini, allow me to present to you Mr. Sidney Rammage, secretary of the Society of American Magicians."

"A very great pleasure," Rammage purred unctuously, shaking hands.

"I'm surprised we haven't met before," replied Bess with a modest smile.

"My loss entirely. Harry, I wanted you to see this deck." Rammage produced a pack of cards, handing it to Houdini. "In England, it's called 'Instanto.' The invention of one Billy O'Conner. Bills himself as the 'King of Kards.' "

"Easy enough. I was a card king myself once upon a time back in the nineties." Houdini opened the pack, fanning the cards with a deft flourish. "What's the gag?"

"The deck is rigged. You can call any card before you cut to it."

"Marked edges?"

"No. It's a variation on Walter Gibson's 'New Spelling Trick.' I thought you might like to have it for your collection."

"Very thoughtful of you, Rammage. Many thanks." Houdini slipped the deck into his pocket. The lobby lights blinked off and on.

"Don't mention it. There's the warning. Better get to our seats." Rammage gave a short bow. "Delighted to have met you at long last, Mrs. Houdini." The bald man turned to leave, then paused, seemingly on the spur of the moment. "Say, Harry. You're friends with Conan Doyle, aren't you?"

"I have that distinct honor," Houdini replied.

"Think you might introduce me to him?" Rammage twisted his lips into an expression more grimace than smile, as if even he found his servile toadying unpleasant.

Houdini felt trapped by the slight weight of the trick deck in his jacket pocket. Rammage bought this requested favor cheaply and he resented him for it. "Sir Arthur and Lady Conan Doyle are to be my guests at the S.A.M. banquet," he said without enthusiasm. "I'll present you to him then at the McAlpin."

"Righty-o." Rammage clicked his heels and hurried off into the dwindling crowd.

The magician and his wife followed an usher down the aisle. With every seat taken, the capacity audience numbered over thirty-five hundred. An almost palpable heat filled the thirty-year-old concert hall.

"What a distasteful little man." Bess broke a tense silence.

"An utter cad," Houdini agreed as they sat down.

"Why do you put up with him?"

"Politics."

She patted his arm. "Harry, dear, you were never much good as a politician."

"Nor am I getting any better at it now. Rammage is secretary of the Society and I must treat him square, although I opposed his nomination. Fate is a curious thing, Bessie. Before he left England for keeps, Sidney Rammage performed as Ali ben Haroun, the Wizard of the Rif."

Concentration creased her brow as she sifted through memories twenty years old. "Wasn't he the one who . . . ?"

"The very same. Tried to steal my thunder with a handcuff challenge act during our first European tour."

"I thought he was supposed to be some kind of bedouin."

"He was an Arab like William Ellsworth Robinson was a Chinaman. A little greasepaint turns any man into the League of Nations."

"Too bad Rammage didn't do a bullet-catching act." Bess referred to Robinson's accidental death onstage five years earlier while performing as Chung Ling Soo.

"Mike . . ." Using his wife's nickname softened Houdini's stern moral tone. "Dear, sweet Mike. . . . Never wish evil on another. Remember what Mama said." The houselights dimmed as the curtain rose. All around them, the murmuring of the audience fell away to an expectant hush. " 'Every dark thought returns to your heart,' " he whispered, " 'as surely as swallows return in the spring.' "

Pale blue light bathed the stage area. A committee of dignitaries sat like a small congregation behind the podium, their features barely visible in the crepuscular dim.

"Who are they?" Bess's breath tickled Houdini's ear.

"Well-known mediums." The magician strained to make out the faces. "There's Leonora Piper . . ." He held his breath when he recognized Opal Crosby Fletcher. ". . . and V. T. Podmord . . ."

"Isn't the woman in black that Isis person?"

Houdini cleared his throat with a half-cough. "I . . . believe you're right."

"You'd think she wouldn't have the nerve to show her face in public after you exposed her as such a fake."

The applause greeting Conan Doyle's entrance spared Houdini the necessity of a reply. The front-row crowd reached out. Pausing on the apron, the gracious knight touched their beseeching hands. Hamlin Garland stepped from his position of prominence on the platform and welcomed Sir Arthur.

After a brief introduction from chairman Garland, Conan Doyle began his lecture, his voice measured and calm. Much the same talk he had delivered countless times before; at home, in France, on tour in Australia, and in the United States the previous year. Utterly down-to-earth and without pretense of any kind, he conveyed an absolute and unwavering sincerity.

Sir Arthur spoke to them of the chemist Sir William Crookes, discoverer of the element thallium and the first resident in London to have a house lit by electricity. "A thoroughly practical man, not given to fancies. This eminent scientist used laboratory methods to investigate the Florrie Cook phenomena in 1874 and pronounced the manifestations genuine. Here we have a tangible proof instead of mere wishful speculation."

Telling the audience of his Catholic upbringing, Sir Arthur described his schism from the Church and eventual atheism. "I could not believe in what I was unable to experience directly." Gradually, he became converted to spiritism, being led forward by degrees into acceptance through direct communication with loved ones on the Other Side. This contact was always facilitated by the intervention of skilled mediums. "They have something like an 'ear' in musicians. They are like telegraph boys bringing messages."

Sir Arthur went on to detail those instances of spirit contact he had experienced at seances, the many messages coming through from his son, Kingsley, and his brother, Innes, both dead of pneumonia as a result of the war. "Evan Powell is outwardly a simple man, a Welsh coal miner, yet at his best as a medium is at the top of the list. Three years ago, in the darkness at his humble cottage in Merthyr Tydfil, where the windows were ablaze with the flare of a nearby ironworks, my wife and I sat listening to the whispered voices of the dead, voices full of earnest life, and of desperate endeavors to pierce the dull barriers of our senses."

The sounds of sobbing disturbed the ecclesial hush in the shadow-shrouded auditorium. Sir Arthur's countenance expressed kindness and sympathy. "There is no shame in weeping for the loss of loved ones," he said softly. "I wept at Powell's cottage. But they were tears of joy when I realized that our beloved dead are with us still. Is not this knowledge the supreme comfort for our bereavement?

"My own dear mother, to me always 'the Ma'am,' was in life a disbeliever. When she passed over two years ago, my grief was alleviated by the knowledge that contact was possible. Last year, at a sitting in London, the estimable spirit medium Ada Bessinet of Toledo, Ohio, a woman of the first psychic quality, materialized the Ma'am, producing a spirit letter which included her private pet name for me and containing her apology for any skepticism concerning life after death. The Ma'am was there, resurrected before me. I swear by all that's holy on earth I looked into her eyes."

A startled gasp from the balcony produced a further round of sobbing and Sir Arthur suggested a moment of silence and prayer to comfort those who were disconsolate. Suddenly, an unearthly piping pierced the hush like the shriek of a demented banshee.

"There is a spirit manifestation among you, is there not?" called out V. T. Podmord from the platform as a thin, high whistle shrilled in the darkness.

Near-hysteria swept the audience. Sir Arthur pleaded for calm as the panic spread. Far in the back of the hall, an old man rose from his seat. "No . . . ," he called in a frail, emaciated voice. "It's not a spirit. It's my hearing aid."

After a moment of incredulous silence, a sharp burst of laughter broke the tension. Even Sir Arthur smiled in his pleasant, good-natured way. "I appreciate that you didn't wish to turn the instrument off," he joked.

The remainder of the lecture accompanied a series of photographic slides projected onto a large screen suspended behind the seated committee. Suitably mysterious phonograph music played backstage to accompany the presentation. The first slide showed Crookes with "Katie King," the spirit control of Florence Cook. An ephemeral presence shrouded in phosphorescent veils seemed to float beside the stolid, earthbound form of the black-clad scientist.

Other slides pictured dark-haired Marthe Beraud, the famed Parisian medium known to the world as "Eva C." Quantities of a curious amorphous substance extruded from her mouth. Sir Arthur identified it as ectoplasm. "Isn't this, without a doubt, the most fantastic thing the mind can conceive?" His voice trembled with genuine awe. "Before such results the brain, even of the trained psychical student, is dazed."

These slides had an unsettling effect on the audience. Excited screams punctuated Conan Doyle's calm presentation. A woman fainted in the front row. Throughout the hall, general commotion indicated a level of discomfort exacerbated by the stifling heat.

"I should like to conclude with a remarkable series of spirit photographs." Sir Arthur spoke in a soothing tone, trying to quell the unease the way one quiets an angry dog. "These are the work of William Hope, who is employed as a carpenter in Crewe."

There followed a number of slides showing men and women in formal studio portrait poses. Above their heads, disembodied faces floated in the air, hovering in individual cloudlike nimbi. With each successive image, the audience grew increasingly restless. The moans and screams multiplied. Many wandered aimlessly up and down the aisles. Several fainted.

Houdini watched this spectacle in amazement. "Remarkable how easily crowds are duped," he whispered to his wife. "A simple double exposure is all it takes."

Bess smiled in the darkness. "Not so very different from what you've been doing all these years."

"I never claimed to be supernatural," came his quick, indignant reply. "Everybody knows what I do are tricks."

Bess said nothing but her smug smile remained unchanged.

The abrupt end of the lecture seemed almost an anticlimax. A final slide faded from view. Sir Arthur thanked his dazed audience for coming, gave a short bow, and walked off the stage. He received only a smattering of applause. Even this much seemed inappropriate, like clapping in church.

Backstage, the crush surrounding Conan Doyle's dressing room prevented Houdini and Bess from any immediate attempt to get near. The magician knew enough of personal fame and had no desire to intrude on Sir Arthur's glory. While Bess excused herself to seek out a ladies room, Houdini lounged against an ornate cast-iron radiator, ironically the coolest object in the ovenlike heat.

"Why have you been avoiding me?" The soft, melodic voice took the magician by surprise. Opal Crosby Fletcher fixed him with her penetrating gaze. She looked indescribably lovely in a sequined black Molyneux frock.

Houdini glanced about nervously. "I haven't been avoiding you. What gives you that idea?"

"Your manager never got back to my secretary. About a séance . . .? Remember?"

The magician stammered. "Well . . . I mean . . . there must've been some mix-up."

Her knowing, confident smile disarmed him. "You forgot all about it, didn't you?"

"No. Certainly not."

"I took you for a fair man, willing to be an impartial judge." Isis reached up and straightened his bow tie. He flinched at her touch. "Evidently, I was misinformed."

"Look . . . Mrs. Fletcher, I am——"

"Isis." Her voice rang clear and cold as crystal.

"I beg your pardon . . . ?"

"My name is Isis."

Houdini looked away from the penetrating cat-green eyes. "Isis it is then. . . . Please understand, I am a man of my word. If I said I would attend a séance, well, then——"

"It's not a question of if. When is more to the point."

"Whenever you say."

"Tonight . . . ?" The mysterious, mocking smile was more than a little bit wicked.

The magician drew back from her burning intensity. Who was this woman? "I have a prior engagement," he said.

"Break it."

Houdini felt a loss of equilibrium, as if the floor opened up beneath him. No one ever spoke to him in this manner. His fuse burned extremely short and any opposition to his will invariably detonated a temper tantrum. Vickery, Collins, and the rest of the staff had long ago learned to tolerate his extreme bursts of uncontrollable anger. This time confusion, not rage, gripped him. By nature chivalrous, he felt unsure how to react to such a bold feminine challenge. "I . . . ," he started, managing no better than, "I'm afraid that's impossible."

"I thought you were the master of the impossible." Her mocking smile transfixed him, like a pin through the butterfly's heart.

"Look," the magician said, "I don't know how to put it any plainer: I have another engagement and can't get out of it."

Isis laughed. "Something you can't get out of. Must be a first for the great escapologist."

His exaggerated sense of his own dignity normally could not allow him to tolerate being teased, but something about her dancing eyes and the musical chime of her laughter charmed him, scribing a mooncalf's grin onto his usual stern expression. "If it were possible, believe me, I would change my plans to accommodate you, but unfortunately——"

"What's so unfortunate, dear?" Bess appeared unexpectedly out of the shadows in the narrow corridor.

Houdini's lunar grin froze, a startled grimace advertising unspeci-
fied guilt. "Oh, Bess . . . here you are. I . . . I was just explaining to Mrs.
Fletcher that we were unavailable tonight."

"Unavailable for what?"

"To attend a seance." The magician looked clearly uncomfortable.
"I know you haven't met. Mrs. Houdini, allow me to introduce Mrs.
Opal Crosby Fletcher."

"My friends call me Isis." The delicate oval face remained serene
and composed, radiant in its unearthly beauty.

Bess ignored the slender outstretched hand. "A distinct pleasure,
Mrs. Fletcher," she said, each word distinct, as if individually carved
from ice.

"Yes. I'm sure." Isis looked straight past Bess, focusing her intense
attention on the magician. "I'll expect your call," she said softly, gliding
off down the hall, her midnight dress melting into the shadows.

Houdini stared after her. "Consorting with the enemy?" Bess jibed.

"She asked me to act as an impartial psychic investigator at one of
her séances."

"My knight in shining armor." Bess gave him a big hug. "Be careful
of that one, Harry. She's dangerous."

Twenty minutes later, the press of true believers diminished suffi-
ciently to allow the Houdinis to join Sir Arthur and Lady Conan Doyle
for their planned evening of dining and dancing at the Central Park
Casino. They stepped out of the stage entrance onto Seventh Avenue,
confronting a crowd of reporters between them and the hired horse-
drawn hansom cab waiting at the curb. Sir Arthur bristled at the sight of
the gathered newsmen. "Damned jackals," he muttered to Houdini, half
under his breath.

The reporters immediately recognized the two couples and closed
in, all shouting questions at once. Conan Doyle remained polite, replying to the predictable queries with appropriately monosyllabic answers.
How much did he enjoy America? Did he feel tonight's lecture had gone
well?

"What progress has been made in the *Scientific American* competition?" asked a whippet-faced journalist.

Sir Arthur seemed pleased with the question. He answered with a smile. "Well, as you all must know, a twenty-five-hundred-dollar prize has been offered to the first person producing a genuine psychic manifestation. Malcolm Bird, the magazine's associate editor, came over to London at the beginning of the year, and together we attended several séances. We had sittings with Evan Powell and with another medium named John Sloan.

"Unfortunately, in both instances the results were inconclusive, but I expect to continue these investigations with Bird while on tour in the States and have every expectation that we shall be awarding the prize before long."

A woman from the *Herald,* whose long neck, pallid face, and taupe cloche hat made her head appear to be a monstrous mushroom, tried to interject a literary note into the proceedings. "Are you influenced by Edgar Allan Poe?" she asked in a reedy, strident voice.

Conan Doyle hesitated. Those of the press familiar with the author knew firsthand his aversion to questions of this sort and grinned in anticipation of his sardonic rejoinder. In fact, Sir Arthur was jolted into a startling recollection of the morning's apparition. Had he really seen the specter? Did his profound belief in spiritism cloud his reason? The circle of waiting, expectant faces brought him back to the moment. "Poe . . . ?" He blinked, seemingly bewildered. "Oh, immensely. His detective is the best in literature."

The woman from the *Herald* scribbled furiously in an F. W. Woolworth notebook. "You mean, except for Sherlock Holmes?"

Conan Doyle stiffened, his face registering subtle degrees of displeasure. "I make no exception!" he bellowed.

The knight's brusque bark had those in the know grinning. No one much cared for the gangly woman from the *Herald,* and her blunder provided general amusement. Still, the reporters found it hard to fault her motives. Sherlock Holmes remained a subject of interest to most readers, whereas all this spiritualism business seemed a touch loony.

A young reporter wearing eyeglasses as thick as the bottoms of beer mugs unfurled a copy of the late edition of the *American*. A bold Hearst headline blared: POE MURDERS GRIP CITY. "Seeing how much you like Poe," he said, "what do you think of Runyon's notion that we've got some kind of well-read maniac running around town?"

Sir Arthur grinned. "As you all know, I am a devotee of homicide, but alas, I've been much too busy lately preparing for my lecture tour to pay close attention to any recent local bloodletting."

The bespectacled man handed him the paper. "Here. Read all about it."

"I certainly shall, and with great interest."

"Any advice to give the boys in blue?" asked another reporter.

"Boys in blue . . . ? I don't follow."

"You know, the cops. New York's finest. The police. Any inside tips on how to go about finding a literary killer?"

Sir Arthur glanced down at the headline on the newspaper he held. "I daresay it would be best to be apprised of the facts in the case before endeavoring to give advice."

"Boys . . . boys . . ." Houdini strutted before them on the sidewalk. "Let me tell you something. If anyone's gonna get to the bottom of this mystery, it'll be Sir Arthur Conan Doyle. And you can take that one to the bank."

"Is that right, Sir Arthur?" a reporter shouted. "You gonna crack the Poe case?"

The noble knight looked a bit bewildered. "I wouldn't say that. . . . I don't have any of the facts at my disposal."

"He's being too modest, fellas." Houdini gestured like an energetic carnival pitchman. "This is the mind that gave the world Sherlock Holmes. Here is a master of deduction! This man is, in fact, Sherlock Holmes personified. Who else better suited to solving crime than the greatest detective on earth?"

Like scraps tossed to mongrels, the magician's remarks unleashed a frenzy of questioning among the rabid reporters. They danced about the two couples, an agitated wolf pack with the scent of blood in their nostrils.

Conan Doyle flushed pink with embarrassment. "Gentlemen, please," he pleaded. "I am not a detective. I am an author. Let us not confuse fiction with reality."

"What about the Oscar Slater case?" a reporter yelled.

"What about the George Edalji mystery?" another joined in. "The business with the mutilated cattle?"

"I'm afraid you must excuse us now." Sir Arthur shouldered through the yammering reporters, clearing a path to the waiting cab for his wife and the Houdinis. "We really must be on our way. Thank you very much indeed."

Once the cab door closed, the driver flicked his buggy whip and the swaybacked mare pulled the hansom out into traffic, passing in front of a streetcar pausing to discharge passengers at the Fifty-seventh Street corner. Sir Arthur's breath came in labored, choleric gasps. "How could you?" he said to Houdini, struggling for composure. "All that balderdash about the greatest detective on earth."

The magician smiled like a kid who's just hit a home run. "Where's the harm in a little ballyhoo?"

"Harm? Why, it's utter nonsense."

"No need to get upset. Just publicity."

"Bad publicity."

"No such thing . . ."

9

TRIPPING THE LIGHT FANTASTIC

Bitter thoughts crowded Mary Rogers's head as she struggled to stay awake. After more than thirty-six hours on the dance floor she felt giddy with exhaustion. Her hard, brassy, marceled hair hung lank and disordered about her aching neck. Sweat wilted the pleated green silk Charmeuse frock she'd paid nearly eight dollars for at an after-Christmas sale. It was her favorite outfit and had been marked down from $11.98. She had worn it not for comfort but because of how good she imagined she would look for the publicity pictures following her triumphant victory.

Mary Rogers exemplified the epitome of a modern flapper, a sheba who might have stepped straight from one of John Held, Jr.'s racy cartoons. Her hair was bobbed and peroxided, she smoked in public and rolled her hose below the knee and, while still in high school in Teaneck, New Jersey, flopped about wearing unbuckled galoshes and rode with her date to the prom in an open flivver painted with catchy slogans: "99 44/100% Pure," "Lizzie of the Valley," "Mrs. Often," "Four Wheels, No Brakes."

College was never an option for a girl from a working-class family, so after graduation, armed with her stenography certificate, Mary headed straight for Manhattan, found a two-room Greenwich Village apartment, and secured employment at the Consolidated Life Insurance Company. To her Irish immigrant family, none of whom had gone beyond grade school, this seemed a remarkable achievement. Although she felt proud landing a job usually reserved for men, Mary wanted something more out of life than just taking dictation.

She spent her free time in movie palaces and vaudeville theaters, fueling her dreams of glamour and fame. One Saturday afternoon, coming out of a matinee at Loew's New York on Times Square, a man stopped her on the street, gave her his card, and inquired if she'd be interested in working in pictures. Her life changed forever on that day.

Although the promised work turned out to be three days as an extra in a production starring Babe Ruth across the Hudson in Fort Lee, Mary promptly quit her steno's job to pursue a career in show business. A total lack of talent hindered her in this occupation. She didn't sing, dance, or act, and soon discovered a pretty face only landed her a regular spot on the casting couch.

To make ends meet, she took a position as a cigarette girl at Barney Gallant's ultrafancy Washington Square speakeasy, where they served the hooch in ginger ale bottles and printed a set of mock rules on the menus admonishing patrons to "make no requests of the leader of the orchestra for the songs of the vintage of 1890. Crooning 'Sweet Adeline' was all right for your granddad, but times, alas, have changed."

Mary's salary seemed little better than a joke, but she picked up good tips and figured the convenience made it worthwhile. The Club Gallant was close to her apartment on Bleecker Street and working nights allowed her to tramp from audition to audition during the day. She studied the daily *Variety* religiously, attending every advertised open casting call. She became the uncrowned queen of "cattle calls." Herded onto a bare stage under a single, dangling incandescent bulb among dozens of other aspiring chorus girls, and given less than a minute to strut her stuff, Mary felt a bovine weariness settle into her bones.

And what had she to show for all the worn shoe leather and broken dreams? A few days' work here and there for Selznick and Biograph and other local film production companies. Two weeks dressed as Little Bo Peep, handing out free scented Lady Janis Complexion Soap samples at Macy's department store. A session with a photographer, modeling corsets for the B. Altman catalog. And, although she fantasized about becoming a Ziegfeld girl in the "Follies," the closest she ever came to realizing that aspiration remained a two-week engagement in the company of a vaudeville magician.

It would take a bit of her own magic to make the leap to stardom. At a time when entire careers centered on such dubious accomplishments as flagpole sitting and winning crossword puzzle tournaments, anyone with ambition might pluck fame from obscurity, like a rabbit from a silk top hat, by some single act of notoriety.

When Mary Rogers read the newspaper accounts of the first dance marathon contest held in the United States on March 31, she hardly gave the article a second thought. The novelty had originated in England and didn't seem likely to appeal to American tastes. She'd been dead wrong on that score. By the middle of April, more than a dozen competitions had been staged coast-to-coast, with a current endurance record of over ninety hours. Another fad off and running. On the day Roseland Ballroom advertised a May marathon featuring a grand prize of $500, Mary headed the line forming on Fifty-second Street, among the first five contestants to pay the required two-dollar entry fee.

Her partner was a waiter from the club, an affable young man named George Paterson Dobbs, who everyone called "Pumpkin" or "Pummie" for reasons completely unknown to Mary. An aspiring poet, he had lived in the Village for several years before the war, returning to a garret on Carmine Street after being demobbed. Pummie knew Max Eastman and all that gang at *The Masses,* and had published some slight undistinguished work in *The Quill* and *The Dial.* Mary asked him to dance with her in the marathon contest mainly because no romantic attachment connected them. This was strictly business.

Halfway through the second day, Mary Rogers felt sure she hated Pummie. His head rested heavily on her shoulder and the sickly-sweet odor of the Glostora he used to groom his hair made her stomach queasy. His face turned away and at least she didn't suffer the rasp of his beard or smell his sour, tobacco-stale breath. She wondered if he was sleeping. His feet dragged mechanically across the polished hardwood floor, but that didn't prove anything. She'd fallen asleep herself on several occasions and danced on like a zombie, never missing a step.

Every hour, the contestants enjoyed a fifteen-minute recess, barely enough time for a cup of coffee, a bite of a sandwich, and a couple of puffs on a cigarette before the most recent orchestra struck up another fox-trot. Mary no longer distinguished one tune from the next. To her weary ears, "I Ain't Got Nobody" might just as well have been "Ain't We Got Fun."

Of over one hundred couples starting the marathon, fewer than thirty-odd remained on the dance floor. Even the musicians looked rumpled and fatigued, "The Sheik of Araby" sounding like a dirge. Mary cursed her fashionable high-heeled pumps. Why hadn't she had the foresight to wear something more sensible? Her feet were killing her. Not even a massage from one of the attending nurses during the last break had been much help. When she saw two young women in ballet slippers and another wearing rubber-soled gymnasium shoes, she lost hope entirely. There was no way she could go the distance.

Suddenly, Pummie screamed and fell to the floor clutching his right calf.

"Get up!" she shrieked, tugging at him.

"I've got a cramp." His face contorted with pain. "Oh, my dear God!"

"Get up, you bastard! We'll be disqualified."

"I can't move. Feels like it's broken."

She kicked at him. "Get up! Get up! Get up! . . ."

Whirling coin-sized spots of light reflecting from the rotating mirrored ball flickered across her furious, imploring features. "Please, Pummie," she pleaded. "Please, please, please . . . get up and dance."

"I can't, Mary. Honest." George Paterson Dobbs stared at her with the pain-heightened innocence of a chromolith martyr. "I'm finished."

"Piss on you then!" Mary turned with a sneer and hobbled unsteadily off the dance floor, the sad complaint of the orchestra droning a mournful rendition of "Toot, Toot, Tootsie" behind her.

Outside on the sidewalk, daylight took her by surprise. A flock of pigeons whirled into the angled sunlight, turning in a single motion like leaves caught in a whirlwind. Still early, and the shops, theaters, and restaurants had yet to open. Broadway was not an A.M. boulevard.

Mary walked to Forty-seventh Street, then changed her mind and headed east. She didn't feel like taking the subway downtown. A huge painted spectacular advertising Piedmont Cigarettes high above the intersection of Broadway and Seventh Avenue made her crave a smoke, but she'd done the last of her coffin nails almost an hour ago. "My lucky day," she said out loud, her laugh a bitter echo of her emotional state.

Every hotel had a cigar stand, but Mary didn't want to enter a lobby unescorted and reached Fifth Avenue without passing another establishment selling cigarettes. She caught a downtown number four bus, paid her ten-cent fare to the conductor, and climbed the curving rear stairs to the upper deck. Trolley cars and the subway cost only a nickel but, after thirty-six long hours at Roseland, Mary craved fresh air.

It felt good to sit in the open with the sun on her face and a brisk wind tangling her bleached blond hair. A man across the aisle lit up, the flat green metal tin still in his hand. Mary bummed a Lucky Strike, although she adroitly avoided being drawn into any sort of conversation.

Exhaling, she felt her bad mood flowing away on the breeze along with curling wreaths of smoke. Before reaching the Waldorf-Astoria on Thirty-fourth Street, the bus passed a parade of great department stores: B. Altman's, Lord & Taylor's, Tiffany's, Gorham, Best & Company. Mary indulged in a fantasy shopping spree. Something to wear while strutting along Peacock Alley.

Dream-shopping was all Mary could afford these days. Things had seemed more promising a couple of months ago when she landed a job in Harry Houdini's vaudeville company. The pay topped $35 a week and she was giddy in anticipation of buying a fabulous new wardrobe. Next thing you know, the stuck-up little runt docked her a fin because she forgot some dumb part of her costume and after they played the Palace she got notice she wouldn't be needed for the short tour of New Jersey and Pennsylvania. Still a chance she might be asked back for ten weeks on the western circuit later in the summer, but something told her not to hold her breath on that score.

The boy sitting in front of her looked to be about eight. Mary wondered why he wasn't in school. He kneeled on his seat, leaning over the rail and pointing out passing automobiles to the plump, dark-haired woman with him. Canvas-topped cars constituted the large majority, but many enclosed sedans and coupes joined their ranks. Most were Fords—high, black, boxlike Model Ts—the only vehicle Mary could identify by brand name.

"There's a Jordan Playboy, Blair," the little boy cried, pointing to a rakish roadster. "Look, Blair. An Apperson Eight! And a Barney Oldsmobile! There's a Franklin, it's got an air-cooled engine. . . . And a Milburn Light Electric. . . . Hey! Hey! A Kenworthy! A Chandler! . . . An Auburn! . . . A Maxwell! . . . A Roamer! . . . A Peerless! . . . A Locomobile! . . . An Owen Magnetic! . . . A Grant Six! . . . A Jewett! . . . A Haynes! . . . A Cadillac! . . ." The automotive litany continued unabated until Blair and the little boy got off the bus at Fourteenth Street.

Mary Rogers wondered about their destination, having already decided they were filthy rich, a latter-day Buster Brown and his governess. Who else but a millionaire's brat could rattle off fancy car names like that? Were they going shopping? Did they live in one of the old family mansions on lower Fifth? Mary occupied herself with such speculation for the final few blocks past the Salamagundi Club and the gleaming, white brick Brevoort Hotel. At the last stop, she stepped down onto the pavement opposite Washington Mews.

She headed south into the park under the ceremonial marble arch designed by Stanford White. Washington Square before noon retained the serenity of a village green. A few nursemaids and mothers sat knitting on benches beside hooded perambulators. Sunshine burnished the dusty rose facade of a northern row of century-old town houses. Water splashed in the central fountain where once the civic gallows stood. Small children played hopscotch. Idlers listened to an old Italian cranking a hurdy-gurdy.

Mary lingered on the fringes of the group, humming along with the sad sounds of the barrel organ. The Italian had a little monkey on a leash all dressed up in red like a bellhop. Double rows of brass buttons flashed sunshine along his tunic. He looked so cute in his pillbox hat, scampering among the onlookers, holding a tin cup. Mary's happiness gradually gave way to an uncomfortable feeling that someone was watching her. She looked all around and saw no one suspicious. Still, it gave her the heebie-jeebies.

Lacking spare coins to drop into the monkey's cup, Mary turned and walked off before the animal came her way. She followed a brick-lined diagonal path under the arching sycamores to the southeast corner of the park, exiting onto MacDougal Street and walking slowly south into the midmorning sun, past dim aromatic coffeehouses and shuttered basement restaurants. The nagging, creepy feeling persisted. She sensed a shadow on her tail and paused frequently to glance over her shoulder.

At the corner of MacDougal and Bleecker, Mary Rogers turned west, toward Sixth. She lived in a gabled brick building in the middle of the block, a survivor from the second decade of the last century. A Sicilian bakery beside the entrance sweetened the air with delicious aromas. Mary stared past her reflection in the show window at stacked pyramids of fresh-baked loaves. She killed time, not wanting to go inside until sure the coast was clear. A man with his dog on a leash stood nearby while a tiny leg lifted by a fire hydrant. Some kind of miniature schnauzer. After a couple of hard-won drops, they continued on their way. She watched them turn the corner. Why should he be tailing her?

Bleecker Street looked peaceful as a country lane. Neither the heavy-set woman selling roast corn nor the white-clad streetsweeper pushing his barrel-shaped Sanitation Department cart appeared in any way suspicious. Mary sighed, laughing inwardly at her foolishness. She climbed the two front steps and stepped into the tiny vestibule, ignoring any bills lurking behind the narrow, filigreed door of her brass mailbox.

Mary Rogers unlocked the front door and climbed the sagging wooden stairs. Her apartment was on the third floor. One flight up, she paused and looked over the railing. What did she expect to see? Nothing.

Not even a stray cat. No sound disturbed the enclosing silence. She continued on her way, taking each step with slow caution. Outside her apartment door, she fumbled in her purse for her key-ring, clumsily trying the wrong one in the lock. Damn! What was wrong with her? Was she so tired she imagined things?

Mary found the correct key. A soft footstep from behind made her freeze in terror. Before she could turn, strong hands pulled something over her head. Some kind of sack. Her outcry went unheard, stifled by a cloth inside the bag reeking with a strange chemical. Moments before plunging into the black well of unconsciousness, Mary Rogers thought of the hospital where she'd had a tonsillectomy when she was six. The nauseating drip of anesthesia onto the gauze cone covering her face . . .

10

METAMORPHOSIS

It was an hour before dawn. Sir Arthur Conan Doyle sat on a striped divan in the front room of his hotel suite, listening to the slow clop of hooves outside as ice wagons and milk delivery vans made their early morning rounds. Night's dark winding sheet shrouded the still-sleeping city in shadows. Faint as the promise of an afterlife, electric streetlamps cast a dim glow on the uncurtained windows. Up well before his usual time, a practice the author initiated following his first Carnegie Hall lecture, Sir Arthur waited, patient as a hunter in his blind, his keen eyes fixed on the writing table in the corner alcove.

Although ordinarily he withheld nothing from his wife, he had not spoken a word to Jean of these nocturnal vigils. He didn't want to cause undue concern. Not that he doubted his reason or his sanity or anything so melodramatic. First and foremost, he needed to determine if the apparition was merely the by-product of an overactive imagination. His faith in a spirit life remained unshaken in spite of the fact that he had conjured up a ghost costumed like a West End stage illusion.

After many such early mornings spent waiting and watching, whenever he was back in New York between speaking engagements, the knight wondered if his doubts were indeed justified. The specter made no reappearance. Perhaps it had been nothing more than the aftereffects of a bit of undigested beef, as Scrooge supposed upon first discerning his dead partner's features staring dolefully at him from off the door-knocker. Marley's ghost was no figment of the miser's indigestion. On he came, dragging his chains and ledgers.

Sir Arthur rubbed his eyes. What was he thinking of? Investing fictional characters with a reality even Dickens never intended. He suppressed a laugh. His detractors would have a field day with such thoughts as these. How they ridiculed him when he wrote of his belief in fairies, leprechauns, and other wee folks. Not that he blamed them. It did all sound preposterous, until one considered the evidence.

A soft, mournful sigh brought him back from his self-absorbed meditation. He thought it the wind, soughing outside. Another sad, weary exhalation clearly came from the corner of the room. Sir Arthur squinted into the shadows. A faint shimmering outline took shape before him. Undeniably the same ethereal form he had seen before, a seated man in garments stylish three-quarters of a century ago. "Are you Poe, the poet?" Conan Doyle inquired, awe reducing his words to a hushed whisper.

The specter turned, his hollow, haunted eyes burning like embers. "What apparition is this?" The voice seemed to come from very far away, a distant echo muffled by fog and rain.

"Can you see me?" Sir Arthur leaned eagerly forward.

"Alas. Must I surrender what little sanity is left to me in admitting that I do?"

"You are Edgar A. Poe, are you not?"

"I have that distinction." A thin, languid hand the consistency of mist pointed toward the knight. "You are dressed very strangely. What manner of creature are you? Why have you come to torment me?"

Sir Arthur felt an eerie thrill, tempered by a certain confusion. "Have you not come to me?"

"I'd prefer not to think myself that mad. How is it you know my name?"

"I, too, am an author. I've admired your work since I was a student. But, surely, you're accustomed to recognition. You must have known considerable fame when you were alive."

The specter smiled, wistful, distant. "Do you take me for a corpse?"

For a few seconds, Sir Arthur sat dumbfounded, near incapable of speech. In all his experience with spirit contact, always previously guided by a medium, never had anything so inexplicable occurred. Nor had he ever before seen so clear and distinct a manifestation. "My dear Poe," he began slowly, managing at last to find his voice again. "Do you not know . . . ? This is the year of our Lord one thousand, nine hundred and twenty-three."

Poe's ghost, if such it was, threw back its vaporous head and howled with laughter; a wolf's cry, utterly without mirth. "How excellent a jest!" The laughter ended in a sudden choking silence, like hearing a condemned man's final protest cut short by the jerk of the noose. "A traveler from the future. . . . It might be a tale of my own invention."

Conan Doyle felt truly puzzled. How does one persuade a dead man he is indeed a ghost? "What year is it for you, Mr. Poe?" he asked gently.

" 'Forty-eight . . . or 'forty-nine . . . thereabouts. . . ." The incorporeal hand described a listless half-circle in the air.

"And where do you suppose you are right now?"

"Why, New York City . . ." Poe's mouth twisted into a sneer. "The Empire City," he added with some bitterness.

"What is it you see when you look out the window?"

"Very little, for it is yet dark. Nights are long . . . so interminably long."

"So I should imagine. It must seem an eternity for you."

Sir Arthur was perplexed. He had come to believe that, by and large, spirits were a contented lot, at peace at last with their fate, freed forever from the pain and restraints of material existence. Not only were the dead aware of their condition, they sought contact with loved ones still living to reassure them of their well-being.

He learned this lesson from countless séances attended over the past two decades. Face to face for the first time with a visible manifestation, and able to speak without a medium's intercession, he confronted a sudden reevaluation of all his beliefs. He thought of Saint Anthony alone in the wilderness. Could this be a demonic hallucination sent to test his faith?

"Tell me . . ." The specter interrupted his musing. "This future you inhabit, is it a pleasant place?"

"Compared to the world you knew, I should think not. We have had wars more terrible than anything you might imagine. There are flying machines now, and horseless carriages, and submarines, and—" The mocking smile on Poe's face drew him up short. "You think I'm joking, don't you?"

Poe grinned with disdain. "Oh, no, no. . . . Not a whit. Tell me about travel to the moon and transmuting lead into gold."

Another stunning revelation. The spirit knew nothing of the present-day world and all that had transpired in the many long years since his death. Could he be stuck forever in an unchanging past? "Let me ask you a question . . ." Conan Doyle met the tormented, spectral stare.

"I am at your service."

"How do I appear to you?"

"A large man. White mustache. Oddly dressed. I'd guess at a florid complexion, but that is difficult to ascertain."

"Why?"

"Because you emanate a certain unearthly light. There is an almost palpable opalescent cast to your features."

The knight's heart raced. "What is it you think I am?"

"A ghost, of course." Poe's derisive smile eased. "What else could you be?"

"Arthur . . . ?" Jean stood in the open doorway, holding her dressing gown close about her. "With whom are you talking, dear?"

"Darling. . . . Come in. This is most extraordinary."

"What is?" She stood beside him by the divan.

Sir Arthur looked over at the writing table. Dawn's pearly light gave the flanking alcove windows a nacreous sheen. The chair next to the writing table sat unoccupied. Poe's ghost had vanished. "Sit down, my dear." The knight took his lady's outstretched hand. "I'm afraid we have a great deal to talk about."

* * *

At eight o'clock in the evening, Sir Arthur and Lady Jean sat beside the Houdinis on the dais in the main ballroom of the McAlpin Hotel, among the guests of honor at the annual banquet of the Society of American Magicians. Initially, Conan Doyle had declined the invitation, writing to Houdini from Boston that he feared the evening's entertainment would include "bogus spiritual phenomena" and thus make a mockery of a subject he looked upon as sacred. The magician responded by post immediately, assuring his friend as a gentleman "nothing will be performed or said which will offend anyone." This letter did much to put Sir Arthur at ease and he wired Houdini the next morning that he and Lady Conan Doyle should be delighted to come.

The other guests at the head table included Adolph Ochs, publisher of the *New York Times;* Edward F. Albee; Melville Stone, founder of the Associated Press; master magician Howard Thurston; and the department store magnate Bernard Gimbel. As president of the Society, Houdini had planned this evening and personally invited all the distinguished individuals assembled on the dais. He smiled with smug satisfaction, pleased as if he'd materialized them all with a wave of his magic wand. The muted conversation of powerful men intoxicated him. Wouldn't his mother smile to see him in such distinguished company?

Houdini's self-satisfied expression altered imperceptibly into a frown on seeing Sidney Rammage rise from an adjacent table and head his way. Pompous little bastard's probably going to make a stink about not having room at the main table for the secretary of the Society. "Enjoying yourself, Rammage?" He gave him the benefit of his best smile, hoping to deflect any undue criticism.

"Righty-o. Couldn't want for better company." The diminutive conjurer nodded his bald head in Sir Arthur's direction. "Remember, Harry. A promise is a promise."

For a moment, Houdini felt confusion, until their conversation in Carnegie Hall came flashing back. "Of course, of course . . ." Catching Sir Arthur's eye, he said something about presenting a fellow countryman and the proper introductions were made.

"I've been a fan of yours ever so long," Rammage gushed unctuously. "So devilishly clever, and every word born of inspiration."

The knight's amiable chuckle rumbled out of his chest. "Perspiration's more like it."

"You're far too modest, Sir Arthur. To read your books is to feel the presence of the keenest of minds."

"Very kind of you to say so. Afraid the old blade's been a bit dull of late."

Rammage nodded as if sharing a confidence. "A touring schedule's a grueling thing. . . . Tell me, any progress made on this Poe case?"

"I beg your pardon?"

"These beastly Poe murders. I read somewhere in the papers you were having a go at it. Any chance of cracking it soon?"

Sir Arthur shot Houdini a withering glance. "Look here, old chap," he said to Rammage, "all that's nothing but a lot of newspaper blather. You mustn't take such balderdash so seriously."

"Unduly modest once again, I'm afraid." There was no stopping Rammage. "I've read of your success in solving several celebrated cases, and not just fictional ones, either."

Conan Doyle exuded discomfort. "It's true. I have in the past been able to provide the authorities with some assistance from time to time—"

"The mind of Sherlock Holmes," Houdini cut in.

"They were relatively simple affairs." Sir Arthur ignored the magician's remark. "This ghastly Poe business is another matter altogether."

"In what way is that?" asked Rammage.

"Well, the killings are quite obviously the arbitrary acts of a maniac. Very like the atrocities committed by our own Jack the Ripper. There's precious little any one single individual can do in a case such as that. It calls for massive amounts of manpower. Without reliable witnesses and lacking any rational motive, I can't see how the police can do much except hope for a lucky break."

Rammage nodded with earnest sagacity. "You paint a very bleak picture indeed."

"Random murder is not a pretty subject."

Determined not to let such morbid considerations dispel the evening's bonhomie, Houdini did his best to strike a note of enthusiastic good cheer. "Much better to talk about happy subjects," he burbled, clapping Rammage on the shoulder. "What's this I hear about you taking a new show on the road?"

"Well, it's not me exactly . . ."

"No false modesty, Rammage, I read what Sime Silverman had to say in *Variety*. Return of the Sufi mystic. Ali ben Haroun resurrected. Dervish delights."

Sidney Rammage permitted himself a sly smile. "I've resurrected the name, I'll admit. This time I'm only managing the act. I've found a young man, very agile, an adept, really. . . . To be honest, he's no more a Sufi than I was. He's half Greek and has a dark, mysterious look. I think he's going to be very big." Rammage pulled a handbill from the inside pocket of his dinner jacket and handed it to Houdini. "We open at the Albee in Brooklyn next week. I'll comp you at the box office." Turning to the Conan Doyles, he bowed slightly, said what a great honor it had been to meet them, and sauntered back to his table, secure in the knowledge of having scored a direct hit.

Houdini seethed as he read the handbill, a frozen smile disguising his true emotions.

ALI ben HAROUN

Master MYSTIFIER from the ORIENT

Schooled by SUFI MYSTICS & DERVISHES

His psychic power will amaze you. See him lie upon a bed of needle-sharp nails. Marvel as skewers pierce his flesh.

WONDERS NEVER SEEN

BURIED ALIVE!

While in a cataleptic trance, Ali ben Haroun is nailed into a coffin and BURIED ALIVE on stage in full view of the audience. With only enough oxygen to sustain

five minutes of life, Ali ben Haroun will remain
entombed for a FULL HOUR! See him emerge alive
and unharmed at the end of the show.

DON'T MISS THIS SPECTACLE

Houdini read the handbill over a second, and a third time, feeling
rage build inside him like steam in a pressure cooker. He wanted to
scream and tear the paper to shreds but instead kept the false smile fixed
on his face through sheer act of will. Looking up, he saw Rammage
watching him, anticipating a tantrum.

With deliberate care and practiced nonchalance, Houdini folded
the handbill and placed it in his pocket. It took every ounce of self-control in his possession, but he'd be damned if he'd give that shrimp of an
S.O.B. the satisfaction of getting his goat. Resuming his seat, the magician did his best to appear interested in the conversation buzzing around
him. In actuality, his thoughts remained focused on the fake Sufi and his
advertised onstage burial.

For years, Houdini had contemplated staging just such a stunt as
part of his act. Once, in California, he attempted being buried alive
without a coffin, but the weight of the earth almost proved too much for
him and he'd barely been able to claw his way to the surface, emerging
with bleeding hands and broken fingernails. In the end, he'd abandoned
the idea because he couldn't think of how to stage it successfully. No
audience would sit still staring at a sealed coffin for an hour.
Nevertheless, this Ali ben Haroun business burned him up. There was no
way under heaven he'd let some second-rater like Rammage steal his
thunder.

Dinner went untasted, ashes in Houdini's mouth at the thought of
the phony Sufi grabbing headlines rightfully his. Bess covered for him as
best she could, being long familiar with the dark depths of his brooding.
After dessert and coffee, it was time for the entertainment. The magician paid no attention to the card tricks and sleights of his colleagues. He
remained lost in thought until his own turn came.

Bessie joined Houdini on the makeshift stage. Vickery and Collins carried in the familiar wardrobe trunk from behind royal blue drapes. Houdini acknowledged the applause. "This little girl has been doing this illusion with me for thirty years. Since back in a Coney Island dime museum a month after we got married." Bess blushed at the applause.

Houdini introduced Sir Arthur Conan Doyle, beckoning the knight to join them onstage. He received a warm reception crossing from the dais. The magician clapped loudest of all. "We would be honored, Sir Arthur, if you consented to assist us in this endeavor."

"The honor is mine." The merry blue eyes sparkled with anticipated fun.

"I must ask to borrow your dinner jacket." Houdini helped Sir Arthur shrug out of his tuxedo and slipped into it himself. Following Houdini's instructions, Sir Arthur tied the magician's hands behind his back. "Make it tighter. This is one occasion when a gentleman need not be so gentle." The knight did his best, tying sailor's knots learned during two seasons at sea as a youthful ship's surgeon. He thought of hard men he'd known on a seven-month whaling expedition to the Arctic and later aboard a cargo schooner bound for the Gold Coast of Africa. They would have had no compunctions about binding Houdini's wrists tight enough to cut off all circulation.

"Excellent." The magician stepped to the front of the platform. "And now, ladies and gentlemen, it is with great pleasure that I present to you the great mystery known as 'Metamorphosis.' "

Bess held a large canvas sack with leather straps. "A regulation United States Post Office mailbag, ladies and gentlemen."

Houdini stepped into the sack. Bess fastened the buckles with a padlock and gave the key to Sir Arthur. At this point, the two Jims, Collins and Vickery, lifted the mail sack into the trunk, again handing Conan Doyle the key. The author locked the wardrobe and they bound it with lengths of hemp rope, wrapping it as if in a giant spiderweb.

"That should hold even Houdini for a while," Bess quipped as the Jims placed a folding screen in front of the trunk. "And now, ladies and gentlemen . . . Metamorphosis! I will count to three." She clapped her hands. "One!"

Bess stepped behind the screen. Another handclap. "Two!"

CLAP! "Three!" This time the voice was Houdini's. The magician emerged in his shirtsleeves, pulling the screen aside to reveal the still-bound trunk. The ballroom rang with cheering.

"Let's have a look inside, Sir Arthur . . ." The two men busied themselves untying the rope from around the wardrobe. The knight first unlocked the trunk; next, the mailbag. Bess stepped smiling from the canvas sack, wrapped in Sir Arthur's dinner jacket. She looked all the more waiflike lost in its voluminous folds, a little girl dressed up in Daddy's clothing, and turned so the audience could see her hands securely tied behind her back. The entire Society jumped to its feet, the ballroom thunderous with applause.

Houdini untied the rope and took Bess by the hand, bowing gracefully with her, a lifetime together distilled into a single harmonious movement. Clapping enthusiastically, Sir Arthur felt awkward, sharing the stage in their moment of triumph. When the ovation subsided, the magician pulled Rammage's handbill from his pocket. Everyone fell silent, expecting an encore. "Ladies and gentlemen," he said. "Thank you for the kind reception. I have here a challenge from Ali ben Haroun, an Oriental master of mystery. He proposes to be buried alive for an hour in a coffin onstage and challenges me to duplicate his feat.

"Naturally, Houdini accepts! But no duplication. Houdini follows in no man's path. In two weeks' time, I will be sealed in a coffin and submerged beneath the surface of a swimming pool, remaining under water for a period of three hours!" The audacity of this proposal had the gathering of magicians buzzing. Sidney Rammage feigned disinterest. Houdini held up his hands for quiet.

"An impartial committee will witness this test and verify its legitimacy. Houdini never backs down from a challenge."

11

PERCHANCE TO DREAM

Sir Arthur Conan Doyle had been in Baltimore for over forty-eight hours and still had no idea what the place looked like. He'd gone straight from the railway station to the hotel and then on to the lecture hall, with various stopovers in tea rooms and restaurants. His view of the city remained entirely interior. The past two weeks had likewise gone by in a similar blur of activity, the speaking tour taking over almost every aspect of his life. During the few days left to them in New York, Lady Jean sat up with him every morning into the dawn. No further Poe manifestation was observed.

Exhausted by the grueling schedule, Jean had been sleeping late since they resumed the tour. Ever the early riser, Conan Doyle got up in the dark and prowled the unfamiliar terrain of each successive hotel suite. Because it was his second morning in Baltimore, he knew where to avoid a barked shin. No teapot waited outside the door, in spite of specific instructions the previous evening. Sir Arthur sighed in exasperation. He greatly missed the comforts of the Plaza.

Groping for the light switch, Sir Arthur stopped dead in his tracks. There he sat. A will-o'-the-wisp casting a faint blue-green glow in the far corner of the room. "Poe . . . ?" The knight stumbled forward, mouth agape in disbelief.

The luminous specter wavered before him, moving in and out of focus like a magic lantern image projected onto drifting smoke. Sir Arthur stopped, standing stock still in the center of the room, a hunter stalking his prey, afraid any slight motion might drive the spirit from the room. "You are indeed Poe?" the knight insisted.

The poet's tormented eyes sought his own. What horrors had they observed? Conan Doyle recoiled inwardly at the misery embodied in so bleak a stare. Here were eyes that had seen Purgatory, and worse.

"Indeed, I am . . ." The manifestation spoke with unhurried languor, the sound of his words soft as footsteps in the snow. "Poor, wretched Poe . . ."

"I am not a ghost," Sir Arthur said. "In spite of what you may think."

"It matters little what I think. There you stand. If I thought you the Archangel Gabriel, it would be of no consequence. You would stand so before me all the same. Whether you be Lucifer or Ligeia or the ghost of Hamlet's father seems but trivial speculation. The indisputable fact is your presence. Of that much I am sure, for I do not think myself mad."

Conan Doyle's mind raced down corridors of limitless possibilities. "I mean you no harm," he murmured, not certain quite how to start.

"Very reassuring . . ."

"Do you know where you are right now?"

The specter laughed: links of rusted chain dragging up cold stone steps from the mossy depths of some forgotten cellar. "Are you lost? A poor peripatetic spirit doomed to an eternity of wandering? Content yourself in the knowledge of inhabiting the handsomest city in the Union, fair Baltimore, home to four generations of my distinguished family."

"It is the city where you died." Sir Arthur couldn't help himself. The words were out before he realized their impropriety.

"You anticipate my obituary prematurely, or do you mean to be prophetic?"

Once again, puzzled by a ghost refusing to acknowledge its own demise, Sir Arthur felt ancient doubts welling up within him. He rubbed his eyes, as if attempting to wipe the apparition from his sight. "Don't you remember seeing me in New York?" he asked, blinking.

"I can scarce remember New York. Such memories are painful to me. There in that cold city my beloved Sissy was taken from me forever."

"Your wife . . . ?"

"My life. . . . My soul. . . . The entire essence of my being! You asked if I were dead. A question more astute than you might ever realize. My life ended on the afternoon of February 2, 1847, the hour my sweet angelic Virginia was laid within the icy vault. What you see before you is but a husk, the hollow shell of one who loved and laughed and dreamed. He is no more. He is truly dead. Defunct!"

Sir Arthur felt the specter's chilling words resonate within his spirit like the stark tolling of a death knell. A chill chime for each loss in his life; Touie, Kingsley, Innes, the Ma'am, a list of loved ones growing longer with every heartbreak. His belief in spiritism had alleviated the pain, the thought of gentle, happy shades waiting to greet him across the final divide. And here stood Poe's ghost, lost in nothingness, trapped forever by unending tragedy, making a mockery of all he held sacred.

"Is there no hope?" Sir Arthur's face looked old in the gray dawn light. "No hope at all . . . ?"

The specter wavered, dissolving like mist. A bitter smile played about his thin lips. "Hope . . . ?" His laugh came from someplace far away, the sound of childhood games fading in the evening twilight, of friends never seen again. "Hope? Pity the poor dreamer . . ." And he was gone.

The coffin cost $3,500. Cast from bronze, ornate and ponderous, the sort of casket Mussolini would order for his state funeral, it sat on the tiled edge of the Biltmore Hotel swimming pool, bold as an avant-garde art installation. Recent modifications included a battery-powered alarm bell and a telephone. These instruments squatted like black mechanical reptiles on the pleated white satin interior. Death in the Jazz Age.

Reflected light from the Olympic-sized pool undulated across the tiled arabesques of the Moorish ceiling. The close, humid air reeked sexually of chlorine. A crowd of reporters looked down from a viewing gallery. Their muffled wisecracks echoed in the low-vaulted space.

Official witnesses and others with special invitations clustered around the far end of the pool, where a physician took Houdini's pulse and measured his blood pressure. The magician sat, naked to the waist, clad in just the drawers of his bathing costume. At a time when men never went without undershirts or bared their chests in public, this alone ensured him center stage. His superb physical condition prompted more than one envious jibe about vanity.

The Jims—Collins and Vickery—ran a final check on the alarm bell and telephone. Perfectionist jacks-of-all-trades, they were never satisfied until assured the equipment for the Boss's stunts functioned without a hitch. Jim Collins had been first assistant of the troupe ever since signing on along with fellow countryman Jim Vickery back in 1912. The two were working-class English, very alike in their London slum background, sharing a bawdy cockney humor. This proved an asset in overseeing a company at times numbering thirty.

"Everything okay?" Houdini stood at their side, ready to go.

"Copacetic, Boss." Vickery's fish-and-chips accent put a new spin on the stale collegiate slang.

Houdini stepped into the coffin. Ever the showman and unable to resist the pull of any audience, he gestured for attention, his voice echoing in the tiled enclosure. "Medical science states this coffin contains a volume of oxygen sufficient to sustain life for five or six minutes." The magician spotted Sidney Rammage in the gallery and focused his manic intensity upon his rival. "Recent stage burials have suggested the impossible. Houdini now gives you the impossible."

The magician got down into the coffin. Resting on his elbows in the quilted satin, he glanced again at the gallery, straight into the eyes of Isis, her perfect oval face framed in black. Houdini sat bolt upright with a startled gasp. In her jaunty turban and sable stole, she looked as out of place next to a swimming pool as the coffin.

"Problem, Boss . . . ?" Jim Collins knelt instantly by his side.

"I'm okay, Collins . . ." She smiled above him, cool and serene as a hothouse camellia. "Just remembered something."

"You're ghostly pale," Collins whispered. "Take a minute and recover your breathing."

Houdini pulled his eyes away from her stare by pure force of will. He filled his lungs with great inhalations, oxygenating his blood, at the same time seeking the calm center he inhabited when confronting danger. At this, he proved less successful. He closed his eyes and lay back in the coffin.

When he opened them again, it was dark; the lid sealed. He ignored the quick scraping sounds of Vickery and Collins caulking the outer seam, trying to concentrate on total relaxation, limiting his breathing to short, shallow sips. His mind refused to clear. Isis lingered, jade eyes and mocking smile accelerating his heartbeat. Imperative for his metabolism to slow. By sheer determination he brought his pulse under control. He felt the coffin lift and tilt.

Vickery, Collins, and two assistants lifted the Imperial casket down to three lifeguards standing in the pool. They guided it under the surface. The coffin's near buoyancy made it easy to hold the sculpted sides level as it settled to the bottom in five feet of water. The seal held; no telltale air bubbles. Seen from the surface, distortion enhancing its rococo excesses, the coffin seemed mythic, the nautical tomb of a minor sea deity.

Enclosed inside, Houdini felt distinctly mortal. Seeing Isis out of the blue had shocked him into remembering his dreams. Not just the two jolting him up in a midnight sweat, trembling, while Bess gently snored beside him, but dozens of others, wild erotic fantasies he was ashamed to recall. Never in his life had he experienced such dreams. Not even in an adolescence awash in nocturnal emissions.

Isis appeared in these dreams, utterly dissolute, surprising him in unexpected places. Stripped naked for an escape from a nameless prison cell, he turned to find her sprawled on the narrow bunk, her bare, lissome legs spread and inviting. As he sank to the bottom of the harbor in a weighted packing case, she writhed on top of him, playfully hiding the key to his handcuffs, all the while stroking his genitals. Once, they became animals mating in the jungle. Sleek leopards dancing in mottled sunlight, all muscle and sinew; the nape of her neck caught in his curved, ivory teeth.

The telephone rang. It was Vickery. "Boss. Everything's in place. Timing's begun. No leaks. . . . Just checking in."

"Things're fine down here."

"Check. Call you again in fifteen minutes." Vickery hung up the receiver and raised his eyebrows at Collins.

"Guv'nor off on a tear, is he?" Jim Collins wiped the sweat from his smooth bald head with his handkerchief.

"Working up to one. He's brooding on something all right."

Collins glanced at the wavering image of the submerged coffin. "If you was him, you'd be brooding, too."

"If I was him, I'd've retired before it killed me."

Encased within the soft confines of the coffin, Houdini wrestled with his demons. Lying motionless in the utter dark, breathing lightly, his mind isolated from sensory contact, he felt hallucinations creep like shadow-rats across the edges of perception. A thousand times before, in similar enclosed situations, he kept continually busy, working through the arranged stages of the escape. He hadn't considered the psychic effects of lying alone in darkness for an hour. No sound. No sensation.

Isis was with him, filling the tiny space with her powerful presence. Try as he might, Houdini remained unable to rid his mind of the woman. Dark hallucinatory demons swirled up around him. A flock of shrieking succubi thrashed in the blackness, flaccid breasts leaking venom, tattered wings rank with decay. They pressed in around him. Every pale, savage face wore identical features. Green-eyed and raven-haired, they all looked exactly like Isis.

The magician could not slow his headlong descent into madness. Nothing in his experience readied him for this unexpected torment. He thought himself prepared for any emergency; a man who sat for hours in a bathtub amid floating cakes of ice to accustom his body to the cold encountered during bridge jumps and underwater escapes. Who exercised his fingers until they grew strong enough to unfasten buckles through a heavy thickness of canvas.

Unprepared for a situation over which he had no physical control, the magician felt powerless. Guts and grit were no help at all; concentration and willpower less than useless. The hallucinations refused to diminish. For the first time in his life, the magician confronted an unfamiliar emotion: the rigid, irrational beginnings of fear.

He told himself, over and over, the ragged wings sweeping across his body weren't real. He denied the frenzied howls and wailing. Shutting his eyes didn't help. Isis tormented him in all her many guises. Paralyzed by pure terror, Houdini surrendered as the wings folded about him, arms gathering him to her in a dank embrace. He confronted the glowing green stare. Her lips parted for a kiss. In place of her tongue, a writhing snake appeared. When the phone rang again, Houdini was screaming.

Vickery hung up the receiver, his joker's face creased with worry. "Something's wrong with the Boss," he muttered to Collins. "He sounds frantic."

"He in some trouble?"

Vickery shrugged. "Said everything was going fine."

"What's the problem then?"

"Don't know there is a problem. It was just his voice. Rattling on a mile a minute. Seemed a bit weird, is all."

"Maybe I should have a word with him." Collins reached for the phone.

Vickery shook his head, adopting an officious demeanor. Over the years, he frequently appeared in the act as an insane asylum attendant or police detective or whatever dignitary the circumstances demanded, and he had come to assume an air of mock authority even offstage. "Not such a good idea," he said, his voice as comically officious as Groucho Marx pretending to be a judge. "He didn't ask for any help. There's the alarm bell if he's in trouble. My vote is leave him alone. What is it they say about letting sleeping dogs lie?"

"I don't know, what do they say?" Ever the willing straight man, Collins screwed his face into an approximation of curiosity.

"Why, let them lie there, that's what they say. Especially if it's a dog."

"And if it's a cat . . . ?"

"If it's a cat, you kick it in the bloody ass, is what you do. But, never a dog. No, sir. Not on your life. Encounter a sleeping dog and you'd be well-advised to let the beast lie."

"Is it lie, or is it lay . . . ?"

"Depends entirely upon the disposition of the dog."

They continued along with this aimless banter, trading sallies like Gallagher and Shean in the good old days at Hammerstein's Victoria, and all the while, their employer raged in his tomb at the bottom of the pool. Looking at the placid surface, no one guessed what wild orgiastic nightmares transpired just a few feet below the undulant reflections.

The telephone saved Houdini from complete insanity. Every time he was poised to plunge into the final abyss, Vickery or Collins called from the real world and pulled him back. Speaking with them each quarter hour, he managed by supreme effort to keep his voice normal; all the while Isis-faced harpies involved him in previously unimagined sexual perversions. The coffin's narrow boundaries enclosed an infinite landscape of utter damnation. A lifetime of puritanical self-control left the magician unfamiliar with the labyrinthine delights of depravity.

After his first hour underwater, Collins and Vickery telephoned their boss at five-minute intervals. He raved at them but, accustomed to his temperamental outbursts, the Jims took it all in stride, joking between calls about the old man blowing his stack. The next hour passed in this fashion, with Houdini insisting in a ferocious manner that he meant to remain submerged for eternity. His assistants took it all as an angry joke, failing to detect the dissonant note of desperation corroding his voice.

At the end of the second hour, the lifeguards brought the bronze casket to the surface in accordance with prearranged instructions. Although trial runs in the workshop had Houdini remaining sealed in a glass-topped box for nearly twice that length of time, some concern persisted regarding a build-up of excess carbon dioxide. Might it affect the magician's ability to reason? The Jims decided to end the challenge after two hours in spite of any protests to continue.

They unfastened the hasps securing the lid. Because the caulking proved tenacious, Collins and Vickery opened the coffin only after considerable effort. It sounded to them like Houdini was singing, but as they helped him into a sitting position it became embarrassingly obvious that he babbled nonsense. He dripped with sweat and his skin had a dull, ashen pallor. The blue-gray eyes blinked in bewildered disorientation.

The physician stepped in to take his pulse. Only 84 before he'd been sealed inside, it thundered now at 142. His diastolic blood pressure looked even more alarming. At the start of the experiment, it had also measured 84, but had dropped drastically to 42. Houdini looked haggard and drained of all vitality. He found it hard to focus. Those around him appeared blurred, as if seen from under water. Their voices sounded muffled and distant. The bright artificial lights seemed another hallucination. Closing his eyes, the magician prayed for sanity.

Vickery and Collins did their best to hold off the reporters while the Boss pulled himself together. In their zeal, they failed to notice a slender woman dressed in black approaching the magician from the other end of the pool.

"You were quite impressive," Opal Crosby Fletcher said, regarding the pale middle-aged man with an appraising eye. "Death and resurrection. How very, very appropriate for you, my dear Osiris."

"Don't call me that!" Seated on his coffin like some medieval effigy, Houdini avoided looking at her. His voice sounded cranky and feeble; the whining of a frail old man.

"My, my. . . . Aren't we snappy? What's the matter, not getting enough sleep?"

"I get all the sleep I need. Four hours a night is plenty for me."

"Only four hours? Seems hardly enough time to dream."

"Some people have more important things to do with their lives than waste it in bed dreaming."

Isis cocked her head as if considering what sort of meal he'd make. "Dreaming is never a waste," she said. "Nothing is more important in life than the nature of one's dreams. Been enjoying yours?"

"My dreams are none of your business!"

"You are touchy. And here I thought you the master of self-control. Maybe you've been having too many nightmares. Too many wild jungle cats raging in your subconscious?"

Houdini stared at her. "What do you know of my dreams?"

"More than you could ever imagine." Isis walked over to the group of men standing by the end of the pool. "Excuse me," she interrupted with a smile. "Has anyone got something to drink? My tongue is as dry as a snake."

Houdini found it difficult to breathe. He felt powerful electric spasms surge through his body, leaving him gasping and all atremble. Although he didn't make the connection, this sense of dumbfounded amazement was exactly what his audiences had experienced for years, viewing his mysterious and inexplicable escapes.

12

SAYS DAMON RUNYON . . .

Lissen up, little children, and listen good, your kindly old uncle means to tell you a Tale of Two Chippies. One sunny A.M. last week, tug-boat skipper, Anthony "Toot-Toot" Scalisi, spots something strange floating in the harbor just south of Governor's Island. The deck-hands place bets as to whether it is a baby whale or maybe young Johnny Weissmuller having made a wrong turn after he wins a half-mile free-style.

Turns out, once they gaff it, to be the corpse of a young doll. A bottle blond, her hair still bright as a double eagle even if there's not enough face left to form an opinion concerning her looks. A strip torn from her chemise is tied loosely around her neck with a sailor's knot. Her dress is ripped upward from the hem, another strip wrapped around her waist like a sash. Capt. "Toot-Toot" is of the opinion this makes her easier to carry.

At the morgue, county coroner Albert L. Portman discovers the cause of death to be a lace collar. This is put on so tight it is now buried out of sight in a fold of her flesh. It takes a couple more days, but the doll is eventually identified as one Mary Rogers, reported missing two weeks ago. Until her demise, she is employed as a cigarette girl at Barney Gallant's gin mill on Washington Square.

Mary Rogers lived alone in the Village but is really more a Broadway doll than a bohemian. Last seen as a contestant in the recent Roseland bunion derby, she is said by those in the know to be a carefree kid without an enemy in the world. So far, this tale is not so very different from a hundred others like it happening every year in the city O. Henry called "Baghdad on the subway."

What sets this murder apart from other recent rubouts is the distant echo of another crime which made the headlines in Gotham eighty years ago. Here, too, we have a young doll named Mary Rogers who earns her living selling cigars. All reports indicate she is the main attraction behind the counter of John Anderson's tobacco shop at 319 Broadway. Anderson is well known around town as a top-notch snuff manufacturer but it is Miss Mary's considerable charms that keep a steady clientele coming through the doors of his establishment. A pretty face sells a lot of cigars.

As it happened, this Mary Rogers likewise turns up missing back in July of 1842. She leaves home one Sunday morning and isn't seen again until the following Wednesday when her body is found floating in the Hudson off Weehawken Heights. Other eerie similarities raise a fine crop of goose-bumps eight decades later: the same lace choker, the torn bits of clothing, a delay in identifying the body.

About now maybe you are thinking, what's the big deal? Mary Rogers is not some uncommon monicker.

Lots of sweet innocent dolls get bumped off in this wicked city in close to a century's time. Talk to your bookie, he'll give you the odds on such coincidences as this and chances are they'll go no better than three to five.

Maybe so. But you won't be in the money unless your bet-taker knows as much about how to read a book as how to make one. Let me tip you to something on the emmus. These two cigar-selling dames are neck-and-neck on a dead track. If you don't believe me, check it out with the noted scribbler, old pal Edgar A. Poe.

If you remember, your tipster calls your attention once before to the Poe connection in the recent rash of rub-outs plaguing Gotham. What makes E. A. Poe such a kick in the pants is a story he writes not long after the first Mary Rogers gets bumped off. The title of this tale is "The Mystery of Marie Roget" and it lays out all the details of the cigar doll's death, except he gives her this frenchified alias and moves the local to gay Paree so as perhaps to protect the innocent.

Talk to the coppers working homicide and their official line is that Poe is strictly from hunger. But, just between you and me and the lamp-post, if someone is to offer you a tall drink of amontillado, tell him you're on the wagon.

13

BY THE SEA, BY THE SEA

A clown on stilts paraded down the boardwalk wearing a sandwich board advertising FELTON'S AMAZING SALT WATER TAFFY. His chalk-white face boasted a clown nose the size of a golf ball and red as his curly fright wig. A painted grin stretched from ear to ear, concealing the clown's somber scowl. The children laughed at him and never noticed his true expression.

Two boys and a girl, sturdy, tow-headed rapscallions whose bright gales of mirth turned the heads of other, more mature, vacationers, followed after the clown, imitating his stiff-legged gait. Denis, the oldest at fourteen, marched in front, clearly the leader, although his brother, Malcolm, who wouldn't turn thirteen until November, compensated by being the rowdiest of the three. In this, he received effusive competition from their ten-year-old tomboy sister, Jean, who insisted on being called "Billy."

They paraded behind the clown, shouting, shoving, and giggling, from the Ambassador Hotel, where they were staying with their parents, their governess, and a tutor, all the way past the stately ornate Marlborough-Blenheim, facing the ocean like a prim, parasol-toting Victorian matron decked out in seaside layers of lace, pleated petticoats, elaborate furbelows.

Halfway to the Steel Pier, the giant glowering clown came to a lurching stop in front of Felton's Taffy Shoppe, a one-story establishment wedged between a Planter's peanut roasting emporium and a small penny arcade housing twin rows of cast-iron clam shell Mutoscopes. All three children felt the pangs of a false nostalgia for these turn-of-the-century flip-card film devices. Watching the brief flickering images seemed like peeking through the keyhole of time at their father's youth, or at least how he was before they were born, which seemed an impossibly long time ago.

The clown leered down at them, his big rouged grin masking an angry grimace. He jabbed his white-gloved forefinger at the open, sweet-smelling doorway, indicating in furious mime the time had come to stop fooling around and go inside and buy some damn candy.

The children ignored his aggressive gestures, staring through the shop window at the comic gyrations of the chain-driven taffy-pulling machine. They had no shortage of funds, their pockets bulged with change, but the coinage was unfamiliar and they didn't want to appear foolish in front of strangers. After a sudden whispered exchange, the three children darted whooping between the tent-pole legs of the looming clown and ran like mad back up the boardwalk.

Halfway to the hotel, they spotted their father approaching through the crowd. He was a huge man, towering over most others, and easy to see at a distance. "Papa!" Billy waved and shouted. Someone walked with him. A much smaller man wearing a white linen suit and a straw boater. He was clean-shaven, unlike their papa, with his thick white mustache.

"It's the magician!" Denis recognized him and doubled his pace, pulling ahead of the others.

"Who?" Billy hated being the youngest and always the last in the know.

"Houdini, stupid," Malcolm said, hurrying to catch up with his brother.

Sir Arthur scooped his daughter up in his massive arms, tousling her short-cropped blond hair. "Stop that," she protested, happy laughter belying her objections.

Houdini amused the boys with a few easy sleights, pulling coins from their noses and ears. Solemnly pronouncing a "magic" phrase he'd invented at the beginning of his career, "Anthro-pro-po-lay-gos," the magician extracted a pink-dyed baby chick from his mouth and handed it peeping to Billy. The little girl was delighted. Conan Doyle's expression revealed the displeasure of a parent having to deal with unwanted pets while traveling.

They decided to return immediately to the hotel so that the "kiddies" might teach Houdini how to swim. All of them regarded this as a great joke as even Billy knew of the magician's famous underwater escapes. The remainder of the morning passed in the pool at the Ambassador, a wild splashing frolic, laughter echoing off the tiled walls. Sir Arthur floated on his back, spouting like a happy walrus; Houdini demonstrated holding his breath for extended lengths of time. The boys had a grand time challenging the magician to races, he swimming beneath the surface while they thrashed above like frantic spaniels.

After lunch, the knight and the magician sat on canvas beach chairs in the sand, watching the waves curl and fall. Houdini had come down to Atlantic City alone, planning for Bess to join him the following day. His private meeting with Sir Arthur prompted the early arrival. "I felt such an urgency to speak with you I almost telephoned," the magician said, "but decided the matter demanded privacy."

The knight chuckled. "Servants and telephone operators hear all."

"Perhaps an even more sinister eavesdropper is listening."

"I say. You do have a flair for the dramatic, what?"

"I'm serious, Sir Arthur. Do you recall your remarks at the banquet, about how difficult it is to track a random killer?"

"The arbitrary mind of a madman is impossible to anticipate."

"Yes. But what if the acts are not random?" Houdini gripped Sir Arthur's arm. "What if the murders were somehow connected? Did you know Mary Rogers worked for a time recently in my company?"

" 'Marie Roget . . .' Poe again."

"She was with me when I played the Palace the first two weeks of April. Another murdered woman, Violette Speers, was half of a dancing team on the same bill."

"Coincidence."

"That's what I said, and then Ernst made a stray comment. You remember Bernie Ernst, my lawyer?"

"Of course. He urged you to refute my claims of your mediumship by explaining how you did the slate trick, and you refused."

"No conjurer ever reveals his secrets." Houdini's grim smile lacked any trace of joy. His hawklike eyes glistened. "Ernst and I were going over the contracts for the summer tour yesterday and he says to me, 'Curious thing. That Esp girl murdered by the Poe killer? Well, she was a secretary at Dumphry, Hale, and Simmons, the accounting firm that does our books.' Another connection or just coincidence?"

"The young woman up the chimney . . . ?"

"Ingrid Esp. She worked for my accountant!"

"Did you know her?"

"Never heard of her until Bernie mentioned it the other day."

Sir Arthur stared at the sand between his feet, lost in concentration. "Nothing you've told me makes me doubt that we are dealing with a maniac."

"Maybe so." The magician's intensity seemed itself manic. "But his acts are not random. They're connected by Poe, and . . . they're connected by me."

"Let's assume there is a connection." Sir Arthur smoothed the sand between his feet. "We observe that each of the victims was better known to you than the last."

"I didn't know the Esp girl in the slightest."

"Exactly." With his forefinger, Sir Arthur drew a series of concentric circles, shaping a target in the smooth sand. "Here we have a pattern of behavior." He marked the outermost circle with a white fragment of clam shell. "This represents Ingrid Esp." He placed a second bit of shell on the bull's-eye. "And this is you. Now, if the Speers killing goes here, and Mary Rogers maybe here . . ." Two more shell fragments joined in orbit on the diagram. "There is an observable progression. The logical assumption is that the next victim will be still more intimate with you. One of your staff. A good friend . . ."

Houdini flipped a wedge of shell onto the target like a kid shooting marbles. "Everybody I know is in danger."

"Precisely."

"Especially those closest to me. You yourself are at risk, Sir Arthur."

"So it would appear . . ." The knight studied the diagram between his feet. "It seems logical the killer is someone close to you, or at least, someone you know."

"I can't believe it." Houdini's innate sense of fair play made it hard for him to accept the contradictions implicit in such betrayal. "No one who loved me could do such things."

"No. Of course not. But what of those who don't love you? My dear Houdini, I'm sure you recognize that you are one of a brave new breed; a creature concocted of celluloid and newsprint, of radio waves; a twentieth-century hero, beloved by millions, all of whom feel that they know you intimately, that you belong to them."

Houdini scowled. "The curse of fame . . ."

"Much more than that, dear chap. It's the future. What terrors await in an age wedding mass destruction with mass communication?" Sir Arthur chuckled, teeth clenched around his pipe. "Such speculation is of little use to us in our present predicament."

"What should we do?"

"Don't know there's much we can do, other than to stay on guard at all times." Puffing at his pipe provided only the briefest pause. "You might think about possible enemies; someone wishing to do you harm."

"Houdini has no enemies; there are only friends, throughout the world."

Sir Arthur sighed. What was one to do with a living, breathing circus poster? "I ask you to seriously look beyond hyperbole. Is there no one who might harbor some grudge? Can you not recall any threats from disgruntled fans?"

Houdini said nothing but thought immediately of Isis. How he sat exhausted on the bronze coffin as she came pacing back along the pool's edge, sipping from a folded paper cup filled for her at the water cooler in the men's locker room. "You must be careful," she said, in passing. "I get a very strong feeling they're going to bury you in that casket." He didn't think of it as a threat when she said it, but remembered the unfamiliar prickle of fear, instigated a second time that day by just the sound of her silken voice.

"Well . . . ?" Sir Arthur cut into his reverie. "All that cogitation uncover any likely suspects?"

"No," the magician blurted, altogether too quickly. Sir Arthur raised a bushy eyebrow. "Jess Willard and I once exchanged heated words," Houdini continued, visibly annoyed. "I was onstage. He sat in the balcony. The audience hooted him from the theater. That was in Los Angeles in 1915. He's not champion anymore. Maybe he's a bitter man. Maybe he's had it in for me for the last eight years. Maybe he reads a lot of Poe!"

Sir Arthur patted Houdini's shoulder, as if he were comforting a nervous pointer. "I quite sympathize with the impossible enormity of the task I've given you. Looking back over your long career, you undoubtedly could name a thousand such chance encounters. How many of those led to lasting enmity? It's impossible to tell. So, in essence, we're back where we started, confronting a faceless madman."

"Wrong. We started out among the spectators. Now we're on the program with a faceless madman topping the bill." .

"Or madwoman . . ." Sir Arthur drew thoughtfully on his pipe. "Last seen dressed as a gorilla."

The windows of Conan Doyle's suite looked out across the boardwalk to the wind-tossed Atlantic. From where he stood, Sir Arthur could easily see the children sprawled on the beach with young Ashton, their tutor. He'd warned the apple-cheeked Oxonian to keep a weather eye out for strangers, saying there'd been veiled threats from the anti-spiritualist factions. As a further precaution, he checked the loads in his service revolver, a .455 Webley-Green he kept in his desk drawer at Windlesham and hadn't seen since packing it deep in one of the trunks at the start of the mission.

The Webley's weight felt reassuring in Sir Arthur's jacket pocket. There it would reside until all were safely home. He held back the lace curtain and watched his children frolic in the angled afternoon sun.

Houdini hadn't told all he knew. It wasn't the man's nature to share secrets. Sir Arthur saw him flinch when he mentioned the possibility of a mad "woman." Not that the knight had been altogether candid with his magician friend, having made no reference to communicating with Poe's spirit. Without witnesses, he knew any such claim would be dismissed by Houdini as mere "ghost stories."

Sir Arthur had begun a journal on the Poe manifestation in tandem with the study of a two-volume biography. He marked critical observations with an asterisk in the notebook's margin.

·Spirit shows itself only to me.
·Spirit only visible in cities where Poe actually lived. No sightings in Atlantic City after ten days.
·Spirit regards ME as a ghost. Is very calm and rational regarding this belief.
·Spirit does not acknowledge own death!
·Spirit mourns death of wife (Virginia Clemm).
·Is there a way to test the spirit and my own runaway imagination? I must phrase a question for which I haven't the answer, then check Poe's response with a known authority. A correct match-up proves me sane . . .

Reading through these made him pause and uncap his fountain pen. He jotted this note:

Must ask spirit about murders.

Also, get NYC newspaper accounts of all three "Poe" murders.

Is it a puzzle? Can it be solved? Poe a student of cryptography. Victims' names?

The following afternoon, Bess Houdini snuggled her head against her husband's shoulder, safe in the relative privacy of a rented wicker-and-canvas cabana, a bit of welcome shade on the blaze of sunbright beach. Bess felt romantic by the sea. Their whirlwind teenage romance had been a Coney Island courtship and ever since that hot-blooded time it took the merest whiff of salt air, of cotton candy and Cracker Jacks, or the distant calliope waltzing of merry-go-rounds, to make her weak in the knees around Harry.

He was such an old poop. Brooding, his mouth clamped in a scowl, eyes fixed on the horizon; he might as well be a million miles away. Bessie forgave his introspection. She had long ago. At least he was sitting beside her, his arm hugging her to his side. Always such a struggle to get him to take a vacation, even harder to make him relax. It pleased her to have him close, her love a balm for his turbulent thoughts.

The magician's mind filled with targets, all whirling like pinwheels. A knife-thrower's blade flashed through his imagination, thudding among the red concentric circles, anchoring runaway images with a frightening finality. He pictured Bessie framed within a target, the bull's-eye as red as her heart. As red as blood, he thought. Red as death.

He felt numb from the futility of knowing a task to be impossible. His whole career consisted of performing miracles. Easy enough with everything safely rigged beforehand. But what about a challenge from a madman? How do you protect someone you love from the unknown?

Young Billy's breakneck zigzagging through the sand interrupted this desperate meditation. She skidded giggling to a stop on her knees in front of them. Sir Arthur trudged up behind in his dark wool suit, as out of place among the supine sun worshipers as a missionary surrounded by naked heathens.

"My . . . my . . ." Billy caught her breath. "My mother wants to . . . to invite you up to her room. She means to conduct a séance and wishes you to be her guest."

Sir Arthur towered behind her, blocking the sun. Oddly enough, he considered himself a missionary, his speaking tour a mission proselytizing spiritism. Not a religion, actually, but a faith offering more comfort than wearing out your knees on the cold stones of some damp cathedral. His somber get-up was in no way meant to emphasize his beliefs. He'd had a breakfast meeting with local business leaders and a dark suit had seemed appropriate. "Excuse Billy's enthusiastic excesses, but please accept her invitation." Sir Arthur smiled down at them. "It's not a séance, actually. As you may know, Jean has a gift for automatic writing."

"My goodness, yes," Bess piped up, having straightened primly at Sir Arthur's approach. "She was telling me what a thrill it was to feel the spirits take possession."

Sir Arthur coughed. "Well, you know. . . . The experience can be quite an emotional one. It was my wife's expressed feeling that contact with Houdini's dear mother should be attempted. She knows your sentiments and wishes to help."

"Nothing could bring me greater joy." Houdini sprang to his feet, his desire for contact tempered by a natural skepticism. "To speak once again with my sainted mother is a dream I cherish."

"Perhaps we can put you in touch with that dream. Unfortunately, these things go better if it's a private sitting. Having two subjects present might confuse matters. I do hope Mrs. Houdini won't think me rude, but—"

"Sir Arthur, please!" The magician took his wife by the hand. "Under the circumstances, I am certain you realize I cannot allow my wife to leave my side."

Sir Arthur nodded quickly, the revolver heavy in the pocket of his dark wool suit. "Yes. Of course. Quite right."

The windows were left open in the Conan Doyle suite at the Ambassador as a concession to the season. A stiff sea breeze rippled the drawn drapes, allowing in occasional flashes of sunlight and a muted chorus passing along the boardwalk below. Pads of paper and a pair of ordinary yellow pencils waited on the table around which they sat. Sir Arthur stood beside Lady Jean. He bowed his head. "Dear Lord," he prayed in a gruff whisper, "send us a sign from our beloved friends who have gone on before us." Houdini thought he looked like a simple child.

Lady Doyle had been charming. "Now, Mr. Houdini," she said when they first arrived, "I trust you're on your best behavior and won't try and embarrass me with any mischief this afternoon?"

The magician blushed at her forthright manner. He turned to his wife and stammered, "I . . . I have always been a good boy, have I not?"

Even Bess seemed surprised by his emotional exposure. She caught Sir Arthur and Lady Doyle exchanging a quick glance. "Why, Harry," she said, "you're never anything less than a perfect gentleman."

"I should think not," Lady Jean said, guiding him to a comfortable chair. "No true hero ever is . . ."

Houdini pondered the nature of heroism as he studied her face, so utterly without guile. He noted her sincere smile as Sir Arthur sat beside her and lovingly covered her hands with his own. Across the way, Bess waited with her eyes shut. To assist, if possible, Houdini closed his own eyes, calming his mind with thoughts of religion.

A sharp rapping put an end to his meditation. Lady Jean gripped a pencil, her arm jerking with galvanic spasms, the tip pounding against the tabletop. "They have me now, Arthur," she said. "It's never been stronger."

"Allow it to flow, my darling." The knight gently kneaded the back of her regal neck and the corded tension relaxed somewhat.

Houdini watched the spasmodic jerking of Lady Jean's hand. He had no doubt the seizure was genuine. A thrill of anticipation prickled through him, generated by his overwhelming desire to feel his mother's presence once again. He wanted desperately to believe, at the same time recognizing this to be a sucker's impulse. All deception begins with the deceived's willing trust.

Jean regarded her trembling right arm as if it were a foreign crea-ture; fingers bloodless from the strain of clenching the pencil in a death grip. "Spirit," she cried. "Do you believe in God?"

As if in reply, her hand beat three times upon the table.

Jean looked straight into Arthur's eyes when she said: "Then I will make the sign of the cross."

The agony showed on her face as she directed her vibrating hand to scratch a cruciform on the top sheet of a pad. "Who is there?" Jean implored. "Is it Mrs. Weiss, mother of Houdini the magician?"

Again, her hand tapped three times, the pencil scrolling across the page, words shaped by a jerky scrawl. "Oh my darling," she wrote, "thank God, at last I'm through—I've tried, oh so often—now I am happy—"

The large letters filled the first page quickly. Sir Arthur tore it from the pad and handed it to Houdini. The magician read all in an instant, his face grim and pale. Clearly possessed, Lady Doyle scribbled on, page after page. Sir Arthur ripped each free as she finished, tossing it over to Houdini. "Use me, use me . . . ," Lady Doyle moaned.

"There, my dear . . ." Sir Arthur rubbed her neck. "Be gentle with her. Gentle . . ."

The pages flew from her spastic hand. Sir Arthur ripped them off the block, passing each to the magician. Houdini read on and on, loving, eager thoughts, the promise of a better world to come: "I want him to know that—that—I have bridged the gulf—That is what I wanted, oh so much—Now I can rest in peace—How soon—"

Sir Arthur interrupted at this point to ask the magician to think of some sort of private question, a silent test to see if the spirit at their side was truly his mother. Houdini nodded in agreement, thinking, "Can my mother read my mind?" Lady Jean continued to scribble.

The next sheet began: "I always read my beloved son's mind—his dear mind—there is so much I want to say to him—but—I am almost overwhelmed by this joy of talking to him once more—" Houdini nodded at Sir Arthur as he read it.

"She got it right?" Sir Arthur beamed. "You lucky man . . ." And he smiled with pure pleasure and pride as the scribbled pages continued to flow until a pile of fifteen or more lay before the magician.

After the séance, Lady Doyle lay back on the couch, exhausted and unable to speak. Sir Arthur saw to her comfort, placing a damp, folded washcloth on her forehead. Houdini stacked the sheets of notepaper, feeling both grateful and embarrassed. The silence made him uncomfortable and he spoke mainly to sidestep such feelings, just aimless banter about automatic writing. Houdini picked up a pencil. "Maybe I should try it myself at home," he said. "How do you start? Just write the first thing that comes to mind?" He printed a name on the pad: POWELL.

Sir Arthur glanced over the magician's shoulder. "Powell!" he exclaimed with considerable excitement. "Great God! Truly Saul is among the prophets! You are a medium."

"Powell, the magician," Houdini said. "He's down on his luck in Texas. Used to be big. A headliner. Mrs. Houdini and I were talking about him just the other day."

"No, no, that's but your conscious mind searching out a logical explanation. Dr. Ellis Powell, a dear friend and fighting partner in the great cause, died recently in London. I am certain it is he, seeking contact with me."

"Just a coincidence. I was thinking of Frederick Eugene Powell."

Conan Doyle grew red in the face. "You deny the indisputable evidence before you out of your obsession with discrediting spiritism."

"No. It is you who distorts the truth in support of your own beliefs." Houdini gathered up the leaves of the "spirit" letter. "Thank you, Lady Doyle, for your earnest efforts on my behalf." He held out his arm for Bess. "Come, Mrs. Houdini. Good afternoon, Sir Arthur." With exaggerated dignity, the magician escorted his wife from the room.

On the train back to the city, Houdini tried to mollify his Bess, but she was in no mood for conciliation. "A seaside holiday is supposed to last more than one afternoon." Bess stared out the window, refusing to look at him. "At least among sane people it does."

"There was no way I could stay, Bess," he pleaded. "Lady Doyle was so well-meaning. She believes the letter to be genuine. I know it's bogus. Mama couldn't write English. She would never mark a letter with a cross. Bess, for crying out loud, today is Mama's birthday! Don't you think she would have mentioned that?"

"Well, I suppose, knowing Mama . . ." Bess smiled and gripped his hand. "Do you think it's all in her subconscious? Lady Doyle's writing, I mean."

"I believe an alienist would say so." Houdini sat straight-backed beside her like a boyish suitor. "I've seen every kind of fake in the world, and wherever it comes from, I know Lady Doyle to be sincere. But, even so, sincerity doesn't make the letter genuine."

"Harry? You don't suppose the Conan Doyles might take offense from the note we left, do you?" Bess looked like a little girl when she worried.

"Of course not. I explained we were called away unexpectedly." Houdini cupped his wife's small hands within his own. "Maybe it'd be safer for them to put some distance between us."

"What do you mean, Harry?"

"Oh, just a premonition. I'll explain it to you someday, kiddo."

14

MAKING WHOOPEE

Houdini walked uptown on Madison. He'd already been around the block once, having asked the cabby to drop him at the corner by the DeLuxe French Dry Cleaners, where his reflection wavered a second time in the plate glass window. He had approached a lifetime of challenges with the same precise caution. Whether piano case or iron boiler, glass box or wooden barrel, the challenger always left his container on display in the theater lobby for a week prior to the performance, giving the magician and his crew ample time to examine the problem and build an appropriate gag into the challenge, rigging it so the eventual onstage escape went off without a hitch.

He turned west on Eighty-fifth Street, walking back toward Fifth, on his own for tonight's challenge. He saw the dark turrets crowning Opal Crosby Fletcher's mock chateau and the darker silhouette of the trees in Central Park across the avenue. Considering the evening as a problem to be solved, as an undercover investigation, cloaked the adventure in propriety and masked the giddy erotic excitement gnawing at Houdini's gut. The magician's heart raced as he mounted the stone steps to the arched entranceway. He told himself it was stage fright.

Maybe I'm walking straight into the spider's den, Houdini thought, handing his hat to the elderly housekeeper who opened the door in answer to his ring. He followed her tidy gray bun across a vast shadowed foyer, illuminated by a single wall sconce. Other broad dark rooms gaped on either side; the whole place silent as a foreign embassy closed for the night. A huge unlit chandelier hung like an outstretched midnight octopus in the gloom above the curving stairs. He stayed one step behind the prim old woman. She led the way without saying a word.

Bess had gone to the opera with Dash. The magician took comfort in the safety of crowds. Houdini told his wife nothing of his fears. He saw no point in having her worry. All the same, he hired the Burns Detective Agency to conduct a 24-hour surveillance of his home. His brother was the only person, other than Conan Doyle, with whom the magician discussed the Esp girl and the connecting web of murdered strangers in which he found himself inexplicably enmeshed.

The library door stood open at the end of a long hallway on the second floor. It was a spacious room, warm with woodwork, gold-tooled leather bindings, and thick Caucasian carpets. A gas fire flickered in a marble-faced hearth under a Georgian mantel, giving no warmth but casting an agreeable light. Several bright candles augmented the mood of comfort and intimacy.

Isis sat by the fire, looking altogether radiant in a clinging midnight-blue velvet gown with a considerable décolletage. Firelight cast a rosy glow on her bare neck and shoulders. She wore a single ornament between her breasts: a large Mayan moon-face of hammered sheet gold. Originally part of an ancient funeral necklace, it had been adapted by Walter Clarke Fletcher into a pin as a present for his teenage bride.

She extended her slender hand to Houdini. "Welcome at last," she said. "Will you join me in something to drink? I'm having absinthe." She gestured at a green bottle and a cut-crystal water pitcher on a tray beside her. "I remember you don't drink spirits, but Martha can bring you anything you like; apple cider, coffee, tea, milk . . . ?"

"Tea would be fine." Houdini took a seat opposite her. "Two sugars. And in a glass, please."

"Martha. Some tea for Mr. Houdini, served in a glass."

The old woman made no reply, slipping away like the shadow of a crow when the sun goes behind a cloud. The magician never noticed her silent passage, so intent was he on the delicate young woman deftly preparing a drink on the low table between them. She poured a portion of the pale green liqueur into a tall stemmed glass and placed a silver absinthe spoon shaped like a miniature trowel across the rim. Centering a single sugar cube on the spoon, she slowly trickled a thin stream of water over it, a sly sweet rainfall dripping through the ornate perforations. Within the glass, the absinthe occluded, the emerald clarity misting into milky opalescence.

"The green fairy unfolds her cobweb wings," Isis purred softly. She looked up, and was surprised to find Houdini's gaze had strayed to a gleaming object on the mantel. At first, he assumed this to be a crystal ball but realized on prolonged inspection that it took the form of a human skull.

"Aztec," Isis said, catching his eye. "Amazing·work. Shaped from a single large quartz crystal. Done entirely with abrasives. They had no metal tools, you know."

"Looks like blown glass."

"Yes. It's that perfect. Belongs in a museum."

The cat-silent Martha arrived with the tea. She set down a tray and was gone before either of them noticed.

"Very quick," Houdini said.

"Martha takes good care of me."

Houdini dropped two sugar cubes in his glass, added a spoon, and poured the hot tea. Isis watched as he stirred and sipped.

"Interesting flavor," he said.

"Herbal. My own blend. Mainly mint and sassafras. I pick and dry the plants myself every summer. When I visit my parents in New Hampshire."

Houdini put down his glass. The strange taste remained in his mouth. "Your own recipe, huh?" Some secret agent. She might have slipped him a mickey. He thought of Lucrezia Borgia and put on an urgent face, an expression of discomfort calculated to make a request for the lavatory sound natural. Immediate regurgitation was the task at hand.

"Is it brewed too strong?" Isis reached across the table for his glass and took a long thoughtful sip. "No. Seems about right . . ." Her knowing eyes stared past his clumsy disguise. She took another sip. "Way too sweet, though . . ." Handing him back the glass. "Don't you think?"

Houdini didn't know what to think. He suddenly felt very thirsty and swallowed the rest of the tea. She looked so innocent, yet dressed with such confident sophistication. The intensity of her power terrified him. "I like it that way," he said. "Sweet."

Isis sipped her absinthe. "You're in luck then . . ." She pushed a gleaming silver sugar bowl in his direction. Houdini fixed himself another glass of tea. "If you're agreeable," she continued, "I thought we might conduct the séance right here. Are you comfortable with that?"

"Right here is fine by me. What sort of séance did you have in mind?" Houdini immediately cursed himself for any unintended innuendo.

Isis stood, her sleek velvet gown sweeping down in a fluid rush to puddle about her feet on the floor. Her ironic smile announced a connoisseur's appreciation of the double entendre. "It has nothing to do with the mind, my dear Osiris . . ." She picked the crystal skull off the mantel and sat back down with it cradled in her lap. "We are entering the realm of the spirit."

"No cabinet . . . ? No controls?" The magician did not attempt to hide his ironic smirk.

"No props, Osiris. This is not a sideshow." She stroked the sacred Aztec skull and smiled. "All I ask is your concentration. Think of the one you wish to contact. Fill your mind with her presence."

Houdini nodded and swallowed hard. Who said anything about "her"? A light film of sweat formed like dew on his forehead. How does she know so much? "And you?" he asked, struggling to keep his voice even. "What should I watch for?"

"Nothing." She closed her eyes. "I am nothing. I wish to lose myself. To let go. . . . My only desire is to serve as your conduit, oh my lord, Osiris . . ."

Houdini squirmed. A tumult of conflicting emotions raged within. He felt in awe of this young woman. He feared her. God help him, he desired her. The shame engendered by his lust burned with intensified heat, fueled by a desperate yearning to communicate with his dead mother. At heart, he was a sucker. He longed to believe. At the same time, a cold, cynical eye watched to see what sort of "ectoplasm" she conjured. She had to be good, working in the firelight. Most mediums demanded complete darkness to manage their trickery.

At length, he relaxed. Time ticked on. Isis sat motionless, a center of calm. Her hands stroked the incredible carving she held like a pet. Rosy light glimmered on her serene features. Houdini thought she looked like the carvings of saints he'd seen in European cathedrals. He felt his mother's beatific presence surging within his breast.

A violent tremor seized Isis. Her back arched from the force of the spasms. She clung to the crystal skull as her body trembled and ropelike tendons appeared on her straining neck. A rasping raven-croak rattled out of her throat.

Here it comes, Houdini thought, watching her with his raptor's intensity. What came was something the magician never expected.

His mother's voice burst from Isis in a guttural rush of rapid-fire German, the pent-up words escaping like steam through a safety valve. "Ehrie. . . . Mein Ehrie. . . . Kannest du mich horen, mein geliebter Sohn?"

"Mama . . . ?" Houdini's emotions overcame his reason. She called him by his childhood nickname. "Bist du das, Mama?"

"Aber. Ja, ja . . . ich bin bei dir, Ehrie. Ich werde immer bei dir sein."

Overwhelmed by a joyous flood of love, Houdini found it difficult to speak. The voice was his mother's, exact to her slight Hungarian accent. He asked if she could see him. She told him she no longer had sight and tried to describe empathy beyond understanding. She remained with him always, her spirit linked to his. It was impossible to explain with words. How can you tell a blind man what "blue" is? She knew danger surrounded her son like an angry cloud. She had to warn him. Danger, Ehrie . . .

He asked if she'd tried to use Lady Doyle as a medium. Isis relaxed. She smiled and spoke with Cecilia Weiss's voice, quoting an old country folk saying he remembered his mama telling him as a small child in Appleton, Wisconsin. Something about how you can teach a dog to roll over but only a cow gives milk. Houdini had never been sure exactly what it meant.

If he didn't look at Isis, he felt his mother there in the room beside him. The intensity of his love coursed through him like a narcotic. He wanted so badly to believe in the illusion. Watching Isis, he marveled at the simplicity of her performance. His logical nature insisted on thinking of it as performance and illusion. The voice sounded perfect. She'd done her homework, the nuance and details all right on the money.

Isis sagged. The German she spoke slowed and slurred into an unintelligible growl, like a distant radio station fading out of reception.

No! Don't go, Mama! Houdini reached across the table and grasped the delicate hands clutching the crystal skull. "Blieb, Mama! Bitte geh nicht fort!"

Opal Crosby Fletcher opened those clear jade eyes that seemed to see so much. "Oh, dear," she said in her own voice, sweet and pure as a child. "How very powerful."

Houdini blinked, his face etched with grief. The pain in his eyes seemed almost palpable. "Ma . . . ?" His mouth hung open after the first despairing syllable.

"What's wrong?" Isis stood up. "Are you all right?"

The magician cursed himself. The moment he began to doubt, his mother was lost to him. "I'm to blame," he said, tears starting in his eyes.

Isis came around the low table and knelt before him. She took hold of his hands. "There's no blame," she said. "Only fear . . ."

"All my fault," he blubbered, tears streaming, his breath coming in hysterical gasps.

"Don't . . ."

The magician's overloaded emotions got the best of him. He slid off the chair and collapsed sobbing into her arms. She hugged him, crooning soft noises, and he wept helplessly on her breast.

"There now. . . . Let it out . . ." She gently massaged his temple. "Let all the poison and fear flow out."

At length, his pathetic sniveling came to a stop. He dried his eyes with his handkerchief and blew his nose. "She was really here," he said in wonderment. "My sainted mother . . ."

Isis felt him tremble and averted a second onslaught of crying by kneading the knotted muscles in the back of his neck. Her fingers felt remarkably strong for someone who looked so frail. "She's always with you. Every minute of every day," Isis murmured softly in his ear. "There's no death or separation in the realm of the spirit."

"I wish I could believe that," Houdini sighed. He closed his eyes. "You've got magic fingers. Thought my head was gonna bust apart."

"Belief is all there is. It's all that stands between us and nothing-ness." Isis eased her hands under his jacket collar. "Here. Take off your coat. You'll be more comfortable that way." There was no complaint as she eased him out of his rumpled worsted jacket. At her direction, he moved to the center of the thick wool carpet, stretching out on his stom-ach among the swirling multicolored arabesques. She slipped off his shoes and knelt beside him. "Feel better . . . ?" She worked her fingers up and down the bunched muscles along his spine.

"God, yes . . ." He surrendered to her gentle, powerful massage. How did she know him so well? She somehow anticipated his thoughts, expressing concern for his every need. Her touch seemed nothing short of enchanted, all his tension dispelled by her skillful manipulation. And she must have a good heart. Why else would Mama choose her as a medium?

Houdini moaned aloud with pure animal pleasure as Isis went to work on his taut shoulders. Conflicting thoughts crowded his conscious-ness. Maybe she's faking. Gotta keep a healthy skepticism alive. Even so, how can her motives be impure when she had Mama's blessed voice so perfectly right? Every inflection. His nickname. Every . . .

Houdini drifted off into a deep, dreamless slumber. For the briefest moment, he fought the impulse to sleep, a strong survival instinct warn-ing him of the danger inherent in unconsciousness. Unable to resist as a rising tide of darkness flowed around him, he felt drugged, numb; his limbs leaden, his mind a blur. Even the distant crooning of Isis worked as a soporific. Letting go completely, the magician disappeared in the black sea of night.

He had no idea how long he was out. Opening his eyes, he experienced a sudden surge of panic when the world remained dark. He reached up and touched a silken mask bound across his eyes.

"Don't take it off." By the sound of her voice, Isis spoke from the far end of the library. "Not yet. I'll tell you when."

Houdini lay quite still, wondering what made him obey her gentle command. Something else was different. He wore a silk robe. Feeling the smooth cool fabric against his bare limbs brought the incredible realization that she had undressed him while he slept. "What have you done with my clothes?" he demanded.

"Don't worry, Osiris, they're safe. Martha is ironing out all those wrinkles." Her musical voice sounded closer now. "You looked so uncomfortable, sleeping completely dressed like that."

Houdini sniffed. The air smelled strangely fragrant with incense. He thought of frankincense and myrrh and remembered the smells in the European churches he'd visited; thick aromatic white smoke streaming from the swinging censer. Another odd smell, sweet and oleaginous, he recognized as melting wax. What the hell was going on here?

"All right," she said, her voice barely more than a whisper, "you can take off the mask now."

The magician pulled the band of cloth from his eyes, blinking in wonderment and disbelief. At first, he thought he saw stars. Hundreds of candles had been arranged around the commodious room, their tiny flames bright as a flight of fireflies in the gloom. Glittering on every possible level and surface; on the floor, on chair seats and tabletops, staggered along bookshelves, in a line over the mantel; they transformed the formal library with their mysterious dazzle.

Propped on his elbows, taking it all in, Houdini watched Isis approach from the far end of the room, her face startlingly painted. The left side gleamed chalk white (white as a geisha, white as a clown, white as death) while the right side had been done in vivid green, like the absinthe she drank earlier. The colors met in a straight line dividing her features down the bridge of her nose from forehead to chin. Both shocking and weirdly beautiful, the whole effect framed by a glossy oval of black hair gleaming with candlelight. The bizarre makeup distracted his attention from the diaphanous chartreuse chiton she wore.

She swept toward him, a carved wooden casket the size of a cigar box in her hands, her limber body clearly visible through the sheer apple-green fabric. He caught his breath at the sight of her rose-tipped breasts and the small, dark delta of her sex.

In spite of his world travels and long experience in show business, the magician was in reality quite naive and unsophisticated in carnal matters—a bit of a prude, if the truth be known—a man who had never once visited a brothel or cheated on his wife, not even stolen a single kiss from the legion of chorus girls he'd worked with over the years. He never used profanity and blushed when told off-color jokes. The utter novelty of the lust gripping him added greatly to his excitement.

Isis settled beside him, seeming to float. The pale, transparent green gown wafted about her like tangible smoke. "Relax," she said, opening the carved lid of the sandalwood box and removing a blue orb-shaped flask. She poured a small amount of warm, scented oil into her cupped hand, smoothing it across his chest with gentle circular motions. Houdini sighed and closed his eyes. "Good . . . good . . . ," she purred. "Just relax . . ."

Her touch felt different from when she massaged him earlier. More a caress this time. Her fingertips lightly traced the tepid oil over his flesh, circling his nipples, which tightened like tiny wrinkled raisins in anticipation. When she pinched them, an electric shock shuddered through his body all the way to his arching toes.

She hummed as she stroked him, a throaty, aimless melody more a low animal moan than anything musical. The magician drifted in the primal sound. His body tingled with pleasure. It felt so good. He never wanted it to stop. Her hands swirled across his abdomen, spreading a scented sheen of oil. She moved down over his thighs and his body glistened in the candlelight. All resistance ebbed away, any thought of protest vanished, he surrendered to her completely.

"Stay still," she whispered, smoothing oil along his erection. Both her hands urged its straining length up inside as, straddling his loins, she lowered herself upon him. He opened his eyes with an astonished gasp. Seeing her without the gossamer gown added to his pleasure: her slender, girlish waist and the nubile uplift of young breasts. Bucking upward, he reached out his arms to draw her into a grateful embrace. "Be still," she repeated. This time it was an order.

She pushed his hands away, forcing his arms to rest along his sides. Making him lie inert, his head back against the bold Moroccan pillow she had settled there while he slept, she rose and fell above him, rose and fell, rose and fell, all in a slow, steady rhythm much more natural than the usual energetic frenzy of his marital coupling.

Houdini had never made love in this manner before, the woman riding on top. At first, he felt odd remaining so quiescent, the passive partner for once in his life. Gradual delight overcame his reluctance. He closed his eyes again, letting go at last of any impulse to dominate, feeling the moist, sliding motion become an undulant, rippling grip unlike anything he'd ever experienced.

Opening his eyes, he saw Isis with her head bent back, her hands on her breasts, the rosy nipples caught between grasping fingers. She no longer moved. Her pelvis pressed tightly against him, vaginal muscles contracting in some totally inexplicable manner.

Again, his eyes closed. Not even his wildest adolescent dreams had imagined such sensations. Sex never ranked as a high priority in his life. He knew only the tender moments shared with Bess, but didn't think of them now or of his wife. Houdini had been transported beyond thinking.

The magician heard Isis moan and looked up at her reddened neck and grimacing, painted face. She started to climax, the contractions grown so powerful they almost forced him from her body. Her moaning built to a wild animal howl as a pulsing flow of warm fluid fountained out of her vagina, flooding around him onto his belly. Utter delirious astonishment triggered the beginning spasms of his orgasm. He groaned in mindless ecstasy.

At this moment, Isis groped blindly in the sandalwood box beside her, feeling for a carved ivory dildo, greased with Vaseline, its hollow interior filled with heated milk. Taking hold of the smooth, slippery shaft, she reached behind her and pushed its full length into Houdini's rectum. The magician screamed as he came and came and came, his back arching, his brain skyrocketing into exploding pyrotechnic oblivion.

15

ASK ME NO QUESTIONS

Poe smiled at Sir Arthur Conan Doyle. Much more than the mere ghost of a smile, a mocking irony twisted the misty lips; the sardonic arching of his bushy tangled eyebrows suggested eternal cynicism. Sir Arthur thought those eyebrows resembled nothing so much as fat black caterpillars crawling across the poet's high-domed forehead. An unfortunate comparison putting him immediately in mind of worm-eaten corpses wrapped in grave-tattered winding sheets.

The knight sat in the front room of his suite in the Bellevue on Broad Street several blocks off Philadelphia's Rittenhouse Square. An open notebook rested on his lap. It was that gray hour before dawn when even the birds were not yet awake and the busy world remained blunted by a sepulchral stillness. The specter faced him from the corner of the room farthest from the darkened window. Sir Arthur learned from past experience to keep his distance. Like a mirage, the manifestation faded and vanished if approached too closely.

The Conan Doyles had been in the City of Brotherly Love for three days of a projected eight-day visit and, in spite of his hectic lecture schedule, Sir Arthur was up every morning before daybreak waiting for Poe's supernatural appearance. He had not been disappointed. The ghost materialized, bright and early, the very first day.

When Sir Arthur described the ghastly murders committed in

Manhattan, detailing how the killer duplicated crimes Poe had created in his fiction, the ghost opened wide his moonbeam mouth in a caterwaul of chilling laughter. And as he laughed, he slowly dissolved, whirling away like wisps of smoke in an icy wind until nothing remained but the disembodied laughter, a terrifying echo seeming to resound from the very bowels of hell itself.

Waiting in the predawn dark that morning, Conan Doyle remembered yesterday's outrage, pondering the absurdity of his emotional reaction. Why should a spirit long deceased have any sympathy for the newly dead, no matter how grotesque their ends? And how absurd to assume the concerns of the living meant anything at all to those who had already passed beyond. Resigned to these disquieting realizations, Sir Arthur had a pleasant surprise when Poe's ghost materialized as if on schedule and immediately brought up the subject of the murders.

Apparently intrigued with the notion of homicide as an art form, the specter continued: "It's one thing to write about murder in the abstract, to invent a blood-drenched fiction is a fine fancy. But, how much more sublime to populate a narrative with actual corpses and render the scene in crimson gore instead of printer's ink."

"It's not a matter of aesthetics!" Conan Doyle sputtered with indignation. "People are dying. Lives are at risk. My own quite possibly among them."

This last remark prompted the ghost's mocking smile. "Does a phantom worry about mortality?" The frosty eyes danced with irony.

Sir Arthur eased into an answering smile, his wit too keen not to see the humor inherent in the situation. "A metaphysical conundrum, I'll admit," he chuckled. The ghost stared at him. The knight felt a chill deep in his bones. "A more deadly riddle concerns me now. I rather hoped your fondness for problems of this sort might induce you to assist me."

"It is indeed a mystery worthy of analysis." Poe's shade shimmered in the gloom. "Let us examine the elements already in play. The seemingly random nature of the crimes has convinced the authorities they investigate the work of a madman. Perhaps they are correct in this assumption, but it must be remembered there frequently is much method in any presumed madness. What better way to mask a murderous motive?"

Sir Arthur jotted down a quick note. "I quite agree. However, the possibility still exists that we're dealing with a madman pure and simple."

"If that were true there is no purpose to this exercise and we would be well advised to abandon any effort. Better to assume a discernible pattern and hope our investigation bears fruit." The specter's tented fingertips tapped against his pursed and pensive lips. "The sequence of crime was, I recollect: 'Rue Morgue,' followed by 'Black Cat,' followed by 'Marie Roget.' This progression duplicates the order of the stories' publication. Logical to assume the next atrocity, when it occurs, will take as its inspiration one of my tales published at a later date."

"Check Poe chronology," Conan Doyle wrote in his notebook. "Are there any other aspects of these stories that strike you as fitting a pattern?" he asked.

"I can imagine a number of possibilities. The killer has a fascination with my work. It stands to reason, he must be aware of my interest in cryptography. Perhaps he's creating a cipher for us to solve. The problem is knowing where to start. The letters comprising the titles of my tales might be one possibility. And what were the true names of the victims? See what can be made of the letters in their names."

Sir Arthur busily scribbled notes. "Seems impossible," he muttered, writing: "Mary Rogers. (Marie Roget?) Violette Speers. Ingrid Esp. Mrs. Esp. (What was mother's first name?)"

"Nothing is impossible." The ghost fussed with his disheveled cobweb hair. "Merely difficult. . . . Another avenue of investigation might be the victims' street addresses." Poe's thin smile indicated his pleasure with the punning word-play. "Perhaps a numerical sequence will reveal itself . . ."

Impelled by his love of games, Sir Arthur jotted anagrams in the margin of his notebook. Working first with MARY ROGERS, he immediately saw MY RAGE, but that left SORR. He tried SORRY RAGE, and wondered what to do with the leftover M. "It could be anything," he mused, half-aloud.

"That's the beauty of it, wouldn't you say?" Again, the wistful, mocking smile.

"SORRY GAMER . . . ?" Sir Arthur tapped his pen against the page, wondering if he should try the letters from all the names at once. Even then, how could he be sure of finding a hidden message? Perhaps the names of unknown victims not yet dead were needed to complete the anagram. Absolutely no way to tell. "Beautiful in the abstract," he said. "Unfortunately, this is very real. A life and death matter."

"Arthur . . . ?" Jean looked in at him from the bedroom doorway. "Are you all right?"

"Couldn't be finer, darling. Come join us. There's someone here I'd very much like you to meet."

She sat beside him on the sofa, teasing: "Is it a life and death matter?"

"In a manner of speaking." He clasped her hand in his. "My dear, allow me to present to you, Mr. Edgar Allan Poe."

Jean glanced all around. "Where, Arthur?"

The knight gestured at where Poe's ghost had moments before been seated. The empty space looked all the more void for having been so recently occupied. "Why, he was just there. Big as life, if you'll excuse the inappropriate simile." Sir Arthur's brave smile verged on bewilderment. "You do believe me, don't you?"

"Of course, my darling." Jean hugged her husband, kissing him tenderly on the cheek. His skin had a sickly gray pallor and dark circles underscored his eyes. "You really should get more rest, poor dear."

"Poe was here, Jean," he insisted, "right in this room. It's not merely exhaustion."

"Of course not. I wasn't doubting your veracity. But, I'm worried about you. Your lecture schedule is so demanding, and now with you investigating this Poe phenomenon, you're getting even less sleep. I know your energies are equal to those of ten ordinary men, but even the stalwart need rest occasionally."

Sir Arthur patted her hand. "My sweet guardian angel . . ."

"Don't patronize me, Arthur. I love you and want the best for you.

Now, remember your luncheon engagement. It's a newspaper interview and you know how grueling they can be."

"I'd much prefer climbing into a cage with a man-eating tiger."

"And, there's the mayor's reception tonight after the lecture. Not to mention dinner with Leopold Stokowski. You'll need all the rest you can get and I'm taking charge."

"Are you, indeed?"

"I am, my darling. You're coming straight back to bed and get some decent sleep."

The knight gave his wife's knee a gentle squeeze. "Perhaps if something a bit more indecent were being offered . . .?"

"Oh, Arthur, you are a such a charming rogue." She rose to her feet and held out her hand. "Come on then, I'll tuck you in and we'll see what can be arranged."

At one-thirty that afternoon, sipping a cup of black coffee, Damon Runyon awaited his luncheon appointment at a table in Bookbinder's Restaurant. He looked very dapper in a double-breasted blue linen blazer, white flannel trousers with a pale blue pinstripe, and a bold red silk necktie from Sulka. He was in town to cover a doubleheader the next day between the Yankees and Connie Mack's Athletics. A scheduled interview with the New York manager, Miller Huggins, had been canceled at the last minute and the enterprising reporter cast about for another story to fill his column. Sir Arthur Conan Doyle fit the bill exactly.

The knight arrived fifteen minutes late, apologizing for his unfamiliarity with the city and a cab driver who seemed determined to take him on a scenic tour. "When I saw the historic steeple of your esteemed Independence Hall for the third time, I realized I was on a wild goose chase."

"You got taken for a ride, all right," Runyon smirked. "Once a cabby gets an earful of your limey accent he figures he's found himself a mark. Then, watch out, brother, let the sightseeing begin."

Without further ado, they settled in and went to work on the warm Parker House rolls. "Mr. Runyon, I understand you to be a sporting reporter." Sir Arthur plucked a fat green olive from a bowl of crushed ice studded with celery and carrot sticks like jewels in a crown. "I seem an odd subject for someone of your professional interests."

"Not a bit. Didn't you once score a century at Lord's? Not to mention bowling W. R. Grace."

"Good Lord, old man, are you a cricket fan?"

"Not exactly. Baseball's more my game. But I do know your bit with Grace was comparable to striking out Ty Cobb."

"I take that as a high compliment, although I cannot speak from any experience. Been told your national pastime is rather like our game of rounders."

"You've never been to a ballgame?" Damon Runyon watched the negative shake of the Englishman's head. "When do you plan on being back in New York?"

"Perhaps for a short bit in July. I can't say with any certainty. But definitely in the fall, before we sail home."

"Tell you what. The Giants are the world champs for the past two years. If they win the pennant again, I'll get you a seat in the press box for a Series game."

"Capital! That would be jolly nice of you."

"Don't go pinning any medals on me just yet." Runyon glanced at the menu. "Heard you were quite handy with your dukes, once upon a time."

"I beg your pardon?" Sir Arthur frowned.

"Word has it you were a top-notch amateur boxer."

"Pugilism was indeed a favorite activity as a younger man. Still like to spar a bit with a suitable partner."

"A heavyweight from the look of you. Been to any fights in this country?"

"Alas, my schedule has kept me far too busy."

"Firpo goes up against Willard next month in Jersey City. I'll be at ringside. Say the word and I'll save you a seat."

"That would be jolly kind of you. I'd very much enjoy taking in a prizefight."

The waiter asked if they were ready to order. Damon Runyon said he'd like the mixed grill, while the knight opted for crab cakes and a salad. "What I'd really love is a decent drink," Sir Arthur confided to the journalist. "A good stiff scotch and soda or, at the very least, some claret at mealtimes. It strikes me as patently absurd that your congress has legislated a man to be a criminal merely for enjoying one of life's civilizing amenities."

Damon Runyon sipped his coffee. "Got no opinions on that score. I went dry ten years before the rest of the country followed suit."

"Is your abstinence of a religious nature?"

Runyon shook his head, tapping the middle of his chest with a slim finger. "Ticker," he said, his eyes glazing with disinterest. He seemed eager to change the subject. "You ever hear the story of the time Bat Masterson washed his hair with whisky?"

"Who is Bat Masterson?"

"Friend of mine. Sportswriter for the *New York Morning Telegraph*. Before that, he was a lawman and gunfighter on the western frontier. Rode with Wyatt Earp. I grew up in Pueblo, Colorado, listening to stories of Wild Bill Hickok and the Earps and Bat Masterson. Couldn't get enough of those stories when I was a little shaver. Never dreamed one day I'd be hanging out with Bat on Broadway."

Sir Arthur's eyes twinkled. The notion of a gunslinger turned reporter appealed to his sense of the bizarre. "Did your friend find the pen to be mightier than the six-gun?"

"Bat had no literary style but he had plenty of moxie. There was nothing he was afraid to say in print. Cashed in his chips two years back. Must've been sixty-five or better. Found him slumped over his typewriter one morning at the office. His last words were written there for everyone to see: 'In this life we all get an equal share of ice. The rich get it in the summer and the poor get it in the winter.' "

"Pure prairie poetry."

"That was Bat."

The food arrived. Both men praised its excellence after a quick sampling. "Best grub in town," came Damon Runyon's succinct assessment. Between contented mouthfuls, the reporter spun the web of his interview. He had an infallible method for conducting such inquiries.

Meet the subject in a first-class restaurant. Unload a few anecdotes to set him at ease. Grease the wheels with plenty of bullshit and compliments. Offer up tickets to some sporting event, always a good ploy for creating a sense of gratitude. Finally, when the subject was lulled by fine food and, better still, strong drink; time to unload the heavy artillery. Damon Runyon narrowed his eyes behind his round, rimless glasses and drew a bead on Sir Arthur Conan Doyle as the knight started in on his second crab cake.

"About this spiritualism business . . . ?" The reporter avoided Sir Arthur's blue eyes, looking instead at a bit of grilled tomato harpooned on the tines of his fork. "Would you say it was some new form of religion?"

"It's certainly not a religion in any traditional sense." The knight spoke with quiet gravity. "Although it shares the notion of faith. Without a profound personal belief no religion could exist for long. Certainly spiritism is not incompatible with any existing religion. I know of many practicing and devout Christians who regularly attend séances."

"And do you regard your current work in this country as 'spreading the faith'?"

Sir Arthur wiped his mustache with his napkin. "I can only relate the great degree of comfort and serenity my belief has brought to me. At the risk of sounding altogether immodest, I feel it is my duty to share this profound solace with as many who will listen to my message."

This time, the newspaperman's glacial gaze met Sir Arthur's eyes directly; his voice cracked like a whip. "And how do you feel about the pain and suffering caused by your words of faith?"

"I beg your pardon."

"I'm talking about the rash of suicides that have occurred as a direct result of your recent lectures."

"Suicides? I'm not aware of any suicides."

Damon Runyon's predatory shark-slit smile softened just a touch. "They've been front page news back home. Even the august *New York Times* devoted three inches above the fold to the Maude Fancher affair. Haven't you seen any clippings?"

"My manager, Mr. Keedick, sends me the reports from the press. I don't recall reading anything about anyone by the name of Maude Fancher."

"Odds are he only sends the good news. Maude Fancher murdered her two-year-old son and then swallowed a bottle of Lysol."

"Good heavens. How utterly horrible."

"You might say that. It took her a week to die. She left a letter stating she was inspired by your lecture on spiritualism."

"Surely she must have been mad."

"Maybe so. She had plenty of company. There was the guy who killed himself and his roommate. His note said there were no gas bills in the great bye-and-bye. Another character over in Brooklyn, a potter name of Frank Alexi, he stabs his wife in the forehead with an ice pick while she is sleeping. He tells the coppers there is an evil spirit shaped like a raven sitting on her head. Said it flew over from Carnegie Hall while you are giving your talk."

Sir Arthur's face reddened with anger. "I certainly hope you don't mean to imply I am responsible for these deplorable incidents."

"I'm just a reporter. My job is to get the story. I leave the sermonizing and finger-pointing to the Bible-thumpers." Damon Runyon pushed his plate aside. He enjoyed this immensely. "Quite a story, don't you think?"

"It is a grotesque story. Clearly these people were not in their right minds. I have every sympathy for the tragedy involved, but you must understand that such actions as you have described to me represent a complete misunderstanding of what spiritualism is meant to be."

The newspaperman stuck a Sweet Caporal in the corner of his mouth. "So, you tell me, just what exactly is spiritualism meant to be?"

Sir Arthur appeared distracted. He ignored Runyon's last question while he pursued another thought. When at last he spoke, an edge of incredulity shaded his voice. "Did you say that man, the chap who murdered his wife, did I hear you say he thought he saw a raven on her forehead?"

" 'Once upon a midnight dreary . . .' " Damon Runyon thumbed a flame from his gold Dunhill, exhaling a plume of smoke through his nostrils. "You still working on that case? The Poe murders?"

"That was a misunderstanding. But surely, this raven business must be of interest to the police?"

"Even odds they gave Alexi a little taste of the third degree. But, it's no dice, far as I know. The bit with the ice pick was strictly a family matter."

The knight stared off into the drifting smoke above the reporter's head. "A raven," he muttered. "How extraordinary."

Damon Runyon tapped his cigarette ash into the saucer of his coffee cup. "So, I gather Houdini had it all wrong, touting you as your own Sherlock?"

"Mr. Houdini has a genius for hyperbole."

"He knows how to blow his own horn, that's for sure. Not very often he plays a fanfare for anyone else."

"I take it then I should be complimented by his enthusiasm?"

"Taking it at face value would be your best bet. That way you won't notice when he bad-mouths you."

"Sorry. I don't follow." Sir Arthur's puzzled expression appeared almost comical.

"All the noise in the papers last week?" Damon Runyon stubbed out his cigarette. "Guess you didn't see Houdini's comments on spiritualism."

"No, sir, I did not."

"Not surprising, since your manager keeps such a tight rein on what you get to read."

Sir Arthur sat ramrod straight, fixing the newspaperman with a look of stern outrage. "I trust you won't spare me the bad news, as you seem so keen on rubbing my nose in it."

Damon Runyon laughed, his mirthless chuckle like the lonely bark of a stray dog. "Only thing wrong with your nose," he said, "is how far out of joint you let it go. Me . . . ? I've got a nose for news. Now, when Houdini says the creator of Sherlock Holmes is going to play detective and track down a killer who imitates Poe, that's news. And when a bunch of citizens take to committing suicide after they hear Sir Arthur Conan Doyle lecture on spiritualism . . . well, that's news, too. And sometimes, the news is bad news."

The knight relaxed his stiff attitude somewhat, the grim frown easing into a neutral expression. "You'll have to forgive me. Although I'm often impatient with the inventions of the press, I'd very much appreciate hearing what Houdini had to say about me in print."

"Well, the story ran in the *Sun* sometime last week. As I recall, it concerned a séance you arranged for him in Atlantic City. Something about automatic writing and a letter your wife supposedly received from his dead mother . . ."

"Yes? Go on, please."

Damon Runyon lit another Sweet Cap. "Houdini claims the letter is a phony. Said your wife puts a cross up at the top, something his ma would never do. Said the letter is in English, a language the old lady didn't write and barely spoke. Said, to put it bluntly, that you and your wife are well-meaning dupes."

"Did he, indeed?" Sir Arthur bristled with ill-concealed indignation.

The reporter leaned forward in a confidential manner. "Always interested in hearing your side of the story."

"It hardly qualifies as news, but I will say this: the séance was held at Houdini's express request. I know the purity of my wife's mediumship and saw what the effect was upon him at the time. As for the cross at the top, my wife puts it above the first page of all she writes, as a protection against lower influences."

"What about the difference in language?"

"There really is nothing in that. Only a trance medium gets unknown tongues. Any trance or half-trance medium might get the

Hebrew through. I don't think a normal automatic writer ever would. It would always come as a rush of thought, as was the case in this instance."

"Do you think Houdini is cashing in on your celebrity?" The reporter exhaled twin plumes of smoke through his nose. "As a way of hyping his self-declared war on spiritualism, I mean?"

"I cannot speak for his motives, but such behavior must of necessity put a strain upon our friendship."

"Are you quits with Houdini then?"

Sir Arthur folded his massive hands on the tabletop in an attitude of prayer. He sighed and shook his head. "Friends must be permitted their differences," he said. "Besides, we are immutably linked by certain unfinished business."

"What business is that?"

"I am not at liberty to discuss the details at this time."

"Must be some kind of big deal."

"The very biggest, I assure you."

16

-- -- -- -- -- -- -- -- -- -- --

AND IF I DIE

Jim Vickery woke up in the pitch dark, his nostrils alive with the sour smell of vomit. A lingering chemical stench revived his nausea and he gagged back the rising bile. The caustic medicinal odor reminded him of the time a veterinarian put down his son's collie after a neighbor boy playing Geronimo in the backyard shot an arrow through its lungs. He inhaled the last sickening traces of chloroform. The smell was not something Jim Vickery could associate with a name.

He felt warm and comfortable. Soft satin-smooth cushions enfolded him in a secure, womblike embrace. None of this made him feel any less sick. His temples throbbed with migraine intensity. He wondered where he was and who had put him to bed.

Starting to sit up, Jim Vickery bumped his head into a padded barrier above. What the hell? He pressed his hands out to his sides in the darkness, feeling the abrupt dimensions of the quilted enclosure surrounding him. With a dizzying rush of horror, he realized he was shut inside the expensive bronze casket the Boss had bought for his underwater stunt.

Vickery lay very still, trying to piece together the fragmented puzzle of the recent past. He had been working in the shop with Collins and a couple of the other guys, repairing equipment in preparation for the upcoming summer tour. When everybody knocked off for the day around six o'clock, he was still having trouble with a cranky safety valve on the Chinese Water Torture Cell, the trick Houdini's crew always called the "Upside Down." He told Collins he'd work out the problem and lock up later. After a bit of teasing about him being a slave drudge, the boys left him alone in the shop.

Fifteen or twenty minutes later, he had the valve operating smoothly and figured he'd truly earned the quart of cool home-brewed beer waiting in the cellar of his semidetached house in Riverdale. Turning off the lights, he heard a strange noise coming from the store-room. It sounded like a stray cat might've gotten inside and knocked something off a shelf. He went back to investigate.

The storeroom was actually bigger than the shop floor. All the props and magical apparatus used in the show were housed there, along with equipment Houdini had purchased from other magicians. The col-lection included such treasures as "Psycho," Harry Kellar's famed automaton; Robert-Houdin's invention, "The Crystal Casket"; the origi-nal cabinet used by the Davenport Brothers; Bautier de Kolta's final cre-ation, "The Expanding Cube"; and many other classic illusions. Most of the equipment was crated and ready for transport. The baroque bronze coffin from the Biltmore Hotel swimming pool rested on a pair of sawhorses near the back wall.

Nothing seemed amiss. All the inventory stood in place, neatly stacked. Vickery took a second look around, just to double-check. On his way out, someone jumped him from behind. Someone small and very strong clung to his back like a demon, forcing a kind of mask over his face. A wad of cotton wool inside was saturated with chloroform. The nauseating medicinal fumes overwhelmed him. Vickery collapsed with-out a struggle, plummeting into vertiginous darkness.

And he returned to consciousness sealed inside a coffin. It must be a prank, some kind of joke the fellows were playing on him. Not terribly funny. He wondered which of the blokes was in on it. The new guys probably, led by Enrico whatsizname, the disgruntled Cuban who always chaffed under authority. He'd show them who was boss. "All right, you bastards!" he hollered. "Fun's over! Lemme out of here!"

Jim Vickery strained to make out some slight sound in the soul-numbing silence. "Goddamnit!" he yelled. "I'll kill you bastards! Open it up!"

The ensuing quiet presaged the tomb. This thought didn't trouble Jim Vickery. He didn't think about death yet. He thought about getting even. Kicking the ass of the sonofabitch who pulled this stupid prank. "Fuck you, shitheads! It's not funny anymore!"

The plush padding muffled his screams, blunting the sound even on the inside. He wondered why they bothered putting cushions in coffins. Surely not for the comfort of the dead. He screamed again, a wild animal cry he punctuated by furiously kicking his feet.

This last outburst had a calming effect on Jim Vickery. An ironic notion made him smile. Perhaps caskets came with cushions to silence any protest from a corpse who might change his mind. He lay very still, chilled by his bitter mirth. It took no great leap of the imagination to picture himself a corpse laid out within the sumptuous satin. What if the pranksters left him sealed for too long in the casket? What if they'd gone out to drink at some local blind pig and got so ossified they forgot all about him?

Jim Vickery struggled to remember the tests they'd made over a month ago. He recalled the coffin contained a volume of air sufficient to sustain life for more than four hours. And the Boss remained underwater at the Biltmore at least two. He felt some reassurance in this knowledge. But, he would have to remain very still. Immobility was the trick. In order to conserve every precious lungful, he must concentrate on not moving a muscle.

Lying rigid in the dark, Jim Vickery wondered how much time he had left. He had no idea how long he'd been enclosed unconscious in the casket and thus had no way to determine how much of his limited oxygen supply he might already have breathed. And his violent struggling a few moments ago, what percentage of the available air did that futile exercise consume? An icy panic gripped his abdomen. He might have less than an hour. If those bastards were out drinking, an hour could go by in no time at all.

What a stupid way to die, he thought. Not that it mattered once you were dead whether you'd fallen leading a bayonet charge across no man's land or merely choked on a gluttonous unchewed mouthful of rare prime rib. Dead was dead, a condition equal for heroes, martyrs, cowards, and fools. What mattered was dying and how you went about it.

Jim Vickery tinged his self-pity with bitterness. He didn't want to die like this, suffocating in a prop shop coffin because a prank backfired. Where was the dignity, the nobility? He imagined being condemned and making a brave speech to the crowd gathered at the foot of the scaffold. Or, a different sort of death sentence, the kind delivered by a doctor, allowing courage in the face of pain and gradual deterioration. Sealed inside this damned bronze box without a soul to witness his final heroic behavior or acknowledge his ultimate suffering seemed to Jim Vickery the supreme insult, an end rendering his entire life devoid of meaning.

"Vickery . . ." A high fluting voice whispered outside the casket. "Can you hear me . . . ?"

"Enrico? Is that you, you bastard?"

The mysterious voice hissed inches from his ear. "Tell me how the Milk Can works?"

No way it could be the Cuban. The voice was all wrong. Way too high, like a woman's. "Are you crazy?" Vickery shouted. "Let me out of here!"

"First, the Milk Can. What's the gag?"

It had to be the guys having fun with him. The milk can was advertised in the Mysto Magic catalog. Pricey at $35 a pop but no big secret.

"Tell me!"

"Okay. Save yourself a week's pay." Someone was teasing him. "The whole top half lifts off from inside. . . . Satisfied . . . ? The rivets on top are dummies."

"What about the Chinese Water Torture?"

Vickery concentrated on the strange voice. He just couldn't place it. Where had he heard that feminine accent before?

"You want to get out?" The voice had a lethal edge. "Tell me about the Water Torture."

Jim Vickery tempered his anger, confident the casket was not airtight. He had himself drilled the hole for the alarm bell and telephone line. The high, piping voice came through so clearly he knew it wasn't plugged. He felt an enormous relief. No chance of asphyxiation. Vickery laughed out loud. "The stocks holding the feet are rigged," he chuckled. "When the bolt is thrown to lock them, the mechanism actually opens."

"What else . . . ?"

"There's a safety valve down at the bottom. If something goes wrong, the Boss opens it and lets the water out. Now, how about you letting me out . . . ?"

"After you tell me what I need to know."

For the best part of the next hour, the funny-sounding voice questioned Vickery about Houdini's secrets, asking for details of the disappearing elephant illusion and the glass box escape. The Englishman answered every query patiently, bargaining for his freedom with conciliation. The give-and-take reassured him. He felt an odd rapport with his tormentor.

"Hey," Vickery called, after several moments passed without a question. "Learned all you need . . . ?"

His only answer was continued quiet. "I told you what you wanted to know," he shouted, "so get me the hell out of here!"

Silence enclosed him like a preview of eternity. His anger returned in full volcanic intensity. He raged inside the casket, roaring at the top of his lungs in a single sustained wordless protest like some wild jungle beast giving voice to an ancient wrath. Insane with fury, he beat his fists against the coffin lid and kicked his feet in stiff-legged frenzy.

The violence of his renewed outburst set the ornate coffin swaying upon the paired sawhorses, a precarious perch at best. The sudden motion upset a delicate equilibrium. Wobbly wooden legs proved insufficient for the task of supporting such weight. The sawhorses shifted and slid, causing the casket to topple. It fell to the floor on its side with a loud crash.

Jarred from the force of the impact, Vickery pushed against the stubborn lid. Well beyond reason now, shouting and kicking, cursing furiously, he tore at the padded satin lining like a savage animal, ripping through the cloth with his nails until his fingers raked against solid metal.

If anger and blind hatred had been enough to sustain him, he might well have clawed his way to freedom, for he kept at it until his fingertips were torn and bloody, stopping only when the flesh rubbed away to the bone.

17

THE MILLION THINGS SHE GAVE ME

Harry Houdini lay sobbing on his mother's bed. Curled like a fetus, he clutched her framed photograph to his breast, the wrinkled brocade bedspread beneath him darkly splotched with tear stains. If they cared to listen, the servants in the kitchen downstairs could hear the pathetic strangled groans lamenting through the spacious house on 113th Street. The staff had been instructed earlier not to receive any callers.

The magician's wife had gone out for the day with three girlhood friends from Brooklyn. These middle-aged matrons had known her since way back when she was a soubrette appearing as one of the Floral Sisters, a Coney Island song-and-dance act. Whenever they wanted to tease, her friends called her not Bessie, nor Beatrice, but Wilhelmina, the actual given name she had abandoned so long ago. They determined this to be a Wilhelmina day, a carefree time of laughter and teasing. First, a morning spent shopping, then lunch at Child's, followed by a matinee. Harry's recent grim mood, him brooding around the house for weeks with a scowl on his face, made it a pleasure for her to be out from under the prevailing gloom.

Bess remained in the dark as to the true nature of her husband's despair. Unlike all of life's other problems that he discussed so freely with her, he told her nothing about his current troubles. Only in the shadows of his mother's candlelit third-floor bedroom could Houdini find any solace. Spending time alone there was not unusual and at first he made no excuse for sneaking off to rest his head on the pillow beside Cecilia Weiss's photograph. His secret shame felt so enormous, rotting within him like a cancer. The sessions in his mother's room became more and more frequent, until he found himself pretending to work on research in his crowded study, only to close the door and tiptoe back down the hall to Mama's bedchamber.

"I've sinned. . . . I've sinned. . . . I've sinned . . . ," the magician sobbed, clasping the photo-studio portrait to his heart. "I'm a bad boy, Mama. . . . A bad, bad boy . . ." Houdini lay blubbering on the narrow bed in his private confessional, desperate to cleanse his troubled soul of guilt.

"Mr. Houdini . . . ? Excuse me, sir." Lee, the houseboy, stood shyly in the open doorway.

The magician peered up from the shadow-cloaked bed. "What is it?" he barked hoarsely. "Whaddya want now?"

"So sorry to disturb. A gentleman downstairs wishes to see you."

"Darn it all, Lee. I told you no visitors."

"Yes, sir, I know, but—"

"I don't care who it is. No means no! Not even President Harding is welcome here today."

"No president, Mr. Houdini. It is a policeman."

"What?" Houdini sat on the edge of his mother's bed. "What in Sam Hill does he want?"

"He says very important to talk to you. He is a lieutenant, sir." The young man in the white housecoat looked shyly down at the floor.

Houdini forced a grim smile onto his face. "A lieutenant, you say, Lee?" He walked unsteadily out of the darkened room. "I guess that means he's not here about some parking violation."

Lt. Frederick Bremmer stood in the downstairs front parlor engrossed in a large eighteenth-century engraving of a mountebank performing the cups and balls. "Lieutenant . . . ?" Ever the showman,

Houdini put aside his melancholy and bounded energetically into the room.

The two men shook hands. The detective, who prided himself on his strength, marveled at the power of the magician's grip. "Fred Bremmer, homicide," he announced, rasping like a cupful of gravel in a coffee grinder. "Been a fan of yours for years, Mr. Houdini, since I was a rookie. Remember the time you escaped from the Tombs back in 'ought-six. There're plenty of jailbirds wish they knew how you pulled off that trick."

"Too bad you weren't around six years later. Could've used a fan on the force then."

"Yeah? What was the problem?"

"Oh, I had an underwater packing case escape planned to publicize my opening at Hammerstein's Roof Garden. I'd done bridge jumps and jailbreaks before, but this was to be a first. The stunt was set for a pier on the East River. We were just setting up when a bunch of New York's finest roared in like the Keystone Kops and shut me down. Had to hire a tug to haul me out into the harbor where the long arm of the law don't reach."

Bremmer chuckled. "I remember that all right. You carried a pack of reporters along for the ride, so I guess you got plenty of press out of it."

"No complaints, Lieutenant. I ran for eight weeks at the Roof Garden. Packed 'em in every night."

"I'll bet you did. But, don't be thinking the law's got short arms in this town. We just reached right up into your front parlor."

"Boys in blue're always welcome here." Houdini gestured toward the best chair in the room, indicating that the lieutenant should take a seat. When Bremmer did so, the magician perched on the overstuffed arm of a nearby couch. "Say, you want something to drink? Did Lee offer you anything?"

"You mean the Chink?"

"He's from Siam." Houdini no longer smiled.

"Whatever. . . . Yeah, he offered some tea. Not exactly my favorite beverage."

"Well, we run a dry household, Officer, and that's not just a line I hand out only to the law. How about coffee or some fresh-squeezed orange juice?"

Bulldog Bremmer shook his head. He looked as out of place in the chintz-covered easy chair as a toad on a slice of lemon meringue pie. "This ain't exactly a social call, Mr. Houdini." The lieutenant felt uncomfortable with the seating arrangements. He didn't like the magician looming over him from the arm of the couch; his authority felt diminished by occupying the inferior position. "It's more in the line of a murder investigation," he said, getting to his feet.

"Murder . . . ?"

Now the subject looked up at him. Much more to the lieutenant's liking. One thing he knew backwards and forwards was how to conduct a proper interrogation. "I guess you must've heard about these so-called Poe killings?"

Houdini endeavored to keep any trace of scorn out of his voice when he said, "Mary Rogers was a member of my company."

"What can you tell me about James L. Vickery?"

"You've found him?"

"Not yet. That's why I'm here. What do you know about it?"

"Jim's my second assistant. We've been pretty busy the past couple of weeks, getting ready for our summer tour. It's two tours, actually. A short one here in the east, then ten weeks out west. This means plenty of long days for the crew, so when Emma—that's Mrs. Vickery—when she called the other day to say Jim hadn't been home that night, at first I didn't think anything of it. Figured Jim'd been working late and just camped out on a cot in the shop."

"Your men do that often? Sleep in the shop?"

"Not often. Sometimes. In this instance, I had it wrong. When my first assistant, Jim Collins, checked over at the shop yesterday morning there was no one there. The place was locked up tight. The other Jim remained behind when the crew knocked off. Last they saw of him. Collins said it looked like he'd finished his work and closed up for the night."

"How many have keys to your shop?"

"Just me and the Jims."

"Come again?"

"Collins and Vickery. Both named Jim. So, when we couldn't find him the next morning, I told Emma to call the police."

"Officially, this is still missing persons." Lieutenant Bremmer toyed with his watch fob, a bronze medallion advertising the Stutz Motor Car Company. "I wouldn't even've known about it, except for a pal of mine over there gave me a call when he made the connection with Mary Rogers. Not everyone in the department's got shit for brains."

Houdini, who never used profanity, made a slight face of displeasure. "Don't sell your own side short," he said.

"Never do. But you know how it goes. Most get by just doing their job and marking time. Going the extra distance is something special." The lieutenant deliberately cultivated a confidential manner, a technique developed over years of dealing with liars and hard cases. When he asked the tough questions they almost always came out of left field. He gave the magician a knowing wink. "So," he said, "your man Vickery? Did he fool around?"

"What?" Houdini didn't get it.

"I know he's married, a regular upstanding guy and solid citizen. Just wondering if he liked to get a little extra piece of tail on the side."

The magician felt stabbed straight to the heart and his pained expression showed it. To cover up, he assumed an earnest display of self-righteous indignation. "Just because a man is in show business, Lieutenant, it doesn't mean he's a two-timing louse."

"I was thinking about this Mary Rogers. I understand she was some kind of looker."

"All the women in my troupe are the bee's knees. It hardly makes sense to hire ugly ones."

"Vickery ever flirt with any of 'em?"

"Jim is a fun-loving guy. Likes to joke around. So, if you've heard any stories about him cracking wise to the ladies, talk is as far as it went. I'll swear to that, but you know how some people have to gossip."

"Where there's smoke, there's fire."

"Meaning what, exactly?"

"In my experience, when someone gets gossiped about he usually deserves it."

Houdini jumped to his feet. "What've you heard about Jim Vickery?"

"Relax. I ain't heard nothing. Not yet anyway. I was hoping you might fill me in. Tell me about your assistant and this Mary Rogers."

The magician's anger boiled. "There's nothing to tell. Jim was a loyal husband."

"Was . . . ?"

"Stop putting words in my mouth!" Houdini sagged onto the couch like a fighter exhausted between rounds. "A better man than Jim Vickery hasn't been born."

"What about Mary Rogers?"

"I hardly knew her. She was hired for our Palace run. Two weeks in April. What I remember most was she was sloppy about her work. Missed her cues. Always forgetting parts of her costume. I had pretty much decided not to include her in the company for the summer tours."

"You were gonna give her the sack?"

"She wasn't on the payroll after the Palace. I didn't need to can her. Just wasn't going to ask her back."

Bulldog Bremmer leaned over the dejected magician. "Because you caught her at some kind of hanky-panky?"

Houdini's voice betrayed his utter emotional weariness. "Because she wasn't any good," he droned. "I already told you that."

"Vickery ever have any special dealings with her?"

"Jim's my second assistant. A swell guy. Helps run the rehearsals, looks after the costumes and props, handles transport and travel arrangement, designs new equipment, fills in onstage when needed. The list of his duties is a mile long. Any 'dealings' he might have had with Mary Rogers were strictly business."

Lieutenant Bremmer shrugged. "Okay. I'm sold. He's aces far as I'm concerned. Everything's jake. Except one of your people's been murdered and another turns up missing, and me, I feel like I'm getting the runaround."

Houdini's fierce eyes blinked, blunted by sadness. "Lieutenant," he said, "I pray to God nothing's happened to Jim Vickery. If I knew anything more, I'd tell you. Anything at all to help."

"Fine." Bremmer pulled a calling card from a compartment in his billfold. He handed it to the magician. "Here's how to get in touch with me. In case something comes up." Houdini stared silently at the cheaply printed card. "No need to see me to the door," the lieutenant said, leaving the room. "I know the way out."

Houdini listened to the glass in the entrance rattle as the front door slammed with somewhat more force than necessary. Why hadn't he mentioned Ingrid Esp to the detective? Who was he trying to protect?

18

GHOST OF A CHANCE

Sir Arthur Conan Doyle stood on the curb of Pennsylvania Avenue watching a parade. The lure of martial band music had proved irresistible to the subject of an empire fond of public spectacle and he followed a gathering crowd across the Mall, toward what he assumed would be the sort of regimental pomp and circumstance so dear to English hearts. Instead, he found a procession more bizarre than anything encountered in a lifetime of exotic travel. In ranks straight as the trolley tracks, twenty thousand hooded members of the Knights of the Ku Klux Klan marched with military precision, their white robes flapping like acres of laundry hung out to dry.

The Capitol dome towered above legions of small-town druggists and accountants, lawyers and dentists, community leaders, churchgoers, a battalion of family men parading toward the White House dressed like spooks. In place of the torches used to set flaming crosses alight, they carried American flags, the bold stripes and bright stars fluttering past peaked, dunce-cap hoods.

How banal, Sir Arthur thought, aghast at the procession of organized bigotry. He contrasted this sorry spectacle with his memories of the perverse nobility depicted in D. W. Griffith's grand motion picture *Birth of a Nation*. These klansmen resembled nothing so much as a pack of poorly costumed ghosts in some provincial amateur theatrical. Bumpkin bully-boys whose benign comic appearance camouflaged true blackshirt Fascisti menace.

Walking away across the Mall, Conan Doyle had occasion to meditate upon Benito Mussolini's recent appearance on the spring Honor's List. The Italian dictator was now a Knight Grand Cross of the Order of the Bath. What had King George been thinking of, conferring a G.C.B. on such a brute? He remembered the KKK also called themselves knights. How sad a reflection of the chivalrous ideal.

Sir Arthur meandered past the Gothic Revival turrets of the Smithsonian Institution with no particular destination in mind. The puzzling murders in New York occupied more and more of his mental attention. He regretted slighting the demands of his mission but felt it couldn't be helped. Not when the safety of his family remained at risk. Every afternoon recently, instead of napping as Jean recommended, he took long solitary walks, smoking pipe after pipe as he cogitated on the baffling conundrum.

Twenty minutes of aimless wandering led him to a grove of trees planted along the bank of the Tidal Basin. Philadelphia had been an excellent walking city and Washington promised to go it one better. Due back at the Madison Hotel at four to discuss the logistics of tonight's lecture in the ballroom, he savored his solitude and introspection.

Although the morning had bloomed bright and sunny, by noontime storm clouds had gathered and the sky darkened with the threat of rain. A brisk wind corrugated the slate gray surface of the Basin, erasing reflections of the government buildings on the opposite shore. The dim penumbral light gave an unearthly feeling of twilight to the elm grove. Sir Arthur strolled between the trees, puffing on his briar pipe, troubled about what he had read of the Esp murders. Did the killer dress as a gorilla because his madness required the masquerade, or was this a deliberate stunt, some piece of macabre theater? The evidence suggested the former, yet a nagging doubt persisted.

As he pondered, the knight failed to notice a shadowy figure leaning against the pale gray bark of a slender elm. Sudden, extravagant flailing caught Conan Doyle's attention. Arms windmilling, the stranger lurched into an open space and seemed to vanish in the dull metallic sheen reflecting off the wind-riffled water. Sir Arthur gasped. The figure reappeared, racked by spastic shudders and staggering blindly through a narrow rectangle of shadow. Poe's ghost shimmered like gossamer.

"I say . . ." The knight took a tentative step forward. "Poe . . . ?"

The specter glanced up at him, face pale as moonlit ivory. Dark hollows encircled the pain-blunted eyes. "Go away," he said, the haunted voice a distant echo resonating from the depths of a bottomless well. "Leave me alone."

"Do you remember me?" asked Sir Arthur.

"All too well." Poe's ghost groaned, wrapping its misty arms around a tree trunk. He stared up at the knight after a seizure of violent retching. "God. . . . What breed of monster are you, to take such pleasure in my shame?"

Conan Doyle stood dumbfounded. Although he neither saw nor smelled any illness, the apparition clearly vomited before him, contradicting everything he believed about the beyond. Ghostly nausea violated the basic tenets of his faith. The afterlife as he conceived it was not a place of illness or passion or regret. Earthbound woes remained behind forever. Or so he wished with all his heart.

On closer inspection, the knight took note of Poe's disheveled appearance. Cravat undone and waistcoat unbuttoned, the specter lurched about in torn shirtsleeves, having somehow lost his jacket. "You still here?" he bellowed, swaying unsteadily. "Have you nothing better to do?"

The distant, hollow voice sounded slurred and Sir Arthur recognized with chilling certainty that Poe was in an advanced state of inebriation. How could a spirit be drunk? His very soul rebelled at the thought. "Are you not well?" he asked softly.

"I am . . . indeed, indisposed . . ." Poe's ghost sagged, slumping onto a cast-iron bench overlooking the Tidal Basin. "This pestilential city. . . . Capital of despair."

"Why are you here?" Conan Doyle's brain reeled with confusion.

"What business is it of yours, Sir?"

"I . . . I am a friend."

The specter laughed, a sound as dreadful and shrill as the scream of a dying animal. "There are no friends . . . only sycophants and damned leeches. Why, I was to see Rob Tyler today, the president's son himself." Poe stared at Conan Doyle with malevolence, silently challenging him to dispute his boast.

"That certainly . . . is a great honor," Sir Arthur stammered, unsure of what to say.

"It is utter humbug!" The ghost staggered to his feet. Unsettling to see so ethereal a creature move with such total lack of grace. "The man was not at home to me, Sir. . . . He, who had pledged to secure me an appointment . . . at the Philadelphia Custom House. . . . He . . . refused to see me . . ." Poe wandered off, strangling a sob.

The knight started after him. "Don't you remember me from Philadelphia?"

"I don't want to remember." The ghost's doleful eyes brimmed with despair. "I want to forget. I crave oblivion!"

The spectral melancholy proved contagious. Sir Arthur felt the first pangs of ineffable sadness enter his spirit like an infection. "Is there not sufficient oblivion after dying?" he asked, his voice weary and dull.

"Presumably. . . . I'll let you know when I'm dead."

"Damn it, man. You are dead!"

The ghost laughed, shrill as breaking glass. "How true. . . . How pathetic and true. I can picture my epitaph, carved on a cold marble slab: 'Here lies Eddie Poe, / Wearing yet a new disguise. / He lived a life so full of woe, / Thus welcomed death as no surprise . . .' "

Mind near blank with morbid despair, Sir Arthur silently watched the phantom drift off between the trees, dissolving like fog in a sudden shaft of sunlight piercing the ragged storm clouds.

The Friars Club in Manhattan, founded in 1904 by a group of Broadway press agents who wanted a place to conduct business while letting off a little steam, became a favored watering hole of actors and journalists looking to grab some midnight supper or find a friendly gin rummy game. Harry Houdini was not a member, but frequently dined late at the Monastery with friends who were longtime Friars. Tonight, he planned to join his lawyer and the songwriter Billy Rose, whose most recent Tin Pan Alley hit was a catchy little ditty about Barney Google, the comic-strip con man.

Houdini entered the Tudor-Gothic building at 110 West Forty-eighth Street whistling the Billy Rose tune more than slightly off-key. He was notoriously tone deaf. Heading for the grill room, he spotted Sidney Rammage waving a newspaper at him from across the wood-paneled lobby. "Harry! What an unexpected coincidence." The slight, bald-headed man hurried to his side. "Just reading about you."

Houdini beamed. "Never hurts to get your name in the paper."

"Depends what they say, I suppose."

"As long as it sells tickets, they can say anything they like."

"Righty-o . . ." Rammage indicated his seriousness of purpose with a deliberate frown. "I gather then you haven't seen this morning's *American?*"

"I'm taking my show on the road end of next week. Think I've got time to sit around all morning reading the papers?" Houdini said this with a certain malicious pleasure, knowing full well his underwater stunt at the Biltmore had closed down Rammage's buried alive act.

"Just thought you might be interested because of your friendship with Conan Doyle." The little Englishman's smile revealed more than a trace of smugness.

Houdini took the bait. "Sir Arthur had something nice to say about me?"

Rammage shrugged. "It's about your mother, really. Some séance he claims put you in touch with her spirit. Says you deny the truth only to further your own vendetta against mediums."

"Gimme that!" The magician grabbed the newspaper out of his rival's hands. His brow wrinkled in furious concentration as he devoured the brief article. "That bastard," he muttered. "Dirty limey rat!"

"I take it you're not pleased?" Rammage suppressed a grin.

"Damn him. I'm gonna tell my side of this."

"Thought you already did?"

Houdini ignored the jibe. "He wants to tell the truth? I'll give him the truth!"

"Well, you won't have to wait long for that."

"What're you talking about?"

Sidney Rammage positively gloated. "Damon Runyon's sitting in the bar right now, even as we speak. It's his byline."

The magician's intense eyes gleamed. "Runyon, eh? Never met him. What's he look like?"

"A little man." Rammage caught Houdini's raised eyebrow. "Well, he's taller than I," he conceded. "Wears cheaters. Round lenses. Nicely dressed; gray sharkskin suit. Say, you know Bill Fields?"

"The juggler? Of course. Worked the three-a-day with him years ago."

"Righty-o. Then you'll spot Runyon straight away. He's sitting with Fields and another guy with a uke who I—"

Houdini made a beeline for the bar before Rammage could finish what he had to say. He stood in the doorway a moment, looking over the crowd, and found his party right away. W. C. Fields he knew by sight, and there sat the little man strumming a ukulele. Houdini made out the lively strains of "I Want What I Want When I Want It." The third man with the eyeglasses and narrow smile must be Runyon.

When Houdini approached their table, he overheard Fields improvising bawdy lyrics to the old Victor Herbert tune. The comedian had come directly from the Apollo Theater on Forty-second Street, straight from a dress rehearsal for "Poppy." Traces of his stage makeup showed on his neck and forehead.

"Hello, Bill," the magician said. "Still three-sheeting, I see."

Fields interrupted the song and touched his neck, smudging a dab of pancake onto his fingertip for investigation. "Harry, Harry, Harry," he rasped in his Eustace McGargle voice. "Never hurts to advertise. . . . Been getting out of any tight spots lately?"

"Every chance I get." Houdini looked at the man sitting opposite

Fields. Unlike the other two, he drank coffee. "Say, aren't you Damon Runyon?"

The fixed, mirthless expression remained unchanged. "Last time I looked I was."

"Boys, boys . . . excuse my execrable manners." W. C. Fields waved his arm like a snake-oil salesman. "Allow me to introduce the illustrious escapologist, Mr. Harry Houdini. Runyon you've correctly identified. Our croaking troubadour here is another scribbler, Mr. Hype Igoe, sportswriter for the *World*."

"I also break in Runyon's shoes." Hype Igoe displayed a dainty foot, shod in an expensive bench-made calfskin wing tip.

"It's hard to find another guy who wears a size 5 1/2 B," Damon Runyon smirked. "When I do, I make him a friend for life."

"Best part of the deal is I get to wear a new pair of custom clod-hoppers every couple months and it never costs me a red hot cent." The sportswriter accompanied his remarks with ascending ukulele chords.

W. C. Fields patted the seat of an empty chair. "Don't be such a stick-in-the-mud, Harry. Join us for a libation. Needn't be ashamed of your abstinence, Runyon's a teetotaler, too."

"Hate to spoil the party, fellas. I'm meeting some friends in the grill." Houdini leaned against the back of the chair. "Just wanted the opportunity to give Mr. Runyon my side of the séance story now that Conan Doyle's put in his two-cents'-worth."

Damon Runyon's smile widened to show his teeth but still revealed no trace of mirth. He slid his snakeskin notebook from his inside jacket pocket as easily as a killer might draw his weapon. "Shoot," he said. "I'm all ears."

"Okay. Here's the skinny." Houdini's voice softened to a conspiratorial hush. "We're down in Atlantic City about a month ago. My wife, Bessie, and me. Visiting Sir Arthur and Lady Jean. He sets up a séance for us one afternoon, an automatic writing session. There was no hocus-pocus or the usual spook show flim-flam. Lady Jean closed her eyes and just started writing. She maybe trembled a little bit but that was all. No external evidence of any possession."

"What about this writing? Supposed to have been a letter from your dead mother."

"That's all applesauce! First of all, it was Mama's birthday. I made no mention of it to anyone at the time, and naturally there was not one word about it in the so-called letter. If the deal was legit, don't you think Mama would have said something?

"Stands to reason." The reporter never paused in his note-taking.

"You bet it does. And another thing, the letter was in English, a language Mama couldn't write and barely spoke. Then Conan Doyle goes and makes some crack about Hebrew. That's all horsefeathers, too. Kind of remark only a Jew-baiter would make. Mama was Hungarian, but we spoke German at home. Only that, never Hebrew or Yiddish."

"You think Conan Doyle was pulling a con?"

"Say, you wanna sell patent medicine, you better put on a good show. He's here promoting spiritualism, ain't he? What better sales pitch could he want than to get an endorsement from me? Ain't I known as the greatest debunker of fake mediums the world has ever known?" In his excitement, Houdini lapsed back into the gutter slang of his youth.

Damon Runyon pointed a fountain pen at the magician. "Have you never encountered a medium you believed was honest?"

"Never."

"Not once?"

"Nope."

"Let me put it another way. In all your long career—what is it now, twenty, thirty years?"

"Close to thirty."

"Okay. In all that time, didn't you ever meet up with some sort of supernatural phenomena that you couldn't explain? Some wizard or shaman with genuine power?"

An almost imperceptible sweat beaded the magician's brow. "No such thing," he said. "You can go all the way back to Merlin. Nothing but tricks and mumbo-jumbo." He snapped his fingers and a half-dollar appeared between them. "Hey, presto. Just like that."

"Do it again, Harry, and buy me a drink," W. C. Fields quipped.

"You see, Mr. Runyon, all it takes is a little sleight-of-hand and the true believers start forming in line." Houdini spoke with a glib smile. More than anything, he wanted to believe in the truth of his own uneasy convictions.

19

FINDERS KEEPERS

A heat wave gripped the East Coast. In Washington, D.C., President Harding's staff announced the chief executive's departure for cooler climes. The presidential tour of the territory of Alaska began after a four-day Shriners' Convention when twenty thousand fez-wearing delegates visited the White House, the largest number of guests ever to call in a single day in all the Republic's history. The president shook over ten thousand hands, hoping to make an undeclared statement by receiving the Shriners so soon after refusing to meet with members of the Ku Klux Klan.

In a sweltering Federal courthouse in New York, the government rested its mail fraud case against Marcus Garvey, Provisional President of Africa, Commander of the Order of the Nile, and Distinguished Son of Ethiopia. Garvey, his black nationalist movement already in ruins, planned to argue in his own defense following a weekend recess.

These events dominated the headlines. Making final preparations for the summer's short tour through New York, New Jersey, and Pennsylvania, Houdini had no time for newspapers. Last spring, box office receipts had gone down considerably from the previous year and now the magician gave more and more thought to his plans for a full-evening show. He saw nothing from the press but the clippings Ernst sent at the end of each week. He read Damon Runyon's version of his remarks at the Friars Club on a tear-sheet. Seen through the eyes of the cynical Coloradan, he came across as harsh and cruel.

Runyon's column also brought Sir Arthur's reply. It came tucked in a manila envelope among a batch of clippings from small-town papers along the route of the upcoming tour:

> "I hate sparring with a friend in public, but what can I do when he says things which are not correct, and which I have to contradict or else they go by default. Our relations are certainly curious and are likely to become more so, for so long as he attacks what I know from experience to be true, I have no alternative but to attack him in return. How long a private friendship can survive such an ordeal I do not know, but at least I did not create the situation."

Houdini wrote a brief note of apology to Sir Arthur and received no reply. Caught up in the final preparations for the tour, a task greatly complicated by Jim Vickery's continued disappearance, he gave no further thought to it. Collins traveled in advance to Trenton, setting up a challenge, the first such promotion in almost ten years.

Houdini undertook a task normally Jim Vickery's, the final equipment inventory. Not trusting anyone else to do the job, the magician spent his last free Sunday wandering the shelved aisles of his storeroom, clipboard in hand. In the summer heat, the atmosphere inside the windowless chamber was stifling. The drone of unseen flies provided an unwelcome annoyance. A putrid, sickly-sweet odor hung in the air. Something had died. A rat caught between the wall studs, Houdini reasoned. That explained the smell.

Houdini's master list cataloged every illusion, enumerating the backup hardware each required. The magician checked off the main gags, including such related items as "20 loose pin hinges," "2 dozen cleats," and "5 extra angle irons."

The telephone rang in the shop. Houdini made a beeline for the rolltop desk. He dropped into a swivel-chair, grabbing the phone attached to an X-Tendo wall-mount.

"Hello," he said.

"Hello, Morningside seven seven nine four?" chirped central.

"Speaking."

"Go ahead, Regency." The operator made the connection.

"My lord, Osiris . . ." The silken voice purred in the receiver.

Houdini's throat clenched. "How did you get this number?"

"Why haven't you called? Why haven't I seen you?"

What could he say to her? That he felt ashamed and afraid? "It's impossible," he said.

"Nothing is impossible for the courageous."

Anger surged through the magician. "What're you talking about? Courage has nothing to do with any of this. I love my wife. Respect her feelings. I don't want to see her get hurt."

"And what about me? What about my feelings?" Her voice sounded without emotion.

"You're a big girl. You knew what you were getting into." His words cut like an Arctic wind.

"You, I think, have gotten into something you know nothing about."

"What's that supposed to mean? Some kind of threat?"

"Take it to mean anything you like. And remember this: I am not some cheap showgirl you can dally with and then discard."

Houdini resisted an impulse to hang up. "Look," he said, "what happened was a mistake. One I deeply regret. I'm sorry if I've caused you any unhappiness. You must realize that what occurred between us was an accident. This can't be allowed to go any further."

A long silence followed. He heard the chill hiss of her breathing. When she spoke again, her words came slowly, deliberately. "For once in your life, you are involved in something over which you have no control. Larger forces are at work, sweeping us along with them. To resist is to invite destruction. I have looked into your coffin. I see you lying there. Who will throw the first handful of earth into your grave?" She hung up abruptly.

Houdini stared at the telephone with distaste, as if he held some loathsome creature. He replaced the receiver. The X-Tendo contracted, scissoring back against the wall, the movement reminding him of a coiling snake. An involuntary shudder prickled up his spine.

Houdini cursed the day he first laid eyes on Isis. No serpent seemed more lethal. He sensed her venom spreading through his entire life. Hadn't she threatened him twice with odd remarks about his coffin?

The magician headed back into the storeroom, anxious to finish the inventory and get on with more pressing demands. Tolerable before, the smell of rot now struck him as foul and cloying. Some impulse, perhaps occasioned by his conversation with Isis, impelled him to walk behind the storage shelves for a look at the expensive bronze coffin. Above his head, flies buzzed in the shadows like angry demons.

Houdini saw straight away the casket had fallen from its sawhorse supports. It lay on its side in the dim light. The magician approached to investigate. What were the men thinking of? How dare they treat his equipment in so cavalier a fashion? His rage simmered, calling to mind last week's police search. Undoubtedly, this piece of clumsiness was their work. He'd have a word with Lieutenant Bremmer.

The casket weighed too much for one man to handle alone. Houdini did not attempt to lift it. He knew the limits of his considerable strength. The overwhelming smell of decay surrounded the magician like a poison cloud. A thrill of dread apprehension trembled through his fingers as he unfastened the clasps securing the coffin.

The lid fell open. Houdini recoiled from a noxious blast of putrescence strong enough to turn his stomach. Jim Vickery's blackened hands curled into rigid claws. Arrested in a final scream, the teeth in his open mouth looked impossibly white against the bloated, purple lips. Flies had already been at their obscene work and masses of squirming maggots writhed in the hollow eye sockets. The whole of the rigid body hummed with the macabre music of their intense corruption.

Houdini screamed. His terror echoed around him in the windowless room.

20

GIFTS

Lt. Fred Bremmer surveyed the crowd gathered in the lobby of the Essex Market Court. He leaned against a balustrade checking out the hard cases mingling with the merely curious below. He'd seen a majority of their mugs in lineups over the years. The young torpedoes in their flashy suits worried him most. Never trust a hot-head, especially one who went heeled.

Bremmer had been assigned to the courthouse at the last minute, part of a special police detachment numbering nearly one hundred men. Fifty uniformed patrolmen stood positioned at strategic points on the stairs and out on the street. Almost as many plainclothes detectives roamed the halls. All this force just to cover the ass of a mobster named Nathan Kaplan, alias Kid Dropper, who until today everyone in the department thought was headed up the river.

A raid two weeks ago on a bookie joint in the Putnam Building on Times Square, across Forty-fourth Street from the staid Astor Hotel, yielded Kid Dropper, "King of the East Side racketeers," among a dozen others. In the end, the only charge to hold him on was carrying a concealed weapon and this morning he beat even that rap; case dismissed due to lack of evidence.

The biggest problem for the police involved keeping Kid Dropper alive until they released him from custody. A long-standing feud raged between the Dropper's gang and a rival outfit headed by Jacob "Little

Augie" Orgen, who wore on his cheek a curving five-inch scar—Kid
Dropper's trademark, he being a handy guy with a can opener. Jack
"Legs" Diamond, former strong-arm man for gambler Arnold Rothstein,
worked as Orgen's bodyguard and sometime partner in the labor rack-
ets. When Legs and several members of Little Augie's gang were spotted
loitering about the courthouse before Dropper's trial, the commissioner
decided to take no chances and ordered in a big detachment of police.

Capt. Peter Tighe commanded the entire operation. A veteran of
the Bowery gang wars of the 1890s, when the Daybreak Boys from Five
Points and the Pug Uglies and the Dead Rabbits shot it out at night under
the Second Avenue El tracks, Tighe knew firsthand the homicidal incli-
nations of the underworld.

The gangs weren't gone. The Gophers still ran the West Side
docks. Owney Madden, pint-sized limey killer, walked out of Sing Sing a
couple months back with the state's complimentary double-sawbuck in
his pocket. A week later, he strutted around town in hundred-dollar
suits, flashing a bankroll provided by shady Larry Fay, the man who gave
Texas Guinan her stake at the El Fey Club. Just another Gopher eight
years ago, banty-rooster Madden had gone to the big house for bumping
off Little Patsy Doyle of the rival Hudson Dusters and had emerged a
Prohibition entrepreneur. Tighe now wore gold captain's bars. Under
the fancy veneer, neither had changed.

Captain of detectives Cornelius Willemse, another old-timer, had
personal charge of Kid Dropper. Lieutenant Bremmer was assigned as
his backup. A taxicab had been ordered for the strutting gangster, and
two uniforms brought word of its arrival. Captain Tighe made a withering remark about apple-polishers on the beat. Kid Dropper got a big
laugh out of that one. Tighe ignored him and okayed the start of the procession from the courthouse.

Wearing a blue serge suit and straw skimmer, Captain Willemse
led the way down the wide staircase. Kid Dropper followed, his wife,
Irene Kaplan, clinging to his arm. Cocky George Katz, a criminal associate also recently acquitted on the gun charge, strode along on the Kid's
left, a triumphant sneer mocking the assembled forces of law and order.
Bulldog Bremmer brought up the rear.

All along the way, Kid Dropper nodded and smiled like a visiting head of state. The small party passed through the parted crowd in the lobby, between twin ranks of uniformed policemen. Out on Essex Street, a Yellow cab waited at the curb. Several curious onlookers stood about rubbernecking. The gangsters gripped their hands above their heads in the victorious gesture of triumphant prizefighters. A couple of bystanders even applauded.

Captain Willemse held open the cab's rear door, beckoning the mobsters inside. "In you go, boys," he said. "Only sorry we didn't hang the rap on yez."

Katz climbed in, sliding across the backseat. Kid Dropper grinned at the policeman. "Ain't none a you bulls gonna make me take a fall." He followed his compatriot into the cab. The captain made no reply, slipping in next to his charges. Bremmer glanced up and down the street, eyes flicking like an eager watchdog. He took Mrs. Kaplan's arm to guide her inside.

Distracted by the rudiments of gallantry, the lieutenant missed seeing a pasty-faced runt in a drab six-dollar suit dart out of the crowd and run to the back of the cab. Before anyone could shout a warning, the little guy was up on the running board, a snub-nosed revolver in his hand. He fired three shots in quick succession through the open rear window.

Whatever, if anything, the shooter called out was lost in a general outcry from the surrounding crowd. Wild-eyed, Irene Kaplan screamed and threw herself at the diminutive gunman, seizing him by the lapels in a maniacal frenzy. She shrieked and shrieked, waltzing the tiny killer around in circles.

Bremmer pulled his roscoe from under his armpit, holding the .38 Smith & Wesson out of sight along his side, not wanting to alarm the gunman when the woman stood in his line of fire.

Wailing like the noonday whistle, Mrs. Kaplan suddenly let go of the baby-faced torpedo. He dodged around her, dropping his cannon in a sprint across the street.

Captain Willemse had his head out the cab window, shouting at Bremmer, "You get the man, I'll grab the heater!"

The lieutenant took off after the suspect like the "Flying Finn." The little guy ran with the street smarts of someone who'd grown up snitching fruit from pushcarts and had lots of practice ducking away through crowds. This time, more was at stake than stolen apples. Most onlookers, intimidated by the feral savagery gleaming in his wild wide eyes, stepped aside as he wove between them.

"Stop that man!" Bremmer shouted. As if on command, a white-haired grandmother in a long dress fashionable before the war stuck out her umbrella, tripping the fugitive.

Sprawled like a drunk on the sidewalk, the gunman offered no resistance when Bremmer pounced to make the collar. Anyone caught in his iron grip understood immediately why the lieutenant was known as "Bulldog." Hauling the punk to his feet, Bremmer gave him a little taste of the .38. Nothing serious, just a tap on the head to get his attention.

"What's your name, big shot?" Bremmer barked, dragging the punk back toward the waiting cab.

"Cohen," he snarled, sounding tough. "Louis Cohen. Make sure you spell it right for the papers." He was no more than a kid, peach fuzz sprouting on pale cheeks that had never known a razor.

"We'll spell it right when we book you, asshole!"

The skipper waited beside the cab, murder weapon dangling from a beefy forefinger. George Katz had his arms around a weeping Mrs. Kaplan. A couple of uniforms stared in at what lay on the backseat. "Dropper's sneezed," the captain grunted as Bremmer stood the teenage killer before him. "You did us a favor, kid. I couldn't ask for a better gift if it was Christmastime."

"Chloroform . . . ?" Damon Runyon asked.

"Chloroform," Sergeant Heegan repeated.

They sat in a back booth at Lindy's. Runyon picked at the gefilte fish special with horseradish and boiled potatoes "How'd they know?"

"Medical cotton was found in the coffin with Vickery." The sergeant helped himself to a piece of gefilte fish from off the reporter's plate. "The lab boys picked up traces of chloroform in it."

"What about the others?"

"Mary Rogers was too far gone. A week in the harbor is hell on a corpse. We got lucky with Violette Speers and the Esps. They'd all been embalmed."

"Exhumed?"

"All three. Chloroform in every one of 'em."

"How can they tell that?"

Heegan pinched a slice of potato. "Hell's bells, man, I'm not the coroner. It has something to do with pink fingernail beds is all I know."

"Not much of a lead." Damon Runyon sipped his coffee. A born Westerner, he drank it with all his meals.

"Better'n nothing. Gives the boys something to do, checking all them pharmacies and medical supply houses."

"What for?"

"Anyone recently buying chloroform not known to be a sawbones of some kind."

"Long shot."

"Routine. No shortage of shoe leather on the force."

Damon Runyon scraped the last of the gefilte fish onto his fork. "What can you tell me about the Kid Dropper rubout?"

"Open and shut."

"Give it to me. All the knockdown."

Heegan grinned like a man in the know. "The chopper's just a kid," he said. "Only seventeen. Gave his name as Louis Cohen, but his real moniker's Louis Kushner. Still lives at home with Ma. One-sixty-four East Seventh Street. Three miserable little rooms, and there's three more brothers and a sister packed in there like sardines."

"He one of Little Augie's boys?" Runyon never looked up from his notebook.

"Nothing but a runner. Down on the books as the driver of a laundry truck. Claims he was tipped off the Dropper fingered him for the songbird what put him on the mark."

"You buy that?"

Heegan laughed. "Wanna buy the Brooklyn Bridge? There's a witness puts Cohen at the courthouse in the company of Little Augie and Legs Diamond two days before the trial."

"Thanks, Heegan." Runyon gave him a thin chill smile. "Open and shut . . ."

"The kid's game. He won't peach on his pals. No matter Little Augie left him hung out to dry. Didn't even send a mouthpiece to the kid's arraignment. Should've seen the look on the punk's face when it dawned on him he was on his own. God loves an idiot, I suppose. You'll never guess who the court appointed to defend him. Your old pal, the state senator."

"The Honorable James J. Walker."

"The very same."

"Ah, Jimmy. . . . He'll get him off."

"No way. This one's gonna fry."

Dressing rooms, boarding houses, and cheap hotels shared a common melancholy, decades of transience leaving an impalpable residue of loneliness and despair. Houdini learned from years on the road how a few personal touches kept the sad eaters of soul-carrion at bay. Snapshots of Bess and Mama were tucked around the mirror frame like votive offerings. A small square Persian carpet from home made a glad pattern at his feet. Bright bouquets stood at either end of the makeup table, a reminder of his wife, who always ordered fresh flowers wherever they were showing.

Bess had gone out for an hour's shopping, what they used to call "a stroll between turns." The familiar rattle of eggs boiling atop the old hot plate they'd traveled with since their carnival days dispelled the pangs of solitude. Had he been able to set his mind at rest, the brooding magician would have ordinarily devoted free moments to reading. Always sensitive to his standing in show business, Houdini chafed at being spotted fifth in a nine-act bill. Getting the star's dressing room didn't compensate for seeing the name of an Irish tenor above his own on the program.

A year ago, when he last appeared in Hoboken to promote the

opening of his film *The Man from Beyond,* six motorcycle policemen met his car at the ferry and gave him an escort to the Roosevelt Theater, sirens blaring. The mayor himself introduced the magician to a sellout house. From that to fifth billing in a year's time. No crystal ball revealed the future with greater clarity.

Since the war, vaudeville had clearly changed. The trend today veered toward the sentimental; songs and comedy, that's what they wanted. Many vaude houses alternated Hollywood films with the live entertainment. The new magic of the movies, a camera its enchanted wand, one crank making impossible wonders commonplace. His was a more demanding art, born of ancient traditions. How long before the flickering light from the silver screen eclipsed them all?

Houdini knew mounting a full-evening show remained his only possible salvation. He'd lost a bundle in the movie business. His Hoboken Film Development Corporation was up for sale. The big show remained the only answer.

The magician gave it a lot of thought, deciding to divide the production into three acts, the first to feature standard magic. Maybe some of the great classic illusions he'd bought in Europe. Finish with the Needle trick. Act two would be escapes. A strait jacket; perhaps an idea he had about being quick-frozen into a block of ice. The Upside Down remained his most popular attraction; a guaranteed lollapaloosa end for act two.

The third act occupied the greatest portion of his thoughts; something altogether new. Over the past year and a half he'd delivered many public lectures denouncing fraudulent mediums. Houdini planned to spice up these sermons with showbiz razzle-dazzle, surefire bits like revealing the secret behind the rope-tie escapes of the Davenport Brothers and other tricks used at fake séances to delude a gullible public. It would be a wow finish. A flag-waving finish. Leave 'em wanting more.

A knock at the door brought the curtain down on his jubilant musing. "Yes?" Houdini snapped.

The house manager stuck in his head. "Something arrived for you, Mr. Houdini. Special messenger." He reached in an arm, extending a flat twine-bound package wrapped in brown paper. The magician took it with a distracted nod of thanks.

Lingering behind the half-open door, the house manager cleared his throat with obvious embarrassment. "I . . . er, tipped him two bits."

Houdini flipped back a quarter. "Thanks, Lloyd," he said. "Half a buck next time."

"Right . . ." Lloyd withdrew with a wink, closing the door noiselessly.

The magician slit the string with his penknife. The package was addressed simply: Houdini, Roosevelt Theater, West Hoboken, N.J. No return address. He unwrapped the brown paper on his lap.

Inside lay a fat book, bound in red morocco with gilt-edged pages. A white card of the finest stock rested on the cover, embossed with the ankh of ancient Egypt and with a name; Opal Crosby Fletcher. Houdini turned it over. In ink, she had written:

Osiris—
For your edification . . .
                    Isis

The magician looked at the book. Gold-tooled lettering spelled out the title along the spine: THE COLLECTED WORKS OF EDGAR A. POE.

21

THE PLEASURE OF YOUR COMPANY

Damon Runyon spotted Sir Arthur Conan Doyle on his way into the men's bar set up in the billiard room of the Fifth Avenue home of Mr. and Mrs. Vincent Astor. The women's bar was located in the library. The reporter leaned against a pillar along the colonnade surrounding the main ballroom. There by invitation with hundreds of others for a charity entertainment, an "All-Star Cabaret" to benefit the Lenox Hill Neighborhood Foundation, Runyon preferred his entertainment in nightclubs or at ringside. Still, it promised to be a good show. Headliners from Broadway and vaudeville had donated their talents.

Damon Runyon followed the knight into the impromptu bar. A haze of cigar smoke drifted between the crystal chandeliers. Billiard balls clicked. Peals of laughter outside drowned out Ed Wynn's distant punch-line. Scores of gentlemen in tuxedos and evening dress stood about, stiff and formal as the stuffed penguin diorama at the natural history museum across the park. Damon Runyon asked the bartender to pour him a cup of black coffee and surveyed the crowd. Having just accepted an invitation to join in a game, Sir Arthur leaned against the middle of three billiard tables, a brandy snifter warming on his palm.

The reporter observed Conan Doyle and his partner select cue sticks, following the intricacy of their play as they stalked about the table, lining up shots. Sir Arthur made a brilliant three-figure break. His opponent applauded. Players from the other tables offered congratulations. Damon Runyon left his cup on the bar and approached through the crowd.

"Nice shot," he quipped out of the side of his mouth, shaking the knight's hand. "Runyon of the *American*."

"I remember you, Mr. Runyon." Sir Arthur chalked his cue. "Our pleasant luncheon in Philadelphia."

"Firpo knocked out Willard in the eighth. I have it from Tex Rickard that a title bout is set for September. If you're in town, I'll save you a seat. Watch old Iron Mike work his magic."

"Iron Mike . . . ?"

"It's what the Manassa Mauler, that's Dempsey, the heavyweight champ—"

"I know the name of the world champion!" Sir Arthur's brusque manner betrayed his short temper. "England is not some isolate outpost removed from all civilization."

"Civilization you've got in spades . . ." Runyon faked a quick laugh. "Anyway, Iron Mike is what Dempsey calls his right hand. Offer's still good for the ducat."

"Well, sir, I greatly appreciate your generosity. I will be in New York in September. A championship prizefight sounds capital."

"Be World Series time, too. Maybe you'll take in a game?"

"By Jove, that would be splendid!"

"I can't guarantee splendid, but I'll give you two-to-one it's the Giants at the Polo Grounds." Damon Runyon tapped a cigarette on his thumbnail. "They just took a doubleheader from the Cards." He stuck the Sweet Caporal between his thin lips and tipped it into the flame from his lighter. "Having any luck with the Poe caper?"

Sir Arthur chuckled. "An abstract problem, at best."

"Not so abstract for Houdini's assistant," Runyon said, filtering his words through a long, slow exhale. "The magician nominated you for the Sherlock role, maybe the chickens are coming home to roost."

"I take that colloquialism to mean you consider Mr. Houdini or myself to be in jeopardy?"

"You made all the papers. Even mad killers read the news."

Harry Houdini hurried up the broad marble steps to Mrs. Vincent Astor's mansion. The orchestra's jumpy syncopations resonated with the strains of "I'm Just Wild About Harry" from the ballroom within. He was scheduled to go on in a half an hour and looked forward to his turn, planning some sleight-of-hand, a disappearing watch trick and, of course, finishing with the Needles. Entering, the magician surprised a couple necking behind a bone-white statue of Poseidon. They ignored his startled gasp.

The encounter triggered a prudish embarrassment common to his generation. An angry pink flush colored Houdini's cheeks and neck. He fumed, finding no one at the cloakroom to help him. It was a hot summer night and he came without a topcoat, but wanted to check his black homburg. A millionaire family can't afford proper help? He pushed inside the narrow room, sighing in exasperation.

Rows of rented wooden coatracks bulged with sable, fox, and marten. Houdini edged between the ranks of fur, looking for a place to hang his hat. Not one man had checked his coat here. This discovery brought on a smile. Had Bess come along, she'd doubtless be wearing her silver fox.

"Looking for someone . . . ?"

The familiar silken voice made him jump. Isis! He took a step backwards into a soft cloud of sable. "M-Mrs. Fletcher," he stammered.

"Such needless formality, my dear Osiris. We know one another far too well for such sham."

"It is you who pretend. I told you continuing this thing is an impossibility." A furry tickle caressed the back of his neck.

Isis stepped close to him, pressing her delicate hand to his starched shirtfront. "We are bound together by impossible forces," she whispered. "Timeless forces . . ." Her face mere inches from his, the dusky smell of jasmine wafted from her bare shoulders.

"Why did you send me that book?" Houdini demanded.

She smiled. "To further your education . . ." Her hand slipped across his onyx studs, lingering on his cheek as her lips closed over his astonished mouth. Houdini made no effort to push her away. His heart raced, propelled by the intensity of the kiss. Fear provided a potent fuel for passion. It came as a shock to realize how much he feared her and how much that aroused him.

And when she reached down and stroked him, he thrilled to her brazen touch. It was not the magician who ended the kiss. His lips continued to seek hers as she pulled away, nibbling his chin and neck. At the same time, nimble fingers unbuttoned his trousers and deftly plucked his manhood into view. The magician gasped as she stroked him, his eyes darting about in panic lest someone come upon them unexpectedly in such a public place.

Isis slid slowly to her knees, her cheek rubbing along Houdini's shirtfront. He thought she swooned and reached for her when something utterly astonishing occurred. Isis placed him in her mouth. What little the magician knew of fellatio was restricted to blue jokes overheard backstage. Houdini had never before in his life had a blow job. He couldn't imagine a decent woman doing such a thing. The overwhelming trembling excitement made him nearly nauseous.

Lost in a fur-lined fog, Houdini ran his hands up along her jawline, sifting the gleaming black hair through his fingers. "Isis . . . ," he groaned. "My God . . ."

She did amazing things with her tongue. Pleasure rippled through him at every flicker. His legs trembled. Sudden terror jolted open his eyes. He stared at the vacant doorway, seeing no one. The fear of discovery added a titillating excitement to the perverse ecstasy overwhelming him. Houdini closed his eyes, blissfully surrendered to hedonism.

Isis brought him to climax very quickly. The magician's knees buckled as he ejaculated. Unbelievably, she continued the eager sucking. He fought for balance, teetering on the edge of blackout. Utterly helpless, Houdini felt the dim beginnings of dread. What if Isis meant to kill him? She had him at her mercy, toying with him, a cat teasing her prey.

A soft kiss on his shrinking penis marked her parting. Isis rose to her feet, holding on to his hips. She slid up, pressing against him. Her lips brushed across his ear. "I'm pregnant," she whispered and was gone.

The blueblood audience gave Houdini a good hand in spite of what he considered a lackluster performance. Everyone loved the Needles, even this crowd who knew nothing of vaudeville. The magician had never been more glad to conclude a performance. The incident with Isis so distracted him, he came close to fumbling the simplest moves. Worse, he almost didn't make his curtain. For fifteen long minutes before going on, Houdini sat huddled on a folding chair in the rear of the cloakroom, trembling with emotion. It took a supreme act of willpower to get up on that stage.

Fanny Brice was showing next. Houdini gave the "Follies" star a big hug as he passed her in the wings. The portable stage and painted scenery imported for the occasion had been assembled at the far end of the ballroom. After shaking hands backstage with those in charge, the magician slipped away as the orchestra struck up "My Man."

Houdini walked along behind the colonnade, deaf to the comedienne's big hand. He wanted to be far from crowds, alone in the evening's comforting dark. The magician burned with a shame far hotter than his recent lust. He felt somehow defiled, a partner in perversion. The implications of her pregnancy were too dire to contemplate. How could he have let a total stranger gain such control over his life?

The magician slowed his pace. He didn't want to appear in a great hurry to depart. Making sure he was unobserved, Houdini caught sight of Sir Arthur Conan Doyle chatting with a woman off in a corner of the ballroom. With sinking dread he recognized her as Isis.

They hadn't seen him and he knew he might escape undetected. Mustn't let guilt blind my reason, he thought. It's imperative to know what she's saying to Sir Arthur. Both our lives are in grave danger.

Houdini stepped down into the ballroom, weaving through the sparse crowd at the back of the hall. Most guests crowded around the stage, cheering Fanny Brice. "Sir Arthur!" he called jovially the moment the knight's eye caught his gaze.

"Houdini. I daresay . . ." Sir Arthur gestured toward Isis. "Do you know Mrs. Fletcher?" He caught himself with a self-deprecating chuckle. "Isis, I mean."

"We've met . . . previously," the magician said, striving to keep any trace of emotion out of his voice.

"Isis is a most remarkable medium."

"Mr. Houdini knows that far better than you, Sir Arthur." Her voice remained musical and subdued. "He once sat for a séance with me."

"By Jove! Is that a fact? We were just discussing the possibilities of conducting a session for me." Sir Arthur beamed. "So, what was your verdict, Harry? Don't mean to embarrass Mrs. Fletcher by asking such a question in front of her, but I know you never to let etiquette stand in the way of candor."

"Fear not. I've been embarrassed by Mr. Houdini before, Sir Arthur."

"Indeed?"

Houdini swallowed hard.

"He interrupted a public séance of mine, but I forgive him."

"And why is that?" Sir Arthur cocked an ironic eyebrow.

"Because I know he respects the truth." Isis licked her lips, savoring every word. "The naked truth . . ."

"Ah-hah. And what is the truth regarding your impressions of Mrs. Fletcher as a medium?"

"Very . . . impressive." Houdini glanced quickly at Isis.

Sir Arthur bobbed on the soles of his feet like a fencer about to lunge. "No sign of fraud then, what? Would you say she is a candidate for the *Scientific American* prize?"

The magician squirmed. "The results were . . . ah, inconclusive. It would take . . . another sitting."

"Would you categorize her séance as 'tricks and mumbo jumbo'? To cite a recent newspaper quote."

"No," Houdini blurted. "Of course not."

The knight's eyes blazed triumphantly. "Then here is a medium who is not a complete fraud?"

"Possibly, yes . . ."

"What an admission! Would you be willing to make such a positive statement to the press? You certainly never hesitate to spread the bad news or blacken my reputation."

Houdini felt a profound weariness settle on his shoulders. "I never meant to discredit you personally, Sir Arthur. You must know that. I'm a fair man. I keep my eyes open and tell the truth about what I see."

"Mr. Runyon is here tonight. You've never been shy about talking with the press. Why don't we go collect him so you might express your true opinion regarding Mrs. Fletcher's abilities."

Isis grinned. "Yes," she said, "I should think he'd have quite a lot to say on that subject."

"Now is not the right time," Houdini said, a little too quickly. "I . . . ah, require at least another sitting before making any formal statement."

"Join me for the séance Isis is planning. Of course, Mrs. Fletcher, this invitation is subject to your approval."

"Personally, I prefer private sessions," she purred, fixing the magician with her catlike stare. "But, I'll gladly make an exception in this case."

"We leave tomorrow for the western portion of our pilgrimage. Texas . . . California . . . Colorado . . ." Sir Arthur counted the destinations on his fingertips. "Every other wild and woolly place you can think of. Won't be back until mid-September."

Houdini fidgeted. "Our schedules don't coincide. My summer tour doesn't end until October tenth."

"Well then, Jean and I don't sail until the ninth of November. That should be ample time, if there's an opening in Mrs. Fletcher's calendar?"

Isis smiled. "My calendar is at your command, gentlemen."

"There's still a problem." The magician avoided meeting her gaze. "I begin a three-week fall tour almost immediately. October fourteenth. Boston, Syracuse, Rochester, Buffalo, Detroit, and ending up in Chicago. When I return from the West Coast, I'll need every available minute just getting things ready."

Sir Arthur exchanged a conspiratorial wink with Isis. "Why do I get the feeling Mr. Houdini is avoiding us? Can it be he regrets his pledge to make an honest and unbiased report to the press?"

"No! I stand by my word of honor!"

"I suspect our bold magician is afraid of me." The bewitching feline eyes danced with mockery. "I know too many secrets . . . universal secrets."

"Secrets be damned!" Houdini blurted. "Sir Arthur, as soon as time permits, I pledge to form an impartial committee to investigate her claims. Whatever I observe will be honestly reported." The magician stared hard at Isis, who gestured teasingly with her black mesh purse. "And now, if Mrs. Fletcher will excuse us, I truly need to have a word with you in private."

"I'm sure that means he has something nasty to tell you about me." Isis plucked a strand of hair from the corner of her mouth. "Nasty and unflattering. Sir Arthur, you know how to reach me. I will schedule time for you in the fall. À bientôt . . ." She took three steps and turned. "I don't know which of you this concerns. . . . The room is so crowded. I'm receiving a clear and terrifying message. Beware of Halloween. Darkness, pain, and death await you on the Night of All Saints." She turned quickly and hurried away.

"By God, sir, you are the rudest individual I've ever encountered," Sir Arthur fumed.

"Better rude than dead."

"What can you possibly mean by that intriguing remark?"

"Just this. I have reason to suspect Isis of being the Poe killer."

"Are you mad? I should certainly like to hear any evidence."

"I'm not at liberty to reveal it at present. She has good cause to hate me. I disrupted an important public séance of hers. A big fundraiser for the Temple of Isis."

Sir Arthur took this in, tugging his earlobe as he thought. "Was this public séance before or after the Esp murders?" he asked at last.

"Well, after . . . but, think of my reputation as an enemy of mediums."

"There are many mediums. Given what you've told me, I see no reason to accept your thesis. Perhaps if you shared the other evidence."

Houdini glanced away. "Can't do that. Not yet. Look. All the killings took place in New York. You leave the city tomorrow. I go out on the road next week. Bess and Dash go with me. I think we're all safe as long as we're away."

"I've given it some thought." Sir Arthur nodded. "And I quite agree."

"Just be careful when you get back. You'll be in town on Halloween."

"Boo!" Sir Arthur barked, laughing gently, while his right hand sought the cool solid weight of the revolver in his jacket pocket.

22

IN THE GOOD OLD
SUMMERTIME

An unrelenting sun burned down on the transplanted palms. Eucalyptus scented a hot desert wind with their pungent medicinal smell. Pepper trees added astringent spice. Sir Arthur stared up into an empyrean sky as brilliant and magical as any Tiepolo ceiling. High on a rolling golden hillside, abrupt above the yucca and live oaks, letters tall as billboards welcomed the visiting knight to HOLLYWOODLAND.

Conan Doyle was having the time of his life in California. Unlike the East Coast, so like home with its lush, verdant springtime and glorious summer, the western half of the United States struck him as exotic as Africa; the perpetual sunshine and fierce azure skies above an unfamiliar terrain. Crossing Arizona, he saw his first large saguaro and felt very far from yew trees and boxwood hedges.

Their first week in Los Angeles had been extremely busy. Sir Arthur delivered a lecture at the Trinity Auditorium to an enthusiastic reception. He and Jean were the guests of Sid Grauman at his palatial Egyptian Theater on Hollywood Boulevard for a showing of *The Hunchback of Notre Dame,* starring the protean Lon Chaney. A twenty-five-piece orchestra accompanied the film. The lush music and opulent, gilded make-believe presaged their entire stay among the movie colony.

Louis B. Mayer treated the Conan Doyles like visiting royalty. He personally escorted them around the M.G.M. back lot, having only recently added his own initial to the studio monogram. They dined with Doug and Mary at "Pickfair," and found America's Sweetheart and her swashbuckling husband to be a charming couple.

Visiting Chaplin the next day on the set of *A Woman of Paris,* they chatted about Pickford and Fairbanks, sharing the intimacy of fellow countrymen in an alien land. Chaplin praised his new partners in United Artists, calling them his only equals in the profession. Even so, he confided, for all their talent, they were little more than Babbitts.

The red carpet remained out for the Conan Doyles' entire stay. Hollywood craved their proper British respectability. The previous year had been a time of dreadful scandal for the motion picture industry. Director William Desmond Taylor's unsolved murder had ruined the careers of Mary Miles Minter and Mabel Normand. The third Fatty Arbuckle trial, although it ended with the comedian's acquittal, ruined his. Clean-cut Wally Reid, "the King of Paramount," had died a morphine addict in a padded cell. A visiting knight provided a momentary veneer of honor and dignity. Sir Arthur found himself assiduously courted by former junk dealers and ragmen grown rich merchandising celluloid fantasies of the American dream.

Manifest evidence of an underlying decadence provided ironic counterpoint to the self-congratulatory adulation. At the intersection of Sunset, Prospect, and Talmadge near the eastern end of Hollywood Boulevard, mission-style bungalows and unpaved streets surrounded the decaying remains of ancient Babylon. The Los Angeles Fire Department had condemned the towering set from D. W. Griffith's 1916 epic, *Intolerance,* as a fire hazard, but still it stood, a wall three hundred feet high fronted by giant columns topped with crumbling plaster pachyderms.

Conan Doyle frequently came here. His favorite walk took him across Mulholland Dam and around Lake Hollywood, a rustic ramble providing astonishing glimpses of wildlife. Sighting deer and coyotes within the city limits of a large metropolis delighted Sir Arthur but, in

spite of such sylvan attractions, he was invariably lured back to the bogus
Babylon.

The knight stared up at the immense ramparts, grander in concept
than any wonder of the ancient world, yet utterly insubstantial, the lath
already showing through a deteriorating plaster surface. Here stood the
very soul of America, he thought. Such introspection suited his mood. A
certain ironic bitterness had replaced the uneasy dread of knowing one's
family to be stalked by a predator. His peace of mind increased with
every mile he traveled from New York. He began taking a perverse pleasure in a dispassionate examination of the strange land he traversed. In
Texas, he had stopped carrying his service revolver.

After their first few days in Hollywood, the children tired of
searching for movie stars and instead rode the Red Line trolley with
their tutor every afternoon out to Santa Monica and the glories of the
beach. Jean had embarked on a round of tennis lessons under the tute-
lage of Big Bill Tilden's coach. With one remaining lecture scheduled in
Pasadena, Sir Arthur felt free to roam as he pleased, after writing for
several hours early each morning.

The knight had a lot on his mind. Curiously, the further he dis-
tanced himself from the macabre Poe business, the more it occupied his
thoughts. He had not seen the ghost again since the unpleasant encounter
in the capital a month ago. No other murders followed Jim Vickery's
death in June. Sir Arthur felt certain none would occur while Houdini
and his family were away from New York for the summer.

There had been no contact with the magician since their chance
meeting at Mrs. Astor's gala. Twice, after reading Houdini's continued
attacks on spiritualism in the newspapers, Sir Arthur started to write
angry letters. Both times, he'd thought better of it. As long as no
mention had been made of him personally, there seemed little point in
retaliating.

"If thinking pained me as much as it looks like it does you, I'd give
it up."

An unexpected voice interrupted Sir Arthur's musing. The knight
turned and saw a sad-faced man staring dolefully from behind the wheel

of a sporty yellow two-seater Pierce-Arrow runabout parked at the curb. There was something familiar about the fellow, and although Sir Arthur couldn't immediately pin a name on him, he answered without hesitation. "If you must know, I was thinking about the magician, Harry Houdini."

The stranger nodded, his woeful countenance unchanged. "Small world," he said. "Houdini's my godfather."

"Are you serious?" Sir Arthur masked his suspicion with a jovial smile.

"Don't I look serious?" the stranger deadpanned. "I was born in a trunk, as the saying goes. A vaudeville brat. My parents worked a double on the same bill with Harry and Bess. It was him named me Buster."

Of course. Conan Doyle immediately recognized the dour comic actor. He also detected the fruity aroma of alcohol. The man was drunk. The knight decided not to introduce himself. No point in getting embroiled in any inebriated misunderstandings.

Conan Doyle was unaware that he too had been recognized. Buster Keaton spotted the author from familiarity with his photo in the Sunday rotogravure of the *Los Angeles Times*. The coincidental meeting struck the comedian as an almost divinely inspired stroke of luck. For weeks, he'd been wrestling with the scenario for a new motion picture, an off-kilter fantasy about a projectionist who walks into the movie he's showing, stepping through the screen like an electric Alice to join the other characters in a detective plot. The working title was "Sherlock, Jr."

Keaton's company owned the production; he was both director and star of the five-reeler. With the start of principal photography scheduled for next week, he had yet to decide on an ending: a problem of ulcer-inducing proportions. The comic had fled to the old *Intolerance* set to drink and brood. Conan Doyle arrived like a gift from heaven.

"What brings a proper English gentleman like yourself down to the corpse of this colossal flop?" Keaton asked.

Sir Arthur gestured at the framework towering above them. " 'My name is Ozymandias, king of kings,' " he quoted. " 'Look upon my works, ye Mighty, and despair!' "

Keaton's face remained impassive. The appraising hangdog eyes never missed a trick. This blowhard's more Watson than Sherlock, he thought. Just what the doctor ordered.

When Houdini's troupe embarked by train for their ten-week Western tour, the magician remained behind in New York. He told Bess certain business matters required his immediate attention, promising to rejoin her in two or three days. When she insisted on staying, he dissuaded her, explaining he needed her to manage the company accounts in his absence. "Without Jim Vickery, poor Collins has his hands full. He won't have time to look after the books." In the end, Bess did as Harry wished, just like always.

Houdini had a busy schedule in the city. He spent most of the first morning at the Pine Street offices of Dumphry, Hale, and Simmons, his accounting firm in the financial district. The magician spoke with those who had known Ingrid Esp, asking many of the same questions the police had asked back in April. The secretaries and stenographers cooperated because they knew him to be a famous man and an important client.

Secretly, they wondered what point there was in going over it all again. He repeatedly inquired about clairvoyants or mediums or whatever. Ingrid had been a quiet Norwegian girl who kept pretty much to herself. She lived with her mother and didn't have any beaux, as far as anyone could recall. One thing sure, she wasn't the sort to waste her hard-earned paycheck on fortune-tellers.

After a quick lunch on the fly, grabbing a hot dog and a dope from a pushcart vendor, Houdini set about tracking down "Dapper Dave" Conrad, first stopping at the Palace, where the house manager obliged him by searching through his April booking sheets for the name and address of the hoofer's agent.

Arnold Small's office consisted of a single dusty room above a pawnshop on Forty-fifth Street. The agent was a lean, nervous man with springy red hair thick as an Airedale's. His natural arrogance transformed instantly into obsequious flattery upon recognizing the eminent magician. Small assumed his client was up for a job and Houdini did nothing to correct that misapprehension.

"Call it luck, call it fate," Small gushed, "Dave Conrad is at this very moment auditioning around the corner for the chorus in the 'Vanities.'"

Despite Houdini's protests, Arnold Small insisted on walking him to the Earl Carroll Theater. They entered by the stage door and waited in the wings, watching a succession of energetic tap-dancing young men buck-and-wing and shuffle-off-to-Buffalo. Dapper Dave's turn came at last and he was half a minute into his triple-time step when an unseen voice in the darkened house called, "Next!"

The disgruntled hoofer stalked offstage scowling. He brightened into a smile immediately upon spotting his agent. By the time introductions were made, the three men were out in the street. Small proved harder to shake than a summer cold, but Houdini managed to give him a polite brush-off, saying he needed to speak with the client alone. Never one to queer a deal, the agent motioned them off, standing on the corner of Fiftieth and Seventh, waving like someone left behind on the station platform after the train pulls out.

The magician and the hoofer walked across Times Square to the Automat on the west side of Broadway between Forty-sixth and Forty-seventh Streets. This was the first of Horn & Hardart's popular novelty cafeterias. It opened a decade before and now a dozen others flourished around town. Entering a gleaming white-tiled room, they passed beneath the two-story stained-glass window designed by Nicola D'Ascenzo into a poor man's palace complete with grinning plaster gargoyles and elaborate frondescent moldings. The white marble-topped tables hosted an early afternoon crowd of out-of-work vaudevillians nursing cold java and leafing through the *New York Star* or the daily *Variety*. Many of these old-timers recognized Houdini and stood to shake his hand as he headed for the chrome-plated coffee urn.

"Let me level with you," the magician said. He dropped two nickles in the slot and filled a pair of mugs with the steaming brew spouting from dolphin-shaped spigots. "This isn't about a job. I want to ask you some questions about Violette Speers."

"That bitch!" sneered Dapper Dave. "What d'you give a damn about her for?"

"Curious about her murder."

"Whoever knocked her off did the world a favor."

"That kind of talk can get you in big trouble."

"You're telling me. The cops tried to frame me at first because it's no secret we hated each other's guts. They figured I was sore because she broke up the act. Bitch was going on the road with a new partner. Lucky thing I had an iron-clad alibi."

"What was that?"

"I was in the hospital close to a month. Appendix operation. She was still alive when I went in and they found the body before my discharge."

"Good break for you."

Dapper Dave sipped his coffee. "In more ways than one. They caught that appendix just in the nick of time."

"So, listen." Houdini leaned forward, his intense, burning stare locked on Dave Conrad. "What can you tell me about Mrs. Speers?"

"Anything you want to know. She was no Mrs., for one thing. She never married Freddy Speers. Not in church, anyhow."

"What about him? This Speers? Think he might've had it in for her?'

"Not a chance. Freddy shook my hand and wished me luck when she jilted him. Turns out, cutting in on his gal was the best favor I could've done him."

"She broke up your romance and your act at the same time. Sounds like enough motive for playing outpatient with an axe."

"You're all wet, brother. There was no more romance. Not for bet-ter'n three years. It was a business arrangement, pure and simple. Can't even tell you the names of the cake-eaters she was screwing. Didn't give a damn."

Houdini winced at the profanity, his reaction occasioned more by guilt at the thought of his own screwing around than from inherent prud-ery. "Okay. I don't see this as any crime of passion."

"Some crazy maniac with a library card."

"Maybe. . . . Maybe crazy like a fox." Houdini patted the edge of the table. "This might seem like a funny kind of question, but, what do you know about her beliefs?"

"You mean like how did she vote and what church didn't she go to . . . ?"

"Actually, I was thinking about ghosts."

"Did she believe in ghosts . . . ?"

"Mediums. . . . Palm readers. . . . Crystal balls. . . . Did she go in for that kind of thing?"

Dapper Dave scratched behind his ear and grinned in unconscious imitation of Will Rogers. "Now that you mention it, she was goofy that way," he said. "Used to get her horoscope done. You know, couldn't make a decision without checking on her stars."

"What about séances?" Houdini's eyes gleamed with anticipation.

"Well, I didn't exactly follow her around." Dave Conrad silently shook his head at the absurdity of this thought. "I remember once she told me about going to a spook show at some spiffy Fifth Avenue joint. There was this stage-door Johnny squiring her around. Must've been twice her age, but ultra swank. He took her someplace very hoity-toity."

"Opal Crosby Fletcher?"

Dapper Dave looked puzzled at the magician's enthusiastic outburst. "Who's that?"

"The medium. Was she called Isis?"

"Search me. All I recall is how gaga Violette was telling me about it. Said all the other guests were these top-drawer blue bloods. Said it was like dying and going to heaven. I guess she knows more about that stuff now."

A flush of excitement tinged Houdini's cheeks. "Did she say anything about her hostess being the medium?"

"Maybe. To be honest with you, I didn't pay much attention. It was just Vi, hogging the spotlight, like always."

"But you remember her saying Fifth Avenue?"

"I wouldn't swear an oath on it. Maybe it was Park. What difference does it make?"

Houdini looked grim. "Perhaps the difference between life and death," he said, one showman to another, milking the moment for all it was worth.

* * *

A fresh, crisp breeze whipped in across the harbor, making white-caps dance around a Staten Island–bound ferry. Gulls wheeled shrieking above a tug-towed garbage scow heading for the Narrows. The salty sea air tasted clean and invigorating to Sgt. James Patrick Heegan, accustomed to breathing a poisonous midtown miasma composed of equal parts truck exhaust and coal furnace fumes. He sat on a park bench behind the aquarium in Castle Clinton, staring out at the Jersey shore and the distant, arsenic-green Statue of Liberty.

The sergeant had arranged to meet Damon Runyon in Battery Park. It wasn't far from headquarters on Centre Street and he wanted the reporter to come see him for a change. At the same time, it seemed a little too close for comfort, being as he was in uniform. Rather than some more convenient spot near City Hall, Heegan suggested the park as neutral territory, not wanting another cop to see him talking to the press.

The sergeant clutched a rolled copy of a novelty publishing experiment, a weekly news magazine called *Time*. The first issue had appeared five months earlier. Heegan didn't give it much chance of success. He only bought the magazine as a silent rebuke for Damon Runyon. Give the arrogant bastard a clue. Let him see maybe his future wasn't all that secure.

The reporter strolled into Battery Park after walking down Broadway from Trinity Church, where he'd mistakenly asked the cabby to drop him. This wasn't his part of town. The last time he'd been down on Wall Street had been three years before when anarchists exploded a junk cart full of scrap metal in front of the House of Morgan, killing thirty. Although Runyon considered himself a sportswriter, William Randolph Hearst liked having him cover certain big stories of a criminal nature. In 1916 he'd even jogged along on muleback beside Black Jack Pershing at the head of the Thirteenth Cavalry, chasing after Pancho Villa in Old Mexico.

Runyon dressed like a sporty racetrack tout in two-tone tan-and-white shoes, a pale blue linen suit, and polka-dot bow tie. His heartless eyes swept the benches behind Castle Clinton, spotting the bulky blue figure of Sergeant Heegan alone by the iron rail at the water's edge. The taxpayer's burden, he thought.

"What have you got for me today, Sergeant?" asked Damon Runyon, settling himself on the opposite end of the bench.

Heegan fixed the reporter with his sternest third-degree stare. "The question is, Mr. Runyon, what've you got for me?"

Time to nip this deal in the bud. Behind the implacable round-lensed glasses, the Westerner's eyes narrowed with anger. "Don't confuse newspaper work with how you coppers conduct business," he said. "I don't pay for favors."

The policeman affected a pained expression. "I'm not asking for grift. What I want is a favor from you."

"Name it."

"Well, I been feeding you all the lowdown for some time. That Ed Poe caper come from me. Seems like you've been scoring big points with that one." He waved the copy of *Time*, a pen-and-ink portrait of treasury secretary Andrew W. Mellon staring furtively off the cover.

"Give it to me straight, Heegan."

"Look. I read the papers every day, year in and year out. I see how you put your friends in your column. Make a big deal up out of nothing . . ."

"You'd like to see your name in the paper?"

"Sure would tickle my wife and kids."

"Heegan. You're on." Damon Runyon sprang to his feet and clapped the sergeant on his shoulder. "In two paragraphs, I'll make you the biggest hero in the city. The little woman and all the rug rats will fight for the privilege of bringing your pipe and slippers."

Much further uptown, another al fresco meeting had been planned for that afternoon. Harry Houdini sat on a green-painted bench in the garden mall extending down the center of Park Avenue. A cobbled pedestrian walkway divided the grassy islands, connecting ovals in the middle of each block where benches were arranged. A single lane of traffic ran along either side. Houdini faced west, into the sun, watching taxis race downtown.

After parting from Dapper Dave Conrad, the magician telephoned Isis at her home, arranging a rendezvous in an hour's time. She suggested he drop by for tea, but he decided against taking chances. No more private séances and cloakroom encounters. He wanted to get together in the open without any furtive hanky-panky.

She, of course, was late. The magician managed a grim smile at his own annoyance. Considering the woman might well be a maniacal killer, it seemed a bit silly to worry about her tardiness. He tried to imagine Isis in the act of murder; driving an axe into Violette Speers's skull; costumed as a gorilla, carrying Ingrid Esp down a midnight street. The graphic mental pictures came all too easily.

"Penny for your thoughts . . ."

Jolted from his homicidal reveries by the unexpected sound of her voice, Houdini gasped with surprise. "Do you always sneak up on people like that?"

"There was no sneaking." Isis smiled slyly. "You just weren't paying attention." She sat next to him on the bench, so close their shoulders touched. "I missed you," she said, tracing a familiar finger along the crease in his trousers.

Houdini got abruptly to his feet. "If we're to have this conference, I must insist you keep your hands to yourself."

Isis made an exaggerated show of sliding to the opposite side of the bench. "Please, sit back down. I won't bite. Honest." She watched him settle as far from her as possible. "After all, you were the one who called me."

"Yes, but not with any romantic intentions, I assure you."

"Romance is not an attribute I would ever make the mistake of associating with you, my elusive Osiris."

Houdini looked puzzled, unsure of his feelings. If she didn't want him, why had her pursuit been so ardent? "Well," he said, primly folding his hands on his knee. "Fine. It seemed to me we needed to have a talk, especially in light of your recent allegations."

"Am I accused of not telling the truth?"

"What makes you so sure I'm the father?"

Isis smiled. "A woman knows these things. Although you've been unchivalrous enough to suggest promiscuity, I've been with no other man this past year but you. We can always let a judge decide."

"No. There's no need for something like that." Any inquiry would immediately become public knowledge and Houdini dreaded the adverse publicity. "For the sake of argument, let's say I believe you. What is it you want from me?"

"Not a thing. I've already gotten everything I need."

"Everything . . . ?"

"Separated from Osiris, Isis is incomplete. So, she sets out in search of him. I found you. Life comes full circle. I am fulfilled. Whole at last."

A numb outrage blunted the magician's self-righteous piety at this unexpected rejection. He felt violated. Outmaneuvered. "What about me?" he blurted. "Don't I count for anything?"

Isis rose and looked him straight in the eye, her schoolgirl features hardening into an ageless indignation. "Quite honestly, Mr. Houdini," she said. "I no longer give a damn if you live or die!"

23

GAMES

Upstairs in their suite, the Conan Doyle children sat on the carpet around a Ouija board. Drawn drapes shut out the midday Colorado glare. After the glories of Hollywood, such enticements as the Mile-High City had to offer lacked a certain luster. Only the roller-coaster at Elitch's Gardens provided sufficient temptation, and Sir Arthur had put a ban on further trips to the amusement park until the weekend. Making contact with the spirit world seemed a better adventure than roaming the streets of downtown Denver. They had already gone exploring for cowboys and red Indians, sadly encountering only businessmen, just like anywhere.

Denis, Malcolm, and Billy all believed in spiritual survival after death. Ghost stories did not frighten them. Although the Ouija was much more than a game, it still seemed mountains of fun. They knelt together on three sides of the board, with Billy in the middle, gently resting their fingertips on the triangular three-legged pointer. As the oldest, Denis assigned himself the task of recording any spirit contact. Several sheets of hotel stationery and a pencil lay on the carpet beside him.

"Are there spirits present?" Malcolm asked, without a trace of boyish irony. All three children concentrated very hard on clearing their minds of extraneous thought. They wanted to be open transmitters for visitors from the other side.

"Keen!" enthused Billy when her fingers started tingling.

Almost imperceptibly, the tripodal pointer began to tremble. The vibrations grew stronger and the little platform took on an independent life, pulling inexorably across the arcing alphabet, sweeping back and forth before coming to a resolute stop above an ornate letter.

"P!" shouted Malcolm.

Downstairs, in the soaring golden onyx lobby of the Brown Palace Hotel, Houdini and Conan Doyle sat in wing chairs, facing one another over a tea table. Sir Arthur sipped legal sherry. A local physician on the chamber of commerce wrote him a prescription for it. Nerve tonic. The magician had tea. He wore a black mourning band on his right sleeve.

Since the death of popular president Warren G. Harding from cerebral apoplexy in San Francisco five days before, the nation had plunged into a collective sorrow. Flags fluttering in patriotic Independence Day profusion only a month ago drooped at pathetic half-mast. Across the country, bereaved citizens dressed in black in spite of the summer heat. Theaters closed everywhere as a show of respect.

The Orpheum in Denver, where Houdini topped the bill, remained dark for a perfunctory single night. The magician, an intensely patriotic man, instructed his company to wear signs of mourning onstage at every performance. Most other acts followed suit. Viewing the program, this gesture deeply touched Sir Arthur, bringing back memories of his own personal grief amidst the national mourning for Edward VII.

Conan Doyle, together with his wife and children, had been Houdini's guests at the previous night's performance. Visiting backstage afterwards, there had been no opportunity for private conversation. The magician gave Billy a box of chocolates and Jean a pretty bouquet of violets.

They chatted for a few somber minutes about the national tragedy. Houdini mentioned he'd spent fifteen minutes with President Harding a year ago, recalling the vigor of his appearance. Shocking to contemplate how a simple case of ptomaine poisoning led, in just a week's time, to such fatal conclusions. Human existence seemed pitifully fragile when life and death hung on a balance as trivial as a meal of dubious crabmeat. A somber silence precluded any further conversation and the two men soon parted, planning to meet again the next afternoon.

The second encounter began with some awkwardness, owing to Sir Arthur's embarrassment over a story in the morning Denver *Express:* DOYLE DEFIES HOUDINI; OFFERS TO BRING BACK DEAD. He felt once again manipulated by the press. Clearly, they had put words in his mouth. A damned awkward business after all his sanctimony.

Houdini brushed aside the knight's apologies. The magician hadn't seen the papers. As a master manipulator of journalism's propensity to exaggerate, he knew all too well how an innocent remark might be misquoted.

Sir Arthur looked remarkably fit. His tour had been the most successful since the final lectures of Mark Twain. Everywhere he traveled, he felt buoyed anew by the great affection the American public showed for him. In contrast, Houdini appeared pinched and drawn with worry. He carried the weight of weary sadness.

"It's been what . . . ?" Sir Arthur pondered aloud, lighting his pipe. "Seven weeks since you discovered Vickery's murder?"

"Almost eight."

"Hmmm. . . . Twice the time as that between any of the other killings. And you were for the most part away from New York during the same period."

"Supports your theory that I'm the prime target." Houdini rested his elbows on his knees, cradling his chin on upturned palms.

"At the very least, it doesn't dispute it . . ." Sir Arthur puffed in silence. "Perhaps the atrocities have simply ceased; inexplicably, like the Ripper."

"I doubt it." Gloom clouded the magician's features. "I did a little poking around two weeks ago, between tours. I have testimony that Violette Speers attended a séance at the home of Opal Crosby Fletcher."

"Pure circumstance."

"There's more. She sent me a copy of Poe while I was showing in Hoboken."

Sir Arthur leaned forward, eagerness brightening his blue eyes. "Think she's toying with you or merely exercising a remarkable gift?"

"Gift . . . ?"

"Clairvoyance, old man."

"You know I don't buy it. Bess and I worked a mentalist act in our circus days. All the great 'mind readers' use trickery. You'll never believe that, so I'm not gonna argue the point. I'm not interested in exposing Isis as a fake medium."

"Might that not be because you know her abilities to be genuine?"

"I know plenty about her abilities. In fact, I know a whole lot about little Miss Isis." Houdini caught his breath. Mustn't let a burst of temper reveal too much. "I've been . . . conducting a . . . a . . . an undercover investigation." Even as he said it, he knew it sounded absurd.

"Father!"

Malcolm's voice, calling out high above, saved the magician from the knight's quizzical eyes. Sir Arthur glanced up into a huge atrium. The lobby of the Brown Palace rose eight stories to a stained glass ceiling the size of a rugby field. Houdini peered upward at the surrounding vortex of filigreed cast-iron balconies. Hard to tell from which tier the sound had come.

"Over here, Father!" Denis called this time. All three children waved from the sixth-floor railing. The eldest boy held a paper glider, folded from a sheet of hotel stationery. "Here it comes," he cried, launching the glider out into open space.

Sir Arthur watched the lazy downward spiral. "The children are having a séance," he told the magician. "Said they'd send me details of any contact."

The glider turned over the tops of the potted palms. Sir Arthur crossed the lobby to intercept it. Houdini followed him.

"A message from a ghost," announced the knight, snatching the drifting glider from overhead. The magician stood beside him as he unfolded the intricate origami. Together they read the message. It consisted of a single syllable: POE.

Tucked between the matching stoops of twin brownstones, the entrance to the Zebra Club on West Forty-eighth Street sported a black-and-white canvas awning stretching to the curb. In the evenings, a uniformed doorman strutted between the polished brass poles. He knew the regulars on sight, greeting them cheerfully; one of the things Damon Runyon liked best about the place.

The reporter was also quite fond of Leon Fishkin, the jovial proprietor, known as "Smiley" to the racetrack crowd who congregated at his speakeasy. A born handicapper, he could always be counted on for the inside dope. On slow nights, Runyon sat with the rotund little man by the hour, listening to his comic tales of bookies and touts.

The Zebra Club had a floor show, and a certain long-legged, brunette songbird in the chorus was the main reason Damon Runyon spent so much time in Smiley's joint. A handsome, dapper Irishman, with a similar eye for showgirls, lounged beside him tonight. Decked out in evening clothes and patent leather shoes, state senator James J. Walker wore the look of success easily. The talk along Broadway was that he planned to challenge Mayor John F. Hylan in the next election.

The reporter took a keen interest in his friend's political career, judging its course with the jaded eye of a lifelong newspaperman. From the press perspective, Runyon remarked, it was a damn shame Walker had been handed Kid Dropper's killer, a losing proposition bound to see a lot of local coverage.

"Wrong call." Jimmy Walker sipped champagne. "This thing's going to make me shine."

"Having a client go to the chair never looks too good in the papers, Jimmy."

"Relax, pal. I'm going to win this one."

"Win . . . ? You've got a self-confessed killer who's made a point of repeating his story to anyone who'll listen."

"Look. I know it's water-tight. Saving Louis Cohen's life will be a win."

"How you gonna do that?" Damon Runyon lit up a Sweet Cap. "Pay somebody off?"

Senator Walker grinned. "You know I don't do business that way. This will be a courtroom victory. I plan to obtain a verdict of second-degree homicide."

"You and what magic wand?"

"If I reveal my strategy to you now, it is with the understanding you won't use any of it until after the trial."

Damon Runyon nodded, at the same time flicking his earlobe with his forefinger. "On the Eire . . ." He used an underworld expression warning of possible eavesdroppers.

Walker refilled his glass, pushing the empty bottle neck-first into the ice-filled bucket. "Here's the law," he said. "Unless the murder is proven, it is impossible to convict for first-degree murder, even with a signed confession."

"So, how do you figure to disprove the murder?"

"There's no need to 'disprove' anything. I merely have to introduce the shadow of a doubt."

Runyon grinned. "Shade on, McJames . . ."

"You remember Willemse, the bull-necked captain in charge of the prisoner . . . ? Well, he was in the cab with Dropper, an eyewitness to his untimely end. After the dust settled, he went back in an alley and shot a hole through his straw skimmer. Then he bragged to all the boys about his close brush with death."

"I like it," Damon Runyon said.

"You're going to love it." The elegant politician signaled a waiter, a turn of his hand ordering another bottle of bubbly. "All witnesses agree Cohen fired three shots. That many spent shells were found in his revolver. Three bullets were recovered from the cab. One came out of the roof; one out of the floor. The third was in Kid Dropper. My client's a terrible shot. Even at close range. No better than one in three. Terrible shot."

"So . . . ?"

A cork popped. The waiter refilled Senator Walker's glass. The senator waited for him to leave before resuming. "So, the one through Willemse's hat makes four. Four bullets, but only three from Cohen. Which one killed the Dropper? Who fired the other shot . . . ? Voilà! Reasonable doubt."

Runyon sipped his cold cup of coffee. "Pretty cute. Think it can win?"

"It can't lose. The proverbial sure thing."

24

BUY ME SOME PEANUTS AND CRACKER JACK

When Sir Arthur Conan Doyle and his family returned to New York on September 14, the desk clerk at the Plaza handed him an envelope emblazoned with the logo of Hearst's *American*. A note inside from Damon Runyon: "Tonight! Polo Grounds. 8:00 P.M. Runyon." Clipped to it, a ringside press pass for the Dempsey vs. Firpo championship bout.

Although initially Sir Arthur protested he wouldn't dream of leaving Jean alone on their first night back, she told him not to be silly, what a shame to miss it. She'd have dinner with the children, perhaps take them all to the cinema. Not to worry. She'd be fine.

The Polo Grounds turned out to be a major league baseball stadium and not the elegant greensward the knight pictured in his imagination. Located alongside weed-choked vacant lots in the far upper reaches of Manhattan, the old, girdered, tin-roofed grandstand looked right at home among the surrounding warehouses and factories. The ring had been set up in the infield. Sir Arthur found his way to the press seats, pushing down a crowded row past peanut sellers and hot dog vendors.

Damon Runyon stood to greet him at ringside, the roar of the crowd making anything more than perfunctory conversation impossible. Runyon introduced the knight to his fellow sportswriters, Ring Lardner and Gene Fowler. They joked about the million-dollar gate and the slowness of the preliminary card. Sir Arthur marveled at how blasé they seemed, while he soared with giddy excitement.

After the long-winded oratory of the introductory remarks, the main event exploded in a blaze of savagery. The champion, his blunt, bulldog face a mask of determined rage, stalked the lumbering. Argentine, knocking him to the canvas seven times in the first two minutes of round one. Bloody and bewildered, Firpo fought on with pure animal fury. A massive haymaker sent Dempsey hurtling back on the ropes with enough force to propel him through, tumbling pell-mell into the uplifted arms of the startled spectators.

Sir Arthur and Runyon were among the half-dozen or so laughing men who pushed the dazed fighter upward, eagerly helping him back into the ring. "By Jove," the Englishman enthused. "Capital sport, what?"

"Go get him, Jack!" Runyon hollered.

Although stunned and confused, Dempsey avoided the contender's wild punches until the bell. At the start of the second round, the "Mauler" surged forth renewed. A punishing series of jabs brought the "Wild Bull of the Pampas" to his knees in the first thirty seconds. Firpo's massive strength willed him to his feet one more time, but a short right to the jaw floored the Argentine giant for keeps.

Sir Arthur couldn't take his eyes off Dempsey as the referee emphatically counted Firpo out. The champion relaxed in a neutral corner, arms angled along the top rope, a confident gladiator, at home in the arena.

The ref lifted Dempsey's arm in victory. "Wanna meet the champ?" Runyon shouted into the tumult.

"By a knockout . . . ," the announcer droned.

Conan Doyle nodded yes.

It took some time to get past the mob to Dempsey's dressing room. Damon Runyon knew all the cops by their first names. An obliging patrolman ran interference. The spare, concrete room under the bleachers was already packed when they arrived. Dempsey sat on a workout table. A trainer poured a bottle of champagne over his head.

Spotting Runyon, the champ waved the reporter over. "Thanks for the lift," he grinned.

"Don't bullshit me. You didn't know what hit you." Both men being from Colorado, they shared the Westerner's instinctive easy familiarity. Damon Runyon introduced Sir Arthur to the heavyweight champion.

"You the fellow wrote that Roomorg mystery?" asked Dempsey. "The one Runyon told me about?"

"I'm afraid not. You're thinking of Edgar Allan Poe."

"Oh, yeah. Right." The champ rubbed his thumb along his broken nose. "Poe. . . . The guy doing all those killings around town."

The final eight weeks of the Conan Doyles' American visit had been intended as a winding down of official activities. Only five lectures remained on the schedule. The knight and his lady looked forward to evenings at the theater. Sir Arthur began a new Professor Challenger story in California and thought to reserve mornings and most afternoons for spinning the remainder of the tale.

By the first week of October, Conan Doyle had accomplished no literary work at all. A writer famed for jotting Sherlock Holmes stories in his notebook while chatting and drinking with friends now found it impossible to concentrate in the privacy of his hotel suite. The Poe mystery occupied his every thought.

Up each morning before dawn, he saw no further manifestation of the author's spirit. During the day, the knight roamed the victims' neighborhoods, asking questions of shoemakers, hotel managers, greengrocers; anyone who had served the Esps, Violette Speers, or the Rogers girl. He again carried a loaded revolver in his jacket pocket.

After pounding the pavement for a fortnight, Sir Arthur learned nothing new of any consequence and had heard altogether far too much scurrilous gossip. He knew the futility of searching for clues in such a random fashion, yet persisted, a gambler's instinctive hope for the lucky break augmenting his tenacious curiosity.

One clear morning in early October, the knight prowled the

streets of Jim Vickery's Bronx neighborhood. Broad sycamores shaded comfortable lower-middle-class streets. Movie-music from numberless electric pianos drifted through the open windows of identical semidetached homes. After interviewing a battalion of bored housewives, hearing them repeat pointless stories already told several times to the police and anyone else who'd listen, Sir Arthur conceded he'd had enough sleuthing for the day.

As they were already in the borough, he instructed the driver of the hired car to motor him over to Fordham, asking directions at two filling stations before finding the Poe cottage on East 192nd Street. Paved streets enclosed the barren little hilltop park crowned by a dilapidated one-and-a-half-story frame farmhouse. A sign erected by the Bronx Society of Arts and Letters identified the hundred-year-old structure as the home of the noted poet from May 1846 to June 1849. The cottage had been moved to the park from an adjacent site in 1913.

Sir Arthur left the car and walked up the packed red earth of the grassless hill. Standing on the porch, he tried to picture the place seventy years before, when it sat in the middle of rolling farm country surrounded by fruit groves and hay meadows. How isolated from the city Poe must have felt. Did his macabre imagination ever envision this nightmare encroachment of pavement and brick?

The little farmhouse stood locked up tight. Conan Doyle tried the front door, noting a placard listing the stated hours of public visitation: Open MON. WED. FRI. The knight shaded his eyes, stooping for a look through the front window into a spartan parlor contained no furnishings other than a pair of spindly chairs and a small pine table.

A shadow flickered across the polished wood floor. Sir Arthur caught a glimpse of Poe passing an open doorway. He rattled the window, finding it latched. Six swift strides carried him around the corner. He peered through the kitchen window with his heart racing. The apparition swayed in the center of the tiny room, a foxfire phosphorescence emanating from the stooped shoulders and tousled head.

Sir Arthur tapped gently on the pane. Poe's ghost looked over at the window. His melancholy eyes met the knight's gaze, an almost palpable sadness hovering between them. The knight cupped his hand, motioning for the spirit to join him. Turning with the underwater sluggishness of someone in a dream, the luminous figure drifted slowly out of the room.

Conan Doyle hurried around the rear. He glanced through a tiny window into an empty bedroom not three paces across and scrambled in a most undignified manner to complete a circumnavigation of the cottage. Reaching the porch again, he found the apparition standing by a pillar, staring past hanging electrical wires and rooftop water towers.

The knight stepped up beside the misty specter. Poe glanced at him, expressing less interest than a man encountering his reflection in a glass. "Must you torment me even here?" the spirit asked in weary resignation.

"You remember me . . . ?" Their last confrontation in Washington, D.C., seemed eons ago.

"Would one easily forget a phantom from the future?"

"Tell me what you see." Sir Arthur pointed toward the surrounding urban blight. "Over there . . ."

Poe gazed out across a forgotten landscape. "Cherry trees grow close by. An apple orchard at the bottom of the hill. Beyond the meadow, on the far side of the second fence, stands the Beauchamp cottage. About a half mile beyond their farm you can just make out the Croton Aqueduct. A grassy footpath runs along atop it. I often stroll there as far as High Bridge. Fine view of the city from High Bridge."

Conan Doyle shuddered at the discrepancy between what the ghost described and his own dismal urban view. "Have you . . . lived here long?"

"Three years; although I'm no longer a tenant Whenever my journey takes me to New York, I come up here for a visit. A vacant house is memory's tomb."

"What are you searching for?"

"What, indeed . . . ?" The specter laughed bitterly. "Sadly, such as you, yet at once so different your presence is a painful rebuke. My own dear wife, my Sissy, died here. A dreadful, cold winter day . . ."

Pathos gripped Sir Arthur. "You seek her spirit . . ."

"We both find that ironic." Poe's ghost grinned in a ghastly manner. "For reasons neither of us will ever fathom."

"I find it painfully sad." The knight sagged against a pillar, grateful for its firm support.

"Your vicarious sympathy disgusts me! Tell me instead how progresses that clever killer who imitates my tales?"

Sir Arthur jumped. "There have been no further murders in more than four months," he said.

"Ah. . . . Then, the perpetrator is close to his intended victim."

"How do you deduce that?"

"The first crimes were to establish a pattern of madness. Having achieved that result, the assassin has the leisure to wait. When the time is right, he strikes, confident an unknown lunatic, a character of his own invention, will receive the blame." The specter began to fade, features a sudden blur.

"Wait!" Conan Doyle threw open his arms in supplication. "Stay! How can you be certain the killer isn't simply a madman?"

"Oh, he's mad enough . . ." The ghostly voice sighed like a distant wind. "But not at all simple. His crimes are complex. Although seemingly without motive, we must ask ourselves, for what purpose is such maniacal ingenuity intended? Logic suggests a plan of this complexity must be designed to serve some grand ambition . . ." Sir Arthur Conan Doyle strained to hear the ghost's last words even after nothing remained of Poe but a faint dust-devil whisper.

The end of the second week of their short autumn tour found the Houdinis in Detroit. They had a room at the Statler. Riding back up in the elevator after a shave and a haircut in the basement barbershop, the magician felt a pang of dread at the thought of returning so soon to New York. Out West for the summer, he knew they were safe. No harm would come to Bess as long as they stayed on the road.

The three days back in the city between tours had been a constant torment. He had the Burns Agency put a man on Bess round the clock and still he worried. Logistics and equipment repair kept him and Dash busy for long hours late into the night. There had been no time to meet with Conan Doyle, but they did speak twice over the telephone.

Sir Arthur told the magician of his recent detective work and of the negligible results. The knight warned him to stay on his guard, convinced the length of time since Vickery's murder indicated the killer prepared for his prime target. Easy enough to theorize, Houdini thought, if you were sailing home to England in two weeks.

As he let himself into their room, Bessie got up from the desk by the window and approached him with a puzzled look. She carried a red, white, and blue Cracker Jack box in one hand. "Harry . . . ?" she said. "We got something peculiar here."

"What is it?"

She handed him the Cracker Jacks. "This came in the mail."

"You didn't eat any of it, did you, Mike?" He followed her over to the desk, greatly agitated.

"Didn't even open it." She handed him a letter. "This came with it."

Houdini stared at the expensive linen stationery. An embossed ancient Egyptian ankh served as a letterhead. In a loopy feminine hand it read:

Osiris:

What is sweeter than going for the prize? Do you eat the candied popcorn and peanuts first, or do you immediately dig deep for treasure?

Guess what I do . . .

Consider Cracker Jacks a form of modern augury, dependable as the intestines of doves. The package comes to you at random. The unknown prize within is an omen. Look inside to know the future.

Isis

Houdini tore the wrapper and cardboard lid off the oblong box, pouring the contents out onto the desk blotter. "Don't eat this stuff!" he cried, sifting through the sticky kernels to uncover a square cellophane envelope. The magician scooped it up, the pink rubber pacifier clearly visible inside.

"What . . . ?" Bess wrinkled her nose in baffled exasperation.

"That woman means to destroy me."

"Who?" Suddenly frantic, Bess grabbed the prize from her husband's hand. "What's going on here, Harry?"

"Opal Crosby Fletcher . . ."

"What does she want with us? Tell me! Harry—"

The magician's eyes moistened with guilt. He trembled from an overwhelming urge to confess. To throw himself on his knees before Bess and beg her forgiveness. Unable in the end to confront the shame, Houdini took his wife by the hand and said: "God only knows how her mind works. Maybe she wants me to stick it in my mouth and stop giving lectures exposing phonies like her."

Bess giggled. "You'd look cute with this in your kisser," she said.

Houdini took the pacifier from her and tossed it on the Cracker Jack–littered desk. "I'm getting this stuff tested," he said. "Maybe it's poisoned."

"Oh, Harry. You're so melodramatic." Bess kissed him. "Just like one of your movie serials."

He held her close, wishing life guaranteed happy endings the way the flickers did.

25

TRICK OR TREAT

On October 31, 1923, Damon Runyon's column in the *New York American* ended with the following:

TRICKS . . .

All the spooks and goblins running around the streets tonight bring to mind a certain local ghoul who has been out of the action as of late. It is close to five months since we last hear a peep from the Poe Killer. Perhaps he has hung up his spurs.

Little Hymie says the P.K. went on summer vacation and so must be a swell. Nick the Greek offers three to five he strikes again before the year is out.

AND TREATS

Or, it just might be the P.K. is taking a powder as a result of the diligent police work of such as Sgt. James Patrick Heegan of homicide. It is Sgt. Heegan who first puts the department wise to the fact that gorillas plus blonds equals Poe. This selfsame triple-striper also turns up the only eyewitness to have seen the mysterious murderer in action.

A twenty-four-year veteran of the force, Sgt.
Heegan represents the finest tradition of law enforcement. He is part of a legion over 25,000 strong. No
wonder the Poe killer is on the run.

Of the four annual Grand Sabbaths celebrated in the Middle Ages,
Candlemas, Walpurgisnacht, Lammas, and All Hallows' Eve, when
witches and horned warlocks danced and fornicated under a full moon,
only one of the revels survived the Inquisitions of the Mother Church,
evolving over time into an innocent children's masquerade. Although
Halloween wasn't any sort of holiday back home, Sir Arthur and Lady
Jean both enjoyed dressing up and were delighted to receive an invitation
to a Grand Costume Ball downstairs in the Gold Room.

Jean took charge of the costumes, after a brief conference con-
firmed commedia dell'arte as their theme. With the help of the front
desk, she located a theatrical firm called Brooks and conducted the
entire business over the telephone. When Conan Doyle saw the selection
delivered to their suite, he patted his tummy, protesting he was only fit
to appear as the portly Mountebank or the bombastic Capitano.

"Nonsense," Jean chided. "I'm going as Columbine, so you'll have
to be either Harlequin or Pierrot."

Sir Arthur fingered the gaudy fabric. His good-natured grumping
masked extreme pleasure. "If I wear the particolor tights I'll look like a
circus ball. And Pierrot is so wistful. The unrequited lover. Might make
me too dour."

Jean laughed. "I remember you as an unrequited lover," she said,
kissing his cheek. "You were never, ever dour."

"Never in public anyway."

In the end, he went as Pierrot, spared the discomfort of a mask
with his face powdered white. The flowing white garments concealed
more than mere girth; his service revolver hung at his side, the swivel
mount in the butt clipped to a lanyard looped over his shoulder.

Conan Doyle carried the Webley-Green with him everywhere since returning to New York. It stayed snug in his pocket when the knight made another trip to the Polo Grounds, three days after seeing Poe's ghost in Fordham. He was once again the guest of Damon Runyon, only this time to witness a World Series game. Knowing nothing of baseball, Sir Arthur listened intently as the reporter provided a play-by-play description. Runyon called it a "subway series," with the National League Giants pitted against the formidable Yankees of the American League. This was the second game of the contest, the Giants taking the opener by a single run in brand-new Yankee Stadium across the Harlem River in the Bronx.

Sir Arthur sat with Runyon in the first row of the press box behind home plate, peering through protective chicken-wire mesh. The reporter hammered at his portable typewriter, a narrow plank serving the press as a work table, and commented on the action out of the corner of his mouth between staccato bursts of two-fingered typing. To the Englishman, there didn't seem to be much action, as the game moved slowly as cricket, always more fun to play than watch. He appreciated the information nevertheless.

In the fourth inning, with the count at two and one, the big Bambino, Babe Ruth, knocked one out of the park. In the fifth, Ruth homered again with a long line drive into the right field stands. Even the placid Runyon seemed excited. "That ties the record," he shouted. "Only two other players have ever scored two home runs in a single World Series game."

When Ruth stepped to the plate in the top of the ninth, the crowd went wild with anticipation. "They'll walk him," came Runyon's laconic comment. The sportswriter was wrong. At manager McGraw's signal, the pitcher threw a low curve and the Sultan of Swat hammered the ball deep into center field. The entire crowd jumped, screaming, to its feet. It looked certain to be another home run. Sir Arthur found himself hoarse with cheering. Two strides from the backfield fence, Casey Stengel, the lithe Giant outfielder, leaped high into the air and did the impossible, snagging the ball at the top of his reach.

"Tough luck," muttered Damon Runyon. The knight detected a slight frown of disappointment on the reporter's implacable poker-faced features.

The Gold Room pulsed with boisterous confusion, overflowing in an exotic carnival cavalcade of costumed celebrants. Although an occasional devil or witch acknowledged the evening's occult heritage, they were lost in a backlot polyglot of Napoleons, Arab sheiks, mikados, Buffalo Bills, Marie Antoinettes, Joans of Arc, matadors, knights in armor, Little Tramps, and Argentine gauchos.

Paul Whiteman's orchestra blared above the general hubbub. Just back from a triumph in London, the portly "King of Jazz" bobbed up and down on his toes, waving his baton with an air of self-importance wondrous to behold. His music, a bubbling confection of bouncy dance tunes only a white audience would ever call jazz, had charmed His Royal Highness, the Prince of Wales, who gave the world the Windsor knot and plus fours. Anyone desiring to hear the real thing went uptown to Harlem and took a table at the newly opened Cotton Club, or at Barron's Cabaret on 134th Street, where Duke Ellington and his Washingtonians played their "jungle music" nightly.

Sir Arthur caught a glimpse of Whiteman's fleshy, pear-shaped face; the tiny, absurd, upturned cartoon mustaches, like a misplaced pair of eyebrows perching above a smug mortician's smile. Quite possibly the most ridiculous-looking human being on earth, thought the knight, twirling his lady across the dance floor in a fast fox-trot.

As they danced, the Webley-Green thumped against his ribs. Sir Arthur wondered at his precaution in bringing it. Surely, they remained safe in a crowded hotel ballroom. The killer required solitude for his sinister work. Solitude and silence. Perhaps a pistol would prove an inadequate defense against this deadly phantom, a notion raising the specter of another, more troubling thought.

Conan Doyle had not encountered the ghost of Poe since their chance afternoon meeting in the Bronx three weeks ago. He'd been back up to Fordham on several occasions, but no further sightings occurred. A curiously disturbing notion began taking shape in his imagination. He had once witnessed the spirit vomiting. This act contradicted everything spiritualism taught him to believe. Were ghosts capable of other, more disturbing deeds?

It seemed a mad thought. Try as he might to dislodge it, the thing persisted in his mind like a pestilence. If the murders were in essence supernatural, every other mystery fell into place: the paucity of clues and witnesses, the inexplicable lack of motive, the very insane, random nature of the crimes.

This notion of insanity troubled him. To most people, conversing with ghosts would be considered insane. And, as no one else had ever seen the Poe manifestation, wasn't it his word against the world? Quite an accurate definition of madness: to insist, in the face of all reason, on the validity of private visions.

The dance ended. Various friends and acquaintances recognized them and stopped to chat. Unable to shake his troubling thoughts, Sir Arthur excused himself, saying he needed some air. He left Jean conversing with Grover A. Whalen and his wife, costumed as Humpty-Dumpty and Little Bo Peep, and with Rodman Wanamaker, the department store heir, wrapped in a toga. The knight supposed he looked equally silly in his melancholy white clown's suit.

Stepping from the ballroom into a spacious corridor, Sir Arthur immediately noticed the figure costumed as the Red Death standing among a half-dozen other masqueraders. A small person, no more than five feet tall; made grand by the voluminous, hooded scarlet cloak; made hideous by an ingenious mask, shreds of realistic rubber flesh peeling away from the Grim Reaper's gleaming ivory skull. Hollow, eyeless sockets stared straight at Conan Doyle.

Against his better judgment, Sir Arthur approached. The grotesque, diminutive Red Death looked up at him and croaked: "Once upon a midnight dreary . . ."

The knight thought the gravelly voice spurious, perhaps designed to disguise the more lilting speech of a woman. "While I pondered weak and weary," he answered.

A high cackling laugh emanated from the grinning, gap-toothed mouth. "Quoth the raven . . . ?" inquired the Red Death.

"Nevermore," answered Sir Arthur Conan Doyle, a tingle of excitement raising hackles on the back of his neck.

"Are you an admirer of Poe?"

The knight marveled at the uncanny realism of the death mask, remembering autopsies performed on putrid cadavers. "The master of all who love the mysterious," he replied.

"Would you say the mysterious murders done in his name were worthy of the master?"

"I haven't considered their aesthetic implications," Sir Arthur snapped.

"But you have given the matter some thought?" The Red Death turned in a half-circle around the knight, the crimson cloak flaring. "The newspapers intimate you have taken on the case. Sherlock on the trail."

Conan Doyle bristled. "You have the advantage over me, as I am unaware of your identity."

"Please . . . indulge my passion for anonymity." The grotesque, hooded figure ceased pacing. "Did you know Hilda Esp worked here at the Plaza?"

"Hilda Esp . . . ?"

"Mother of Ingrid. A laundress. Worked in the basement laundry. Does this interest you?"

"Very much." Sir Arthur studied the mannerisms of the costumed figure, at a loss in assigning any particular sex to the exaggerated gestures.

"If you've had access to the police files, you'll know one of the peculiar aspects of the Esp case is that almost no blood was found in the apartment. Hilda Esp had her throat cut, yet there was hardly any blood. Strange . . ."

"Very strange."

"It is my contention Hilda Esp was killed elsewhere and her body transported from the murder site to the apartment."

"Have you evidence to substantiate this theory?"

The Red Death swept the cloak across one shoulder. "I believe she was murdered in the basement of this hotel. I know the spot."

"How is it that you come by such knowledge?" Sir Arthur crossed his arms on his chest so he might feel the bulk of the revolver under his loose-fitting tunic.

"I have done some investigating of my own." The Red Death took a step down the corridor, beckoning the knight to follow. "Would you care to see what I have found?"

Sir Arthur tried to temper the sudden thrill of the chase with cautious evaluation. He clearly enjoyed considerable advantage in size and weight. Moreover, he carried a concealed weapon. Conan Doyle felt confident of handling any situation that might arise. "I'd be delighted," he said, excited at the possibility of being in the presence of the actual murderer. "Lead on."

A door marked EXIT at the end of the corridor opened onto uncarpeted service stairs. Conan Doyle followed the cloaked figure clanging down the steps. Reaching the bottom, the Red Death held open a scuffed metal door. As Sir Arthur stepped into an arched passageway, he was careful not to turn his back on the costumed stranger.

"We're in the subbasement." The Red Death led the way down the dim corridor. Occasional hanging low-wattage bulbs provided minimal illumination. The shadowy bare brick walls echoed their muffled footfalls. "Not too many ever come down here."

They passed a low-ceilinged chamber heaped with bundles of dirty linen. Two colored women separated the towels from the sheets on a long bleached-plank table. "Sorting room," commented the stranger like a demonic tour guide. "Laundry's around the corner."

The two masqueraders continued to where a drab canvas dropcloth concealed a breach in the wall. It had the look of recent construction, the work unfinished, temporarily suspended; everything tidied up in a makeshift way. The Red Death stood upon a nail keg, taking two electric torches down from a shelf mounted under a row of cast-iron pipes. "We'll need these from here on," he said, handing one to Conan Doyle.

Switching on his light, the stranger stepped behind the canvas curtain. Sir Arthur followed. He found himself in a dark, unfinished alcove. The air smelled of dampness and earth, like a fresh-dug grave. The knight saw the stranger's light about twenty paces ahead. "This way," called the Red Death.

Sir Arthur took his time, flashing the light beam around to get his bearings. He spotted a wheelbarrow and a pile of bricks. The vaulted ceiling dripped with hanging strands of niter, like white moss. The knight stared up. A sudden jolt of apprehension: why had two torches been waiting so conveniently? A reassuring glance at the second light further along allowed him to exhale. He flicked his light in the stranger's direction.

With the unheard stealth of a pouncing cat, something lithe and strong landed on Sir Arthur's back. The knight spun around in the darkness, swinging his torch like a club, as a tight-fitting leather sack pulled down over his head. Inside, it reeked of chloroform. His assailant leapt soundlessly off his back. The torch clattered on the concrete floor.

Desperate, Sir Arthur reached up at whatever enclosed his head. It was a sort of eyeless mask, fastened from behind with buckles. The harsh chemical whirled through his brain. Clumsy fingers fumbled at the straps. Catherine wheels and kaleidoscopes spun before his bound eyes. The knight reached under his flouncy clown shirt for the hanging revolver as he plummeted forward into unconsciousness.

Conan Doyle had no notion of where he was or how he got there when spasms of nausea brought him back from the lost, black depths. A candle flickered on the floor by his feet. He sat on a narrow concrete ledge, one hand chained to a water pipe running along the wall above his head. Only this kept him from falling on his face.

Sir Arthur squinted into the pale corona of light, groggy from chloroform. Beside him on the ledge stood a squat amber wine bottle with the cork drawn. He heard a metallic clink. Looking up, the knight confronted a rising brick wall two arms' lengths in front of him. It stood eight or nine courses high. The Red Death worked with a trowel, smoothing a layer of mortar before setting another brick in place.

"Ah, Sir Arthur, so good to have you awake again." The fake voice rasped behind the macabre mask. "I trust you had a peaceful rest."

Conan Doyle groped for his revolver and found the lanyard dangling free beneath his arm.

The Red Death held up the Webley-Green, pinching the barrel between his fingers like a greengrocer showing off a prize carrot. "I'm certain you appreciate the necessity of relieving you of this."

Sir Arthur heard the pistol clang off in the darkness like a piece of discarded iron pipe. Another course of bricks rose before him. "This addition was scheduled for completion a month ago . . ." The masked stranger talked on as he worked. "Then, the supervising engineer was fired. Now, there's disagreement between the new firm and the city building inspectors. Be at least another month or two before the issue is resolved and any work resumes . . ."

The knight made no reply. He felt thick and drugged. The Red Death set the final row, wielding his trowel delicately as a pastry chef icing a wedding cake. Only one brick remained to complete the wall. "Should you get thirsty . . ." The hideous skull peered through the aperture. "I've left you a very nice wine. *In pace requiescat!*" The final brick slid into place.

Sir Arthur was alone. Far off, penetrating the deathly silence, he heard the steady drip of what he presumed to be water. He rubbed his eyes on the loose sleeve of his absurd Pierrot costume. Be more appropriate if he'd worn Harlequin's lozenge-patterned motley. That costume even had bells to jingle.

He picked up the bottle beside him, sniffing the fruity amontillado. Doubtless poisoned. It would be to the killer's advantage for him to die as quickly as possible. Less risk of premature discovery.

He set the bottle down. Perhaps in a few days' time, he'd welcome a drink. Best thing not to panic, he told himself. It seemed preposterous that he shouldn't soon be found. He resided in one of the world's great hotels, not some forgotten Italian catacomb. Surely those laundresses would hear him.

"Halloo!" he shouted. "Is anybody there?" No answer. He sat very still, listening to the distant dripping.

Conan Doyle lurched to his feet. Even stretching his chain out full-length, he was unable to touch the new wall with his other hand, the wet mortar inches from his fingertips. Don't go yelling your head off before hearing someone approach, he thought. Must conserve my strength.

Stooping, he picked the burning candle off the floor, raising it for a better look at his surroundings. He was immured within a narrow masonry-walled niche twice as long as it was broad, his right hand fastened to a water pipe on the rear wall by a pair of steel handcuffs. He tried tugging on the chain, although attempting to bend the pipe appeared a futile exercise.

Taking a closer look, Sir Arthur noticed the broad arrow and crown marking the case-hardened steel. Jersey Giants! By God, these were Scotland Yard darbies! The knight rapped the handcuff soundly against the stone wall as Houdini had taught him. The lock snapped open at once and his wrist came free.

Wasting no time, Conan Doyle stepped to the fresh-laid wall. The mortar had not yet dried. He leaned his full weight against the bricks and the wall began to bulge. He pushed harder. The bricks sagged outward and Sir Arthur raised his hands above his head as, all at once, the wall collapsed around him.

The knight staggered through the darkened alcove. He pushed the tarp aside and stepped into the corridor. Not a soul in sight. Not a sound.

The two electric torches sat on the shelf. Sir Arthur took one and returned to the alcove. After searching for a few moments, he found his revolver. He picked it up, carefully using his pocket handkerchief. Another twenty minutes' probing revealed no further clues. The knight had learned one thing with absolute certainty: the killer was no ghost.

The diminutive assailant who tackled him from behind had been very corporal indeed.

At 6:00 A.M. the following morning, Harry Houdini and Sir Arthur Conan Doyle breakfasted together in the restaurant at Central Station in Buffalo, New York. The knight's telegram had reached the magician at the Statler in Detroit just as his troupe was making the jump to Chicago. Houdini arranged for them to go on ahead and caught the next eastbound train. Sir Arthur spent the night on the New York Central "Wolverine." Both of them had the rumpled look of men who had slept in their clothes.

Houdini listened intently as the Englishman told his story a second time. Hearing about the Jersey Giants made him grin, although his eyes remained grim and brooding. "Think there's any chance the police might find fingerprints on your revolver?" he asked.

Sir Arthur shook his head. "I didn't call the police. I sent you a wire instead. It was my conclusion the authorities would assume I'd made the whole thing up for the sake of publicity. I can assure you there are no fingerprints. The Los Angeles County sheriff's department gave my boys a fingerprinting kit as a gift. I confiscated it when I found their bed sheets smeared with ink. Last night, I made use of it, dusting the revolver with silver powder. Sorry to say, the only prints I uncovered were my own."

"Let me play the devil's advocate," Houdini said, "and this is not meant to take anything away from what you experienced, but what makes you so certain this really was the Poe Killer and not just some drunken prankster?"

"Because unless it was a policeman versed on the case, which I sincerely doubt, only the actual killer would be privy to such a telling detail as the absence of blood. You didn't know about that. Nor did I."

"Maybe the prankster made it up?"

Sir Arthur pounded his huge fist on the tabletop. "Damn it! This was no prank!"

"Relax. I believe you." Houdini prodded a bit of cold scrambled egg with the tip of his fork. "You're sure it was a woman?"

"She was very strong. But, judging from her size and the way she disguised her voice, I feel reasonably certain in making this determination."

"It's Isis," Houdini muttered. "Has to be."

"Might well be. But you can offer nothing but conjecture. It's proof we need."

"Remember the tone in her voice when she made her dire predictions about Halloween?" Houdini pushed his plate away. "She was threatening us, and she knew it. Easy enough to be a prophet when you carry out the predictions yourself."

Sir Arthur filled his pipe. "I have a séance scheduled with Mrs. Fletcher. Six in the evening, November third."

Houdini's eyes brightened. "I have a plan. Who all knows what happened to you?"

"Only yourself and my wife."

"Perfect." The magician permitted himself a thin smile. "As far as the murderer is concerned, you are a dead man. Nothing must occur to alter that perception. You have to stay out of sight for the next two days. Take a hotel room here in Buffalo. Use an assumed name."

"My dear fellow, what you suggest is preposterous."

"Hear me out. The murderer thinks you dead. I'm safe until I return to New York. Longer, really, because I'm sure the killer won't strike again until after your body is found."

"Whatever are you talking about? There's no body to find."

"Of course not, but the killer doesn't know that. By not revealing yourself in public, she'll continue to believe you're walled up in the sub-basement of the Plaza. Send your wife a telegram so she won't worry. Better yet, have her announce you've turned up missing."

"That's absurd! I could never ask Jean to do such a thing."

"All right. Have her say nothing. Just don't show yourself. Then, when you arrive for your séance with Isis, you'll know immediately by her expression whether she's guilty or not. If she is the killer, she won't be expecting you. She won't have made any preparations for the séance."

Sir Arthur grinned. "What an excellent idea. If Mrs. Fletcher is the woman who attacked me, I'll see it instantly in her eyes."

"Be on your guard." Houdini consulted his watch. "I have a train to catch if I'm going to be in Chicago for tonight's performance." He placed a half-dollar on the table. "Breakfast's on me. You still have that revolver?"

"I'm carrying it now."

"Good." The magician pulled on his overcoat. "Make sure you're armed when you go for the séance. If Isis tries any funny stuff, don't hesitate to shoot her."

26

UNDER THE KNIFE

The Lincoln Gardens on Chicago's South Side featured the hottest musical aggregation in town, King Oliver's Creole Jazz Band. Catering to a rough clientele, the place served as an informal clubhouse for flashy yeggs from the Capone mob and every night saw its share of fights. Occasionally, the lethal staccato of gunfire punctuated the wailing New Orleans blues. Rather than driving people away, impending mayhem proved an irresistible draw and business was booming.

The gaudy barnlike dance hall had walls efflorescent with faded crepe paper blossoms and bright petals of peeling paint. A balcony corralling small, round tables ran along one side. Body heat, tobacco smoke, the astringent smell of sweat sweetened by a potpourri of cheap perfume and scented hair oil coalesced into a volatile miasma suggestive of sex and betrayal.

Slightly after ten o'clock on a weekday evening, the joint was just beginning to jump when Harry Houdini, still dressed in his stage tux, made a furtive entrance. Very much a fish out of water, he quietly took a table by the railing at the end of the balcony farthest from the bandstand. Energetic gangsters and their effervescent molls shook and shimmied, gyrating wildly through the intricacies of the Charleston and the Black Bottom as the band played "Froggy Moore," the "Alligator Hop," and "Canal Street Blues."

The magician held the opinion that he didn't care for jazz, although the music he so designated was a corny Tin Pan Alley hybrid bearing only a passing resemblance to this exuberant improvised polyphony pulsating with the shocking novelty of true art. Almost against his will, he found his foot tapping to the robust syncopations.

"Did this place used to be called the Royal Garden Cafe?" he asked a waiter still sneering in disbelief at his order. Lemonade wasn't the usual bill of fare on the South Side.

"Right. New name. New management," the apron-wrapped Sicilian replied, turning briskly on his heel.

Houdini pulled a crumpled piece of paper from his pocket and smoothed it on the tabletop. A typewritten message read:

Excuse me sir, I beg your Pardon,
I believe you wish to know
The whereabouts of Edgar Poe.
Just ask the King of the Royal Garden;
Say the password: Geronimo.
He will tell you where to go.

The magician found the doggerel in an envelope on his dressing room table after the second show at the Lyric Theater. Reading it made his hands tremble, even as he puzzled over the cryptic meaning. He asked one of the stagehands if there was someplace in town called the "Royal Garden" and received a detailed set of directions leading him to the rainbow-hued railing he leaned against.

Houdini studied the band, a Negro septet featuring two cornets, trombone, clarinet, piano, bass fiddle, and drums. The pianist was a lovely light-skinned woman barely out of her teens. The percussionist seemed not much older, a small, laughing man nearly hidden behind his huge bass drum. Their ensemble playing, collectively improvised, formed a seamless amalgam, with four distinct individual voices weaving in and out around the melody.

The leader stepped forward to blow a cornet solo on "Snake Rag."

A dark, formidable man whose rain-barrel physique recalled turn-of-the-century politicians, he appeared almost twice the age of the other musicians. His cheeks puffed as he blew chorus after chorus with such power his starched dickey popped free, curling up to reveal a red union suit. "Oh, Papa," shouted the bassist, "play that thing!"

Houdini sipped his lemonade, only half-listening. He thought about the mysterious poem, wondering what to do next. Assuming the reference to "the King" must indicate the cabaret's owner, he waved down a waiter to inquire if the proprietor was on the premises.

"You got a complaint?" If looks could kill, the waiter's surly scowl might have caused a massacre.

"No. Not at all. I merely want to talk with him. He isn't a gentleman named King, by any chance?"

The waiter jerked his thumb at the burly cornet player. "Only 'king' we got around here is him."

"Oh?"

"Joseph 'King' Oliver. Cornet king of the Crescent City. Don't you read? Name of the band is posted outside in big red letters." The waiter sauntered off, shaking his head. Rudeness obviously constituted a deliberate part of the dance hall's raffish charm.

Houdini glanced from the crumpled poem to the bandstand. The big man had been joined by the younger second cornet, and the two played a duet in fast, flawless harmony. The magician had performed with the incomparable Bert Williams, but on the whole, Negroes were a rarity on the vaude circuit, although there certainly was no shortage of blackface acts. He marveled at the jazz band's devil-may-care professionalism, at how much fun they seemed to be having.

After another twenty minutes, the musicians took a break. Houdini pushed back his chair and headed for the bandstand.

"Lord, Babe," the clarinet player said to the drummer, "you gonna kill somebody in that big red Oldsmobile of yours, 'specially the way you fill up on rotgut 'fore you drive. I gotta keep my eye on my baby brother."

"The Tiger's safe as they come," the trombone player said. "He fetches me to work every evening, and gets me there all in one piece." The others joined with his laughter.

"Excuse me," interjected the magician from the edge of the dance floor. "Mr. King . . . ?"

The whole band stopped talking, regarding the stocky white man quizzically. "Mr. King?" laughed the affable young second-cornetist. "That's you, Papa Joe."

"How you know that, Dippermouth?" the drummer demanded with a big grin. "Maybe I be Mr. King."

"King of what? King of talkin' trash?"

The imposing band leader stepped forward. "I'm Joe Oliver," he said with quiet dignity. "They call me King."

"Geronimo . . . ?" Houdini said tentatively.

King Oliver chuckled to himself. "So, it's you all right." The musician pulled a sealed envelope from the inside pocket of his tuxedo jacket and handed it to Houdini. "Man said I was to give this to you."

"What man?" He held the envelope with both hands, as if afraid it might get away.

"Man that gave me fifty dollars. Said a gentleman'd be comin' in bye-and-bye, don't matter who. He'd let me know by sayin' 'Geronimo,' and I was to give him the letter and not answer any questions."

Houdini pulled out his billfold. "I've got a hundred here for any information you can give me."

"Mister, save your money. I can't tell you a blessed thing more'n I've already done. It was a white gentleman. 'Bout your size, maybe a little shorter. I didn't pay it no nevermind, as we say down home."

"Bet you paid plenty mind to that there fifty," the impudent drummer sassed. All the musicians laughed, King Oliver loudest of all.

The young cornet player stared at the magician, his generous mouth curving into a smile. "Say. I know you," he said. "You're the Great Houdini. I saw you escape from a strait jacket once in downtown Saint Louie. I was workin' the riverboats with Fate Marable."

"I saw him in that movie," the drummer enthused. "He was froze-up in a great big ol' iceberg."

The magician smiled, nodding in uncomfortable silence. "I am Houdini," he said at last, backing away. "Always a pleasure . . . to meet my fans."

Houdini backed almost to the middle of the empty dance floor before he turned and made a beeline for the exit.

The comely pianist smiled at the boys in the band. "He mailed out the invitations," she said softly, "but weren't nobody home."

The envelope contained a newspaper article torn from a late edition of the Chicago *Tribune*. Four inches on the closing of the historic Majestic Theater, the old vaude house to be converted into a motion picture palace. "I had no choice," the story quoted owner Izzy Finkleman. "Better I should knock it down and open a parking lot?" The address was Sixty-fifth and Cottage Grove.

A lonely survivor from the era of Booth, Drew, and Minnie Maddern Fiske, the Majestic had seen better days, her soot-darkened Moorish details frosted with pigeon droppings like a widow in the snow. Houdini had the cab driver drop him half a block down from the abandoned theater in a dark, deserted neighborhood. Not surprisingly, Mr. Finkleman's box office had fallen off. The magician walked along the opposite side of the street, keeping in the shadows close to the buildings.

Concealed in the darkened entrance of a boarded-up hardware store, Houdini surveyed the surroundings. A narrow, graveled alley ran along the back side of the old theater. No automobiles parked within a block of the building. Traffic on Cottage Grove remained sparse. After waiting fifteen uneventful minutes, the magician crossed the street and ducked into the alley.

He found the stage door sealed tight with a padlock completely familiar to him. Inserting a simple pick formed from a bent piece of wire, the magician bypassed the wards inside. He felt the bolt shoot free and the lock popped open.

Silently, Houdini eased the stage door ajar, confronting an ominous damp darkness as foreboding as the interior of a mausoleum on a moonless night. His every instinct warned of inherent danger, but a lifetime of risk-taking inured him to apprehension and he stepped inside without further thought, pressing his back to the wall beside the open door.

Houdini groped for a light switch. Finding none, he stood motionless, listening to the even beat of his heart. A faint illumination from the alley glowed in the doorway beside him and as his eyes gradually became accustomed to the greater dark within, he made out a black line dividing the shadows above his head. He reached up to grasp a grimy cord and hanging glass bulb. Houdini pulled the short chain. Sudden glare made him squint.

It looked no different from a thousand other stage entrances framing his life over the years: bare brick walls, utilitarian iron-pipe railings on the stairs, a list of management rules (KEEP IT CLEAN) pinned to a call board near the door. Houdini stood very still, studying his surroundings. His footprints marked a scuffed trail through the dust gently powdering the forgotten premises like the ashes of memory. He saw at a glance no one else had entered this way in a very long time.

Houdini closed the door and drew the dead bolt, remembering a prankster who'd locked him in a hotel lobby telephone closet. He never went in one afterwards without wedging his foot in the doorway. The light from the single dangling bulb carried past the dressing room stairs, revealing a portion of bare stage under the flies. A control box hung above the rows of dimmer-switches along the far wall. The magician considered his next move.

Other than his penknife and a couple simple lock-picks, Houdini carried no tools. He didn't consider the implications of being unarmed. Over the years, confronting difficult jailhouse challenges, the magician had made a habit of concealing vital implements on his person; the lock-pick and other tiny devices in his mop of wiry hair, a thin strip of spring steel inserted into the callus on his heel. Once, he hid all his tools in a tiny blue serge sack, which he hooked to the back of the warden's suit collar before being strip-searched, and then deftly plucked free as he was led naked to the waiting cell.

Houdini wrapped one of his lock-picks in a torn corner of a pocket handkerchief and swallowed it. Retroperistalsis gripped the little bundle halfway down his throat. Feeling it there provided a sense of security. He walked cautiously to the dimmers. The magician opened the control box and threw a master switch, turning on the worklights overhead. A second master lit up the house.

Houdini glanced above at the dust-festooned gridiron in the empty flies: ropes, sandbags, and pulley systems long gone. The stage yawned wide and open with the tormentors and teasers removed. Only a memory of the curtain remained in the stark, open proscenium. Some sort of scaffolding stood center stage. Houdini ignored it, looking out at row after row of dusty seats. A man stared back at him from the center of the house.

The magician froze, locking into the stranger's unblinking gaze. There was something vaguely familiar about the old-fashioned clothing and nineteenth-century hair styling; the abrupt mustache. Houdini shuddered. The man's makeup and costume made him resemble Edgar Allan Poe.

The man didn't move. He never blinked. The magician left the stage, finding a set of stairs leading to an exit under the box seats. The man dressed like Poe hadn't moved a muscle. He stared straight ahead like someone in a trance.

Houdini walked between the seats one row in front of the immobile stranger. "I got your poem," he said as he approached. "What's with the scavenger hunt?"

The magician received no reply and saw immediately why. It wasn't a man at all, but a plaster department store dummy togged-out in antebellum clothing and folded stiffly into the theater seat. From up close, the figure looked nothing at all like Poe, but the effect had been very convincing at a distance. A small cardboard sign rested on the mannequin's lap. A single word crayoned upon it. NEVERMORE.

The lights went out. Houdini spun around. Too dark on stage to see who had thrown the master switches. The magician strained to hear if anyone approached along the curving rows of seats. His body tensed, awaiting attack.

It came from behind, where he least expected trouble. An acrobatic assailant leaped onto his back, pulling a hood down over his head. Chloroform! Nauseating. Chemical. Overwhelming. Houdini grabbed hold of his attacker. Whoever it was broke instantly free, jumping away from the magician.

Pulling at the confining hood, Houdini found it tightly buckled in back. The fastenings locked together in some unfamiliar mechanical manner. As the anesthesia rapidly overwhelmed his senses, he groped in his pocket for the penknife, pulling open the single, razor-sharp blade. Houdini willed himself to remain alert. Slicing through the restraining straps, he never stopped working until his knees buckled under him and he collapsed into unconsciousness.

Swimming up from dark, cold depths through the vortex of a powerful whirlpool, Houdini opened his eyes and the world continued to spin, a sickening multicolored blur making his stomach lurch. Attempting to sit, he found himself restrained. He lay flat on his back, arms outspread like a man on a cross, each wrist manacled to the floor, his tethered legs bound together at the ankles. He was stark naked, pinioned on the stage beneath the scaffolding observed earlier.

A strange hooded figure stood on the apron, watching him. The long flowing garment and tall conical hood put the magician immediately in mind of the Ku Klux Klan. Was he the prisoner of racist bigots? On second thought, the sinister garb possessed a stiff formality not usually associated with the hasty bed-sheet habits of night riders. Houdini recognized the traditional robe of the Grand Inquisitor. Just such an anonymous official once condemned heretics to the *auto-da-fé*.

"Awake at last," the Inquisitor said. "I feared you might well sleep through the whole show. Certainly a pity, missing all the action." Houdini found the clipped, lilting voice very familiar. The hooded figure swept toward him across the empty stage. "If I may allow myself a self-congratulatory pat on the back, it was a most excellent trap, and how eagerly you took the bait."

Houdini stared up at the Inquisitor, desperate to control his rising gorge.

The nonstop boasting continued, acidic with scorn. "I'm most proud of the dust by the stage door. Didn't you find it convincing? I used face powder, an ironic theatrical touch, of which I'm quite fond. Ditto, the misdirection of the lights. I convinced you the source was on stage. When I switched everything off, you incorrectly assumed the threat came from the front of the house and most obligingly turned your back to the real danger."

The magician contained a volcanic rage. He didn't like playing the fool. Having his nose rubbed in his own foolishness angered him all the more. Stifling the impulse to curse and shout, he grinned through gritted teeth. No percentage in revealing his emotional state to the enemy. Houdini composed his features, although he feared his blazing eyes gave him away.

"You're strangely silent, Harry," the Inquisitor said. "It's not like you."

Who was this bastard with his easy familiarity, Houdini wondered. Where had he heard that peculiar accent before? The voice sounded definitely masculine. Sir Arthur had guessed wrong. The killer was not a woman.

"I trust you've been keeping up on your Poe . . . ?" The hooded assassin swirled beneath the framework of joined pipes. "I saved the very best especially for you."

Houdini's gaze followed the Inquisitor's uplifted, pointing finger, noting a hairy, muscled forearm when the robe's capacious sleeve fell back. Fifteen feet above his head, he observed a curious mechanism mounted to the top of the scaffolding: an eccentric collection of cogs and gears resembling the innards of a huge clock. In place of a pendulum, a curved, weighted blade hung motionless like the guillotine's infernal knife. A keen razor edge caught the light with a sinister glitter.

"Clever device." The Inquisitor chuckled smugly. "A rachet lowers the pendulum one-quarter inch at every swing. Tested it out on a stray dog yesterday. Most effective. The canine's body did not impede the oscillation of the blade in the slightest. Just like slicing luncheon meat. Beast kept on howling until his backbone severed. . . . Will you howl for me, Harry?"

"Fuck you!" The magician spat the forbidden phrase, the first time in his life he had ever voiced so distasteful a profanity.

"Righty-o. . . . Glad the cat hasn't got your tongue. I'm so looking forward to hearing you beg for mercy."

"Lemme up and we'll see who does the begging," Houdini snarled.

"Still have some fight left? That's good. Very good. . . . I trust you'll put on an excellent show; one of your masterful escape attempts . . ." The Inquisitor produced Houdini's penknife and the extra lock-pick from under the folds of his robe. "Of course, this time you'll have to do so without the aid of these. While you slept like a baby, I took the liberty of conducting a thorough search."

The magician glanced away, spotting his clothing in a discarded bundle several yards off. No help there.

"You should have a word with your tailor," the Inquisitor said, leaning against the scaffold's framework. "Such shoddy workmanship. . . .Afraid I took some liberties with the Poe narrative. As you must recall, his unfortunate hero remains tied for days under the knife. I simply don't have that kind of time at my disposal."

The Inquisitor pulled a cord hanging from the mechanism above. The whir and clank of an escapement and regulator set in motion started the pendulum swinging with a steady sweep. "About two seconds for each complete arc. At that rate, the blade should strike the floor in no more than twenty minutes. Perfect length for a headline act."

"Enjoy the show." Houdini made it sound like a threat.

"Oh, believe me, I plan on doing just that. Your last performance. I do hope the great escapologist won't disappoint."

The Grand Inquisitor hurried off the stage. Houdini watched him take a seat, front and center. Looking away, the magician studied the handcuffs securing him. His right wrist was fastened by a pair of American Bean handcuffs to a ring bolt screwed into the stage. Regulation U.S. Army cuffs secured his left in a similar fashion. Neither presented a real problem. Houdini glanced up at the slow silver sweep of the pendulum, every passage succinctly calibrating the remaining seconds of his life.

Houdini regurgitated the cloth-wrapped pick. As his tongue unwound the torn hanky, he breathed slowly and deeply, willing every muscle to relax. He kept his eyes on the silent swing of the scimitar, matching his heartbeat to the steady metronome rhythm.

The magician stared down at his rope-bound feet, wrapped with a length of chain and padlocked to a ring bolt. He lowered his head, rehearsing the moves in his mind. The Inquisitor presented the biggest problem. Houdini estimated the time it would take the bastard to rush the stage with his chloroform. Fifteen seconds . . . ? Maybe twenty at most, but only if he stayed alert. The magician needed to borrow more time.

Houdini lay motionless, hoping to lull the enemy into inattention. The magician's tongue carefully rolled the torn cloth around the end of the pick to give his teeth an additional grip. Better not wait too long, either, he reasoned. Son of a bitch is sure to get all hot and bothered during the finale.

Houdini stared at the descending pendulum scything ever closer. He'd wait until it closed half the distance. Having made the decision, he gave it no further thought. He used the time to run through the moves, rehearsing them in his mind over and over again, concentrating on smoothness and speed. When the moment for action arrived, the magician would have mentally made the escape many times.

Houdini watched the sibilant swing of the blade and thought of Poe. The unnamed narrator in his story didn't escape until the pendulum actually sliced through the fabric of his robe. He rubbed food on the ropes binding him and rats chewed him free. A true cliff-hanger. Houdini also raced the clock, but it was not the razor's edge he feared. The ten minutes remaining in the pendulum's deadly descent allowed plenty of time to effect an escape. The twenty seconds it would take the killer to gain the stage imposed a more stringent deadline.

The magician planned his first move to be undetectable, slowly sliding the lock-pick up between his lips, grasping the cloth-bound portion in his teeth. He didn't want the Inquisitor to notice. Too early to start the clock ticking.

"What's the matter, Harry . . . ?" the plummy voice called from the auditorium. "Giving up without a try?"

Hasn't seen a thing, the magician thought, imperceptibly tensing his arm and shoulder muscles, drawing his legs ever more taut against the length of chain restraining them. His back arched like a bow. With extreme effort, Houdini slowly crossed his ankles beneath the bonds. He heard the Inquisitor's fitful cough. Bastard didn't have a clue.

The trick was to gain some slack. With slack anything became possible. Houdini didn't mind the pain. He had trained himself to dislocate his shoulders, an excruciating procedure, in order to gain enough slack to slip the cross-bound sleeves of a strait jacket up over his head. The magician's ankles were double-jointed, capable of amazing contortions. He ignored the pain.

The time had come. Houdini thrust violently forward, uncrossing his ankles in the same sudden moment. He gained a few precious millimeters of slack in the loop of chain. Drawing up his knees with a sudden jerk, he bent his feet into an exaggerated dancer's point. The chain slipped free, scraping away a superficial layer of flesh.

"Bravo, Harry!" The Inquisitor applauded. "Well done, indeed!"

Houdini sneaked a peak at the hooded killer. The damned fool just sat there clapping his hands. Perfect. An unintentional gift providing precious extra seconds. The magician's legs remained bound by rope, but this was of little consequence. In a fluid contortionist's move, he lifted them together and plucked the lock-pick from his teeth with the toes of his right foot.

"Harry . . . ?" The Inquisitor rose in his seat.

The next move was critical. The magician bent to the side, his bound feet reaching for his outstretched wrist, turned so the keyhole on the Bean cuffs faced up. His prehensile toes readied the lock-pick. Deftly, he slipped it inside.

"Damn you!" The Inquisitor struggled over the seat in front of him. "You're going to die, Houdini!"

The magician concentrated on the feel of the pick, ignoring the frantic sounds of the killer's desperate scramble. He held his breath, focusing his entire attention on the problem at hand. Years of performing precise manipulations underwater had taught him never to rush or panic. Somewhere, far off, the Grand Inquisitor snorted like a savage beast.

Houdini felt the pick in place. His toes gave it a half turn and the lock snapped open. Wrenching his wrist free, the magician caught a glimpse of the robed killer crashing into the orchestra pit. Ten seconds! Houdini fingered the handcuff, not finding the lock-pick. It had fallen out of the keyhole. He slid his searching hand across the dusty stage floor as the Inquisitor stumbled through a thicket of wooden folding chairs, kicking them aside in a frenzy.

The magician's fingertips slid upon the lock-pick's reassuring shape. He seized it and rolled to his left, inserting the pick into the army cuffs in the same motion. Government issue. Simplest mechanism of all. A slight twist and the lock was open. Houdini sat straight up, turning to face his attacker, expecting to see him mounting the stage. The Inquisitor was nowhere in sight. Suddenly, all the lights went out.

In a single, swift motion, the magician jumped to his feet. He grabbed hold of the scaffolding and hauled himself aloft, working his bound legs like a single appendage. Safe at the top, perched above the clanking mechanism, Houdini untied the knots securing his feet. Somewhere in the distance, he heard a door slam. Assuming this to be further misdirection, he sat very still, listening for the killer's stealthy approach, holding the rope wound tightly around both his hands. When the time came, he would use it as a garrote.

27

BARNSTORMING

Night had never before seemed so dark. Blackness enclosed him in a void made mad by the rain-stung wind and the propeller's deafening roar. Houdini felt no sensation of movement, although the fabric-covered aircraft trembled from the exertions of the V-8 Hispano-Suiza engine. He held the throttle wide open, pushing the tachometer up over 1,200 rpms, higher than safety or prudence permitted.

The magician sat in the open cockpit of a war-surplus Curtiss Jenny, chilled to the bone in spite of an insulated one-piece flying suit with a fur collar, a leather helmet that buckled under his chin, a long woolen scarf, and goggles. Roiling storm clouds obscured both the stars overhead and their mirror-image, the occasional lights lost somewhere on the ground far below. Night and the foul weather commingled, creating a new dimension, one seemingly without space or time, black and empty as death itself.

Houdini gripped the stick in his gloved hand, the throttle in his left, thrilled to be at the controls of an aircraft once again. Famous as a pioneer aviator, the magician hadn't piloted a plane solo since those first flights in Australia more than thirteen years before. His boasts to Conan Doyle had been chiefly exaggeration; the spin in the Stinson while filming in California consisted merely of taking over from the pilot for a few minutes, cruising the clear blue skies above Hollywood. His longest flight in the old Voison was less than ten minutes. Two hours flying the Jenny far surpassed his lifetime total aloft.

Using a flashlight, Houdini studied the gauges on the instrument panel. The oil pressure remained steady; the altimeter indicated twelve thousand feet. Mail pilots never flew above the clouds at night, navigating from one bonfire to the next along their routes. No such beacons awaited the magician. Storm conditions demanded he seek an altitude where the wild, buffeting winds diminished. Upon takeoff, Houdini discovered the ceiling to be under one hundred feet. Afraid of flying so low in the gale's force, he climbed, slowly and patiently, high into darkness.

The magician was flying blind, navigating by the crude kerosene-filled "whisky" compass on the instrument panel. He held to a course of E-NE, according to directions received at the airfield, along with a tattered road map with the estimated flying times between refueling stops marked out in pencil. In many ways, his situation had not measurably changed from that four hours earlier when he had perched naked above the scaffolding on the dark, abandoned stage of the Majestic Theater.

Houdini had clung there, waiting to strangle his attacker, until his eyes adjusted to a faint light filtering into the auditorium. Darkness favored the enemy. Patience, together with a secure vantage point, were on the magician's side. Satisfied nothing moved in the shadows, Houdini climbed down and retrieved his clothes. It didn't take long to find the master light switch two rows behind the dummy. Further search revealed only an open lobby door and the discarded leather mask, still reeking of chloroform. The magician took it with him when he headed out into the night to flag down a cab.

It was 2:00 A.M. before the driver dropped him at an airdrome in Skokie. A light drizzle glistened on the grassy landing field. The place looked deserted. Like earthbound angels, silhouetted biplanes stood randomly grouped in front of darkened hangars. Houdini wasted no time in waking a night watchman from his dreams. At first, the big-bellied guard proved uncooperative, but the magician's intensity and a five-spot convinced him to search out a barnstorming pilot he remembered might have bedded down in Hangar B.

Desperate apprehension gnawed at Houdini. Sir Arthur's séance with Isis, scheduled for the next evening, plagued him with worry. Conan Doyle had every reason for believing her to be the killer. He carried a loaded revolver in his pocket. The unexpected proved commonplace with Isis. What if the knight misinterpreted her eccentric behavior? The chances of an accidental shooting seemed vividly possible. Haunted by an image of her pale flesh torn by bullets, the tiny fetus shattered within her womb, Houdini had attempted to place a toll call to Conan Doyle in New York, but was informed by the long distance operator that trunk lines down in an Indiana storm made this impossible. He had the taxi driver take him next to an all-night Western Union office and sent a wire to the Plaza Hotel, which he knew would not be delivered until the following morning. Following the burly night watchman through the rain, the magician implored him to hurry. Houdini had to reach New York in fifteen hours.

They found the barnstormer, a lanky, sandy-haired Midwesterner who'd flown Spads in France and called himself "Ace" although he hadn't actually seen any aerial combat, bundled in a tattered crazy quilt on a folding canvas cot at the rear of the empty hangar. Rubbing the sleep from his eyes, the pilot blinked at his unexpected visitors. "Fly you to New York, mister?" he grinned. "Sure thing. When do we leave?"

"Right now."

"You mean tonight?"

"The sooner the better." Houdini locked his eyes on the pilot like a man possessed.

"Hell, mister, I don't fly at night."

"I'll pay you fifty dollars."

"You can pay anything you like, I don't go up at night."

The magician remained undeterred. "What's the matter? Mail pilots fly at night."

"Then find yourself a mail pilot." The barnstormer wrapped the quilt around his shoulders, searching along a workbench for a pint bottle he'd hidden behind the metal lath. "We lost fifteen airmail pilots this year alone," he said, taking a slug. "Ain't that right, Charley?"

"It's a fact," Charley agreed.

Houdini looked at his watch. "You do own an airplane?" he asked, his sarcasm born of impatience.

"That's my JN-4D trainer parked outside. It's got an eight-cylinder Hisso engine. Whole lot better'n the Curtiss Challenger driving most Jennies. Sixty more horsepower."

"I'll give you three hundred dollars for it."

"What . . . ?"

"Three-fifty . . . cash."

"Mister, you just bought yourself a damned fine flying machine."

Twenty minutes later, Houdini was gassed up and in the air. Ace gave him the flight suit, along with a well-worn map and laconic directions, adding his personal belief that going up at night in bad weather was certain suicide.

Two hours into his flight, when the rain turned first to sleet and then to snow, Houdini felt inclined to agree with the barnstormer's assessment. Ice accumulated on the wooden struts connecting the wings. The wind licked horizontal icicles into sawtoothed spines along their back edges. The magician estimated a loss of altitude caused by the additional weight. Despite the bronze trophy hanging in his dining room, Houdini was not an experienced pilot. Had he been, he would have put the Jenny into a spin and descended to a warmer altitude. Instead, he gritted his teeth and pushed on into the storm.

Four inches of wind-driven ice encrusted each strut. Houdini heard them creak, a wail of pain above the engine's roar. They didn't appear strong enough to withstand the extra weight. If even one snapped, he was a goner. Without support, the fabric wings would buckle, shredding under the force of the slipstream.

A prolonged groan of straining wood determined the magician's desperate decision. He stabilized the stick, wrapping it in a length of rope tied to either side of the cockpit. Searching under the seat, Houdini uncovered a toolbox. He rummaged among the wrenches jumbled inside until his fingers closed around the haft of a ball peen hammer. With this tool in hand, he eased himself out of the cockpit on the port side, grasping a diagonal guy as he stepped onto the ice-slick wing.

The blast of rushing wind caught him like laundry hung on a line. He clung to the turnbuckle-tightened cable, struggling to maintain his footing as the gale raged, roaring in his ears louder than a passing express train. The magician thought of his Hollywood stunt doubles with their safety harnesses and connecting wires and, for a brief ironic moment, regretted he had no camera present to capture the most daring exploit of his long career.

Edging warily along the wing, left hand gripping the vibrating cable, Houdini chipped ice away from the struts, one at a time, tapping the hammer with the delicate touch of a sculptor, afraid too strong a blow might fracture the frozen wood. Suddenly, the biplane veered, lifting on a massive updraft. The magician's feet skidded out from under him and, for a terrifying moment, he hung in space by one hand, desperately trying not to drop the precious hammer.

Hooking his elbow around the guy, Houdini slid to his knees on the slick, bucking wing. The Jenny yawed and pitched in the wind. Struggling upright, the magician resumed his steady chipping. It took another fifteen minutes for him to finish the job. The starboard wing took twice as long.

The storm raged through the waning hours of the night. Houdini flew on, navigating by compass. Just before daybreak, he again climbed out on the wings to chip ice off the struts. After more than three hours of flight, the Jenny ran low on fuel and the magician spun down through the tempest, emerging out of the clouds in the hazy dawn over the barren, harvested farmland of eastern Ohio.

He soon cut across a muddy highway. Following it for a few miles led to a medium-sized town situated on a railroad crossing. Houdini circled once, close enough to read CHEW MAIL POUCH painted on the side of a big red barn and JESUS SAVES emblazoned on the water tower. As luck would have it, he spotted a filling station and cafe just opposite a fallow five-acre field. The magician throttled back for a smooth, easy landing, barely traveling at the speed of a coasting bicycle when his wheels touched down on the sere grass.

Catering to a farming community, the establishment opened early and Houdini was fueled up and back in the air in under twenty minutes, with a full thermos of hot coffee and a paper sack stuffed with sandwiches. His arrival had not gone undetected. Before he took off, a small crowd gathered around the biplane, mostly curious children on their way to school. They stood staring, somber and silent, breath steaming in the chill November air, while he taxied to the end of the field. Several of the bolder ones waved as he roared past, skimming away over the treetops. Ever the showman, Houdini waved energetically back. Not one of them recognized him.

The ceiling lifted to well over a thousand feet and the magician kept the Jenny below the cloud cover. Daylight made flying much easier. With the worst of the storm behind him, he no longer feared the weather. Although he encountered troubling patches of fog, the danger of ice waned with the warming of the day. Watching the endless gray and brown farmland patchwork pass monotonously below reassured him. He had a strong, steady tail wind and estimated his air speed at over seventy-five miles per hour. For the first time since leaving Skokie, he believed he had a chance of reaching New York before Sir Arthur's séance with Isis.

After failing to reach Conan Doyle, Houdini had phoned Bess and Dash at the Drake Hotel. He stressed the urgency of the situation but offered no explanations, saying only he'd be back in Chicago in two days' time. His brother agreed to cover for him at the shows he would miss. When pressed for details, Houdini said it was a life or death situation. Something in the tone of his voice precluded any further questions.

His final call roused the house detective. Houdini told the man recent death threats endangered his family and offered full salaries plus a bonus for men to guard Bess and Dash round the clock. The hotel dick assured him he knew several city cops who'd be more than happy for the chance to make some extra dough-re-mi.

Shortly before noon, the magician landed on the outskirts of Williamsport, Pennsylvania, for a second refueling stop. He put down, quite by chance, at a small field equipped with a gasoline pump, something not usually encountered except at big city airdromes. Able to fill up and be quickly on his way, Houdini considered himself lucky and, as luck would have it, the field manager provided new directions guaranteed to shave almost half an hour off his flying time.

The man proved correct in this prediction. Houdini adhered to his navigational instructions and the Hudson came into view in under three hours. The magician followed the river flowing southward like a great shimmering highway. Blood-red, the last of the sunset slashed across the western horizon over New Jersey. Ahead in the gathering dusk, the myriad lights of the city resembled a fallen galaxy jumbled in a heap beneath an empty sky.

Smug with satisfaction as he flew past Yonkers, Houdini at first refused to believe the hour he observed on a church clock tower. He'd forgotten the different time zones. It was five-thirty in the afternoon, although his own watch insisted it to be an hour earlier. No time remained to look for a landing field in the Bronx or Queens as he had planned. He had to be at the Fletcher house on Eighty-fifth Street before six o'clock.

Houdini angled into the city over Harlem. Off his starboard wing he glimpsed Morningside Park and the unfinished Cathedral of St. John the Divine. He thought of his beloved home, indistinguishable from so many others in the vast grid below. How odd to view Manhattan this way and see man's grandest achievements reduced to mere geometry. Crossing into Central Park above Harlem Meer snapped him abruptly out of any philosophic musings.

The magician flew due south, beginning a steep descent taking him across Croton Reservoir. Belvedere Castle crowned Vista Rock dead ahead. Off to port, the massive Metropolitan Museum hulked beside Fifth Avenue. To the rear, abrupt as an exclamation mark, the weathered obelisk known as Cleopatra's Needle jutted above the autumnal trees. The Jenny came gliding in over a deserted playground. All along the walkways, in the soft glow of cast-iron streetlamps, astonished pedestrians out for an early evening stroll pointed at its unexpected approach.

Hard to starboard, the double rectangle of the Old Reservoir succinctly defined one boundary of the magician's makeshift runway. A narrow reach of greensward stretched before him. Only a fool would land an airplane here, Houdini thought, setting down slowly in a controlled stall. He grinned at his own audacity, but the urgency of the situation foreclosed on any prolonged felonious pleasure. Touchdown came smooth and easy.

The moment the Jenny rolled to a stop, Houdini gathered up his belongings and scrambled out of the cockpit, the prop still turning. Numbers of curious bystanders hurried toward the biplane, anxious to be part of this miraculous occurrence. The magician dropped to the ground and ran off under the trees before they reached him.

Loping down the steep sledding hill north of the museum, Houdini shed the bulky flight suit like a sleek black moth emerging from its chrysalis. He darted out onto Fifth Avenue through the gate on Eighty-fourth Street. Blasé New Yorkers paid scant attention to the frantic man dressed in evening clothes who dodged between them and raced across the avenue, heedless of the two-way traffic. He made it safely to the other side amid an auto-horn cacophony as demented as a chorus of drunken geese.

When Martha, the elderly, gray-haired housekeeper, opened the front door, Houdini pushed past her without a word. "Wait!" she called, outrage raising her voice an octave. "You can't—"

"Where is she?" The magician started across the huge foyer toward the curving marble stairs. "In the library?"

"You have no right," the housekeeper scolded. "I will call the police."

Somewhere off in the distance a clock chimed six times. Houdini started up the polished steps. In the nick of time, he reflected, just like the movies.

The elderly housekeeper puffed along behind as he hurried down the long hallway. In his urgency, he gave no thought to his previous visit to these elegant surroundings. He thrust through the open doorway into the Queen Anne library and was astonished to discover Isis quietly sipping tea with Sir Arthur Conan Doyle.

"Houdini . . . ?" Sir Arthur rose to his feet, teacup in hand.

The magician understood immediately from the Englishman's astonished expression how alien he must appear in his leather flying helmet and rumpled tuxedo. "Did you get my wire at the Plaza?" he demanded.

The housekeeper fidgeted behind him. "I tried to stop him, Mrs. Fletcher," she whined. "He just wouldn't listen."

"It's all right, Martha." Isis patted the couch cushion beside her. She wore a gold-embroidered green velvet caftan and her pale, oval features gleamed like polished ivory. "Mr. Houdini is always welcome here." The housekeeper left the library with a quiet *humph* of indignation.

Conan Doyle grinned. "Took your advice and remained in Buffalo until this morning."

The magician felt utterly foolish. "Wasn't the séance set for six?"

"So it was, old chap," Sir Arthur answered, "but a scheduling conflict arose and so we moved it back to five. Absolutely astonishing session. The Ma'am was with me, fresh as life. But, you know all about Mrs. Fletcher's remarkable gifts."

Houdini blushed. "Well . . . yes. . . . She's . . . a remarkable woman."

"Won't you join us for some tea?" Isis purred. Her enigmatic smile rivaled the Mona Lisa's. "You prefer yours in a glass, I believe."

"No! Thank you, I mean . . . I'm afraid I must decline. No time to stay." Houdini unbuckled the leather flying helmet. "I hope you'll excuse me. . . . Sir Arthur, I need a word with you in private. It's of the utmost importance."

The knight glanced awkwardly at Isis. "If you insist," he said. "I do beg your pardon, Mrs. Fletcher."

"Not at all," she said. "We all have our little secrets."

The two men stepped out into the hallway, Houdini leading them away from the open door. "Most gifted voice medium I've ever encountered," Sir Arthur enthused. "I'm recommending her for the *Scientific American* prize."

The magician ignored his friend's fervor, drawing him into a small sitting room off the hall. "The Poe killer tried to murder me last night," he whispered.

"What!"

"Suckered me into a trap. Used the chloroform."

"Where? I thought you were away on tour."

"Happened in Chicago. Big surprise. 'Pit and the Pendulum,' only no pit."

"Last night you say? How on earth did you—"

Houdini impatiently cut him off, answering the unfinished question by waving the flying helmet and goggles like props in an elaborate trick. "Best escape I ever made," the magician boasted. "Had me shackled under a blade as big as a manhole cover. He was after me all along, like you said."

Sir Arthur tugged on his earlobe, flabbergasted by his friend's amazing audacity. "You're positive it's a man . . . ?"

"More than that. I know his identity."

"Good Lord! Who is it?"

"I won't make any accusations until I have proof." Houdini strode to the door, clearly constructing a dramatic exit. "I mean to search his home. Top to bottom."

Sir Arthur stepped quickly to the magician's side. "I'm coming with you."

"No!" Houdini placed his hand on the knight's shoulder. The fingers gripped like iron talons. "You've already put yourself too much at risk because of me."

They faced one another in the richly carpeted hall. "I believe I've earned the right to see this thing through to the end." Conan Doyle's resolute manner left no room for argument.

"What thing is that . . . ?" The lilting voice made both men turn. Isis stood watching them from the library door.

"As you wish," Houdini whispered.

Isis glided noislessly toward them. "You're not taking Sir Arthur away, I trust?" she asked, displaying the merest astringent hint of annoyance.

"Mrs Fletcher . . . I beg you to accept my profound apologies." The knight bowed his head like an apprehended truant. "Mr. Houdini and I have some unfinished business requiring immediate attention."

"You promise not to leave for England without a proper good-bye?" Isis clasped Sir Arthur's hand in hers. The magician noted a fecund swell of abdomen barely perceptible beneath the flowing velvet garment.

"You have my word." Conan Doyle beamed.

Isis turned her foxfire eyes on Houdini. He surprised her by holding her gaze. "Take great care, Osiris," she murmured. "The blow that kills you will be completely unexpected."

"They haven't killed me yet," he replied.

"It's only a matter of time." Isis brushed her fingertips across his cheek and left them, drifting off down the hall with a languid wave of her hand.

"The angel of death," Houdini whispered, watching her turn the corner.

Sir Arthur chuckled. "I daresay Mrs. Fletcher hasn't forgiven you yet for disrupting her séance last April."

"Hell hath no fury . . . ," Houdini said, faking a grin as they headed together for the stairs.

28

ELEMENTARY

The cabby left the meter running while Houdini hurried inside his house on West 113th Street. Conan Doyle sat and waited, contemplating the seam sewn along the crest of the leather flying helmet he held in one hand. On the drive uptown from Mrs. Fletcher's, the magician had filled him in on the incredible details of the past twenty-four hours. Exhilaration accelerated Sir Arthur's heartbeat. His physician's nature cautioned that a man his age ought not to get so overexcited, but under the circumstances, any prescribed calm remained impossible.

In his other hand, Sir Arthur gripped the eyeless leather mask, still emanating a caustic hint of chloroform. Closely examined, it seemed a crude affair, very like the flying helmet in overall design. How many victims had it claimed, he wondered. Perhaps this same infernal mask had been forced over his own head.

"Put that stuff in this." Houdini placed a Gladstone bag on Conan Doyle's lap as he slid back onto the seat beside him. "Driver," he barked. "Take us to Herald Square."

"You got it, mister." The cabby adjusted his spark and throttle, engaged the transmission, and they set off, turning the corner and heading downtown on Eighth Avenue.

"You found the correct address?" Sir Arthur asked.

"In here." The magician waved the copy of the Society of American

Magicians directory they'd come uptown to retrieve. He dropped the small, leatherette-covered book into the Gladstone bag.

"And you say I've actually met this Rammage chap?"

Houdini nodded. "Back in May. The S.A.M. banquet."

"How can you be sure you've got the right man?"

"First off, he's the right size." The magician's eager eyes gleamed with predatory intensity. "We were so convinced it was a woman. Rammage is slight; you might even call him tiny. Yet, because of his profession, he is physically very strong."

"Purely circumstantial," Sir Arthur snorted.

Houdini ignored this rebuttal. "It was something he said that gave him away. You yourself remarked about the Red Death's fake tone of voice. I remember you thought it was a woman pretending to be a man."

"There was obviously an attempt made to disguise the voice."

"Yes. But not because of sex. Because of his accent." The magician's enthusiasm made his words tumble rapidly, one on top of the other. "Rammage is an Englishman, like yourself, but his accent is different. Not so educated. More like Jim Collins and poor dear Vickery. But not cockney."

"Working class?"

"Yes, and provincial, too, I'd guess. He didn't try to disguise it with me. Even so, I couldn't put my finger on what sounded so familiar. It nagged at me all through the flight from Chicago. Well, at least after the storm died down. Up there alone, you've got plenty of time to think. It was something he said. I racked my brain, but just couldn't bring it to mind. And then I remembered. It was 'Righty-o.' "

"Righty-o . . . ?" Sir Arthur suppressed a dubious grin.

"Something Rammage says all the time. The Grand Inquisitor used the exact same expression."

"And this is your evidence? Righty-o?" The knight sounded incredulous.

"We'll know soon enough after searching his apartment," Houdini sniffed, looking out the window in a sulk.

Saying he wanted to avoid the traffic on Central Park West, the cabby entered the park at 110th, winding down West Drive. The magician stared silently at the lights from distant apartment buildings flickering through the bare tree limbs.

"You propose to break the law based on nothing more than what you've just told me?" Conan Doyle ended the silence as they passed the Maine Memorial, exiting Central Park and angling onto Broadway at Columbus Circle.

Houdini didn't turn his head. "This man tried to kill me. And you. I don't think he concerned himself with legal niceties."

"Someone certainly tried to kill us," Conan Doyle said without emotion. "A person whose identity remains unknown."

"Not to me." Houdini leaned his forehead against the cool window glass. "I know who did it. Without a doubt."

Neither man felt comfortable with further conversation and they rode in renewed silence as the cab traversed the blazing carnival brilliance of Times Square. Houdini remembered the area as Long Acre Square, when Oscar Hammerstein moved his theater uptown and Rector's and Shanley's and Reisenweber's were the places to be seen. Not another word until Sir Arthur caught sight of the Hotel McAlpin on the uptown corner of Thirty-fourth Street. "By Jove," he remarked, "I know where we are now. This is where we attended the banquet."

"Rammage lives just below Herald Square," the magician muttered, still staring sullenly past his reflection in the window. "If he caught the midnight milk run out of Union Station, he's not due into Grand Central or Penn Station for two hours."

In the nineties, the intersection of Broadway and Sixth Avenue had been the juicy rare prime of the Tenderloin, but the Haymarket and Jim Corbett's place and Koster & Bail's Music Hall were long gone. And, ever since James Gordon Bennett's familiar two-story palazzo housing his *New York Herald* was torn down a year and a half ago, Houdini felt a stranger in this part of town.

"Herald Square," the driver called as the cab passed beneath the dripping iron girders of the El.

Houdini and his wife had showed in many of the surrounding theaters back in the old days. Bess still came here once or twice a month to shop at Macy's. She spoke of the area with nostalgia, but as far as the magician was concerned, each demolished building further eroded his memories of those happy times long ago.

"Where to, mister?" An edge of impatience sharpened the driver's query.

Houdini had the cabby turn left at the Hotel Martinique and drive east on Thirty-second Street. Conan Doyle observed the magician carefully scrutinize the odd-numbered addresses along the uptown side. At Fifth, Houdini settled back in his seat. "Drop us at the Life Building on Thirty-first," he ordered.

"You got it." The driver followed Fifth Avenue downtown for a block before turning west again on Thirty-first. He pulled to a stop in front of the offices of the famed humor magazine, a classical building with iron balconies sporting an ornate pattern of back-to-back *L*'s. Houdini paid the buck-fifty fare with a two-dollar bill and told the driver to keep the change.

The cab's departing taillight faded down the block. Houdini followed its diminishing red stare, Gladstone bag in hand. Sir Arthur paced solemnly at his side. "Look here," the knight said as they turned the corner and headed uptown on Broadway, "what possible motive would this man Rammage have for wanting to kill you?"

"Remember, in Atlantic City . . . ?" The magician cocked his head, eyes glittering in the lamplight. "You asked if I had any enemies? Someone who might have it in for me?"

"It seemed a logical avenue to pursue."

"Well, the avenue leads straight to Rammage." Houdini jabbed a spieler's forefinger at his companion. "We've been rivals since I first toured your country twenty years ago. I totally discredited his handcuff escape act. I'm sure he hates me."

"Two decades later the man decides to murder you? Highly improbable."

"There have been other . . . incidents, over the years. I never did like Rammage. Something instinctive, I suppose. Couldn't ever pass up a chance to take him down a peg or two. I opposed his run for secretary of the Society. Why, just back in June, I torpedoed his swami act with my underwater stunt at the Biltmore Hotel."

A twinkle of merriment brightened Sir Arthur's empyrean eyes. "I daresay I might have a motive for killing you myself, were I he."

The two men paused on the downtown corner of Broadway and Thirty-second Street. The Hotel Martinique, an opulent French Renaissance confection with multileveled mansard roofs, stood on the opposite corner. There was an entrance on Thirty-second. Farther along rose the Alcazar, another midprice hotel, although sporting a less extravagant facade. Number forty-five West Thirty-second Street, sandwiched improbably between them, had once been part of an elegant row of brownstones stretching all the way to Fifth, but now, it alone remained, a quaint knickknack from the past. "That's it," Houdini whispered, though there was no one else close enough to hear. "At best, we've got two hours."

They crossed the street and Sir Arthur stood fidgeting outside on the stoop landing while the magician picked the front door lock. Larceny accomplished in an instant, Houdini bowed from the waist, beckoning his friend inside.

Conan Doyle crossed the threshold with a culpable look over his shoulder. "Swift," he remarked, concealing his guilt under a smoke screen of sarcasm.

"Piece of cake. You can open junk like that with a hat pin."

The two men climbed the dusty carpeted steps. Once a single-family home, the building had been divided into eight small apartments. Sidney Rammage lived in 4-B. The lock was a standard Yale triple-ward. Twenty seconds with the pick and Houdini was inside.

Sir Arthur stood by quietly while the magician closed the door behind them and took a small flashlight from the bag, flicking the beam around the room, making certain the drapes were drawn before he switched on the ceiling fixture. The old gas lamps had been converted to electricity around the turn of the century and the cramped apartment,

with its somber quarter-sawn oak wainscotting and ornate picture moldings, retained a fussy Victorian gloom.

The entire layout consisted of two tiny rooms, plus a kitchenette
and bath. Ancient music hall posters advertising "the Wizard of the Rif"
and framed photos of Rammage costumed as Ali ben Haroun hung
everywhere. Clumsy installment-plan furniture crowded the threadbare
carpet. Curiously, a rusted suit of armor slumped in one corner and an
exquisite fourteenth-century diptych altarpiece stood on the cluttered
desktop, improbable as a perfect rose growing out of a litter pile.

Houdini went in to search the bedroom, leaving Sir Arthur to deal
with the messy desk, a task complicated by the diptych's minutely
detailed beauty. The right-hand panel portrayed the peaceable kingdom
of Eden; the left, Adam and Eve expelled from the Garden. The knight
studied the pair's guilty, hangdog expressions and felt he knew exactly
what they were thinking. How like a lapsed Catholic to be so troubled by
conscience, he thought, sorting through a stranger's correspondence
scattered across the desktop.

Most of the mail was business-related—unpaid bills, letters
concerning booking inquiries, notes from other magicians. A surprising number were from spirit mediums. Apparently, Sidney
Rammage was a believer. Sir Arthur recognized many names, including
some of the most illustrious. Their tone was chatty, occasionally philosophic, and almost every letter contained scurrilous references to
Houdini. " . . . Another diatribe from H.H. I concur with your opinion,
Sidney, the man is truly a menace . . ." "Houdini up to his usual dirty
tricks again. Went in disguise to a séance in Brooklyn and disrupted it
utterly. How much longer must we tolerate such outrage? . . ."
"Saddened to learn the archfiend, Houdini, has once again attempted to
besmirch the integrity of our sacred beliefs. Something must be done to
stop him . . ."

"Look at this, Sir Arthur!" The magician rushed out of the bedroom, waving his arms furiously. "Just look at this!"

Conan Doyle glanced up from his reading. "Hmmm . . . ?"

"I found these searching through a chest of drawers." Houdini held several fragments of cut leather. "Bet my bottom dollar they're the pieces for another mask."

"Perhaps. We'll have to come up with something much more substantial if we wish to make a case."

"I'm just getting started," Houdini snorted, hurrying back into the bedroom.

Conan Doyle next turned his attentions to the contents of the desk drawers. Other than the usual clutter (cheap fountain pens, pencil stubs, a jar of hardened library paste, scattered thumbtacks, postage stamps, rubber bands, several packs of playing cards), he found nothing unusual until he came across a battered volume of Poe resting atop a metal cash box in the bottom drawer.

The knight rifled the pages. Key passages in the stories relating to the murders were carefully underlined in red pencil. "A ground plan for homicide," he muttered to himself, sweeping aside the accumulated correspondence and placing the book on the desk blotter. A quick perusal of the notated tales evoked a lethal imagination. The ghastly underscored details fairly leapt off the page: "a razor, besmeared with blood"; "decayed and clotted with gore"; "completely buried in the flesh"; "a crescent of glittering steel, about a foot in length from horn to horn. . . ." Sir Arthur closed the book, feeling himself in the heartless presence of a murderer.

"Just look at this!" Houdini cried, charging in again from the bedroom. "Here's your proof hanging in his wardrobe." Draped dramatically in a blood-red cloak, the magician held up the rubber skull mask as if it were a severed head.

"By Jove, that's it!" In his excitement, Sir Arthur overlooked his annoyance at the magician's endless histrionic posturing.

Houdini showed him the label: Brooks Theatrical Costumers. "They're a top-notch outfit. One of the biggest. Cater mainly to the profession."

"Odd . . ." Conan Doyle examined the coarse woolen cloak.

"The costumes Jean and I wore that night were hired from the same establishment."

"Like I said, they're tops."

Turning to the desk, Sir Arthur shuffled through the scattered letters. He quickly found a sealed statement bearing the Brooks letterhead and sliced it open with the penknife on his watch chain.

Medieval Death (w/mask)
One wk. @ $3.50 per $3.50
PAYMENT DUE UPON RECEIPT

Sir Arthur handed the statement to Houdini and stooped to examine a stack of paid bills impaled upon the desk spindle. Halfway down, he found another receipt from Brooks Costumers. It was dated March 25: one gorilla suit, black, w/mask. The rate was four dollars per week.

"Now are you convinced?" Houdini exulted, reading over Conan Doyle's shoulder.

"Quite." The knight retrieved the first statement, folding the two together. "How on earth could the police have neglected to consult the records of recent costumes for hire?"

"Probably never thought to check the professional accounts, only one-time customers. What does it matter? We've got the goods on him now. I say we call the cops."

Conan Doyle shook his head. "The Red Death is no good. I never reported the assault in the Plaza. In essence, it's a crime which didn't occur. And the presence of a second receipt only dilutes the import of the first. We need more proof."

"I'll get busy." The magician paused in the bedroom doorway. "Are you armed?"

Sir Arthur patted the slight sag in his jacket pocket. "Revolver. Why . . . ?"

"The trains might be running early." Houdini glanced at his wristwatch. "Rammage could show up anytime. Keep an eye on the door."

Conan Doyle wanted to say he had more important things to do than guard the door, but held his tongue, turning his attention back to matters at hand once the magician left the room. The cash box was locked and heavy. Shaking it revealed no hint of the contents. Sir Arthur placed the box on the blotter for a closer look, but something else caught his eye—something on the blotter itself.

All down the side, etched into the soft green blotterboard, the ghostly imprint of past writing formed a repetitive pattern. The same signature, over and over. Conan Doyle took a number two pencil from the top drawer and carefully rubbed the lead across the blotter, creating a shaded area out of which the signature slowly emerged like a figure approaching through the fog: Opal . . . Crosby . . . Fletcher . . .

"Houdini!" the knight called, continuing to shade the blotter. Multiple variations of the signature came to light; some showing the stilted formality of a copyist, others more fluid and natural. Between them, snatches of the alphabet and stray words appeared in the same forged hand. "Houdini! Come here at once!"

The magician was on his hands and knees, peering under the brass bed. Surrounded by mouse-sized dust clumps, a dented green metal footlocker scraped the springs. He pulled it out into the light and opened the lid. It was filled with scrapbooks and leather-bound photograph albums. "This is most important!" he heard Sir Arthur call from the other room. "You must have a look."

Houdini bounded to his feet and poked his head through the door. "Turn something up?"

"Have a look." Conan Doyle pointed to the desk blotter.

Houdini gasped when he read the name delineated by the graphite mist. "Isis . . . ?" The magician traced his finger over the multiple signatures like a blind man reading Braille.

"Rammage has taken great pains learning to forge Mrs. Fletcher's hand."

"Why?"

Sir Arthur gave Houdini the strongbox. "Open this. It was in the bottom drawer together with an edition of Poe."

The magician surveyed the simple lock with a frown of disdain. A half-turn with his pick and the catch released. Houdini swung back the hinged lid, centering the open money box on the desk. Inside, a pint-sized medicinal bottle with a ground-glass stopper rested atop a pair of books. Conan Doyle picked it up and took a cautious sniff.

"Chloroform?" Houdini asked.

Sir Arthur nodded in agreement.

Houdini seized the uppermost volume, a five-and-dime school notebook with marbled cardboard covers. Flipping it open, the magician immediately encountered an extensive entry in what he knew to be Sidney Rammage's handwriting. Carefully outlined in a neat accountant's script, Opal Fletcher's telephone numbers and addresses in both Paris and London, as well as New York, filled an entire page. The names and addresses of her servants followed ground plans of her home on Eighty-fifth Street, precisely sketched and including various illicit access routes via the cellar and a second-floor balcony.

"Curious . . . ," Sir Arthur murmured, looking on as Houdini turned the pages. Similar entries detailed the movements and habits of Ingrid Esp, Violette Speers, Mary Rogers, Jim Vickery. . . . "By Jove! He's got my tour schedule down exactly," the knight exclaimed, observing the extensive Conan Doyle section. "The man is certainly methodical."

"Dirty bastard." Houdini seethed, reading the scrupulous notes Rammage had compiled on him and Bess. Phone numbers. Itineraries. Floor plans of his house. Finally, sketches of many of his illusions; the Metamorphosis, the Milk Can, Chinese Water Torture, each with an explanatory paragraph.

"Stealing your thunder . . . ?" Sir Arthur queried.

"Most of this I've published myself. But, only the Jims knew the secret of the Upside Down." The magician closed the notebook, a ghastly pallor aging him by a decade. "My God. . . . He tortured poor Vickery . . ."

"Dangerous adversary, this Rammage chap."

"Is that what this is all about? A few cheap tricks . . . ?"

Conan Doyle lifted the second book out of the money box, a small gilt-edged, hand-sewn, red-leather-bound journal with the initials O.C.F. discreetly embossed near the lower left corner. "I believe we'll find his motives a touch more convoluted," he said.

The entries were written in purple ink, the cursive Palmer-method script unmistakably the schoolgirl hand of Opal Crosby Fletcher. "Remarkable forgery . . ." Sir Arthur held the volume so Houdini could read along with him. "Rammage has a deft touch."

1/1/23

A new year. Clean white pages. The blood-red cover strikes me as entirely appropriate. This is to be a diary of doom, an honest chronicle of the death sentence pronounced on Harry Houdini. He must be punished for his blasphemy. The world must know of the pain he has caused innocent believers.

"He's setting her up," Houdini muttered.
"Precisely . . ."

2/17/23

Ingrid Esp is a most obligingly punctual young woman. She puts the Swiss to shame. Every morning, out of the building six-thirty on the dot, brisk march to the subway . . .

4/2/23

The chloroform works like magic. She was out in an instant. I drove to 38th Street and changed into the ape suit. She looked like a sleeper, slumped on the front seat. I strangled her, and ran and ran and ran, her weight barely noticed, limp in my shaggy arms . . .

4/3/23

. . . so easy when they're unconscious. The razor a difficult tool, cutting flesh easily enough, but had to saw and hack through cartilage and windpipe . . .

4/29/23

. . . brought me from the edge of my trance. Incredible! It was Houdini.
He fairly leapt upon the stage. So unwary. So fond of himself. Easy prey.
Even now, the noose tightens. When they find Mrs. Speers someone
will remember Poe. I want H.H. to be terrified when I come for
him . . .

"He must have quite enjoyed this," Conan Doyle said, momentarily
half-closing the book.

"I'm going to enjoy it plenty if I ever get my hands on him."

"Easy, old man." Sir Arthur gave the magician's shoulder a paternal
pat. "Best to let the law follow its own course."

"Let me have a look at that thing." Houdini grabbed the forged diary
from his friend's grasp and thumbed quickly through, reading bits and
snatches at random.

4/20/23

. . . headlines full of Poe mystery. Mr. Runyon is my partner in
vengeance . . .

4/25/23

How divinely inspired! Mary Rogers, a speakeasy cigarette girl, worked
for a brief time in H.H.'s troupe. Here is a sure sign my plan is the
sacred sword of justice . . .

5/7/23

. . . the Village is such a tranquil neighborhood despite its boisterous
bohemian reputation. Strangled M.R. in her Bleecker St. apt. Waited
until after midnight to bring her body down to the sedan. Not a soul in
sight . . .

6/16/23

. . . to the Biltmore Hotel on 43rd St. Watched H.H. as he was
submerged in a coffin in the swimming pool. How provident for him to
supply the equipment I require for my next Poe stunt . . .

"My God!" Houdini exclaimed. "He was there that day observing her, not me."

"A most thoroughgoing and persistent fellow, indeed."

6/28/23

. . . Vickery quite strong and agile, but, as always, chloroform effortlessly did the trick. There's a chance he'll be found before dying. Either way, the Poe fits. They already know about the chloroform. Thanks to Mr. Runyon, I know they know . . .

10/31/23

All Hallows' Eve. The trap in place: bricks, mortar, a nice bottle of amontillado. A.C.D. costumed as a clown! More Divine Intervention. My Red Death proved an enticing bait. With the wine to slake his thirst, he might last a month.

Sir Arthur allowed a grim grin as he read of his immurement. "Cold-blooded rascal. Intriguing to read his thoughts in her hand."

"Still a couple more entries," Houdini said, turning a page.

11/2/23

Another successful trap. The magician fooled by a bit of clever misdirection. My sweetest success enhanced by his desperate terror. I can die happily with the sound of Houdini's final scream enshrined in memory. My revenge is complete. How I wish I still were sitting in that dark theater. The train ride home from Chicago proves to be a terrible bore.

"He wrote this before leaving New York." For the second time in his life, Houdini's expression contained the same look of wonder he had so often induced on the upturned faces of his audience.

"All part of the master plan."

"Last one's got tomorrow's date."

11/4/23

Ennui. Utter boredom. The Poe Killer retires and I slide safely into his legend. Is this all the world is to know? What purpose is served by my revenge if no one understands that Houdini was punished for the shame he inflicted upon the realm of the spirits? How dull life seems bearing this secret to the grave. What better exit than to make death a proclaimer of the truth? My passing to join the shades is a final act of faith. Let this diary serve as an eloquent suicide letter. Chloroform should prove most appropriate.

"He meant to kill her." Conan Doyle took the volume from Houdini, rereading the passage.

"Master plan's kaput now."

The knight pulled his watch from his vest pocket. "What time did you say the Chicago train arrives?"

"Eight forty-five."

"He got in fifteen minutes ago." Closing the watch case, Conan Doyle frowned. "I believe Mrs. Fletcher may be in serious jeopardy. Rammage already made up his mind to kill her. Make her look like the murderess. His plan has altered, but the impulse remains."

"If he caught a cab at Penn Station or Grand Central, he could possibly be there already. He'd be here by now. It's a five-minute walk either way."

When Houdini tried to phone a warning to Isis, central informed him that her line was inexplicably dead.

"We must hurry!" Conan Doyle shoved the forged diary into the Gladstone bag and the two men quickly gathered up the remaining evidence. They were out the door in less than a minute.

29

-- -- -- ---- -- -- -- --- -- -- --

A WOW FINISH

An ominous darkness festered within the Fletcher mansion as Conan Doyle and Houdini rushed from a Yellow cab. They had been lucky, spotting a taxi discharging passengers outside the Hotel Martinique. Traffic was sparse and the cabby got them up to Eighty-fifth and Fifth in ten minutes flat.

"I don't like the looks of this at all," the knight muttered, glancing at the blackened windows.

"Maybe she went out?" Houdini slipped the bent-wire pick into the front door lock.

"Some lights would have been left burning. And surely, there are servants within."

The magician opened the door. The two men whisked inside, stalking into the shadowed foyer. Houdini switched on the flashlight when they reached the stairs, mounting at a silent lope, two steps at a time, to the living quarters. Conan Doyle puffed at his side.

They hurried along the darkened hallway, flicking the light beam into empty rooms. A pungent medicinal reek lingered in the air outside the library.

"Chloroform," Sir Arthur whispered. Houdini probed the shadow-shrouded library with his flashlight.

Distant metallic clanging resonated from somewhere high above.

The magician and the knight stared straight up, straining to hear. Long silent seconds passed. "The roof!" Houdini cried, suddenly recognizing the sound.

No longer concerned about stealth, they ran pell-mell for the service stairs at the far end of the hall. Scrambling up three flights in the dark, footfalls loud on the uncarpeted steps, the two men felt desperation verging on panic.

They paused on the landing below the open door to the roof, instinctively knowing the need for calm and surprise. Loud above their panting silence, a cold birdsong clank rang through the night. Someone dragged a length of chain. Conan Doyle drew the Webley-Green from his pocket, aware of its weight and lethal danger. He pointed the revolver carefully away from Houdini.

The rasping chain chattered like the evil laugh of an incubus. "Houdini will go first," the magician hissed. "No light. Speed'n silence is the ticket."

Houdini climbed the final steps and slipped out like a shadow. Conan Doyle was right behind, astonished at the tom-tomming of his heart. A war hero who never saw combat, he thought ruefully.

A narrow balcony fronted by a crenelated parapet ran along the back side of the house. Facing east, it overlooked a tidy row of brownstones. The two men moved along with deliberate silence. Street light from Fifth provided ample illumination in contrast with the mineshaft gloom of the service stairs. Houdini held the inactive flashlight at his side in much the same manner as Conan Doyle handled the revolver.

Turning a corner, they encountered an iron catwalk arching across a narrow courtyard to a conical slate-roofed turret. A hunched silhouette balanced on the stark skeletal railing, hauling tight on a shadowy chain. "Hold!" Houdini cried, switching on the flashlight.

Rammage squinted into the harsh, unexpected gleam. He perched like a gargoyle on the slender railing. "What in hell . . . ?" Blinded by the light, the tiny Englishman tightened his grip on the length of chain wound around the railing. The chain descended at a sharp angle into the beam's penumbral corona. There, supine on the catwalk, the bodies of two women lay chained together. Cheap rubber novelty monkey masks were secured over both their faces. Neither appeared to move.

Conan Doyle trained his Webley-Green on Rammage's crouching form. The knight could not stop his extended arm from trembling, although he was an experienced shot with his own private pistol range. "I am armed and will not hesitate to shoot you down." He cocked the revolver, struggling to control his abhorrence at the notion of taking a human life.

"Show's over, Rammage," Houdini taunted.

"Harry . . . ?" The rival magician teetered on the rail, clinging to the length of chain. "Is that you?"

"You always were all washed up. You threw your biggest challenge at me and I'm here to tell you it wasn't good enough. You've never been good enough, have you, Rammage?"

"Good enough to create the mystery of the Poe Murders." Rammage crouched on the rail. "You brought a policeman with you. Ask him, Harry. A diverting entertainment this past summer, don't you think, Officer?"

"It is Conan Doyle," the knight called. "You have twice failed."

"Ah. . . . Life is full of mishaps." Clinging like a trained monkey, Rammage shied from the light. "Tell me, Sir Arthur. . . . You are a literary man. Do you recognize the source of my final performance?"

"Poe's 'Hop Frog.' You're shy six orangutans."

"I had to work on such short notice. Bought the masks from a news butcher at the railway station." Reaching between absurdly thrust knees, Rammage groped in the shadows behind the women.

"Mmmmm. . . . Gnmmm. . . . Nnnnnnmmm." Opal Crosby Fletcher's muffled voice sounded a plea of inarticulate desperation.

"She's alive!" Houdini cried.

"Take courage, Mrs. Fletcher." Conan Doyle steadied his wobbling aim. "No harm will befall you."

Rammage grasped something unseen and drew himself slowly upright by pulling on the chain. "I trust you remember the ending of the tale?" Rammage waved a fuel can above his head. "Righty-o!" He poured a stream of amber liquid out over the recumbent women. "Gasoline. . . ." His nervous giggle gave way to eerie maniacal cackling.

"Stop it or I swear I'll shoot!" Sir Arthur braced his shooting arm with his other hand.

"No, you won't." Rammage dropped the can and dug deep into his pocket. "You won't dare. Because you don't know if you can kill me before I strike a spark on my lighter." Sidney Rammage held the regulation R.E.F. trench cigarette lighter triumphantly in his hand.

"He's bluffing," Houdini sneered.

"No. I don't believe he is." Sir Arthur squinted along the revolver's barrel. "Hop Frog, the dwarf, took revenge by costuming the king and his ministers as orangutans and setting them on fire."

"A most exquisite tale," Rammage raved. "The master at his finest. . . . So, back away! Or watch them burn!"

"Shoot him," hissed Houdini. "Now!"

The magician switched off the flashlight. The shadow form of Rammage made an easy target. In the sudden dark, Conan Doyle felt his hand tremble. His aim was unsure.

"Do it!" Houdini's insistent whisper rent the night.

"Shall I count to ten," Rammage teased.

Conan Doyle knew what had to be done. He glanced away for a second, thinking to fire on impulse when he looked back, and to his amazement, he saw the phosphorescent specter of Poe standing on the adjoining parapet.

Rammage gasped. "Poe . . . !" Astonished, he wobbled on the railing, fighting for balance.

"Shoot!" Houdini howled, hurling his Gladstone bag at Rammage.

The leather satchel caught the killer square in the face, spinning him around. Rammage lost his footing, plummeting backwards into the night. With a sharp jerk, the other end of the chain cinched tight around the iron rail.

Houdini leaned out over the edge, shining the flashlight down the taut, swaying chain. "Rammage . . . ?"

Fifteen feet below the catwalk, Sidney Rammage swung on the

chain, hanging on with one hand. His other hand defiantly gripped the cigarette lighter. Caught in the beam, he grinned up at Houdini through a volatile drizzle of dripping gasoline. He thumbed a flame alight. It flickered like a tiny firefly on his fingertips. Rammage stared ruefully at the feeble, wavering flame. "You win, Harry," he said, letting go of the chain.

Rammage fell backwards without a sound, hurtling toward the ground in the flashlight's widening shaft of illumination. He hit the paving stones with blunt finality and lay still. Houdini stared down at him.

"Mrs. Fletcher . . . ?" Conan Doyle knelt beside the recumbent women, slipping the rubber ape masks off their faces. Houdini was suddenly at his side with the light. Isis and Martha were gagged, their eyes wide, alert with fear. The magician unknotted the handkerchief bound across Opal's open mouth. "Did you see it?" Sir Arthur asked, working on Martha's gag.

"See what?"

Conan Doyle glanced at the darkened turret. "Nothing."

"Here is a future I could not foresee." Isis smiled when Houdini removed her gag. "God bless you both."

"I thought for certain we are dead," Martha sobbed, her brittle accent cracking from the strain.

The two men set about freeing them, unwrapping the other end of the chain. Both women were bound hand and foot with strips of canvas webbing. The moment Isis felt her wrists untied, she bent to release her feet unassisted. Houdini watched her toss the military strap aside. "Recognize this . . . ?" She handed him a square of damp cloth: the handkerchief that had gagged her.

The magician noted familiar hem-stitching; a torn corner and the monogram: H.H. "This is mine."

"He also had your penknife. Planned on leaving it behind."

"Make me the fall guy?"

"Last trick up his sleeve." Conan Doyle helped the trembling Martha to her feet.

"How'd you know about the knife?" Houdini asked Isis, as she accepted his proffered arm.

"He told us. Bragged really. Took his time, organizing things. The ether, or whatever it was, soon wore off. Martha and I came to tied and gagged in the library. Mr. Rammage boasted of his clever scheme to 'frame' you."

"Wait! You know his name." Houdini grabbed her other wrist. "What do you have to do with Sidney Rammage?"

She twisted free from his grasp. "As little as possible, I assure you."

Sir Arthur coughed in an obvious, throat-clearing sort of way and glanced over the railing at the shadowy courtyard five stories below. "Well, best thing now is to notify the authorities."

"No. You can't." A note of panic edged her musical voice. "That's impossible."

"I know your telephone is out of order. There must be another somewhere nearby."

"If you make that call, I'll be ruined."

"My dear lady . . ." Sir Arthur glanced significantly at the maid. "Perhaps it would be best to retire inside where this might be discussed privately?"

"I have no secrets from Martha," Isis said, giving the older woman an affectionate hug. "She is my right arm."

"This have something to do with that bastard Rammage?" Houdini bullied. Sir Arthur cocked an eyebrow at such ungallant behavior.

"I met Sidney Rammage in Paris the year after my husband died. I had a flat in the Sixteenth, just off the Bois du Boulogne. Mr. Rammage advertised manuscripts for sale. Alchemical texts on parchment. I arranged for a showing and paid a good price. I believe it was on that first visit when Mr. Rammage conceived a passion for my skull."

"Skull . . . ?" Conan Doyle looked utterly nonplussed. "Most bizarre, what?"

"A pre-Columbian skull, cut from quartz crystal. Mr. Houdini is familiar with the object. I sometimes use it to communicate. There was no need during our session today."

"I imagine it contains great power." Sir Arthur nodded.

Houdini was not interested in any discussion of the occult. "Rammage try to steal the gizmo?" he demanded, glancing over the railing into the shadows below.

"He was far too subtle to try something like that. It's my fault, really. I was guilty of . . . an indiscretion, that year in Paris. Foolish, I know, but I am young and foolish. Mr. Rammage came into possession of certain letters and photographs. I think you get the picture. He threatened to make this material public in New York. It would mean my social ruin."

"Blackmail." Houdini seemed bursting with compressed energy.

"Of the most insidious variety. I can survive anything except scandal."

"Rammage wanted the skull as payment?" Sir Arthur tamped tobacco into his briar pipe.

"Exactly. We engaged in a delicate diplomacy. The skull is important to me. I felt time was on my side. The longer I held out, the more likely Mr. Rammage would accept a cash settlement."

"You can save your money now." The magician poked a thumb at the dark void behind him. "He don't need it where he's going. His murdering, blackmailing days are over."

"Wrong. Mr. Rammage placed the documents in question in the care of his attorney. A sealed envelope. He left instructions that it was not to be opened except in the event of his death. Said it was his life insurance policy."

Conan Doyle leaned on the railing. "And if you surrendered the crystal skull?"

"The attorney has instructions to give me the papers upon delivery."

"No problem then!" Houdini clapped his hands like a wizard dispelling demons.

"No problem . . . ?" Sir Arthur frowned. "Damnit man, of course there's a problem." The knight pointed down at the courtyard. "What about him?"

"Him! To hell with him. He tried to kill the three of us." Houdini paced on the catwalk. "Why should he get away with destroying her life?"

"What do you suggest, then?"

"First, we better drag our friend inside. Get him out of sight." Houdini led the way back to the stairs. "Can Martha help?"

"She will do what you ask of her."

"Good. I have a plan. Sir Arthur? Were you not trained as a surgeon?"

They started down the darkened steps. "I am ever a doctor," Conan Doyle said with pride.

"You travel with your medical bag?"

"It's at the hotel."

"Get it. I have errands to run as well. We'll meet back here in an hour." The magician's swaggering authority proved a welcome reassurance. "It'll be a busy night. If I'm gonna catch the Twentieth Century to Chicago, we'll have to work overtime."

30

LEGERDEMAIN

Police captain Francis Xavier Boyle was furious. Although he appeared outwardly calm, flushed splotches on his cheeks gave away his rage. Sergeant Heegan had learned to recognize these signs of the captain's displeasure way back in the winter of '99 when he walked a rookie's beat out of the Twenty-ninth and Boyle had been precinct sergeant.

". . . As I was saying, Jimmy, any situation reaching my desk automatically becomes a problem." Captain Boyle's bottled-in-bond murmur crooned softly in the wood-paneled office. "And when my good friend Captain Conny Willemse of homicide complains to me of a Judas Iscariot in his department, his problem becomes my problem."

"Judas Iscariot, Captain . . . ?" Heegan didn't like the way things were going. When told to report back to his old precinct, the sergeant had assumed it meant a return to active duty. The red danger signals on Boyle's cheeks warned of the unexpected.

"A stool-pigeon, Sergeant, in the parlance of those we are sworn to guard the citizenry against." Captain Boyle waved a copy of the morning *New York American,* flourishing the headline TELL-TALE MURDER: POE KILLER CLAIMS NEW VICTIM. "Let me read you several lurid highlights. 'Magician Found Dismembered . . . head, arms, and legs bundled around the torso inside a dented green footlocker lodged between the floor joists. . . . Right eye gouged free and replaced with a milky-blue marble. . . . A curious clockwork mechanism wedged inside the chest cavity produced a steady metronome beating. This is the sound, overheard by neighbors, which resulted in the police being summoned . . .' Why is it, do you suppose, the press seems to know the details of this case even before our reports are filed?"

Better cover my ass here, Heegan thought. "You want me to do some snooping around?" he asked. "They trust me down there. Might be able to turn something up."

The captain's thin, tight-lipped smile grew ever more taut. "Are you volunteering to go undercover?" Boyle purred softly. "Is that what you have in mind, Sergeant?"

"It is indeed."

"Ask a few leading questions? Coax the culprit out of the woodwork . . . ?"

"That is my sincere intention."

"You dumb bastard!" Captain Boyle shouted. "You ignorant, conniving, lying mick! Don't you think everyone's noticed that one paper out of all the pack, one paper alone gets the scoop? That paper is the *American*. And is it any coincidence that one reporter there seems always to get the story first?"

"I wouldn't know, sir." Heegan's tongue felt thick in his mouth.

"Wouldn't you, Jimmy . . . ?" Boyle whispered. "Wouldn't you know that Damon Runyon has a little birdie singing in his ear? A little birdie in a blue coat?"

"Surely, Captain, you don't mean to suggest that—"

"Shut your ignorant yap, you damned idiot!" Captain Boyle pulled a second newspaper out of a desk drawer. "I'm not one to read a Hearst rag with any pleasure, so I didn't see Damon Runyon's column of a week ago until it was brought to my attention yesterday." Boyle folded this copy of the *American* to the sports section. "The diligent police work of such as Sergeant James Patrick Heegan of homicide," he read. " 'Sergeant Heegan represents the finest tradition of law enforcement!' " The captain slammed his desk with the folded newspaper. "Don't you think I know a payback when I see one? This is your damn vigorish, Jimmy! You always did have a mouth big enough to stable a horse."

Heegan stared at his scuffed, black brogans. "It was just idle chitchat over coffee," he whined. "No more than that."

"Anyone too dumb to appreciate a sinecure doesn't deserve it." The captain was no longer smiling. He tossed a police whistle into the sergeant's lap. "Starting the noon shift, Heegan, you're back on traffic detail. Better get your white gloves out of mothballs."

A mile or so from the Twenty-ninth Precinct, Damon Runyon threaded his way past the stevedores and embarking passengers crowding into a baggage wagon logjam on Pier 56. The Cunard liner *Aquitania,* scheduled to sail on the afternoon tide, rode at her moorings: immense, immobile, and yet, for all her stillness and majesty, the embodiment of motion and unimaginable power. Above the dockside confusion, a festive mood prevailed aboard the great ship. Runyon ascended the first-class gangway tilting up against the vast, clifflike expanse of her hull, serenaded by the distant strains of a lively string orchestra.

Uniformed deck stewards wandered among the milling passengers carrying trays heaped with noisemakers, sacks of confetti, paper streamers in colorful, compact rolls. A smiling young man handed Damon Runyon a cardboard party horn as he entered the main salon. The sportswriter attempted an experimental *toot* on the grand staircase beneath the gilt-framed Pannini painting of postcard-perfect Roman ruins.

Entering a reception lounge paneled with authentic Grinling Gibbons carvings, Runyon ditched the gaudy horn in a tall, sand-filled brass ashtray, making his way toward a noisy gathering at the far end of the room. A small crowd of reporters and assorted professional well-wishers surrounded Sir Arthur Conan Doyle and his family. "There's a long, long trail a-winding," sang the jovial knight in his off-key baritone.

"It's a long way to Tipperary," his son Denis joined in at the top of his lungs. "It's a long way to go . . ." Together, they made a joyous noise, each singing a different song, their happy cacophony preventing any possible questions.

Runyon hung back a moment to enjoy the spectacle. With his tour at an end, Conan Doyle clearly no longer felt any obligation to cater to the press. His derisively dissonant duet seemed intended as a discreet Bronx cheer, to use the clever catchphrase for a raspberry coined by his friend Bugs Baer. And who was on the receiving end of said insult: the assembled members of the Fourth Estate. Dumb bastards just didn't get it.

"And the pale moon beams. . . ." Catching sight of Damon Runyon, the knight broke off his lusty caroling and pushed through the cluster of reporters to shake the newspaperman's hand. "Good of you to come."

The three children vanished the moment their father stopped the dreadful singing, darting away to explore the labyrinthine mysteries of the enormous liner.

"Wanted to see you off." Damon Runyon fished in his jacket pocket and came up with a baseball. "Brought you a present."

"Jolly nice," Sir Arthur said, examining the stitched horsehide orb with the curiosity of an anthropologist contemplating some arcane tribal artifact. "Thank you so very much."

"It's the one you saw Ruth belt into center field," Runyon lied. "The one Stengel caught. Got them both to sign it." This much was true. Conan Doyle admired the Babe's broad scrawl. "Yanks take the Series, four games to two." The sportswriter spoke in the curious clipped manner he'd made his trademark. "The Giants' only wins come because of Casey Stengel's two homers; the first one inside the park at Yankee Stadium. That's in the opener. Only run of the game. Worth the price of admission."

"Well, sir, I certainly owe a great measure of sporting pleasure to your kindness." Sir Arthur tossed the baseball into the air, laughing as he caught it. When the other reporters edged closer, notepads in hand, he waved them off as one might disperse a swarm of pesky gnats.

"For my money, you're missing out on the best game in town," Damon Runyon muttered as he lit a cigarette.

"And what might that be?"

"Poe murders, natch." The reporter squinted through the smoke of his dangling Sweet Cap. "This last one was a beaut. Regular chop suey. Think of the fun you'll miss, not solving the case."

"I'll leave that dubious pleasure to 'New York's finest,' as I believe your constabulary is designated." Catching sight of Opal Crosby Fletcher entering in her sable coat, Sir Arthur shaded his eyes with a saluting hand; a parody explorer scanning the horizon. "I say," he said, "this is turning into quite a gala fête."

"Hello, Sir Arthur," Isis called out with a smile. "Or should I say, farewell . . . ?"

"Mrs. Fletcher. What a pleasure . . ." He grasped her black-gloved hand. When last he saw that hand it was red with blood. She'd made an excellent nurse in the makeshift surgery she arranged in a corner of her basement furnace room. "How have you been?"

"Very well, thank you."

Sensing they wished a private conversation, Damon Runyon excused himself and drifted off, managing to pick up the words "Did you contact the barrister?" before the rest was lost to him.

Isis waited until the reporter was at a safe distance. "Monday morning," she whispered. "That same afternoon. I felt something close to joy when I burned the file."

"And what of the skull?"

"Sidney Rammage's personal effects are to be auctioned next month. I entered into private negotiation with the executors and I believe my bid has been accepted."

"Congratulations!" Sir Arthur's smile belied the sadness webbing his eyes.

Runyon spotted Harry and Bess Houdini making an entrance and sidled up to them. The magician carried a large wicker picnic hamper tied with a bold red ribbon and bow. "Couldn't miss the bon voyage . . . ?" the reporter quipped.

"Hello, Runyon . . ." The magician briskly introduced his wife without breaking stride. Conan Doyle waved at them with a forced grin.

"Delighted you came." Sir Arthur took Bess's hand. "So good to see you again, Mrs. Houdini."

"Likewise." Bess smiled, immediately seeking out Lady Jean, who sat on a chaise, chatting with a plump woman from the Theosophical Society.

Runyon patted Houdini's basket. "Looks like quite a feast."

"Nothing but the best for the world's greatest author."

Isis took note of the alarming contrast between the magician's brash music hall demeanor and the dead emptiness in his despairing eyes. His pallor suggested incipient illness. "Have you not been sleeping?" she asked softly.

"Rough couple of nights. I'll be okay now the tour is over with."

Taking his arm, Isis led Houdini a few paces away from the general commotion surrounding the departing knight. "I owe you more than my life," she murmured. "I am twice indebted for the life I carry."

"Now, listen . . ."

"Please. Hear me out. After the Christmas season, I'm going abroad to bear my child in seclusion. I say mine, because I absolve you of all obligation. There will be no scandal. The world will be told I adopted Osiris in Europe."

"Osiris . . . ?"

Isis smiled. "I thought you'd be pleased."

Damon Runyon stepped up close, almost coming between them. "What d'ya think about the Poe killer bumping off another magician?" Houdini recoiled from a drifting cloud of cigarette smoke. "I mean, after your assistant was rubbed out like that."

Houdini spoke slowly, choosing his words with care. "The death of a colleague is always regrettable. This . . . tragic horror makes the loss much . . . much more difficult to accept."

"Did you know this guy, Sidney Rammage?"

"Not very well. . . . He was secretary of the Society of American Magicians. I . . . knew him mainly in that capacity."

"Think you're next?"

"I certainly hope not." The magician's doleful gaze implored Conan Doyle to intercede for him.

"Don't mean to be rude," Sir Arthur said, taking the hint. "But I need a word in private with our mutual friend." He thought Houdini's unexpected impotence with the press a most telling sign.

"And I need to hurry if I'm going to make my next appointment." Isis threw her arms around Conan Doyle's neck, giving the burly knight a fervent hug. "Good-bye, Sir Arthur. You possess a radiant spirit."

"Good-bye, dear lady." He kissed her cheek.

She gave Houdini's hand a brisk shake. "Always most entertaining, Mr. Houdini . . ." Isis ignored Damon Runyon, passing him by with a cold smile.

The reporter grinned, wiping his cheaters on his handkerchief. "Hey, everything's jake. I'm not a guy to hog all your time. Answer one question and I'll scram."

"Ask away."

"What's your last word on the Poe murders?"

Sir Arthur glanced at Houdini. The magician stared fiercely at Damon Runyon. "You may repeat what I've always maintained," said the knight. "A random killer, acting out of madness, might be anyone, anywhere. The man standing next to you in a queue might harbor the most dreadful homicidal secrets. The stranger encountered in a pub or on a railway platform could well be the next Jack the Ripper. The monster wears the face of everyman."

Damon Runyon grinned. "Moral being to watch your back . . . ?"

"There is nothing moral about murder, Mr. Runyon." Conan Doyle extended his hand. "A pleasure meeting you."

"Pleasure's mine." A quick handshake and the reporter was gone, snapping the magician a sharp hat-brim salute in parting.

"Let's take a walk," Houdini said.

"I'll show you our stateroom."

After Sir Arthur reassured all present he would return shortly, the two men set off together along a passageway decorated in the stern Restoration classicism of Christopher Wren. They walked a good distance in silence. "Are you all right?" asked the knight at last.

"I'm alive," the magician replied. "Alive and kicking. Both of us . . .

alive and kicking. Our families and friends, safe and sound. What could be better?"

"Nothing better . . ."

The two men paused and faced one another. Sir Arthur pulled a folded newspaper page from his side pocket. "I saved this for you."

Houdini set the gift basket at his feet, spreading the page out on the bulkhead. There was a three-column photo of the Jenny at rest in Central Park. "WAY OFF COURSE," read the caption head. "Saw it on the train," he said. "But, thanks. Flying again was the best part of this whole dirty business."

"No. The best part was renewing my friendship with you."

Houdini picked up the gift-wrapped picnic hamper, handing it to Conan Doyle. "Here."

"Heavier than it looks." Sir Arthur attempted a weak grin.

"There is no heavier burden." The magician's mournful stare burned into the apprehensive knight. "I know you to be a connoisseur of magic. And so, I've prepared one last trick for your entertainment . . ."

Sir Arthur cleared his throat. The utter lack of emotion in Houdini's voice chilled him. He sensed the crossing of an invisible line. "I'm honored . . . to participate," he said.

"Put the hamper away in a safe place. Do not open or unwrap it. At precisely midnight on the third night out, read the card attached to the ribbon."

"What then?"

"The card will instruct you what to do next." Houdini squeezed Sir Arthur's shoulder, one comrade to another. "Good luck in your spiritual search," he said, hurrying off down the passageway with no further word of farewell.

The knight watched his rapid departure. "Good-bye, Houdini," he called, cradling the wicker picnic hamper in his arms. Hanging from a blood-red ribbon, the floral greeting card lay open before his gaze, the unfolded white inside surface completely blank.

31

------·------·------·------·------·------

ABRACADABRA

Down off the ways in 1914, the *Aquitania* was the last of the great four-funneled ships, a floating museum of architectural style. Walking through her public rooms and salons revealed a time machine worthy of Mr. Wells's imagination. Every period from sturdy Tudor to the baroque excesses of Louis XIV awaited the discerning traveler. On A Deck, a number of suites had been named after the great painters. One might choose Holbein, Rembrandt, or Velasquez, among others, each suite decorated with a nod to the aesthetics of the appropriately designated Old Master.

The Conan Doyle family occupied the Romney Suite. Reproductions of his lively portraits hung in every room. Sir Arthur had a special fondness for the vivacious portrayal of Emma Hamilton decked out in a wide-brimmed straw sunbonnet. Her saucy glance beamed down at him from the damask-covered wall of their sitting room. The knight reclined on a comfortable couch, staring up at those dancing eyes that had so bewitched Lord Nelson.

"Land of my dreams . . . into the land of my dreams . . ." He sang the line again and again, softly under his breath. A perverse penance for having taunted the press with his raucous treatment of the cherished sentimental songs of the Great War. "A-winding, into the land of my dreams . . ."

Third night out on a calm passage. Over in the corner, a tall Hepplewhite grandfather clock chimed the hour, the hand-painted phases of the moon waxing on its face. Humming along, Sir Arthur counted all twelve strokes of midnight.

It was time. The knight retrieved Houdini's wicker picnic basket from the stateroom closet. He had concealed it behind a jumble of over-coats and rubberized macks hung out in readiness for their return to the inhospitable climate of home. Turning back toward the couch with it under his arm, he saw the ethereal ghost of Poe sitting, somewhat petu-lantly, on the edge of a Chippendale armchair opposite the couch. A hov-ering luminous fog surrounded him like the haze of cigar smoke.

"So, we meet again . . . ?" The specter's querulous voice whined: a cold wind whistling though the unlatched shutters of an abandoned house.

"Do you know where we are?" asked Sir Arthur, concealing his amazement as well as he could while he resumed his seat. He placed the wicker basket on the low table in front of him.

"Aboard ship. . . . Some miserable packet bound out for . . ." His words drifted into inaudibility.

"Bound for where?" the knight prompted.

"I know not where. . . . I sailed for England once, as a child long ago. In the company of my stepfather and his family."

"Is England your destination now?"

Poe's ghost waved his frost-white fingers in an indeterminate ges-ture. "Does it matter? We're all fellow passengers on a voyage into eter-nity. The ports at which we call along the way are of no real import. Our mutual destination remains the same . . ."

Sir Arthur sagged back against the couch cushions, succumbing to the numb beginnings of despair. "You paint a bleak picture of life," he said.

"Life demands such perspective." The apparition wavered, a dim candle flame in the winds of time. "And such a palette: dismal gray, murky browns, blue shadows, the black of night . . . of the yawning grave."

"Is death truly such a lonely affair!" the knight cried out, his heart sick with doubt.

"You tell me," mocked the spirit. "I can only vouchsafe for the lone-liness of life."

"Then speak for yourself. My life remains cheerful."

"Does it indeed . . . ?" The sepulchral laugh tolled with the hollow chill of a death knell. "Is that why you guard that case like it was a loved-one's casket? What does it contain that is so precious?"

Sir Arthur placed a protective hand on the wicker basket. "I . . . don't know."

"Don't know, or don't want to know?"

"Does it matter?"

"Not to me. I no longer have treasures to cherish." The ghostly fig-ure rose to its feet like a wisp of smoke drifting up from a smothered fire. "I wrote a tale once about a man on shipboard who keeps a clandes-tine container in his cabin."

" 'The Oblong Box' . . ."

"Ah, you're familiar with my work?"

"An excellent story. But, so sad . . ."

"No less true, for all its pathos. How often have I wished to sink beneath the surface along with my dear departed wife." As before, the image of the ghost began to fade; a flight of moths in the moonlight, the dust from their fluttering wings filtering down through the shadows.

"Poe, wait!" Sir Arthur implored. "Please. Stay a moment longer. There's so much I need to ask you."

"Alas, I have no answers . . ." The ghostly voice whispered. "I pos-sess not a single truth to share with you." Just as if the moon had slipped behind a dark storm cloud, Poe's luminous form diminished, leaving only a trace, his vague nocturnal outline hovering in the corner. "I do know this . . .," he said, his voice a thin hiss. "The casket you guard is filled with sin. It reeks of evil. You may think yourself somehow sepa-rated from malfeasance, but you are wrong. . . . You are bonded to the poison. . . . The guilt is yours. It is . . . an eternal chancre . . . upon your soul . . ."

A firefly winked; the wolf's lonely cry lost on the distant wind. Poe was gone.

Sir Arthur Conan Doyle felt very cold. He hugged his arms to his sides and shivered. Perhaps his conscience played tricks on him. The wicker picnic basket squatted on the table; insidious, malevolent, the bright scarlet bow bold as a harlot's leering smile. He reached for the gaudy floral card, plucking it free from the ribbon.

"What magic is in store for me now?" he muttered, half-aloud, thinking all the while nothing would ever surprise him again.

He opened a card no longer blank. A crepe-paper rose bloomed in the fold. Below it, bright green script commanded: "Carry the basket out on deck. Walk aft to the stern rail and pluck this blossom." It didn't seem much of a trick. Some sort of special ink?

Sir Arthur followed the instructions to the letter. He donned a tweed coat, knowing the night air to be cold on deck. A brisk wind blew off the sea from the starboard quarter. It was dark and overcast; not a single star brightened the sky. The knight stood in the lee of a ventilator, the basket at his feet. He pulled the crepe flower off the card. A slip of paper attached to the stem bore a printed message: Look in Your Breast Pocket.

Conan Doyle harrumphed under his breath. It had to be a bluff. He hadn't been wearing this suit on the day they departed. No possible way for Houdini to have slipped something inside when he wasn't looking. He reached under his overcoat into the breast pocket of his Norfolk jacket. He found an envelope there.

Fingers trembling, Sir Arthur ripped open the gummed flap and extracted a plain white card. How did he do it, he wondered, straining to read in the dim light. "Throw the basket into the ocean," it said.

All at once, the card burst into flame. Conan Doyle dropped it, instinctively putting his singed fingers in his mouth as he stamped out the tiny fire. Greatly alarmed, he looked around to see if anyone had noticed the sudden flare. Not a soul in sight. The afterdeck remained deserted.

Sir Arthur picked up the wicker basket. Five swift strides took him to the stern rail. The sea below looked black as the night. Without a moment's hesitation, he dropped the basket overboard and it fell soundlessly into darkness.

All Orion/Phoenix titles are available at your local bookshop or from the following address:

Littlehampton Book Services
Cash Sales Department L
14 Eldon Way, Lineside Industrial Estate
Littlehampton
West Sussex BN17 7HE
telephone 01903 721596, *facsimile* 01903 730914

Payment can either be made by credit card (Visa and Mastercard accepted) or by sending a cheque or postal order made payable to *Littlehampton Book Services*.
DO NOT SEND CASH OR CURRENCY.

Please add the following to cover postage and packing

UK and BFPO:
£1.50 for the first book, and 50P for each additional book to a maximum of £3.50

Overseas and Eire:
£2.50 for the first book plus £1.00 for the second book and 50p for each additional book ordered

---

BLOCK CAPITALS PLEASE

name of cardholder ....

....

address of cardholder ....

....

....

....

postcode ....

delivery address
(if different from cardholder)

....

....

....

....

postcode ....

☐ I enclose my remittance for £...............................

☐ please debit my Mastercard/Visa (delete as appropriate)

card number ☐☐☐☐☐☐☐☐☐☐☐☐☐☐☐☐

expiry date ☐☐☐☐

signature ....

prices and availability are subject to change without notice